The Best
AMERICAN ESSAYS
2017

GUEST EDITORS OF
THE BEST AMERICAN ESSAYS

1986 ELIZABETH HARDWICK
1987 GAY TALESE
1988 ANNIE DILLARD
1989 GEOFFREY WOLFF
1990 JUSTIN KAPLAN
1991 JOYCE CAROL OATES
1992 SUSAN SONTAG
1993 JOSEPH EPSTEIN
1994 TRACY KIDDER
1995 JAMAICA KINCAID
1996 GEOFFREY C. WARD
1997 IAN FRAZIER
1998 CYNTHIA OZICK
1999 EDWARD HOAGLAND
2000 ALAN LIGHTMAN
2001 KATHLEEN NORRIS
2002 STEPHEN JAY GOULD
2003 ANNE FADIMAN
2004 LOUIS MENAND
2005 SUSAN ORLEAN
2006 LAUREN SLATER
2007 DAVID FOSTER WALLACE
2008 ADAM GOPNIK
2009 MARY OLIVER
2010 CHRISTOPHER HITCHENS
2011 EDWIDGE DANTICAT
2012 DAVID BROOKS
2013 CHERYL STRAYED
2014 JOHN JEREMIAH SULLIVAN
2015 ARIEL LEVY
2016 JONATHAN FRANZEN
2017 LESLIE JAMISON

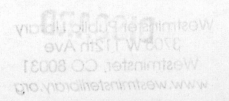

The Best AMERICAN ESSAYS® 2017

Edited and with an Introduction
by LESLIE JAMISON

Robert Atwan, Series Editor

A Mariner Original

HOUGHTON MIFFLIN HARCOURT

BOSTON • NEW YORK 2017

www.hmhco.com

ISSN 0888-3742 (print)   ISSN 2573-3885 (e-book)
ISBN 978-0-544-81733-3 (print)   ISBN 978-0-544-81742-5 (e-book)

Printed in the United States of America
DOC 10 9 8 7 6 5 4 3 2 1

Contents

Foreword ix

Introduction xvi

JASON ARMENT *Two Shallow Graves* 1
FROM *The Florida Review*

RACHEL KAADZI GHANSAH *The Weight of James Arthur Baldwin* 16
FROM *BuzzFeed*

ELIESE COLETTE GOLDBACH *White Horse* 29
FROM *Alaska Quarterly Review*

LAWRENCE JACKSON *The City That Bleeds* 45
FROM *Harper's Magazine*

RACHEL KUSHNER *"We Are Orphans Here"* 60
FROM *The New York Times Magazine*

ALAN LIGHTMAN *What Came Before the Big Bang?* 72
FROM *Harper's Magazine*

EMILY MALONEY *Cost of Living* 82
FROM *The Virginia Quarterly Review*

GREG MARSHALL *If I Only Had a Leg* 91
FROM *Electric Literature*

BERNARD FARAI MATAMBO *Working the City* 104
FROM *Transition*

KENNETH A. McCLANE *Sparrow Needy* 115
FROM *Kenyon Review*

CATHERINE VENABLE MOORE *The Book of the Dead* 128
FROM *Oxford American*

WESLEY MORRIS *Last Taboo* 160
FROM *The New York Times Magazine*

CHRISTOPHER NOTARNICOLA *Indigent Disposition* 176
FROM *North American Review*

MEGHAN O'GIEBLYN *Dispatch from Flyover Country* 180
FROM *The Threepenny Review*

KAREN PALMER *The Reader Is the Protagonist* 192
FROM *The Virginia Quarterly Review*

SARAH RESNICK *H.* 203
FROM *n+1*

HEATHER SELLERS *Haywire* 232
FROM *Tin House*

ANDREA STUART *Travels in Pornland* 252
FROM *Granta*

JUNE THUNDERSTORM *Revenge of the Mouthbreathers:
A Smoker's Manifesto* 267
FROM *The Baffler*

ALIA VOLZ *Snakebit* 275
FROM *The Threepenny Review*

Contributors' Notes 285

Notable Essays and Literary Nonfiction of 2016 291

Notable Special Issues of 2016 301

Foreword

THE DAY I began this year's foreword the news in my inbox reminded me that April 6, 2017, marked the one hundredth anniversary of America's entry into World War I. The momentous decision to send U.S. troops came after years of hesitation and deliberation, and it was roundly applauded by those who thought an Allied victory (as Woodrow Wilson claimed) would make the world "safe for democracy"; H. G. Wells believed it would be the "war that will end war." For the ill-prepared American conscripts, these noble ideals soon found themselves severely tested in the trenches of Flanders and Belleau Wood.

Although most Americans rallied behind the declaration, vigorous antiwar protests left many communities across the nation divided. One of the most interesting voices opposing U.S. entry into the war belonged to a young essayist who would die in the Great Influenza shortly after the Armistice, at the age of thirty-two. Randolph Bourne (1886–1918) remains one of the nation's greatest advocates for peace, social justice, youth movements, labor, immigration, educational reform, and progressive values in general. The historian Christopher Lasch thought Bourne one of the earliest American writers to examine the intersections of culture and politics. Although his professional writing career covered barely eight years, Bourne's literary output as an essayist was impressively prolific and often groundbreaking. In *The Best American Essays of the Century,* Joyce Carol Oates and I included Bourne's "The Handicapped," a moving account of his youthful struggles with two medical misfortunes: a grotesquely disfigured face caused

by a "very messy birth" and severe physical disabilities resulting
from the spinal tuberculosis he contracted at the age of four.

Back when the word "activist" was still a neologism, Bourne
demonstrated what the term actually meant and would mean in
the future. As an undergraduate at Columbia, Bourne confessed
getting into "trouble over some impassioned letters I wrote to the
college daily protesting against the poor treatment of the scrub
women, and the low ages of the children employed around the
campus." Like other universities, he argued, Columbia "does not
hesitate to teach Social Ethics in the classroom and exploit its labor force on the side."

When America declared war, Bourne was shocked and devastated to see that many of his fellow intellectuals supported Wilson's decision. He was especially disappointed that his mentor, the
influential philosopher John Dewey, had also joined the pro-war
ranks. In one of his major essays, "The War and the Intellectuals," Bourne acutely describes how the nation's intelligentsia and
its elite eastern ruling class had surprisingly aligned themselves to
persuade a skeptical and neutral public that going to war would
promote the best interests of both American liberalism and international democracy. As he put it: "Only in a world where irony
was dead could an intellectual class enter war at the head of such
illiberal cohorts in the avowed cause of world-liberalism and world-
democracy."

Bourne's essay appeared in the *New Republic* for April 14, 1917.
A regular contributor to that magazine, Bourne had broken ranks
with numerous colleagues. The magazine's editorial for that
same issue praised America's entry into the war as a "moral verdict reached after the utmost deliberation of the more thoughtful members of the community." It should come as no surprise
that Bourne's reputation expanded decades later with the disasters
brought on in Southeast Asia by the clique of White House advis-
ers the late David Halberstam ironically termed "the best and the
brightest."

A public dead to irony represented one of Bourne's greatest
fears. He strove to be not only a committed political thinker but a
respected literary essayist. He did not perceive committed politics
and a love of the essay as antithetical passions. But he did see the
problems in reconciling the two; that is, how to fuse the essayist's
open-minded, irresolute, and skeptical disposition with the fervor

and conviction that grow from a reformist desire to achieve better government and a more just society. As many writers know, something usually has to give—either we lose the intellectual skepticism or the impassioned resolution. Unlike the essayist, the advocate rarely tolerates contradictory opinions. As Cynthia Ozick put it in her introduction to the 1998 volume: "The essay is not meant for barricades; it is a stroll through someone's mazy mind." Although one needn't accept such a dramatic distinction, Ozick succinctly reminds us of the traditional tension between the reflective and ruminative essay and polemical writing that seeks unqualified assent.

Throughout his tragically brief career as an essayist, Bourne sought to reconcile his commitment to political activism and his love of literary aesthetics. He saw early on that a single intellectual capacity could unite the activist and the artist: irony. In a remarkable essay published in the *Atlantic Monthly* in 1913, the twenty-six-year-old Bourne set out a highly original philosophy of irony that stretches our understanding of the concept far beyond the standard rhetorical definition. In "The Life of Irony," Bourne emphasizes that being ironical is much more than a matter of saying one thing and meaning another (as complicated at times as even that can get). He sees irony as much more than a rhetorical device or intellectual method. It is, instead, an entire way of life; the ironist, Bourne (perhaps punningly) claims, "is born and not made."

For Bourne, irony is the very soul of the essay, the source not only of a transcendent critical judgment but of personal self-discovery. "Not until I read the Socrates of Plato," the youthful Bourne writes, "did I fully appreciate that this irony—this pleasant challenging of the world, this insistent judging of experience, this sense of vivid contrasts and incongruities, of comic juxtapositions, of flaring brilliances, and no less heartbreaking impossibilities, of all the little parts of one's world being constantly set off against each other, and made intelligible only by being translated into and defined in each others' terms—that this was a life, and a life of beauty, that one might suddenly discover one's self living all unawares."

One can imagine a future Columbia student—one who grew up not far from Bourne's Bloomfield, New Jersey—heartened by such words, though I can't be sure he ever read them. Allen Ginsberg would transform Bourne's transcendent irony into a powerful po-

etry that found no disconnect between political protest and literary aesthetics. Add to this Bourne's seemingly paradoxical view
that irony was both essential to empathy and an all-embracing
democratic sensibility, and we come even closer to a vital connection between Bourne and the beat generation.

Bourne's ideas about irony and empathy may seem counterin-
tuitive: after all, isn't the ironist typically detached, sardonic, cyni-
cal, quick to ridicule? In "The Life of Irony" Bourne importantly
distinguishes these lesser qualities from true irony, which brings
us closer to the experience of others—not farther away. The inner mechanism works like this: because ironists readily adopt another's point of view and make it their own, they come to live the
other's experiences with greater understanding and compassion.
"Irony," he says, "is thus the truest sympathy." And this sympathy
is inseparable from social criticism: "Things as they are, thrown
against the background of things as they ought to be—this," he
claims, "is the ironist's vision." (For the greatest example of irony
in the service of a political cause—an essay against colonial exploitation that makes the preposterous sound reasonable—readers
are directed to Jonathan Swift's masterpiece, "A Modest Proposal
for Preventing the Children of Poor People in Ireland from Being a Burden to Their Parents or Country, and for Making Them
Beneficial to the Public.")

Because ironists can't resist applying irony to themselves, Bourne
maintains, they will also be far less prone to egotism and self-esteem. Essayists since Montaigne have often relied on introspection
as the most effective method of acquiring a self-understanding that
leads to the understanding of others. For, as many still think, we
know other minds only by analogy to our own. But Bourne refused
to honor this essayistic legacy. When it came to self-understanding
and self-interpretation, he wrote: "Introspection is no match for
irony as a guide." The dynamics of self-understanding, he suggests,
move not inside out but rather outside in. Only from others do we
learn how to interpret ourselves. "The ironist," he proclaims, "is
the only man who really gets outside of himself."

So, now a key question: How applicable is Bourne's ironic perspective—or, for that matter, Swift's, Twain's, or even Orwell's—
to today's political environment? Wouldn't irony simply be lost in
a Twitter-based discourse? Is it a distracting and irrelevant liter-

ary device, no substitute for chants, mantras, slogans, and sound bites, all designed to convey the absolute absence of ambiguous or ambivalent expression? Maybe Swift really was advocating that the children of Ireland's poor be sold to the rich so they can be butchered for gourmet food. Isn't that how the essay reads? Who can risk irony if the political message might get distorted or complicated? Or the writer or speaker mislabeled? Can irony (or any aesthetic stance) be defended in an age of activism, especially at a time when so many political questions appear to be matters of life or death, when few individuals tolerate opinions different from those of their party?

How does the essay fare in such a politically dichotomized world? How does the many-sided essayist take a side? Can the genuine essay be compatible with the political certitude that usually drives the opinions of advocates and activists? These aren't recent questions. In his sprawling and unfinished novel, *The Man Without Qualities,* first published in the dangerous early 1930s, the delightfully ironic Austrian writer Robert Musil created a fascinating protagonist who realizes that his thinking life has taken on the shape of the essay. As such, he finds himself in opposition to systems, certainty, and consistency, and far more inclined to inertia than action. He terms his resistance to action "essayism," from the way that the essay "takes a thing from many sides without comprehending it wholly." As the novelist Alan Wall puts it, Musil's essayism "is characterised by an aversion to the axiomatic, a deliberated provisionality, an acceptance of uncertainty, an openness to the possibilities of intellectual adventure and discovery which Musil liked to call 'possibilitarian.'" Musil saw this intellectual and emotional tendency as more than a literary phenomenon—it was essentially a conflict between doubt and decision, nihilism and activism.

Bourne believed that without irony the activist essayist would too easily lapse into the polemicist, and he himself had his lapses. Political pressure obviously creates difficult situations for some writers who, though they may posses strong allegiances and commitments, may still feel personally, intellectually, or even artistically compelled to examine unpopular points of view. To take just one example: if in our time being "undemocratic" or "authoritarian" appears to be one of the most horrible attitudes anyone can imagine—both politically and ethically—would a writer risk challenging the unquestioned superiority of democracy to all other political systems? To be perceived as attacking democracy—even hypothetically or in essayistic speculation—could possibly label one for life a fascist, Stalinist, Nazi, or worse. Trigger warning: students may want to avoid Plato's *Republic*.

The poet Robert Frost spent a great deal of time doing what essayists often do—thinking about thinking. In a magazine interview, he once famously pointed out something about the process: "Thinking isn't to agree or disagree. That's voting." To my mind, his remark when unpacked goes to the core of the essay as writers continually search for creative ways to engage and assess a multitude of polarizing current affairs.

The Best American Essays features a selection of the year's outstanding essays, essays of literary achievement that show an awareness of craft and forcefulness of thought. Hundreds of essays are gathered annually from a wide assortment of national and regional publications. These essays are then screened, and approximately one hundred are turned over to a distinguished guest editor, who may add a few personal discoveries and who makes the final selections. The list of notable essays appearing in the back of the book is drawn from a final comprehensive list that includes not only all of the essays submitted to the guest editor but also many that were not submitted.

To qualify for the volume, the essay must be a work of respectable literary quality, intended as a fully developed, independent essay (not an excerpt) on a subject of general interest (not specialized scholarship), originally written in English (or translated by the author) for publication in an American periodical during the calendar year. Note that abridgments and excerpts taken from longer works and published in magazines do not qualify for the series, but if considered significant they will appear in the Notable list in the back of the volume. Today's essay is a highly flexible and shifting form, however, so these criteria are not carved in stone.

Magazine editors who want to be sure their contributors will be considered each year should submit issues or subscriptions to:

The Best American Essays
Houghton Mifflin Harcourt
125 High Street, 5th Floor
Boston, MA 02110

Writers and editors are welcome to submit published essays from any American periodical for consideration; unpublished work does not qualify for the series and cannot be reviewed or evaluated. Also ineligible are essays that have been published in book form—such as a contribution to a collection—but have never appeared in a periodical. All submissions from print magazines must be directly from the publication and not in manuscript or printout format. Editors of online magazines and literary bloggers should not assume that appropriate work will be seen; they are invited to submit printed copies of the essays to the address above. Please note: due to the increasing number of submissions from online sources, material that does not include a full citation (name of publication, date, author contact information, etc.) will no longer be considered.

The American essay lost one of its most impressive and beloved figures with the passing of Brian Doyle on May 27, 2017. His work appeared often in these pages. Fortunately, Brian's genius enabled him to transfer his magnetic presence to the printed word, and his inquisitive, beneficent, and essaying spirit will long survive: "And though the last lights off the black West went / Oh, morning, at the brown brink eastward, springs—"

As always, I'm indebted to Nicole Angeloro for her keen editorial skills and her ability, given our tight schedule, to keep so many moving parts in smooth working order. And for their expertise, a heartfelt thanks to other publishing people with Houghton Mifflin Harcourt—Larry Cooper, Melissa Dobson, Carla Gray, and Megan Wilson. I also want to thank my son, Gregory Atwan, for all of his help in identifying the astonishing number of journals that publish online only. When we launched this series in 1985 such publications were unimaginable; they now comprise an enormous percentage of the material I encounter annually. It was a special pleasure to work with one of the nation's most talented young essayists, Leslie Jamison, whose remarkable essay "The Devil's Bait" was selected for the 2014 volume. Her introduction to this extraordinarily diverse collection explores dimensions of the contemporary essay that the series thus far has only sporadically covered. It is an indispensable contribution to the art of the essay in a worrisome time.

R.A.

Introduction

IN MY TENTH-GRADE English class, we read a short piece about America that was just a catalogue of comparisons: *America is the man sleeping off his bender on the street. America is the cart of fruit, overturned.* It was metonymy I misunderstood as metaphor. *America is . . . America is . . . America is . . .* Back then, I only knew I loved the swell and soar of its prose, the prerogative of rebooting and reimagining, the surprise of following the same phrase to a different place each time.

We were supposed to write our own imitations, and they were supposed to be about high school. I wrote: *High school is a clown holding a gun to his temple. High school is all the children gathered around him, laughing.* I wasn't much for subtlety. My loneliness, then, was not a subtle feeling. I wanted to express what it was like to be young, how it lived in the sudden knot in my gut when a popular girl came up to me in the locker room and asked if I could smell my own body odor. How it lived in the breathless surge of getting into my best friend's car on a Friday night, rolling down the windows and rounding the bend, through a tunnel, where the I-10 became the Pacific Coast Highway, with ocean beyond, its sharp salt wind and dark waves rustling under moonlight. So I wrote: *High school is a clown holding a gun to his temple. High school is carbonation and twilight.* Juxtaposing sad clowns and highways was a way of saying: Sometimes I have someone to eat lunch with, and sometimes I don't.

This was my first taste of the mind as curator, plucking what it needed from the world and finding vessels for feelings without shapes. *Being young is a clown. It's a gun. It's fizz. It's dusk.* This was better than the five-paragraph model. It was better than argument. It was freedom. It was a tunnel opening onto ocean. It was an essay, my first.

I wrote those first three paragraphs in a moment of inspired reverie, during the weeks immediately preceding a presidential election I felt optimistic about. I'm writing this next paragraph on the morning of an inauguration whose prospect has made me sick to my stomach ever since November. In a few hours, I will head to Washington, DC, to march with hundreds of thousands of people so that our bodies can collectively pronounce the basic tenets of the country we believe in. That kind of articulation feels right and necessary in this moment: collective, embodied, populated, unambivalent. Sometimes it feels like the only kind of articulation that matters.

I have been thinking for many months about why the essay matters, too. I have been thinking about what the second adjective of this volume's title might mean for us right now. "American." Is nimble talk about the aesthetics of association and juxtaposition —finding ways to talk about eating alone in high school—is that simply self-indulgent and irrelevant? Talking about aesthetics in the midst of political crisis can feel like surveying the wreckage of a nuclear blast and then treating the charred skeletons of buildings as jungle gyms to play on.

That first morning after the election, I thought maybe nothing mattered but policy op-eds and marching. Maybe nothing mattered but articles about politics with a capital *P*. That first morning, belief in art as a cultural value in its own right felt intellectually correct but deeply abstract, far removed, like an object under water—no answer for what felt sick and broken in my gut when I thought of millions of deportations and the families these deportations would break open, when I thought of years of stop-and-frisk policing, a national *Fuck you* to the idea of police accountability; when I thought of a Muslim registry, or girls driving for days across state lines to get abortions they couldn't afford.

But of course, what had the election changed? I knew it wasn't a glitch in some hypothetical song of American justice but another track in a record of ongoing inequality. I knew our political crisis was ongoing. So what did it mean to sit down and write my essay-

anthology introduction in the face of all that? Put more crudely: Why does the essay matter at all?

If you've ever read an essay about essays, then you've read the root of the word: from the French *essayer,* to try. Etymology arrives as show pony and absolution, along with its attendant permissions: The essay doesn't offer seamless narrative or watertight argument. It investigates its own seams. It traces what leaks. But doesn't this endless permission—the fluttering Monopoly money of *attempt,* its endless currency—ever get a little tiresome? If anything counts as attempt, what could possibly count as failure?

Essays aren't immune to failure. They can fail in a thousand ways—by failing to offer insight, by offering insights that feel too easy, too tidy, too shopworn. They can fail to enchant. They can fail to cast a spell or build a world. They can fail to interrogate their own conclusions. They can fail to render their subjects with sufficient complexity. They can declare themselves done too soon. An essay is not an attempt captured in its first iteration, but in its ninth, or tenth, or fifteenth—honed, interrogated, reimagined. Another word for this is "revision."

But if essays aren't immune from failure, they *are* singularly equipped to metabolize their own failures, to follow the smoke signals of these failures toward better versions of themselves, to take what might feel like an obstacle—shame, confusion, contradiction, muddled memory—and confess it, investigate it, probe it. This is failure as a trampoline rather than a straitjacket. My beloved essayist mentor put it more succinctly, as beloved essayist mentors are wont to do. He told me once: "The problem with an essay can become its subject."

When Guns N' Roses was recording a demo of "Sweet Child o' Mine," a track that emerged unplanned from one of Slash's guitar riffs during a jam session, the band couldn't think of lyrics to accompany the musical breakdown at the end. Axl Rose started muttering: "Where do we go now? Where do we go now?" and those muttered words became the lyrics. The wondering became the song.

When I started writing this introduction in the wake of the inauguration, I realized that my problem had once again become my subject. *Why does the essay matter?* A few months after the election, a friend of mine was teaching a class called Writing After the Election at a writing program in the White Mountains of New Hampshire, where everyone was holed up in an old hotel while the snow came down. By mysterious (and probably illegal) means, one of his students had brought a lynx pelt and skull to the hotel, from an animal he had accidentally struck with his car, and my friend decided he would use this lynx skull as a prop in Writing After the Election. He would set the skull in the middle of his desk—at the front of the room—and begin to speak about the role of creative writing in our time. At a certain point, he would say that writing without letting politics into your work was like trying to describe this room without ever mentioning there was a bloody lynx skull in the middle of it.

This introduction is my way of saying: There is a bloody lynx skull in the middle of the room. There has always been a bloody lynx skull in the middle of the room. We write our essays not despite that bloody lynx skull but because of it. The essay isn't a retreat from the world but a way of encountering it.

After the election, when my students asked me if their "unpolitical" essays even mattered anymore—their essays about friendship and fly-fishing—my first reaction wasn't *yes* or *no*. It was: *Those essays are probably more political than you think.* There are politics in everything. My answer wasn't: *Go looking for politics to put in your work.* It was: *Find the politics that are already in there.*

That November, I was in the weeds of an essay that I'd been working on for several years, about a photographer who had spent more than two decades photographing the same Mexican family —traveling back and forth across the border, finding ways to document the evolving and frictional humanity of a particular cluster of people. I'd been assuming the essay was about devotion or obsession, but now I saw it was also about borders, and the fact that our president wanted to build a wall along the length of ours. It was about twenty-five years of entanglement as the ethical opposite of that wall. It was about encounter. Had there ever been an essay about anything else?

The essay has always courted a reputation as a solipsistic genre; a mind fondling itself on the page. But to me the defining trait of the essay is the situation and problem of encounter. The essays I like are full of the kind of humility and curiosity that make these encounters electric—whether you are regarding the self, the world, the past, the other, the other's mother, the vacant lot next door, the transatlantic flight, the suburb, the city block, the dry cleaners, the burlesque. The essay inherently stages an encounter between an "I" and the world in which that "I" resides; just as politics is a way of examining the relationship between an "I" and whatever communities she finds herself a part of. If one definition of politics is "the total complex of relations between people living in society," the essay doesn't just describe these relations. It unsettles them. It models a certain way of paying attention: awestruck and humble and suspicious all at once, taking as premise —as promise—the limits of its own vision.

The essay is political—and politically useful, by which I mean humanizing and provocative—because of its commitment to nuance, its explorations of contingency, its spirit of unrest, its glee at overturned assumptions; because of the double helix of awe and distrust—faith and doubt—that structures its DNA. Essays are political not just when they take up the kinds of content we call political with a capital *P*—social injustice, civic life, the rule of law and government—but because they are committed to instability. They are full of self-interrogation, suspicious of received narratives, and hospitable to contradiction. They thrill toward complexity. Essays bear witness, and they confess the subjectivity of their witnessing. They need some motivating urgency. Like? Wonder. Trauma. Mystery. Injustice. The essay insists that every consciousness yields infinite complexity upon close scrutiny. This is something close to the precise ethical opposite of xenophobia or scapegoating. Essays take abstractions and make them particular.

How do I make that abstraction particular? I could tell you about Kenneth A. McClane's "Sparrow Needy." It's an essay about McClane's brother, Paul, who died young from drinking hard; who was never fully at home in his own family, or in the world; who moved with his "bones sidling against themselves." It's also an essay about visiting a neighborhood bully at Sing Sing, among tables blistered by ancient gum, and finding this bully so thin it was difficult to summon the memory of how fearsome he had been. To say that "Sparrow Needy" is about urban violence or police accountability or being black in America wouldn't be incorrect, it would just be a refusal to speak the language the essay itself makes gloriously available—which is the language of specificity and precision.

If I'm going to tell you about "Sparrow Needy," it's better to toss topical keywords into the trash bin and say that it's an essay about a sinkhole at Riverside Park, at Seventy-Seventh Street, "brimming with bottles, potato chips bags, broken dolls," with the Hudson River running underneath like blood pulsing through a vein under the skin. It's about the possibility of a lost girl swirling in those waters. It's better to say it's an essay about a particular brother, who collapsed on a particular day when he was four years old, at the unmarked heap of stones marking the slave quarters at Mount Vernon, and died in a particular hospital decades later, creating a particular rift in the world.

Particularity is the native tongue of the essay—at least, the essays I like most—and particularity isn't just an aesthetic code (*be vivid!*) but an ethical imperative that reads more like invitation: *Approach the sinkhole. Look closer. Get dizzy. Every human life is infinite. You will never know the half of it. Here's a half, and then another half, and then another half, that's three—there's more!* No life is a thesis statement. No life is as simple as a threat. Everyone hurts about something. Everyone has feelings about breakfast. Every person is a fucking miracle. These statements might not sound political, but if you really believe them they make political demands. Essays take the political and make it something that lives in a body, that needs to sleep and stay hydrated, that might—for example—drink water as hot as a locker-room shower twenty klicks north of Fallujah.

When I was reading the essays in this anthology—each and every one of them—I found nothing like a retreat from the world. I found the world itself, waiting. I found startling white sneakers in an East Jerusalem refugee camp. I found the names of dead West Virginia tunnel-diggers and the faces of their living relatives. I found rape lurking in a footnote, the possibility of a homeless man called a "body," the possibility of facing a weeping Iraqi bomb-maker and feeling nothing. I found the generative energy of refusal: refusing to stay silent, refusing to call that man a "body," refusing to feel nothing or to pretend it was easy to feel something, refusing to leave the homeless or the dead unnamed.

Many of the essays in this anthology are about things that we'd readily call political: police violence, our national heroin epidemic, the toll of our wars, the brutality of corporate greed and negligence, the unacknowledged rallying cries of class warfare. But all of these essays are examples of the essay itself as a singularly capable instrument of political imagination. The essay asks us to encounter the world as questioning creatures, wary of pre-cooked narratives, attentive to humanity in all its strangeness and variety. The politics of the essay don't just live in content but in form—in narrators willing to question themselves, to admit the "I" as something multiple and contradictory, indefinite, ambivalent, uncertain.

I felt my own uncertain, multiple "I" enlarged by all the essays you'll find here. I was taken to corners of the world I hadn't imagined, or hadn't been able to imagine; corners of the world I had tricked myself into believing I'd imagined, but had gotten wrong —or only partially understood. I was corrected. I was expanded. I was bothered. The power of the essay lives in a certain kind of impulse, a gaze that overturns the easy story and seeks the unseen. When Jason Arment looks at two shallow graves in the Iraqi desert, he sees one meant for his POW and one meant for himself—whatever would be left of him, once the war was done.

What will you find in these pages? You'll find a scientist wondering, *What happened before the beginning of the universe?* You'll find three miner brothers who preserved their lungs in glass jars as proof of the silicosis that killed them. You'll find a female professor describing her decision to make an amateur porn film with her partner. You'll find people who are not walking thesis statements but actual human beings—ecstatic, contradictory, imperfect, hurting, trying again.

In "Dispatch from Flyover Country," Meghan O'Gieblyn describes watching a communion on the shores of Lake Michigan —in golden, gauzy dusk light—and catching sight of a drone hovering over the water. In "Cost of Living," Emily Maloney narrates the fiscal aftermath of a suicide attempt—survival as debt, survival *in* debt, a woman paying for the hospital stay her insurance did not cover.

So yes, the personal is political. When a woman buys a cake to celebrate another year of living on the anniversary of the day she did not die, and can barely afford this cake because she is in debt to the medical system that kept her from dying—this is both personal and political. The brief glimpse of that cake—the kind of impactful specificity, or *telling detail,* that I am always demanding

from my students—suggests we might want to imagine and implement a system where such debts did not exist. I believe in essays
because I believe that it matters to narrate the particular stories of
particular debts, rather than simply Debts Writ Large—so that we
might access broader truths through the fissures of these heartbro-
ken lenses. Every piece of cake has its politics, and its price.

Political discourse can make us forget that abstractions like
"rape culture" are actually the accumulation of millions of particular, lived moments of terror, degradation, disrespect, dismissal,
and violation. But in "White Horse," Eliese Goldbach doesn't let
us believe for a moment that "rape culture" is just an abstraction.
In this essay, rape culture isn't just a phrase; it's a narrator trying
to figure out how to narrate her rape in the aftermath of a disci-
plinary committee that listened to her story—the story of being
drugged at a party, dragged into the woods, and forced into intercourse—and told her she wasn't raped at all. "White Horse" uses
the particular tools of the essay—formal experiment, ruptured
narrative, a voice that admits doubt and questions the terms of its
telling—to fight silencing. Masterful form is often a question of
well-managed rupture.

In "'We Are Orphans Here,'" Rachel Kushner revisits her own
notes from a visit to Shuafat Refugee Camp in order to question
the narrative her memory has sculpted from her time there. It's
this willingness—to return to the original encounter, to question
her own story, to reveal its elisions—that breaks her piece open.
This is the prerogative of the essay: as it witnesses, it investigates
the terms and fragility of its own gaze.

In the months following the election, I went to an exhibition of
paintings by the artist Kerry James Marshall, and found myself particularly moved by one called *Slow Dance*. It's an acrylic painting,
about six feet square, that shows a couple in their living room: a
man in a wifebeater, his wife's light-catching nails on his dark back,
music made visible as notes swirling across the room, a candle glowing in a wine bottle, their dinner plates on the coffee table, each
plate holding a few stray green beans. It was immediately clear to
me that those green beans were *everything*. They were my favorite
part. They turned a constellation of brushstrokes into two particular people with particular appetites, people who had decided to

get up—in the middle of dinner, their vegetables unfinished—and start dancing, because the music had moved them, because they needed a pretext to bring their bodies close together.

Is it ridiculous if I say that's what the essay is, those green beans? The green beans are the detail that recognizes a particular humanity, and helps bring us close to that humanity for a moment—from an oblique angle we wouldn't have expected, an angle we couldn't have imagined for ourselves. What we can't imagine for ourselves: that's why we need to see the world—for a spell—through someone else's eyes.

An essay lives in its details, and argues through them: a little girl dressing up in the stiletto heels sent as charity relief in the aftermath of a disastrous flood, or a woman tasting bitter oranges in the backyard of James Baldwin's home in France, taking stock of what remains from his life there: "a dozen pink teacups and turquoise saucers." This is Rachel Kaadzi Ghansah, who takes a trip to Baldwin's home as part of a larger inquiry into "how his memory abides," and finds it abiding "on the scent of wild lavender like the kind in his yard, in the mouths of a new generation that once again feels compelled to march in the streets of Harlem, Ferguson, and Baltimore."

An essay lives in those high heels, those teacups, that lavender. A Coke and a sticky bun, straight from the oven, on a long day in Harare. A boy dreaming of busloads of Africans on a highway to America, straddling an entire ocean. All kinds of longing. All kinds of violence. A girl playing with a white plastic horse. A woman dreaming of being saved by a man who rides one. A boy weeping at a pile of rocks. A pair of lungs in a glass jar. An addict with vomit as viscous as cake batter. You'll find that addict and his vomit in Sarah Resnick's essay, "H.," in a hospital waiting room, along with a nurse who says the man doesn't deserve help because he brought this on himself. But the essay believes something else. It believes his story holds more. When I talk about the politics of the essay, I am talking about that—an essay's fidelity to nuance, and its belief in the infinitude of every life.

An essay can be a chorus. It can crowdsource. For instance, I could send an email to my students and tell them I'm trying—I mean, *essaying*—to write an essay about essays. I could ask them: *What can an essay be?* I could spur them on: *It can be a protest, a betrayal, an eyesore, a hack job, a salvage yard, a trash fire.*

When I say, *I could ask them,* I mean, *I did.* The essay is more like a student than a teacher anyway. Andrew said: *An essay is what happens when an unfinished thought doesn't get away—it's the fisher-person's story of reeling that thought in. Sometimes we cry: "Bullshit!"* Kate said an essay could be a tapestry, a dishrag, or a plea. Joseph just said: *An essay can be selfish.* Nick said: *Some essays seem to sweat.* Lisa said the best kind of essay reaches you like a letter from an ex-lover. Zoe said: *Not sure what an essay is or can be, now that you mention it. It's the five-paragraph, in-class bane of existence in high school. What it becomes after that? Not a "trash fire" that's for sure. Our president-elect is a trash fire. What else? Does anyone know? No one even gets what I'm saying when I tell them I'm writing essays in graduate school. I'm going to keep thinking on it whether you need me to or not.*

I thought: Good. Do that. An essay is the thing that refuses to be done too soon. It's all of the above: a suitcase, a tapestry, a dishrag, the fisher-person's story. It's always somewhere, sweating. It's the second grave, the one that holds what's left of you. It's the drone over the water, the sudden glimpse that says, *This has always been public.* It's a plate of uneaten green beans. It's a search for just the right metaphor for an addict's vomit, which is made of the same stuff as anyone else's.

The essay resists the easy binaries we might draw between interior and exterior, self-indulgence and curiosity, beauty and ethics, aesthetics and politics. It implicates itself in what it critiques. It makes wild moves but holds itself accountable to truth—and always, also, to spell casting and enchantment. It's the subway-car dancers I saw just this afternoon, on my way home from work, riding the Q train over the late-sun-spackled water of the East River, while I was indulging some foggy reverie about the Statue of Liberty and the hypothetical people to whom it promises refuge, when I was interrupted by the actual bodies of actual people beside me, in motion—dancers spinning on poles and twisting in the air, hanging from metal bars touched by the hands of a thousand strangers. The essay isn't made of distant abstractions but proximate lives and bodies. It disrupts the car. It might kick you in the face. It uses the materials of the ordinary world, things you might see every day—railings and poles and sliding doors—to create a particular choreography that hasn't happened before and won't ever happen again. It turns the common world into generative constraint, into sheer possibility.

America is the Q train at twilight . . . America is a line of barges on the East River . . . America isn't the Statue of Liberty but the subway dancer who blocks your view of the Statue of Liberty. The essay knows that. It knows that America isn't the iconic body of a woman in robes, larger than life, but the stranger's body right next to your own—the stranger's body in headphones, daydreaming, or in the midst of a cell phone argument. The essay lives in moments of disruption. It lives in the belief that no beauty is innocent, no ugliness is fixed or simple, every life is bottomless, and no experience is ever only private. An essay doesn't simply transcribe the world, it *finds* the world. It makes the world. It remakes the world. It puts a boom box right on the floor and starts playing.

LESLIE JAMISON

The Best AMERICAN ESSAYS 2017

JASON ARMENT

Two Shallow Graves

FROM *The Florida Review*

I MET A man who was soon to die. The man had been a farmer or herder in the desert before the war broke out in Iraq; that's what I assumed, anyway, as professions were extremely limited in the middle of the desert. I couldn't see his hands to tell if heavy calluses and cracked nails marked him as a manual laborer because they were zip-tied behind his back, and I couldn't see his feet either since he was on his knees. His head bowed low, he trembled as he sobbed, the noises muffled by the sandbag over his head. What set this man apart from all the other people I met in Iraq who died soon after—Iraqi police at checkpoints who would disappear into the dark hours of night or become balls of flame during the day; Marines I met in passing who would barbecue in their Humvees; Iraqis I barely noticed who'd get run over or fall ill or disintegrate in a hail of gunfire—is that none of them knew. This man did.

Echo Company had driven many, many miles north of Hob—"a shitload of klicks," as a Sergeant had put it during the half-assed company mission briefing. Enormous swaths of the desert were to be swept for Bomb Makers and other, lower-profile insurgents who would carry out the violence. During the brief the Captain had instructed Echo Company to keep an eye out for terrain models, copper plates disguised as ashtrays, wires, and chalky substances while searching peoples' houses. When the company's convoy finished the long trek out to the middle of nowhere, taking from dawn until midday, the gun trucks formed a large circle and faced outward. All of Weapons Platoon stood post in turrets and driver's seats of vehicles for days while the rest of the platoons went hunting. Finally, Third Platoon brought someone in.

The man was guilty; his crying gave it away. The Iraqis we brought in who cried were guilty. They knew they were going to be turned over to the Iraqi Army or the Iraqi Police and from there they would, as the Marine Corps saying goes, be in a world of shit. The IA's brutality toward POWs passed from Marine to Marine as lore, an oral history from those who'd walked into IA or IP prisons outfitted with meat hooks hanging from the ceiling, who'd watched the IA attach jumper cables to scrotal flesh; senior Marines passed these stories to those in their charge. The Marine who told me about the jumper cables coercion also remarked on smelling burnt meat and hair, like a farmer recounting a hog being slaughtered, while the Marine who'd seen the meat hooks just sounded sad when he talked about it. Both Marines were my superiors, veterans of the invasion. Crying wouldn't save the Bomb Maker. It only let us know he was guilty beyond a doubt—the guilty POWs always cried, the innocent never shed a tear. Not that there was much of a doubt after his house was swept for contraband.

Third Platoon found a terrain model of an Iraqi Police station built to a scale on par with ambitious sand castles. Third Platoon also found bomb-making materials: wires, explosives, copper plates, cell phones, beepers, and wind-up timers from old washers and dryers. When Third brought in the man they called him the Bomb Maker, and that's what he'd been known as since. Third also called him a PUC, Person Under Custody. If we called him a POW, Prisoner of War, in any paperwork, the prisoner would have been granted rights under the Geneva Convention. The man on his knees wouldn't have his status change from PUC for about forty-eight hours, when the United States felt it appropriate, and he would become a POW. The seemingly ambiguous number of hours being how far the U.S. was willing to bend the rules of war.

"Who put him on his knees?" I asked Ulrich, who had been pulled off of post to watch the PUC.

"Nobody," Ulrich said, walking forward out of a vehicle's shadow. "He wants to pray."

"He's praying, huh?" I said. "I wonder what he's saying."

The desert's night breeze blew between us with a gentle hiss of sand moving. The man's prayers, interspersed with crying, sounded like nothing more than whispered Arabic to me and I doubted they would save him; it would be left to Allah's vengeance, sometime in the future, to show He had not forsaken His people. How his head bowed made sense now. He was trying to prostrate himself before Allah, but the restraints held him upright. I would like to say that I felt for him. But I didn't. I watched his tears plunging down to become black dots on the desert floor. Great forces had moved us into opposition. I stood on the side of might, and therefore right, while he rested on his knees in the sand with a bag on his head and his hands bound. It was like watching a man being swept out to sea by a rip tide; there was nothing I could do to save him, even if I was as complicit as the moon.

Looking back now I wonder how it didn't weigh more heavily on my mind then, how I remained so aloof. I knew the man's fate as well as he did, knew it to be morally wrong and a mistake by the standards of agreements and policies written long ago. This knowledge obligated me to do something to stop it. I didn't though. I found acquiescence to be a refuge even as I was troubled in a way that touched me deeply. But it's easy for me to forget the hunger, the sun pounding down, sleeping in full gear, the night breeze cracking my skin, how I quenched my thirst with water as hot as a locker-room shower, and the intense solitude of fifteen-hour posts behind a turret staring out into the desert for ten days straight. Right and wrong had boiled down to survival. At this point in the occupation, insurgent tactics revolved around actions by lone wolves. I wasn't worried about FOBs being overrun, as had happened with one of 2/24 Battalion's FOBs during its first time over —another company in 2/24, Fox, had been overrun, but Echo had been spared the baptism by fire. My main concerns were snipers and copper-plate IEDs. This put the man across from me directly at odds with my existence.

As far as I knew this guy had personally made the bombs that killed the guys in Fox earlier in the tour when they ran over an IED and roasted in their vics after being sent out on a fool's errand by their CO. The man fit the profile of a Bomb Maker who would funnel IEDs and munitions to the hearts of conflict in the al-Anbar province. Aside from having the setup and paraphernalia, the man lived far away from the cities where he wouldn't have to worry about the Iraqi Police stopping by his house to discover the large terrain model of their station, nor the blasts from the devices he created. The man had nothing to worry about until Echo formed up its hunting party in a circle facing outward onto the desert plain. Now here he was, on his knees, sobbing prayers to a god that had turned his back on the land between the Tigris and Euphrates. Maybe the man thought about it while he was on his knees, how Saddam's audacity led him to write Allah's name on Iraq's flag as if he had the power to command Allah's blessing; then the Westerners had come with their gun trucks and their young men and their thundering aircraft. War had descended on the land, bringing with it destruction, desolation, pestilence, and finally despair as the Marines rooted out the insurgency.

The Bomb Maker was a "no-joke bad guy." A mujahedin in the language of the Arabs, a "freedom fighter" in my own. He'd be put to death as certainly as the harsh desert sun would sweep westward over the sky in the morning. The same sun that had watched his fathers build and prosper would watch as the IPs loaded him into a truck and took him to a bitter end.

Ulrich and I stood long together in silence; at this point in our tour in Iraq, we'd become like an old couple, able to be quiet in each other's company for days. As with most old couples, the shadow of death never left us. The war was wearing us down in body and mind. Backs ached from supporting body armor for ten days straight. Compacted disks groaned and creaked from the stress. Heels rubbed raw from never leaving their boots. From what I gathered in fleeting glimpses of my reflection in rearview mirrors of trucks, I looked like a street urchin. Ten days of sleeping on the desert sand or in the bed of a truck without washing my hands had left dirt smeared across my face, hands, and forearms. Splotches of darkly discolored skin peppered my body. Unbeknownst to me then, I'd picked up a fungus that liked the damp seams of my uniform and the sweatiest part of my body armor along the collar. After the war I'd go to a store every few months in search of some kind of foot cream to slather over my neck and chest; the rash never went away, though, only went back into remission. Ulrich's filth was only noticeable by how light-colored the desert's fine dust made him. Instead of a deep mahogany, his skin looked like a powdered doughnut, a kind of reverse blackface.

I'd been excited on the drive north from Camp Habbaniyah, in the back of a seven-ton truck, but now my mind strained. No one had told Weapons we'd be standing post on Echo's perimeter for the duration of the operation so I'd thought my platoon would help hunt the Bomb Maker—ten days in and I'd already spent over 150 hours on post. During the day the sun and heat made thoughts jumbled and confused in my head. I would sit on post and think back to before I joined, what I thought war would be like. I'd envisioned the desert version of Vietnam, which, in hindsight, didn't make any sense since the environments stood in near diametric opposition to each other. Vietnam seemed like the Wild West compared to Iraq's Rules of Engagement and Escalation of Force—it was like bureaucrats wrote the rules this time around with future legalities in mind. When I'd enlisted at seventeen, I'd felt like I was fighting for a righteous cause, back when 9/11 was still fresh in my memory. I imagined the towers falling again and again, but unlike years before I didn't focus on planes gliding into obelisks of steel and concrete; instead I focused on the aftermath—the great fall of debris and bodies, the tumult of smoke and great cloud of dust that rose when everything crashed into the ground. This war seemed like a perpetuation of the devastation in the impact, forever, in all directions, until I wonder if that very devastation didn't lie before me in the desert. The mission in Iraq when I'd come over with Echo had been to snuff out the insurgency through what amounted to an occupation turned witch hunt. And here a Bomb Maker was, hunted down in desert bad at the ends of the earth.

The man on his knees in front of me was not a civilian to my mind. I could sympathize with his drive to fight for his peoples' sovereignty, even as his country was on its back in a pool of blood. I'd felt much the same feelings when I'd first left the States and arrived in Iraq—an event that was so remote in my memory it seemed like some kind of creation myth. This was the endgame, taking down the Bomb Makers with terrain models in their lawns. The resistance to Allied presence in the al-Anbar province would be less capable of doing heavy damage to our vehicles. A plan to attack an Iraqi Police station had been thwarted. I continued to toe the party line that had us calling POWs PUCs and handing them over to Iraqi Army nut-zapping butchers. I acquiesced because it would have been hugely unpopular—some would have called it treason—to protest. My dissenting voice would have been crushed by the boots of Marines.

No one in my squad ever regaled the new joins with the story of the man on his knees who cried all night, whose prayers to Allah were filled with snot and salt. After the war our memories seemed to become selective, and the VA hospitals would ask us if we thought we were blocking out parts of the war. Some of us would answer yes, because on dark nights alone with our drink, or smoke, or whatever poison we chose to numb the sleepless hours and ward off nightmares, in those moments some of what we pushed down deep would come bubbling up out of our unconscious. The crying Bomb Maker was one of those memories; the trouble with memories like that was oftentimes they slipped away again, like the tide. I would try to hold on to them by writing them down. I had tried before, but the journal I kept in Iraq wrote right around the memories worth keeping. I penned out how awful a given day was, how my eyes strained on patrol, but not until years later would I glance back through it and wonder why I hadn't written down any of the important stuff. Maybe I couldn't.

The man shifted from one knee to the other, trying to ease the pain of kneeling on rocks. The desert plain we stood on had cracked like a dried-up pond in the hot sun. At some point in months prior, puddles had covered much of the plain. I looked at the man, then Ulrich, and then back to the man.

"Has anyone shown him the shallow graves?" I asked Ulrich.

Ulrich laughed and lit his own cigarette.

"I doubt it," Ulrich said. "Third had him blindfolded the whole time."

Two shallow graves, half-dug, lay just beyond to the southeast. They were the only change on the desert for miles in any direction. I'd first seen the graves by the ruined walls of a brick house when Echo staged its vehicles single file before orchestrating them into a circle. The twin graves were fair warning, and as the trucks circled in a defensive posture the imagery wasn't wasted on me; it made me think of the old Chinese adage, "When embarking on a quest for revenge, dig two graves." Echo's higher-ups hadn't mentioned revenge and probably didn't look at it as any more than another mission in the desert, but we were a part of 2/24 Battalion, and Fox, one of our sister companies, had suffered three KIAs from an IED in the northern part of our Area of Operation.

"You think he should be shot and thrown in one of those little graves out there?" Ulrich asked, giving his cigarette's butt end a couple of flicks with his thumb. Ulrich wasn't one for mercy, but when he looked up at me like he was going to continue, he didn't. Instead, he just laughed a sad laugh.

"Nothing like that," I said. "I'm just saying it seems like much ado about nothing to keep him like this, on his knees crying, if all that is going to happen tomorrow is us handing him over to the IA."

Ulrich's cigarette cast his face in a red hue when he dragged on it.

"I've heard things could get rough for him," Ulrich said. "Intel has been calling in from battalion trying to see if they could see him before we turn him over to the IA."

"Funny how they make zombies look like walking corpses in the movies," I said. "This dude's as close to the living dead as we'll come, and he isn't green or trying to bite people."

"Do zombies drink water?" Ulrich asked. "I'm pretty sure real zombies don't drink water. This guy keeps whining about how the water is hot. Gunny had me rig up some 550 cord to hang a bottle of water in front of the air conditioner in an MRAP. I'm not sure if it cooled it down very much, but that's what I've been giving to him."

"Is that what the hullabaloo was about earlier?" I asked. "When some of the guys from Third were yelling about POWs getting treated better than Marines?"

"PUC," Ulrich said. "He's a PUC."

I took a drag of my cigarette as my eyes narrowed on Ulrich.

"Who gives a fuck?" I asked. "I could boot this dude in the face and no one would touch me for it."

Ulrich laughed grimly.

"Look at you," I said. "All standing guard in the shadows like a salty devil warrior, ready to defend this man's status as a PUC from those who would accidentally give him rights by calling him a POW."

"*Semper,*" Ulrich said. "*Semper fidelis.*"

Always faithful. The Marine Corps motto. I continued without missing a beat.

"Oh yeah, look at you, young warrior from the sea. Between these two Humvees with your head down and your dick hard. You steely-eyed killer. You're going to make sure this guy gets enough to drink so he can keep crying. Devil Dog, you're going to hang water from the ceiling of the MRAP so this motherfucker here can sip on some cool wat—"

"Arment," the Company Gunny bellowed, walking up behind Ulrich. "What the fuck are you doing talking to this Marine while he stands post?"

"Gunny, Sergeant Prockop sent me to see how Ulrich was doing on post. He wanted to make sure he didn't need any food or water."

The Company Gunny walked out from behind Ulrich to stand facing the man bound on his knees, who was still crying softly and whispering prayers. New black spots appeared on the sand as the old dots faded to the color of the desert.

"How long has he been crying for?" Gunny asked.

"As long as I've been here guarding him, Gunny. So about eight hours," Ulrich said.

"Fucking Christ," Company Gunny said. "Keep an eye on him. Make sure he doesn't shuffle off somewhere on his knees."

"Aye, aye, Gunny," Ulrich said as Gunny Vance turned and started walking away from us.

I feigned a gesture of masturbation at Ulrich while keeping a serious look on my face.

"Arment," the Gunny yelled without turning around. "Stow that shit. We don't need another Abu Grave on our hands."

I stood dumbfounded for a few moments; the Gunny didn't usually have a flair for puns.

"How the fuck can he see me?" I muttered to Ulrich.

"Arment!" Gunny Vance bellowed, turning to face me this time.

"Yes, Gunny," I said.

"Ulrich is fine," Vance said. "Now I know you Machine Gunners are thick as thieves, but you are interfering with this Marine's ability to stand post, so I suggest you go back to yours."

So I did.

Back in my post, behind a machine gun in a turret of a seven-ton, I watched the truck's shadow stretch longer and longer before me. I counted myself lucky to be facing outward on the eastern part of the 360-degree perimeter. I didn't envy evening shifts of looking into the sun while it set. My mornings of watching the sunrise left my eyes so fatigued the horizon blurred and twisted. But the first few moments of the sun breaking over the crags of desert crust in the distance made me feel connected to the rest of the world. I thought about how people back home were watching it rise as well, even though in reality it was night in the U.S.

This night I thought about the man on his knees and his prayers. I recalled one of the times I had been told to get on my knees and pray. I was six, and late one night my mother decided it was time for me to accept the good Lord Jesus Christ as my personal savior. I'd asked questions—Will God say no? What if I don't? What if I don't mean it?—to which my mother yelled at me to "shut up and accept the Lord or you'll go to hell!" I accepted the Lord because my mom was yelling at me about hell, if that can be called acceptance; when I was older I realized I had to accept that some people with authority would have me say I accepted the Lord. Did the man on his knees really believe in Allah? Or was this the first time in a long time he'd gotten on his knees to pray? It stood to reason that he was devout since he actively fought against what he probably thought of as Christian forces that had come to his land. We could probably find common ground in our fighting spirits, talk about how the war hadn't lived up to the promises of our respective prophets. But I would never really be able to feel his loss. And he would never feel the numbness I felt as I watched him cry. I wondered if the man's faith would falter and fade like the day's light.

I surveyed my sector of fire with care, squinting to see as far as I could across the flat, cracked desert. As night fell, Marines on perimeter were supposed to transition over to their night-vision goggles as the changing ambient light required. The NVGs were to be mounted and ready to go but not activated since their batteries drained very quickly. I didn't bother putting mine on. If anyone crawled up the front of the seven-ton to check, I'd have them on long before they got to the top. Even with the sun just below the horizon, the desert sky held enough light to allow me to see eight hundred meters, but that gradually decreased down to fifty or so as night fell.

A few hours into night watch I noticed a pack of cigarettes on the dash below me. Quietly I squatted to lower my top half into the cab to find Huelatte, the Marine standing post behind the wheel, sound asleep. I thought about waking him but figured if anything happened my shooting would rouse him. I grabbed the smokes and stood back up and chain-smoked until the pack was empty. Forty-five minutes passed on my watch while I smoked fifteen cigarettes. My lungs felt heavy and my head light. I leaned forward in the turret and rested my helmeted head against the fifty cal's handgrips.

The night air held the chill of a midwestern autumn. The street-lights of a small-town suburb showed broken sidewalks and dark lawns in a neighborhood that looked like any other in the Mid-west. The moon hung full in the sky. People were hunting me. I wasn't sure how I knew, but a horrifying certainty filled my mind, pushing everything else out. I looked down to find myself in a T-shirt, cutoff digital-camouflage shorts, and an M-16 slung to my body. The street stretched before me for a quarter mile before it blurred in the darkness. Behind me the street ran thirty meters be-fore coming to a T intersection. I turned around and started walk-ing for the intersection, then started running. My breath came in short, ragged gasps. I could hear men running through yards, kick-ing leaves; one of them stumbled and fell. I spun around, quickly squeezing the trigger over and over in a long arc of fire that swept through the lawns on both sides of the street. The muzzle flash left negative imprints of bright blue and green in my vision. Dark shapes of men fell down.

One of the featureless silhouettes stepped onto the sidewalk. I trained my weapon on him and pulled the trigger but nothing happened. The human form saturated with blackness sprinted at me as I frantically racked the bolt back and forth while pulling the trigger, trying to find a round that would fire. As the man leaped at me, I took a deep breath to scream and suddenly he and my rifle dropped out of existence like they had never been there at all.

I stood stunned, peering around me in the dim light. The leaves in the yards were upturned where they'd been run through. My breathing returned to normal. From one of the houses, light stretched out from the front door as it opened, like a pale carpet of light reaching out. A strange compulsion drove me toward the door, and I knew as I walked across the lawn I was dreaming. The door closed behind me as I dug in my pocket for a pack of smokes. The large entryway of the house was empty except for ascending stairs and a chandelier above me strewn with thousands of crystals. I heard a soft crying coming from upstairs, a crying that rever-berated through the chandelier and made the crystals sound like hail on a tin roof. I got the pack of cigarettes out of my pocket. It was covered in bloody fingerprints. My fingers dripped red onto the carpet. I tried lighting a smoke, but the blood made it hard to work the lighter, eventually soaking the cigarette all the way through. The crying turned to a wail that oscillated the crystals into a hailstorm. Then the wail stopped and everything was still.

"Time to face it," I said.

Somehow I already knew what I would find upstairs, in the sole room on the second floor of the house. My left hand swung free, splattering blood on the white carpet; my right hand felt along the side of the stairwell, leaving behind a streak of blood that oozed from the wall. The chandelier's crystals reached a frenzy as I stepped from the stairs to the second floor, dropping to thud on the carpet like pouring rain.

The man was on his knees in the room, crying and praying in Arabic. I stood in front of him, my hands still dripping. Around me on the walls hung pictures of my family. They fell from the walls, breaking on the floor. I held my hand in front of my face, feeling the slippery blood between thumb and forefinger. The man started pleading for help in English, told me how his family needed him and that he wanted to see them again.

"I can't help you," I said. "This is a nightmare."

I looked up to see the first rays of the sun cresting the desert horizon. Yawning, I looked down to see Huelatte slumped over the steering wheel snoring. I gave him a few swift kicks in the head to help him get started.

"What the fuck, Big Head? You can't wake me up like a normal person?"

"Marine," I said, "sleeping on post is a very serious offense."

"I woke up in the middle of the night to have a smoke. And guess what? You were having some kind of raving nightmare after smoking all of mine!"

"A pack of smokes is fifty cents in the ville," I said. "I'll pick some up for you next chance I get, you goddamn crybaby."

"When is the next time we'll be back in a town? Fucking days? Weeks? We've been sitting in this circle for ten days now!"

Huelatte started to say something else, but then his voice trailed off for a moment.

"The Iraqi Army is here to pick up the PUC," he said at last.

I twisted my head to the right to see a dozen Iraqi Army vehicles headed in our direction. About the time they pulled into

Echo's circle of vehicles relief arrived for Huelatte and me. My back creaked as I crawled down from the turret; my joints were aching in a way I'd never felt before. Now I was free to sleep on the sand, try to find an open spot in one of the trucks, eat an MRE, drink hot water, smoke, or relieve my bowels in one of the two shit-ters—two bags filled with a sanitizing chemical. But there was one something I could do, and it was the most interesting thing to be done. I could watch the Bomb Maker be handed over to the Iraqi Army in a culmination of the hunt. I started walking toward the center of the circle.

"Sergeant Prockop I'm going to check on Ulrich," I yelled over my shoulder without bothering to stop and listen for a response.

Halfway to the small group of trucks that made up the COC, I realized my slow trudge was more of a stumble. Fragments of the nightmare I'd had already faded to almost nothing. A street, I remembered a street, and lawns. There had been a moon, and a man crying on his knees. Had my family been there, with the sound of rain?

When I saw the man, still on his knees, it was like remembering a forgotten face.

Ulrich stood close by the Bomb Maker, looking like hell after not having slept for over thirty hours by my estimate. He'd wiped the desert's white dust off his face at some point, but hadn't both-ered to touch his neck. Ulrich looked at me as I approached, his face the mask of a Marine on duty. When I drew close he relaxed and exhaustion broke across his face. He tried smiling at me, but couldn't manage more than a smirk, and I could tell that took a considerable effort.

"Time's about here," he said slowly. His eyes held mine, then looked over at the man.

I lit up a smoke and turned to look at the man. Ulrich walked over and pulled the sandbag off of his head.

"He won't need that anymore," Ulrich said.

The man looked around, blinking. In appearance he was just like any other Iraqi male so it was hard to place his age. The desert made young men seem to be about in their midthirties, old men to be really old. The man remained silent on his knees. When he looked at me I felt the same way I did when barefoot, shirtless Iraqi children with bloated bellies playing in lots filled with garbage looked at me, the same way I felt when limbless Iraqis with deep scars webbing their faces would look at me, the same way I felt when I watched Marines hit Iraqis or kill their animals—a nothingness like the cracked floor of the desert I stood on. I couldn't look back at him, but Ulrich stared him down the entire time.

A convoy kicked up a rooster tail of dust in the distance to the south. Marines from Third Platoon showed up to make sure the PUC became a POW with no problems. After several minutes the IA convoy pulled alongside Echo's perimeter and sent a single vehicle into the circle. The man stopped crying as the IA truck reached him. His jaw set as Marines loaded him in, and his eyes searched the sky after they slammed the door. Maybe he took some solace in knowing he'd done what he felt was right. I wondered if I could say the same if the desert's people took my life tomorrow. I tried to think back to the start of Iraq for me, months before, tried to feel the same feelings and commune with the same beliefs. I watched the small Iraqi Army convoy fade into the desert's whitewashed horizon. It was just me and Ulrich standing there.

"I had a strange dream last night," I said.

"What happened?" Ulrich said.

"I had blood on my hands and he was there," I said with a nod toward where the convoy had disappeared on the horizon.

Ulrich followed my gaze without answering for a moment. The wind hissed between us.

"Sounds like being awake," Ulrich said.

We turned and started walking back to the part of the perimeter where Machine Guns stood post.

"You know, I'm beginning to worry about that," I said. "The way that my nightmares and reality are so similar."

"Do you think it has something to do with the stress?" Ulrich asked.

"Maybe," I said. "I think it has to do with a lot of things."

When we neared the truck, Prockop slept, Ulrich broke away from me to find out where his post would be. He needed to get some sleep, pretty obviously; his words slurred and his syntax jumbled. Whatever was happening in his head wasn't translating to his mouth right anymore.

"Well good luck getting a post that's far enough away you can sleep," I said. "I'm heading over to the small contingent of IA that came."

"I forgot they were with us," Ulrich said.

Four Iraqi Army trucks had been tasked by the IA to come along on the safari for Bomb Makers so it could be called a "joint operation." In actuality the IA slept outside of their trucks on cots they had brought; they slept all night and most of the day. I wanted to get their take on the Bomb Maker, see what they thought and ask if they knew what would happen to him. When Echo had trained in Israel with the Israeli Defense Force Counter-Terrorism Instructors a year or so before going to Iraq, I'd asked the instructors what they thought about Palestinians, since there was so much conflict between the two peoples. One instructor, Tom, went on about killing them; how he would sometimes shoot toward their villages in hopes that his stray round might snuff out a life. Another instructor, Gal, told me how they didn't want to kill them, that it was war, an unfortunate circumstance that set brothers against each other. Gal had made certain that I was understanding him correctly, that I knew he didn't take pleasure in killing Palestinians and was only protecting his home and people. I wanted to know if the Iraqi Army had similarly diverse thoughts, or if it was enough to simply be on the winning team.

The four trucks stood parked in a row forty or so meters outside of Echo's perimeter.

"How are you folks?" I asked.

Eight men lay on cots by their vehicles; they were all middle-aged and overweight, with bellies that hung over their belts and bushy mustaches. None of the vehicles had turrets, and only one of the vehicles was armored. The other three were pickup trucks painted Iraqi Army colors.

"Mista, water?" one of the men said without bothering to sit up in his bed.

The man had more rank on his shoulders than the other men, who hadn't bothered to wake or move at all.

"You don't have any water?" I said in complete disbelief.

"Mista, water, water, please!" the man said again.

Another one of the men woke up and started asking me for food.

"I only have enough for me," I said. "I can't help you."

Now more of the men started begging, some of them getting up to show me their empty water bottles and MREs. My mind was boggled. These men who were supposed to be soldiers were begging the same way the Iraqi children begged for chocolate. After a few more minutes of empty water bottles being waved in my face and MRE trash being thrown at my feet I turned and walked away.

"Mista, water, please!" Over and over as I walked away.

"What the fuck were you talking to those Hajjis for?" Sergeant Prockop asked me when I got back to the perimeter. Someone on post must have told him I'd walked out of Echo's circle.

"They don't have any water or food," I said.

"What?" Prockop said. "You have got to be kidding me."

"I shit you not," I said.

"Go talk to Company Guns and see what he can work out for them," Prockop said before climbing back into his truck to sleep.

I made my way back to the center of the circle to find Gunny Vance busy looking at maps and personnel rosters. He informed me that each platoon had given up food and water to the IA that had been sleeping by the circle for the last twelve days. Now it was Machine Guns' turn.

"I know it shouldn't be this way," he said. "But this is the way it is."

I nodded in agreement, a grim look on my face.

"Prockop always says it's the nature of the beast," I said.

Gunny Vance spit a long tendril of chew spit from his mouth to the desert floor.

"That's because Prockop knows not to try and make sense of it," Gunny said. He looked up at me from his map. "That's something you could learn a lesson from, Arment."

I didn't say anything in response. Maybe he was right and I needed to stop thinking. I looked at the circle of trucks all around me, then back at the Gunny deep in thought over his map, then at the four IA trucks. My walk was more of a stumble back to my post. I had to stand watch during the day; somehow the posts had been shuffled around and I ended up with extra. I let a Marine know to run some of our food out to the IA, then I crawled up in the turret. I lit up a cigarette and started chain-smoking and staring into the desert, trying not to think about anything. But it couldn't be helped.

I was standing in the truck's turret that overlooked the graves. When Echo had first arrived in the desert plain, I'd thought the graves could be used for whoever we caught out here. Now I knew better. One grave for the Bomb Maker, and one grave for whatever was left of me at the end of all this.

RACHEL KAADZI GHANSAH

The Weight of James Arthur Baldwin

FROM *BuzzFeed*

IT WAS AN acquaintance's idea to go there, to James Baldwin's house. He knew from living in Paris that Baldwin's old place, the house where he died, was near an elegant, renowned hotel in the Côte D'Azur region of France. He said both places were situated in Saint-Paul-de-Vence, a medieval-era walled village that was scenic enough to warrant the visit. He said we could go to Baldwin's house and then walk up the road for drinks at the hotel bar where the writer used to drink in the evening. He said we would make a day of it, that I wouldn't regret it.

For the first time in my life I was earning a bit of money from my writing, and since I was in London anyway for work and family obligations I decided to take the train over to Nice to meet him. But I remained apprehensive. Having even a tiny bit of disposable cash was very new and bizarre to me. It had been years since I had bought myself truly new clothes, years since going to a cash machine to check my balance hadn't warranted a sense of impending doom, and years since I hadn't on occasion regretted even going to college, because it was increasingly evident that I would never be able to pay back my loans. There were many nights where I lay awake turning over in my mind the inevitable—that soon Sallie Mae or some faceless, cruel moneylender with a blues song–type name would take my mother's home (she had cosigned for me) and thus render my family homeless. In my mind, three generations of progress would be undone by my vain commitment to tell stories about black people in a country where the black narrative was a quixotic notion at best. If I knew anything about being black in America it was that nothing was guaranteed, you couldn't count on anything, and all that was certain for most of us was a black death. In my mind, a black death was a slow death, the accumulation of insults, injuries, neglect, second-rate health care, high blood pressure, and stress, no time for self-care, no time to sigh, and, in the end, the inevitable, the erasing of memory. I wanted to write against this, and so I was writing a history of the people I did not want to forget. And I loved it; nothing else mattered, because I was remembering, I was staving off death.

So I was in London when a check with four digits and one comma hit my account. It wasn't much but to me it seemed enormous. I decided if I was going to spend any money, something I was reluctant, if not petrified, to do, at the very least I would feel best about spending it on James Baldwin. After all, my connection to him was an unspoken hoodoo-ish belief that he had been the high priest in charge of my prayer of being a black person who wanted to exist on books and words alone. It was a deification that was fostered years before during a publishing internship at a magazine. During the lonely week I had spent in the storeroom of the magazine's editorial office organizing the archives from 1870 to 2005, I had found time to pray intensely at the altar of Baldwin. I had asked him to grant me endurance and enough fight so that I could exit that storeroom with my confidence intact. I told him what all writers chant to keep on, that I had a story to tell. But later, away from all of that, I quietly felt repelled by him —as if he were a home I had to leave to become my own. Instead, I spent years immersing myself in the books of Sergei Dovlatov, Vivian Gornick, Henry Dumas, Sei Shōnagon, Madeleine L'Engle, and Octavia Butler. Baldwin didn't need my prayers—he had the praise of the entire world.

I still liked Baldwin but in a divested way, the way that anyone who writes and aspires to write well does. When people asked me my opinion on him I told them the truth: that Baldwin had set the stage for every American essayist who came after him with his 1955 essay collection *Notes of a Native Son*. One didn't need to worship him, or desire to emulate him, to know this and respect him for it. And yet, for me, there had always been something slightly off-putting about him—the strangely accented, ponderous way he spoke in the interviews I watched; the lofty, "theatrical" way in which he appeared in "Good Citizens," an essay by Joan Didion, as the bored, above-it-all figure that white people revered because he could stay collected. What I resented about Baldwin wasn't even his fault. I didn't like the way many men who only cared about Ali, Coltrane, and Obama praised him as the black authorial exception. I didn't like how every essay about race cited him. How they felt comfortable, as he described it, talking to him (and about him) "absolutely bathed in a bubble bath of self-congratulation."

James Baldwin and my grandfather were four years apart in age, but Baldwin, as he was taught to me, had escaped to France and avoided his birthrighted fate, whereas millions of black men his age had not. It seemed easy enough to fly in from France to protest and march, whereas it seemed straight hellish to live in the States with no ticket out. It seemed to me that Baldwin had written himself into the world—and I wasn't sure what that meant in terms of his allegiances to our interiors as an everyday, unglamorous slog.

So even now I have no idea why I went. Why I took that high-speed train past the sheep farms and the French countryside, past the brick villages and stone aqueducts, until the green hills faded and grew into Marseille's tall, dusky pink apartments and the bucolic steppes gave way to blue water where yachts and topless women with leather for skin were parked on the beaches.

It was on that train that I had time to consider the first time Baldwin had loomed large for me. It had occurred ten years earlier, when I was accepted as an intern at one of the oldest magazines in the country. I had found out about the magazine only a few months before. A friend who let me borrow an issue made my introduction, but only after he spent almost twenty minutes questioning the quality of my high school education. How could I have never heard of such an influential magazine? I got rid of the friend and kept his copy.

During my train ride into Manhattan on my first day, I kept telling myself that I really had no reason to be nervous; after all, I had proven my capability not just once but twice. Because the internship was unpaid I had to decline my initial acceptance to instead take a summer job and then reapplied later. When I arrived at the magazine's offices, the first thing I noticed was the stark futuristic whiteness. The entire place was a brilliant white, except for the tight, gray carpeting.

The senior and associate editors' offices had sliding glass doors and the rest of the floor was divided into white-walled cubicles for the assistant editors and interns. The windows in the office looked out over the city, and through the filmy morning haze I could see the cobalt blue of one of the city's bridges and the water tanks that spotted some of the city's roofs. The setting, the height, and the spectacular view were not lost on me. I had never before had any real business in a skyscraper.

Each intern group consisted of four people; my group also included a recent Brown grad, a hippieish food writer from the West Coast, and a dapper Ivy League sort of mixed-race Southeast Asian descent. We spent the first part of the day learning our duties, which included finding statistics, assisting the editors with the magazine's features, fact-checking, and reading submissions. Throughout the day various editors stopped by and made introductions. Sometime after lunch the office manager came into our cubicle and told us she was cleaning out the communal fridge and that we were welcome to grab whatever was in it. Eager to scavenge a free midday snack, we decided to take her up on the offer. As we walked down the hall the Princeton grad joked that because he and I were the only brown folks around we should be careful about taking any food because they might say we were looting. I had forgotten about Hurricane Katrina, the tragedy of that week, during the day's bustle, and somehow I had also allowed the fact that I am black to fade to the back of my thoughts, behind my stress and excitement. It was then that I was smacked with the realization that the walls weren't the only unusually white entities in the office — the editorial staff was strangely all white as well.

Because we were interns, neophytes, we spent the first week getting acquainted with each other and the inner workings of the magazine. Sometime toward the end of my first week, a chatty senior editor approached me in the corridor. During the course of our conversation I was informed that I was (almost certainly) the first black person to ever intern at the magazine and that there had never been any black editors. I laughed it off awkwardly only because I had no idea of what to say. I was too shocked. At the time of my internship the magazine was more than 150 years old. It was a real *Guess Who's Coming to Dinner* moment. Except that I, being a child of the '80s, had never watched the film in its entirety, I just knew it starred Sidney Poitier as a young, educated black man who goes to meet his white fiancée's parents in the 1960s.

When my conversation with the talkative editor ended I walked back to my desk and decided to just forget about it. Besides, I reasoned, it was very possible that the editor was just absentminded. I tried to forget it myself but I could not, and finally I casually asked another editor if it was true. He told me he thought there had been an Algerian-Italian girl many years ago, but he was not certain if she really "counted" as black. When I asked how that could be possible, I was told that the lack of diversity was due to the lack of applications from people of color. As awkward as these comments were, they were made in the spirit of oblivious commonwealth. It was office chatter meant to make me feel like one of the gang, but instead of comforting my concerns it made me feel like an absolute oddity.

On good days, being the first black intern meant doing my work quickly and sounding extra witty around the watercooler; it meant I was chipping away at the glass ceiling that seemed to top most of the literary world. But on bad days I gagged on my resentment and furiously wondered why I was selected. I became paranoid that I was merely a product of affirmative action, even though I knew I wasn't. I hadn't mentioned my race in either of my two accepted applications. Still, I never felt like I was actually good enough. And with my family and friends so proud of me, I felt like I could not burst their bubble with my insecurity and trepidation.

So when I was the only intern asked by a top editor to do physical labor and reorganize all of the old copies of the magazine in the freezing, dusty storeroom, I fretted in private. Was I asked because of my race or because that was merely one of my duties as the intern-at-large? There was no way to tell. I found myself most at ease with the other interns and the staff that did not work on the editorial side of the magazine: the security guards, the delivery guys, the office manager, and the folks at the front desk. Within them the United Nations was almost represented. With them, I did not have to worry that one word pronounced wrong or one reference not known would reflect not just poorly on me but also on any black person who might apply after me.

I also didn't have to worry about that in that storeroom. I vexingly realized three things spending a week in the back of that dismal room. That yes, I was the only intern asked to do manual labor, but I was surrounded by 150 years of the greatest American essays ever written, so I read them cover to cover. And I discovered that besides the physical archives and magazines stored there, the storeroom was also home to the old index-card invoices that its writers used to file. In between my filing duties, I spent time searching those cards, and the one that was most precious to me was Baldwin's. In 1965 he was paid $350 for an essay that is now legend. The check went to his agent's office. There was nothing particularly spectacular about the faintly yellowed card except that its routineness suggested a kind of normalcy. It looped a great man back to the earth for me. And in that moment, Baldwin's eminence was a gift. He had made it out of the storeroom. He had taken a steamer away from being driven mad from maltreatment. His excellence had moved him beyond the realm of physical labor. He had disentangled himself from being treated like someone who was worth less or questioning his worth. And better yet, Baldwin was so good they wanted to preserve his memory. Baldwin joined the pantheon of black people who were from that instructional generation of civil rights fighters, and I would look at that card every day of my week down there.

What makes us want to run away? Or go searching for a life away from ours? The term "black refugees" applies most specifically to the black American men and women who escaped in 1812 to the British navy's boats and were later taken to freedom in Nova Scotia and Trinidad, but don't many of us feel like black refugees? Baldwin called these feelings, the sense of displacement and loss that many black Americans ponder, the "heavy" questions, and heavy they are indeed. Sometime in the early '50s, after being roughed up and harassed by the FBI, James Baldwin realized that while he "loved" his country, he "could not respect it." He wrote that he "could not, upon my soul, be reconciled to my country as it was." To survive he would have to find an exit. On the train to Baldwin's house I thought more about that earlier generation and about the seemingly vast divide between Baldwin and my grandfather. They had very little in common, except they were of the same era, the same race, and were both fearless men, which in black America actually says a lot. Whereas Baldwin spent his life writing against a canon, writing himself into the canon, a black man recording the Homeric legend of his life himself, my grandfather simply wanted to live with dignity.

It must have been hard then to die the way my grandfather did.

I imagine it is not the ending that he expected when he left Louisiana and moved to Watts—to a small, white house near Ninety-Ninth Street and Success Avenue. After his death, I went back to the house in Watts that he had been forced to return to, broke and burned out of his home, and gathered what almost ninety years of black life in America had amounted to for him: a notice saying that his insurance claim from the fire had been denied, two glazed clay bowls, and his hammer (he was a carpenter). My grandfather had worked hard but had made next to nothing. I took a picture of the wall that my grandfather built during his first month in L.A. It was old, cracked, jagged, not pretty at all, but at the time, it was the best evidence I had that my grandfather had ever been here. And as I scattered his ashes near the Hollywood Park racetrack, because he loved horses and had always remained a country boy at heart, I realized that the dust in my hands was the entirety of my inheritance from him. And until recently, I used to carry that memory and his demand for optimism around like an amulet divested of its power, because I had no idea what to do with it. What Baldwin understood, and my grandfather preferred not to focus on, is that to be black in America is to have the demand for dignity be at absolute odds with the national anthem.

From the outside, Baldwin's house looks ethereal. The saltwater air from the Mediterranean acts like a delicate scrim over the heat and the horizon, and the dry, craggy yard is wide and long and tall with cypress trees. I had prepared for the day by watching clips of him in his gardens. I read about the medieval frescoes that had once lined the dining room. I imagined the dinners he had hosted for Josephine Baker and Beauford Delaney under a trellis of creeping vines and grape arbors. I imagined a house full of books and life.

I fell in love with Baldwin all over again in France. There I found out that Baldwin didn't go to France because he was full of naive, empty admiration for Europe; as he once said in an interview: "If I were twenty-four now, I don't know if and where I would go. I don't know if I would go to France, I might go to Africa. You must remember when I was twenty-four there was really no Africa to go to, except Liberia. Now, though, a kid now . . . well, you see, something has happened which no one has really noticed, but it's very important: Europe is no longer a frame of reference, a standard-bearer, the classic model for literature and for civilization. It's not the measuring stick. There are other standards in the world."

Baldwin left the States for the primary reason that all emigrants do—because anywhere seems better than home. This freedom-seeking gay man, who deeply loved his sisters and brothers—biological and metaphorical—never left them at all. In France, I saw that Baldwin didn't live the life of a wealthy man, but he did live the life of a man who wanted to travel, to erect an estate of his own design, and write as an outsider, alone in silence. He had preserved himself.

Decades after Baldwin's death in 1987, what I found left behind in his house was something similar to what I saw as we waded through my grandfather's house after it had burned down. In both houses, I found mail strewn in dirt piles in rooms that no longer had doors or windowpanes, and entryways nailed over to prevent trespassers like us. In each case, someone had clearly forced entry in order to drink beer. In Baldwin's house, the scattered, empty beer cans were recent additions, as were the construction postings from a company tasked with tearing it down. So that nothing would remain. No remembrance of the past. In both places there was not even the sense that a great man had once lived there.

James Baldwin lived in his house for more than twenty-five years, and all that was left were half a dozen pink teacups and turquoise saucers buried by the house's rear wall, a chipped fresco on a crumbling wall, and orange trees that were heavy with fruit bitter and sharp to the taste. We see Baldwin's name in connection to the present condition more often than we see Faulkner's, Whitman's, or Thoreau's. But we can visit the houses and places where they lived and imagine how their geography shaped them and our collective vocabulary. By next year, Baldwin's house will just be another private memory for those who knew it.

I do not know if I will ever see his house again. If I will be able to pull sour oranges from his trees and wonder if they were so bitter when he lived there. But I do know that Baldwin died a black death.

For a while when I came back to the States, I started to send strange, desperate emails to people who knew him that read:

For the last two days, I've basically found myself frantically, maniacally looking for everything that I could find about Baldwin's life there. To be honest, I'm not at all sure what I am looking for, but when I walked up that steep little hill, past the orange and cypress trees out onto the main road, and looked back at his house I just felt a compulsion to start asking people who knew him about his life in that house. The compound is almost gone, as they are in the process of demolishing it and yet something about it and him seemed to still be very much there.

Baldwin once wrote: "Life is tragic simply because the earth turns and the sun inexorably rises and sets, and one day, for each of us, the sun will go down for the last, last time. Perhaps the whole root of our trouble, the human trouble, is that we will sacrifice all the beauty of our lives, will imprison ourselves in totems, taboos, crosses, blood sacrifices, steeples, mosques, races, armies, flags, nations, in order to deny the fact of death, the only fact we have. It seems to me that one ought to rejoice in the fact of death—ought to decide, indeed, to earn one's death by confronting with passion the conundrum of life. One is responsible for life: It is the small beacon in that terrifying darkness from which we come and to which we shall return."

I sent those notes—feeling as hopeless as I sounded—because I wanted to save that building. I did not want it and him to vanish into the terrifying darkness. Because I was scared that no one else would ever be able to see that Baldwin had a rainbow kitchen —an orange sink and purple shelves—in his guesthouse. I wanted someone else to wonder what he ate from this kitchen, who stayed in this annex of his estate, who he loved, whether his love felt free in this kitchen, in this house where two men could embrace in private behind the ramparts of his home in another country. I wanted someone else to understand the private black language found in one of Baldwin's last conversations with his brother David. Frail, sick, and being carried to his deathbed in his brother's arms, what the world thought of him might as well have been an ocean away. In that moment, Baldwin didn't refer to French poets, or to the cathedrals of his genius, he instead returned to a popular song. He loved music, and he told his brother: So it is true what they say —he is my brother and he's not heavy.

There is no great mystery behind why Baldwin's house isn't treated like Anna and Sigmund Freud's in London or rebuilt and replicated like Dante Alighieri's in Florence. "We lost the house because supposedly there was no way to prove that it was his," his niece Kali-Ma Morrison tells me with a slight edge in her voice. "People contested his right to ownership in the French Supreme Court and after ten years of fighting to save it, we lost."

For months, I had wanted to know about the women who read as almost mythical in Baldwin's life and work, the siblings and nieces who are tasked with being the legal keepers of his legacy. I was also curious because in the strange early hours of the morning just before the bakeries open and the fog lifts herself from the mountains, I sat in a village in the South of France and watched Baldwin defend our future as black women on *The Dick Cavett Show* in 1968. My god, how I loved his exasperation and anger as he told primetime television, "I don't know if the real estate lobby has anything against black people, but I know that the real estate lobby is keeping me in the ghetto. I don't know if the board of education hates black people, but I know the textbooks they give my children to read and the schools that we have to go to. Now: This is the evidence. And you want me to make an act of faith—risking myself, my life, my woman, my sister, my children—on some idealism which you assure me exists in America which I have never seen?" In 1968 James Baldwin was already asking, *What is any movement without all of us? What is a black conversation that divides our concerns?*

Kali-Ma—Baldwin's niece—is in her late twenties. She is a visual artist and poet, and although she has piercings and tattoos, she looks like the sort of young woman who once appeared in tintype photographs—patient, timeless, and very beautiful in an intoxicatingly demure way. Her grandmother Gloria is Baldwin's sister, and handles her brother's estate. Her other grandmother is Toni Morrison. Kali-Ma hands me a cup of green tea, reaches down to stroke her purring cat, who has been clawing her ankles for attention, and then goes over to a bookcase that sags with books and pulls out some of her uncle's belongings that she retrieved from Saint-Paul-de-Vence. She hands me a faded copy of his book *A Dialogue* (written with Nikki Giovanni), his copies of *Freedomways* magazine (including one with Lorraine Hansberry on the cover), and a small brass plaque (engraved in French) awarded to him for his commitment to human rights.

We are both very quiet. I trace the Greek severe-style angel on the award with my finger until she shrugs and says, "I know I should probably have this stuff locked away, or covered in laminate, but I like him out here, you know, being here with me and mixed in with the other books. Alive." I came to her place to take a picture of Baldwin's typewriter. This is what I told her. But I think I also came because I wanted to see someone who is his flesh and blood. I wanted to see that he was really theirs, their Uncle Jimmy. Because if he was theirs, the logic followed, then he was also ours.

Baldwin's people have an old-world, sophisticated manner. They offer you three types of tea, whiskey, and their time. They're patient and generous. They never ask me what I'm doing there. They are tolerant of my desire to find the quiet bibliography that he left behind in the small notations, brushes, and ephemera of his life. Annotations I believed when taken together would tell a private story of his battles and alienations as a gay black man who was born into poverty as the eldest in a solar system of siblings (there were nine of them), but who was also singularly rich, with an agile mind, a louche, lithe body, and a long-eyed gaze.

In the twenty-first century, black history must shirk any oversimplification. What I unfortunately realized late in the game was that I had allowed myself to understand Baldwin through a series of abstractions, one that was principally based upon how strangers, outsiders, and gatekeepers had interpreted his life. In their telling, I had never heard how Baldwin had felt like he could make peace with his old friend Richard Wright, but it would take a big bottle of booze and a whole night of talking in that garden in Saint-Paul. They never told me just how much Baldwin loved his records—spirituals and Bessie Smith. Or how he had met with Attorney General Robert F. Kennedy to press the government about its callous response to the civil rights movement. No one had ever told me to study with care the Harlem in the way that he could keep a cigarette dangling from his lips, just so, balanced between a blood's deep blues and a 125th Street cool.

"The American triumph—in which the American tragedy has always been implicit—was to make Black people despise themselves," Baldwin wrote in a foreword to Angela Davis's book *If They Come in the Morning*. He signed the letter Brother Jimmy and addressed Angela Davis as Sister Angela. When I was younger, the way Baldwin explained the conditions of "Negroes" to others made me question his devotion, but as I held his copy of Davis's book in my hands and reread those words, it was evident that America had never triumphed over James Baldwin.

One afternoon, Trevor Baldwin, Wilmer "Lover" Baldwin's son (the younger brother of the nephew addressed in Baldwin's "Letter to My Nephew"), tells me about "Uncle Jimmy's" visits back to the States, when he would return to the house that he had purchased for his mother on Seventy-First Street. Trevor is a down-to-earth, forthright Morehouse man, a Harlem man, and he recalls what both he and his father admired most about Uncle Jimmy. "He walked with a certain sense of manhood," Trevor told me. "You could easily see he was gay but [he] walked with his chest out and he'd cut you with his tongue."

"Which is to say he had self-pride?" I asked.

"Yes!" Trevor said. "He had to move to Europe because he was seriously worried that he was going to kill somebody."

Trevor always knew that Uncle Jimmy was in town because suddenly his grandmother's house would swell with visitors. "Uncle Jimmy," he laughed, "brought everybody to her, Maya [Angelou] included, and Toni, and said, 'Here's something else you don't need, but I got another sister. You got another child.'"

"He was the man of the house. He was the patriarch of us all."

I like this image of Baldwin, it is both vanguard and conventional, but I also enjoy the way Kali-Ma shudders when I ask her if her uncle was a patriarch. Of his sisters? His mother? No, she says.

She looks for a word to describe what he was. I try to help. We are both writers, but we could not find a single word to describe this man who told his adopted sisters that they had to write down their stories and later pragmatically assisted them in their endeavors, who had best friends in many countries in all professions, and who taught his older brother and young nephews a rare, lasting lesson in bravery—that we must be brilliant and big enough to be ourselves. To have pink teacups and brown typewriters. Baldwin defined what made him a great writer on his own terms. He also ensured that his success was not dependent on his silences. He taught us all that the greatest black art demands that there be no "rejection of life, the human being, the denial of his beauty" or our power. Some people will consider this vain, but isn't this what all good warriors have always done: venerating, salvaging, and celebrating ourselves in between battles? Is this not our real inheritance?

I have spent months thinking about something his former agent's granddaughter Eliza Mills revealed to me after she found out that

I had been to his home in France. "James Baldwin used to play dodgeball with my dad and his friends. And he'd stay up and out all night and go to bed when my dad and his sister were going to school in the morning. My grandfather helped sell a couple of his books and would read/edit things. I think he was writing *The Fire Next Time* while he lived there. I've seen a note or two that he wrote to my grandfather in the books he left at their house."

Breathless at the idea of all of this, I asked her if she was for real or kidding me.

"Yeah," she replied, incredulous to my doubt. "One little inscription is written in rainbow ink and half in French."

Last week, when I got back from seeing his brown typewriter, I wrote down the word "joy" and underlined it three times, like it was an obligation, a chore, something that I would have to find, if not fight for. I did this because isn't the more intimate, tenebrous story the one where we recognize each other not only in our despair but also in our joy? In your rainbow ink and your sleepless nights, in your demands, and in your nieces and nephews who love you like a black god. I will find you—in the enthusiasms of our people's style, our verve and our wit, the way you slouched in your seat and crossed your legs, in the ways that they will misunderstand you but we will always know you, in the abridgments that we will make to history, changing it forever.

Because I am telling this now, writing it all down, I am finding time to regard memory and death differently. I'm holding them up in the light and searching them, inspecting them, as they are not as what I want them to be. On that hill, in Saint-Paul-de-Vence, I wanted to alter fate, and preserve things. But why? He did not need me—Baldwin seemed to have prepared himself well for his black death, his mortality, and even better, his immortality. Indeed, he bested all of them, because he wrote it all down—both on the page and in his beautiful gestures.

And this is how his memory abides. On the scent of wild lavender like the kind in his yard, in the mouths of a new generation that once again feels compelled to march in the streets of Harlem, Ferguson, and Baltimore. What Baldwin knew is that he left no false heirs, he left spares, and that is why we carry him with us. So now when people ask me about James Baldwin, I tell them another truth: He is my brother, he ain't heavy.

ELIESE COLETTE GOLDBACH

White Horse

FROM *Alaska Quarterly Review*

ELIESE DAYDREAMS OF rape.[1] She imagines it happening to her in dark alleys, or during partics at swanky nightclubs, or on the asphalt after it's just rained. She dreams of rape during the eighteenth century, under a petticoat. In ancient Rome, under a toga. She dreams of rape perpetrated by kings and princes and vagabonds. By Italians and Russians and Bolivians.[2]

In every daydream—after Eliese has imagined herself bloody, abused, nearly dead—a man will step into her plotline to save her life.

The proverbial man on a white horse.[3] That is always the point.

When Eliese was a little girl, the family handyman used to call her Leesy Piecey. *Helloooo, Leesy Piecey,* he'd say as his eyes walked slowly up the length of her body. Eliese always blushed, but she didn't know why. She loved it when the handyman came.[4] He kept a box of Reese's Pieces in his pocket. Always a box, never a bag. The candies rattled as he walked. He'd give Eliese a handful of candy if she watched him work. Eliese liked to watch.[5] She loved Reese's Pieces.

1. Do you trust me?
2. Six days after my eighteenth birthday, I was raped by two men. They took me into the woods. They stripped me beneath a massive, deeply rooted oak. It was late fall. The leaves of the tree had already browned. Many had fallen away. The few remaining leaves clung desperately to the branches in the breeze.
3. *You can't tell anyone about this,* the men said after they finished. They dragged me back to my dormitory. Dirt and gravel bloodied my palms, my knees. *You can't tell anyone about this. You don't want to look like a slut.*
4. *You don't want to look like a slut.*
5. While the men raped me under the oak tree, I wavered in and out of consciousness. I caught glimpses between blackouts. The sleeve of one man's army fatigue

*

There is a paradox of logic that goes like this: *The white horse is not a horse.*

Eliese heard about this paradox, but she didn't understand it. She wrote to a logician and asked him to explain the matter.

"Suppose a white horse is a horse," the logician replied in a letter. "Then everything true of a white horse is true of a horse. Suppose a brown horse is a horse. Then everything true of a brown horse is true of a horse. So, everything true of a white horse is true of a brown horse. That is, a white horse is a brown horse. But obviously a white horse is not a brown horse. So a white horse is not a horse, and a brown horse is not a horse."[6]

---

jacket. The other man's hand reaching for my hair. My chest covered in vomit. While one of the men moved on top of me, I felt as though I were swimming outside myself. I was around and above. In a place along the periphery. I saw my underwear lying a few feet away. They weren't the lacy panties of a woman, but the white Hanes of a little girl. That's what I thought about while the men finished. *Only little girls wear white underwear. Only stupid little girls.*

6. *You can't tell anyone about this.* At first, I didn't heed the advice of the men. I told a few people what had happened. I told several friends. I told a therapist. I told the administrators of the Catholic college where the men and I were students. I told these administrators what I remembered: I had been under a tree, and one of the men moved on top of me, and the other urged him to hurry—*come on, hurry up, someone's gonna see*—and my white underwear lay in the dirt, and the roots of the tree dug into my back, and the November breeze pricked at my thighs, and the men had given me something to drink in a red cup—a red cup I hadn't watched them pour—and the branches of the tree were mostly bare, and everything blurred after I drank from the red cup, and I could no longer stand, and so much of my memory is unclear—even the tree fades in and out—and now I cannot stop crying, and I cannot get clean, and I can still smell them—I can still smell them on my body after I wash—and I cannot forget their smells, and I cannot forget their voices, and I cannot forget how spectacularly the branches of that god-damned tree forked the moonlight into tiny beams.

Everyone asked the same question. *Well,* they said, *did you say no?*

I don't know, I said. *I can't remember.*

People raised eyebrows. They grew silent. There were awkward pauses.

How can you not remember?

Then the people said other things. The therapist said *date rape,* and the college administrators said *consensual,* and my friends insisted I confess my sins to a priest. The priest said that women who don't love themselves often commit acts of sexual indiscretion.

Did you say no? Well, did you? How can you not remember?

*

Eliese daydreams of rape. She dreams of violent rape—knives and AK-47s stuck inside her. Surprise rape—blindfolded and from behind. Stockholm rape—wanting more halfway through. She dreams of torturous rape and rape under palm trees and gang rape. She has always dreamed these dreams, even as a child. She dreamt of rape long before she had a word for such a thing.

Once, when Eliese was still a girl, she followed the handyman into a garage and watched him change the oil on a rusted Chevette. He promised to give her a handful of Reese's Pieces if she kept him company.

Eliese held a white plastic horse in her hand. The horse wasn't interested in oil changes. It was interested in galloping, so it galloped over wrenches and drill bits. It galloped across the concrete garage floor. It galloped up walls and around windows. It galloped right out of the garage. As Eliese clanked the horse's hooves on the sunlit driveway, the handyman stood in front of her. His hands were black with oil.

That's a nice horse, the handyman said. *What's his name?*

It's not a he, Eliese said. *It's a she.*

She's a very beautiful horse, the handyman said. He wasn't looking at the horse. *Listen, why don't you come back into the garage and keep me company? When I'm done, we can eat some candy.*

The candy piqued Eliese's interest. She restrained the white horse's gallop. She followed the handyman into the garage.

Eliese dreamt of rape long before she had a word for such a thing.[7]

*

---

7. *Did you say no? I don't know. I can't remember.*

I remember this, however: I watched a rerun of *The Joy of Painting* on the morning of the rape. Bob Ross brushed one of his idyllic scenes—snowcapped mountains set behind a twisting, rock-strewn river. When the painting looked complete, Bob turned toward the camera with a smile.

Let's put a happy little tree right here, he said.

He loaded a knife with black paint and pulled it down the canvas.

No, Bob, I said aloud, surprising myself. *You'll ruin it.*

Of course, the happy little tree turned out perfectly. Its branches were full of burnt-umber leaves. Its bark was subtle and knotty. The tree looked like it had been in the picture all along.

This is a strange thing to remember.

Nearly ten years after her eighteenth birthday, Eliese walked down a busy street in San Francisco. An old woman grabbed her by the arm and drew her close.

Your chakras are out of balance, the woman said. *Your chakras are dangerously out of balance. For twenty dollars, I can help you.*

Eliese did not want unbalanced chakras, so she handed the woman a twenty-dollar bill. Together, the two women searched for a quiet place where they could examine the state of Eliese's spiritual health. The street was crowded with tourists. The benches and bus stops were full. The two women could find only one area of relative peace: the display window at The Gap. Eliese and the old woman nestled between mannequins. The mannequins wore knitted, earth-toned cardigans. They stretched their arms toward one another, as if speaking, but they had no mouths, no faces.

When you were young, the woman said, *your life was bright, hopeful. You were on the right path, cosmically speaking. But then something happened. Something happened when you were seventeen or eighteen years old.*

The woman paused, as if consulting the universe.

Yes, the woman said, *something bad happened. This thing threw you off. It unhinged you.*

Eliese thought of the two men. She thought of their smells, their red cup. She thought of her half-naked body beneath the tree. She remembered her white underwear. The day after being raped, Eliese had searched frantically through her drawers. She gathered every single pair of white underwear in her possession. She threw them all into the trash. Even now, she will not wear white underwear.

What happened when you were seventeen or eighteen years old? the woman said.

Eliese started to cry. She looked away, into The Gap.

Nothing happened when I was eighteen, she said. *Nothing.*

The woman offered to align Eliese's chakras for a fee of sixty dollars, but Eliese declined. She knew she was being swindled. Eliese thanked the old woman and left. On her way home, Eliese sat down at a bus stop and pondered her faulty chakras. It would take more than sixty dollars to fix the damage done. While Eliese thought and waited, a man at the bus stop pulled a syringe from his pocket. In the middle of the afternoon, beside several anxious BART riders, this man attempted to shoot heroin into his hand. Everyone at the bus stop looked away. They checked their phones.

They stared at the pavement. But Eliese's attention shifted to the man. She ignored her chakras for a moment and watched him struggle with the syringe. She could not help watching.

A sheer, silk blouse sagged off the man's shoulders and revealed the thin straps of a black bra. He tied a tourniquet. He slipped the needle under his skin, wiggling it back and forth, searching for blood. It took him forever to find a vein. With every failed attempt, the man bit his lip and looked close to tears, itching madly for his junk, his skag, his white horse.[8] Eliese watched the man. Her interest was driven by more than morbid curiosity. To her, watching this man in his desperation was a strange type of reverence—it drew her closer to the nasty, frantic pieces of herself. Those parts of her that bring shame. Eliese hoped that a difficult and excruciating beauty was couched in these pieces. So she watched. When the man finally emptied the syringe, he suffered an unsteady, incoherent relief. He stumbled into the street and removed his silk shirt. He stood, dazed. Eliese watched his shallow breath. She stared at his bra, his belly, his skin-tight, stonewashed capris. She thought again of the old woman's words: *Your chakras are dangerously out of balance.*

Back when Eliese was a very little girl, she wrote her first book. She thought it would be the most important book she'd ever write. In this book, a woman loses herself in a snowstorm. The woman falters. She faints. A man rides over on a white horse. He takes the woman in his arms. He carries her to his home. He builds a fire. He undresses the woman and warms her. He tenderly burns her

8. I told a friend about the man at the bus stop. I told her of the syringe, the tourniquet, the black bra. My friend listened distractedly. She was working on a PowerPoint presentation about preventing date rape on college campuses. She was a high school teacher, and the presentation was intended for the senior class. She barely looked up from her computer while I spoke of the man and his heroin.

I'm not surprised, my friend said when I finished my story. *That kind of thing happens all the time in San Francisco.*

Yeah, I said, *but it was so weird. So difficult to watch.*

Eh, she said, *it's not really weird for San Francisco.*

I brewed a cup of tea.

Hey, my friend said suddenly, *do you mind if I use the story of your rape as an example in my presentation?*

She knew what had happened when I was eighteen years old.

Yeah, I said. *Sure.*

Thanks, she said. *It's a great example.*

Yeah. It's a great example.

clothing. The woman wakes naked and disoriented. She tries to leave, but the man holds her down. *You have no clothes. You can't go anywhere.* At the end of the story, the woman simply agrees to stay. Eliese showed the book to her mother. *It's cute,* her mother said. Eliese didn't know what she wanted her mother to say, but *cute* certainly wasn't it.

In front of the bus stop, the man in the black bra dropped his silk shirt. A car sped past, and the man stumbled backward. When Eliese was a very little girl, she wanted so badly to be saved. The very thought made her woozy, light-headed. The man in the black bra lowered himself onto the curb. His eyelids were heavy with heroin. In a few hours, he would crave more.

Eliese wants to tell you a story. She wants to tell you a story, but there are so many things about which she cannot speak. Particle physics, for example. Also, industrial psychology, protein synthesis, polymer science, and the peculiar magic that makes water bugs skate so perfectly on a pond. She wants to tell you a story, but she lacks so many things. Multivariable calculus. Pie making. And there is so much she has forgotten. The conjugation of the verb *vouloir,* the purpose of a Golgi body, the middle name of her first boyfriend. Eliese does, however, know about horses. She can talk about horses. She knows equitation and conformation and equine disease. For example, Eliese knows that white horses must be bred with care. Sometimes, a white horse is born with a fatal genetic disorder known as lethal white syndrome. A foal with this disorder will appear healthy at birth. It will stand and suckle and sniff its mother's scent. A new, white life. But deep inside the foal's gut, something has gone wrong. Its colon has not formed properly. It cannot expel waste. These foals always die—either naturally and painfully over the course of a few days, or through euthanasia. A white, perfect body splayed dead on the straw. The violence of a harbored, hidden waste.

Do you remember that handyman? Eliese's mother asked at dinner one evening.

Eliese was well into adulthood. Her older sister was in town, and the family had gathered for a meal. It had been a long time since she thought of the handyman.

Yes, Eliese said, *I remember him. He used to call me Leesy Piecey.*

I guess he got caught molesting some kids or something. In a bathtub, I think.

Doesn't surprise me.

At least you and your sister weren't alone with him much.

I was alone with him a lot, Eliese said loudly. Her own voice surprised her.

Everyone fell silent. They looked at their plates. It was difficult to tell whether Eliese's assertion, which was stated with such force, was an accusation or a confession. Perhaps it was neither of these things. The conversation quickly turned to other topics—the weather, the consistency of the mashed potatoes. Eliese grew quiet and swallowed what was left of her dinner.

During her final year of college, Eliese attended a Halloween-themed drag show with her boyfriend. She wore a wine-colored Renaissance dress with a plunging neckline.

A strange man with red hair walked up to Eliese.

You look very attractive in that dress, the man said.

Thank you, Eliese said, ever polite, ever demure.

Do you like men who are well hung? the man said.

Eliese did not know how to respond. To say *yes* would be flirtatious. To say *no* would be a lie.[9]

Well, she said, *what girl doesn't?*

I'm really well hung. And I'm a huge comer.

Good for you.

I really like to masturbate while I watch couples have sex.

Eliese rolled her eyes and turned around without responding, figuring the man would comprehend her lack of interest. She stood behind her boyfriend's shoulder and watched the drag show. On the stage, drag queens paraded around in plumes of pink and purple. Drag kings wore wife beaters and baggy jeans.

The strange man with red hair sidled up behind Eliese. She felt his hot, wet breath on her neck. Her body tightened at his proximity. The music swelled. The crowd sang along to "Thriller." The man unzipped his pants and began masturbating. He stood so close to Eliese that every beat of his hand made contact with her body. Eliese stood, paralyzed. Her muscles went rigid. Her diaphragm would not take in air. The man's breath quickened. He

---

9. *You don't want to look like a slut.*

was enjoying himself. Eliese could not breathe. She pulled at her boyfriend's hand. She tried to call his name, but she didn't have enough breath to form the words. She tried to pull more firmly, but her boyfriend would not turn around. He thought her tug was only a loving gesture. He would not turn around. He would not save her. The strange man drew his body closer.[10] Eliese wanted to speak, to yell, to curse, to cry out. But she stood still. Why was it so difficult to speak? Why had no one taught her the words? Why was she relying on the man in front of her to protect her from the man behind?

Eliese gathered herself. She turned and faced the man. For a moment, she stuttered. The man stood still. He looked Eliese in the eye. Finally, with great difficulty, she spoke.

Can you please stop that? she said, ever polite, ever demure.

At least she said something.

Eliese has a memory. She is in her grandfather's house, but her grandfather is not there. Sunlight slants across the kitchen tiles. She wears a dress. It must be spring. The family handyman walks past her, and a box of Reese's Pieces rattles in his pocket. His fingernails are black with dirt. He leads Eliese to the top of the basement stairs and begins walking down. Eliese does not follow. The handyman turns to her. *Come on,* he says. Eliese stands at the top of the stairs, fidgeting with her dress. The handyman smiles. He promises candy if only she'll follow along.

The memory fades. It goes black. Eliese does not know what happens next. She does not know what lies at the bottom of the stairs. She does, however, know that the memory induces panic. Her chest tightens at the thought of those stairs, but she doesn't know why.

When Eliese was twenty-seven, she encountered the handyman at a family funeral. He had grown bloated and sallow with age. When his eyes fell on Eliese, she immediately looked at the ground. Her palms grew sweaty. She felt a strange and sudden shame. While everyone waited outside for the funeral to begin, Eliese's young niece danced in the sunlight. Instinctively, Eliese stood between her niece and the handyman, shielding the young girl's body with her own. Normally, Eliese encouraged jumping on

10. *Did you say no?*

couches and standing atop tables, but she felt an urgent, primal need to protect the young girl, who was already very beautiful. As Eliese stood with legs firmly planted, she wondered whether the handyman had, indeed, abused her when she was young. He'd done it to other children. Repression of traumatic childhood memories is well documented. And so many of Eliese's childhood quirks suggested abuse. Her toy horses often raped one another. She wrote stories of sexual assault. She wet the bed well into puberty. She wet the bed so often, in fact, that her mother made her sleep on green, plastic sheets. By the age of eleven, Eliese had developed an eating disorder. By the age of sixteen, she had attempted suicide three times. Nothing else in her childhood predisposed her to such dysfunction. Eliese was not the product of divorce. Her family was not especially rich, but nor were they poor. They lived in the same midwestern suburb all her life. Her parents were loving, devoted. They took her to church, sent her to private schools, invested in extracurricular activities. Her childhood troubles do not make sense. They seem, as it were, illogical.

One statistic about childhood abuse strikes Eliese with particular interest: victims of childhood sexual assault are two to eleven times more likely to experience revictimization in adulthood.[11] The sexual violence Eliese experienced at the age of eighteen always felt painfully ambiguous. The two men, who were both freshmen at the Catholic university Eliese attended, had invited her into the woods for a few drinks. She had agreed. No one had forced her into the woods. No one had forced her to drink the red cup. She couldn't remember if she said no. When Eliese told college administrators about the incident, they held a small trial judged by Eliese's peers—mostly undergraduate students with religious, conservative backgrounds. During the trial, one of the men said he hadn't even been in the woods with Eliese. *Eliese is mistaking me for someone else,* he said. *She's not remembering clearly.* The man then attacked Eliese's character. *Sometimes she smokes pot behind the grocery store.* Eliese could have likewise questioned the man's integrity — *You fucked your stripper girlfriend in front of the university field house* —but she didn't want to stray from the matter at hand. She didn't

11. T. Messman-Moore and P. Long, "The Role of Childhood Sexual Abuse Sequelae in the Sexual Revictimization of Women: An Empirical Review and Theoretical Reformulation," *Clinical Psychology Review* 23 (2003), 537–71.

want to play dirty. She still believed in that old adage, *The truth will set you free.* So Eliese championed what was left of her memory. She told the judges of the tree, the white underwear, the red cup. She told them that the man had certainly been there. *I know it was you,* she said. *You were wearing an army fatigue jacket. I know it was you. I remember.* This, of course, created a troublesome paradox: Eliese could remember the army fatigue jacket, but she could not remember whether she had said no. After very little deliberation, the university tribunal reached a verdict. They decided that the man with the army fatigue jacket had been present in the woods. And they decided that any sexual acts had been consensual.

The verdict devastated Eliese. She stopped sleeping. She stopped eating. She'd told the tribunal everything—she'd told the truth as she remembered it—and now she was saddled with this word "consensual." Of course, Eliese had only told the judges about the night in the woods. There were other things she could have said. For instance, she could have told the judges that she'd only ever had one boyfriend, and she'd never done anything more than kiss him. She could have told the judges that her knowledge of male anatomy came from textbooks and intuition. She could have told the judges about the morning after the incident in the woods. On that morning, she showered under scalding water and picked gravel from her palms and knees. She cried until her eyes swelled shut. She washed for hours, but the smell of the men's bodies wouldn't go away. No matter how much she washed, she couldn't get clean. Those phantom smells made her vomit for weeks. Eliese did not say these things to the judges. She didn't want to win her case on pity. She wanted to be judged on the facts. And she was. She was judged to be the type of woman who sneaks off into the woods and fucks men she barely knows. So she stopped giving people all the facts. Even now, she only tells snippets—the tree, the white underwear, the red cup. She fashions her story in a way that does not allow for ambiguity. Sometimes she simply says, *I was raped.* She lets the listener's imagination decide the rest—they likely imagine knives and back alleys, black eyes and cop cars, a particular type of violence. Eliese lets them imagine. She watches their faces twist with sympathy or surprise. Eliese lets the listeners imagine, but she never lies. She never tells an untruth, but there is deceit in what she does not say. There were no knives or back alleys. No black eyes or cop cars. What happened to

Eliese was not so clear. She even flirted with the man who wore the army fatigue jacket. Before drinking the red cup, she'd touched the man's arm and smiled. But Eliese does not disclose this information when she says, *I was raped.* If she touched the man's arm, then maybe she asked for it. It is easier to let people imagine the worst. It is easier to let their minds wander toward sympathy. Do not think, however, that Eliese feels no shame at these intentional omissions. Every time she says, *I was raped*—every time she lets someone imagine what that means—Eliese feels the weight of the judges' verdict inside her gut. *No, sweetie, you were not raped. Remember? You are the woman who sneaks off into the woods and fucks strange men.*

The judges' verdict is, perhaps, the reason Eliese wants so desperately to remember the handyman. Had the handyman abused her as a child, then the violence she experienced at the age of eighteen would not have been her fault. People wouldn't ask her if she had said no. The *no* wouldn't matter—she'd gone into the woods with those men because she'd already been a victim as a child. She'd been a victim when she was pure and naive and too young to know better. Too young, even, to say no. Every symptom she'd ever experienced—the daydreams, the self-harm, the rape itself—would be rooted in an event completely outside her control. She could not be accused of poor decision-making or poor self-advocacy or an unhealthy, rape-obsessed imagination. She could not be accused of crying wolf. In the face of disaster, we want clarity. *You are bad, and I am not. Of course I said no.* Eliese wants to relieve her doubt, her uncertainty. She wants to rid herself of that nagging voice—*no, sweetie, you are the woman who sneaks off into the woods with strange men.* She wants so desperately to free herself from the judges' verdict that she will spend hours trying to remember what happened with the handyman at the bottom of those stairs. Maybe, if she closes her eyes hard enough, a memory will materialize. Maybe, if she closes her eyes hard enough, she will be released from her guilt. Yes, she'd flirted with the man in the army fatigue jacket. Yes, she'd touched his arm and smiled. Yes, she'd gone into the woods of her own accord, but only because she had a history of victimization. She was not at fault. *You are bad, and I am not.* But Eliese never remembers what happened at the bottom of the stairs.

Her desire to remember abuse—her desire to neutralize one

violent memory with another—is, of course, entirely irrational. Even if Eliese were to remember the bottom of the stairs, it would only give rise to a new shame, a new doubt, a new search for yet another ameliorating violence. The handyman will not save her. He will not relieve the shame. The shame is a part of her, and she must find its beauty.

Eliese wants to tell you the story. She wants you to witness a desperate piece of herself. She thinks it's a great example, but she will let you be the judge.

Here is the story: "I have just turned eighteen, and I'm drinking malt liquor in the woods with two men I barely know. One is a lanky, dark-haired recluse from Florida. The other is a clean-cut, pre-theologate student with a killer smile. He wears an army fatigue jacket that accentuates his massive, muscular arms. This is only the second time I've consumed alcohol outside of a family gathering. My buzz is distinct, but seems controlled. I joke with an ease I usually find unfamiliar. I turn to the man in the army fatigue jacket and smile. I touch his arm and smile. I laugh and swill and lick my numbing lips until something moves in the woods—probably a squirrel or a bird. The men get jumpy. Maybe the cops are coming, maybe we should get out of here, so we get up and stow our booze in a backpack and walk through the woods. I follow behind the men, overly conscious of my feet. They feel horribly heavy.

We walk until we reach a field where a group of men drunkenly wield golf clubs. They swing into the darkness. The man in the army fatigue jacket speaks to these men. He drives a ball and decides that we will go to a party with these golf-club-wielding men. The party promises more alcohol. I follow, delighting in my new-found college coolness. I'm being invited to a party by people I don't even know. A far cry from my sheltered all-girls' education, which was punctuated by algebra jokes and *Lord of the Rings* marathons.

The party smells of sweat and moldy dishwater. There are only men at this party. Men in Mötley Crüe T-shirts. Men who seem older, more worldly. *I shouldn't be the only girl,* I think, but the thought turns quickly. *I am the only girl. The tomboy. The girl cool enough to have a one-night pass into this man's world.*

I find myself in the kitchen. I am with the dark-haired recluse from Florida. He hands me a red cup of clear liquid, which I drink quickly to show that I am one of the boys.

Everything suddenly narrows. I can no longer walk without the aid of a wall. *I need to find a bathroom,* I think. *I need to find a bathroom until this feeling passes.* There is only one bathroom, and it is up a steep flight of stairs. I brace myself on the handrail. The dark-haired recluse from Florida follows behind me. This does not strike me as odd. After all, there is only one bathroom in the house, and we have been in the woods for most of the night. He must need to use the bathroom, too. As expected, he waits outside the door. I crouch on the toilet and hug my knees. I need to go home, but I don't know how to get there. I will just wait for the party to wane. I'm sure this vertigo will eventually pass.

I gather myself and walk out of the bathroom, but the dark-haired recluse from Florida pushes me backward. I fall into a bathtub, hitting my head on the faucet. In what seems to be one fluid, instantaneous movement, the man from Florida slams the door and grabs my head and puts his already-hard, already-exposed dick in my mouth. I am not sure what is happening. He is wearing long underwear. There is a knock at the door, and the man from Florida leaves quickly. I grab the bathtub faucet and try to pull myself up before everything goes black.

When I awake, I am outside. I am in the woods again. I cannot stand. I am on all fours. The man in the army fatigue jacket stands in front of me. His hand reaches, as if to help me up, but instead he grabs my head. He pushes himself into my mouth so hard I cannot breathe. *I can't breathe,* I think. *I can't breathe.* I try to pull away, but he is too strong. I vomit. Bile runs hot down my neck. The man in the army fatigue jacket pulls away, watches me vomit, takes me by the hair, and puts himself back in my mouth. I black out.

I awake under the tree with my underwear crumpled a few feet away. My arms won't work. The dark-haired man from Florida is on top of me, inside me.

Come on, the man in the army fatigue jacket says, *we gotta go, someone's gonna see.*

I think of my little-girl underwear and close my eyes."

The white horse is obviously a horse, Eliese thinks to herself.

She asks the logician how to refute the paradox.

"Distinguish the *is* of predication," he writes to her, "from the *is* of identity."

Eliese ponders this distinction, but she finds it difficult to grasp. Logic was never her strong point. She thinks of all those things people say she is. She is a woman, although she feels like a girl. She is an intellectual, although she doesn't sound all that smart. She is a laborer and a writer and an avid equestrian. She is sometimes a liar and sometimes a slut. She is also a prude. She is, perhaps, a victim, although the pamphlets and the self-help books and the therapists say she is a "survivor." Eliese eschews both terms. She would rather think of herself in other ways. For example, she is a woman who can harness an animal power between her legs. She once rode her sturdy, sorrel gelding through the woods at dusk. Together, she and the horse jumped fallen trees. They trotted up steep hillsides and waded ice-cold creeks. Or maybe Eliese is a woman who watched the most stunning sunrise of her life while swimming in a beachside pool on the Atlantic Ocean. A pod of dolphins played in the surf, and a man wrapped his arms around her waist. She did not love this man—she did not want to love him —but his body felt safe and warm against her own. For a moment that was enough. Or maybe Eliese is a woman who recently went off into the woods with a man she wanted to love. They sat beside a creek and watched warblers flit through the trees. They made love against a bank of crumbling shale. *That's a first for me,* the man said. Eliese smiled. *It's a first for me, too,* she said. And she meant it.

Perhaps Eliese does not understand the nuances of the logician. She does not understand the different types of "is"—the different types of "to be"—but she intuits a meaning outside of logic. The tiny, predicated pieces of ourselves—the things attributed to us, contained and experienced within us—cannot be confounded with all that we are. The horse may well be white, yet the white horse is not a horse. Eliese is the girl who has been raped. And she is not.

Eliese stands beside a white mare in a paddock. She has been hired to keep the mare under control during breeding. Flies land briefly on Eliese's burnt and sweating skin. The mare flicks her tail and startles at the slightest shift in the breeze.

A tiny, sorrel stallion approaches with his handlers. His eyes are wide and wild and sickled with white. The stallion is usually a calm, steady horse, but there is something furious in him now. Something frightening. He is already erect and impatient, having caught a whiff of the white mare. As the stallion advances, the mare pins her ears. She prepares to bolt, but Eliese holds her still. The stallion sniffs the mare's hindquarters and lifts his upper lip. He prances and whinnies and tosses his head. When the mare finally raises her tail, the handlers loosen their hold on the stallion. He mounts quickly, and the mare lurches forward.

Dammit, hold her still, someone scolds.

Eliese doubles over and leans into the mare's chest. She presses her cheek against the white fur and smells the horse's sweet must —shit and sawdust like honeyed earth. The mare is sweating, trembling, breathing heavy. *Dammit, hold her still.* With the entire weight of her body, Eliese pushes the mare backward. She pushes the mare into the stallion. When the mare inches forward, Eliese inches her back. They rock together, cheek against fur, bracing for the next blow.

Alongside the mare, Eliese is brought back into remembering. She remembers the men and their violence. She remembers the cold, packed earth beneath her thighs. She remembers the contempt in their voices. *You can't tell anyone about this. You don't want to look like a slut.* Blood and semen drip down the mare's hocks, and Eliese pushes the mare backward. *Helllloooo, Leesy Piecey, helllloooo.* Blood drips onto the mare's white hocks. This is her first breeding. *You can't tell anyone about this. This is a great example.* Eliese remembers the men and their violence. She remembers the handyman and his smile. She remembers sorting his Reese's Pieces according to color—oranges and yellows and browns. *Helllloooo, Leesy Piecey. You don't want to look like a slut.* Sweat lathers on the horse's white neck. Eliese steadies the mare, but she is not steady herself. She shakes with what she remembers, and she shakes with what she can no longer recall. The blackouts. The bottom of the stairs. Things lost. *Did you say no? I don't know.* Eliese breathes the men into the mare. The memories slip between fingers and fur, into the mare's already strained shoulders. The white Hanes underwear. The glint of the bathtub faucet before she blacked out. The judges' verdict. *No, sweetie, you were not raped.* The stallion moves frantically atop the mare. *You are the woman who sneaks off into the woods with strange men.*

The stallion digs his knees into the mare's flanks. *You are the woman who sneaks.* Back when Eliese encountered the handyman at the family funeral, she had shielded the body of her young niece from his gaze. Her niece was pure and naive and too young to know better. Eliese wants to teach this niece so many things. She will teach the young girl to name the breeds and cinch a girth and slip a bit between a horse's teeth. She will teach her the cadence of a lope and the rhythm of a poet, which are not so different at all. Eliese will tell the little girl this: Do not imbibe the belief that you are in need of saving. Do not dream of the man on the white horse. Dream, instead, of the white horse unbroken. The solid power of its hooves. The yellow tint of its shit-soaked mane. Dream, instead, of the white horse circling the herd, its tail lifted, its voice so shrill and potent it makes your own mouth itch to speak. Eliese pushes the mare backward, and the stallion finishes. The fury in his eyes is gone. The fury has gone into the mare.

The handlers take the stallion back to his stall, leaving Eliese alone in the paddock with the white horse. They are both spent, shaking. The mare lifts her head. She pricks her ears and flares her nostrils and bats flies with her bloodied tail. With watchful brown eyes, the mare studies a man unloading hay just outside the paddock. Even with a tangled mane and lathered coat, the mare holds herself with an unsettling poise. Each of her muscles is primed with that wild and fearsome power Eliese so admires in horses. The mare offers no apologies. With the lead line held loosely in hand, Eliese walks forward. The mare follows, shifting her gaze to her handler. Together they walk patterns into the dirt, catching their breaths, drying their sweat. And the white horse looks down into Eliese.

Hello, Leesy Piecey.

Hello.

LAWRENCE JACKSON

The City That Bleeds

FROM *Harper's Magazine*

FREDDIE GRAY'S RELATIVES arrived for the trial in the afternoon, after the prep-school kids had left. By their dress, they seemed to have just gotten off work in the medical and clerical fields. The family did not appear at ease in the courtroom. They winced and dropped their heads as William Porter and his fellow officer Zachary Novak testified to opening the doors of their police van last April and finding Freddie paralyzed, unresponsive, with mucus pooling at his mouth and nose. Four women and one man mournfully listened as the officers described needing to get gloves before they could touch him.

The first of six Baltimore police officers to be brought before the court for their treatment of Freddie Gray, a black twenty-five-year-old whose death in their custody was the immediate cause of the city's uprising last spring, William Porter is young, black, and on trial. Here in this courtroom, in this city, in this nation, race and the future seem so intertwined as to be the same thing.

During a break, I offered Freddie's twin sister, Fredericka, a cup of water, which she refused, perhaps wary of the strangers now expressing concern, the same people who would have ignored her waiting for a bus in the rain on North Avenue. After court reconvened, Freddie's mother, Gloria, balled up a tissue and dropped it on the floor, where it rolled under her seat. She didn't know that in his morning testimony Officer Porter had presented himself as a light of reform, telling the jury how public littering was one of the few offenses for which he issued citations on his beat at the Gilmor Street public-housing buildings, where residents like the Grays regularly gathered to interrogate the police during arrests.

When the prosecutor asked Porter whether he had protected public life, he said yes. Gray's stepfather snorted sarcastically.

While court was in session, Freddie's Uncle Odabe clambered over my knees into the pew behind the other family members. He wore a three-quarter-length black jacket, blue jeans, sneakers, black skullcap. A tall, lean man with close-cropped gray hair, he reminded me of the eighteenth-century Marylander Yarrow Mamout, a Muslim man born in West Africa. Odabe wore his facial hair in a style reminiscent of Charles Willson Peale's portrait of Mamout, which now hangs in a museum in Pennsylvania—clean-shaven save for a thicket of hair underneath his bottom lip—though he was two shades darker than the figure in the painting.

Brother Odabe was slyly and amusedly animated. He announced his presence by touching the shoulders of his nieces and his sister. In lieu of a greeting, he began a kind of banter, but the response of his bunched kin suggested that they were warding off a blow; maybe there had been a recent disagreement or they were embarrassed by his presence. Talking in the courtroom was also prohibited. He introduced himself to me by repeating a rhetorical question: "It's all right for a man to cry? It's all right for a man to cry?" Odabe spoke in Baltimore's vernacular, in a low, garbled register, as if his vocal chords were recovering from a shouting bout. He seemed not unaware of courtroom decorum and protocol, merely disinclined to submit to a force so similar to the one that had claimed his nephew. He picked up the balled tissue from the floor, and his pointed, guttural conversation quickened.

"Is it about the money?" he cried to his family, who had recently received a multimillion-dollar settlement from the city. He had seized a white-noise moment—Judge Barry Williams, who dominated the courtroom like a witty powerlifter, had the attorneys at his bench for a discussion, and the clerks had filled the courtroom with the sound of television snow. No matter. The sheriff's deputies swiftly arrived at the pew. "No noise allowed, sir," commanded the same officer who had earlier reprimanded me when I asked for directions to the courtroom for the "Freddie Gray trial," the inaccurate handle that the television networks were using. The officer beckoned for Odabe, who refused to leave and asserted his right to be in the courtroom. The tension was eased by another deputy, bald-headed and bearded like most of the African American men over thirty who were in the courtroom. He knew Odabe, and he touched his hand soothingly, assuring him that he would be all right. But a third officer, tall and powerfully built, reversed the redemptive gesture and commanded Odabe out. The deputy entered the pew and reached for his slumped prey. They were joined by the shift supervisor, a jacketed female sheriff; the four officers yoked Odabe by the shoulders and feet as he argued his citizenship rights, folding his arms like a mummy, and cast him out.

The family seemed to respond to Odabe's outburst with chagrin, but I was moved by his words and wondered whether he had not sacrificed himself to reveal a greater truth. Because it turned out that the powerful officer was Warren Smith, who had been my section leader in band during middle school. Another of the deputies, all of whom were African American, had saved me from being beaten by a gang of older boys when we were in high school. His name was Troy Jackson. Both of the men had served part of their careers as uniformed patrol officers in the Western District, where Freddie Gray lived and died. In the back of the courtroom the next afternoon, I reunited with the men, who were togged out in brown shirts and ties and Glocks. We laughed at the chance meeting, the old times, and called our town Smalltimore. What united us was the same thing that tied us to Freddie, whom other friends of mine had coached in football, to Porter, who grew up in West Baltimore, down the street from my closest friend. Odabe's symbolic theater embodied the point: a living tissue connecting the litter, the litterers, and the cleaners.

Freddie Gray's fatal treatment in police custody happened partly on camera, during a national mobilization of young people who have awoken on thousands of mornings in a nation with a black chief of state. These young people are inspired by the apparently endless possibility of modern life, and as a result they find it difficult to grasp the bantustans of America where black life is not supposed to matter at all. Not so my grandparents, who migrated up to Baltimore, to the edges of the Sandtown neighborhood, in the 1930s, from one of Virginia's southernmost tobacco counties. Many in their clans, eight out of ten for my grandmother and three out of six for my grandfather, relocated to West Baltimore. My grandmother, the eldest in her unit, said the farmwork was hard; her sister Daisy hated it so much that she said little about her own parents in kindness. Even my farm-owning great-grandparents, the first generation born into freedom since Africa, moved to Baltimore before they died.

Since entire extended families crowded into single houses before there was a cure for tuberculosis, a menace to blacks along Druid Hill Avenue, it makes sense to me that my family moved again as soon as they could. My great-uncle, a combat veteran of two years in World War II and two more in Korea, went from Mc-Culloh Street to the tree-lined boulevard of Bentalou Street. He was the only one of his brothers to take his GI Bill–funded education past high school—to fast-typing record holder Cortez Peters's Business School at 1200 Pennsylvania Avenue. Nobody ever told me why they wanted to leave McCulloh Street or Druid Hill Avenue after the start of blockbusting—domino-theory real-estate tactics to frighten less-educated whites into underselling their homes, which were then flipped to blacks at above market value. Besides, the houses my relatives were able to get as whites fled the neighborhood en masse were so much better than the kitchenette apartments knifed into the row houses of Sandtown, where they still go, religiously, to church.

My entire family seemed agreed on this point after World War II. Their grandparents had been enslaved, and their parents had been wiped out by agricultural pests, tractors, and the Depression; they would move to the cities and prosper by beating the odds and owning homes with luxuries like indoor plumbing and gas stoves. My great-aunts and their husbands and brothers, all veterans, crept westward, buying houses on Bentalou, and Ruxton Avenue and Lanvale Street in Edmondson Village, at Hilton and Piedmont, off Bloomingdale in Rosemont, all, with the exception of one traitor to East Baltimore, part of the steady westward expansion of black plumbers, nurses, Social Security Administration employees, circuit-court typists, dry cleaners, cab and bus drivers, and domestic servants. They loved the amenities of the city, the opportunity for high school, the streetcars, the array of foods and shops and churches, the choice marketplace on Pennsylvania Avenue and the even bigger market downtown on Lexington Street. In the country they had cured ham and drunk dandelion wine, but here in Baltimore there was the delicatessen, soft-shell crabs, steam heating, and the craft world of European immigrants from Greece, Poland, Italy, Ireland, and Germany.

I suppose my mother's parents were real strivers, who took the pay from their service jobs and finagled a house on a block with a few Jewish families and one other black family. But their Scotch-Irish neighbors were recent hillbilly war workers, migrants from West Virginia and Kentucky, not even passably educated. They drank freely. The current publisher of the *Afro,* the only leading black newspaper left in the United States, remembered my mom's block in the era after World War II. Robert Street at Linden Avenue was "something to see Friday and Saturday night," with "blood in the street." He was talking about drunk, brawling white men. Still, when the neighborhood to the north became black, the Downes Brothers Pharmacy near North and Linden took out the soda fountain ("a hindrance") and stocked their coolers with beer and liquor. The neighborhood had changed.

And thus the prime version of black advance under segregation: your strong effort for homeownership, fueled by jobs that leave you ineligible for Social Security benefits, is in a crease beyond a real-estate boundary, next door to illiterate drunkards. Eminent domain turned my grandparents' integrated block into a public park. My grandmother moved happily in 1965 north of Druid Hill Park, to Park Heights, then still a Jewish neighborhood. But by the early 1970s, the whites were gone and the houses in need of updating for a generation that was city-born. When I moved to her house in 1997, near the open-air drug market on the corner of Wylie Avenue, I befriended a fifth grader named Marvin Coston. I would try to get him to talk about his life, to stop smoking cigarettes on his way out the door. "Mr. Larry," he used to say, "I just be worried about some damn maniac coming down the street." I was a young professor at Howard, writing editorials about the murder on my doorstep, and I thought that was eerie clairvoyance for an eleven-year-old. I lost touch with Marvin when I moved from the neighborhood. He made it through the difficult teenage years, though not through the wave of forty-five homicides that engulfed Baltimore last July.

My parents went farther away from the traditional neighborhood in Sandtown, up to Liberty Heights. In the year that I was born, they bought a house on a street that was the dividing line between two neighborhoods, Arlington and Ashburton, maybe ten good blocks from Mondawmin Mall, a shopping center catering to the needs of some of the poorest Americans while also offering an absurdly glitzy high end, silk suits and alligator-skin shoes. Beyond Druid Hill Park, the wide, tree-lined boulevards filled with two-story single-family homes must have seemed an almost different city from the places they knew best. Their college friends Nina and Pete Rawlings, the parents of the current mayor, Stephanie Rawlings-Blake, lived a block west on a broad road shrouded by giant maples. But there was no power on earth that would have granted my parents a mortgage to purchase a home in, say, lily-white Dumbarton, between Homeland and Towson, where the same row house is easily worth two and a half times as much today as my mother's row house in East Arlington. (I have marveled at the Dumbarton houses, the irony, when they are featured on *House Hunters*.)

My grandfather's brothers, who died before I was born, and my neighbors Mr. Grant, Mr. Taylor, Mr. Washington, and Mr. Holman worked for a time at Sparrows Point, Bethlehem Steel's plant. In many stories the crisis of Rust Belt deindustrialization pivots on the sad closing of the key employer. But this mill was crucifier if it was ever savior, and the cross was certainly sunk in the ground by the early 1960s, when it employed about 30,000 men, 7,300 of them black. The history there was one of intense segregation: COLORED signs over the toilets, and black men working with one another on unskilled, dangerous tasks, scraping to keep even that piece of a job. The Department of Labor roused itself by 1974 to disrupt the discriminatory system of promotion at the plant, but the handwriting of globalization was in neon on the wall. Nixon and the Chicago Boys of economic theory were getting going in Chile and Argentina, and Baltimore wasn't in line for the rewards for supporting Nixon that went to the Sun Belt.

The gem of Baltimore's urban redevelopment, the aquarium and the two food and specialty-shop pavilions that make up Harborplace, was first dreamed to life in the 1950s with a bond issue and a development plan by a guy named Jim Rouse, who had worked for the Federal Housing Administration. At the time the redesign was conceived, the city of one million was 75 percent white. As waterfront development, financial services, and the Johns Hopkins University hospital complex became the bedrock of the white middle class, black economics rested squarely on the post offices, local government, and the school system. Teachers and

sanitation workers struck for a raise in 1974, and Baltimore caved
to a fate like that of New York, which submitted to the banks in a
debt crisis that resulted in huge service reductions, layoffs, and the
reintroduction of tuition at public colleges. In Chocolate City we
were lashed more tightly to two beasts, a shrinking municipal government and education system and a private market of unskilled-
service employment that ebbed and flowed. But this was during an
era of extreme inflation, when high youth unemployment, urban
density, and a shifting mission for school programs ran headlong
into heroin-addicted Vietnam veterans, and then crack cocaine.
(We always thought cocaine was a sophisticated and unaddictive
stimulant, hence its street name: "girl.") Public education fell under the wheels of the shrinking tax base caused by white flight—an
exodus federally paved with the highway system and the relocation
of the industrial and finance sectors—and let's just pile on "special" education classes for boys. Empowerment Zones and spectacle sports complexes were inadequate balms. Someone once cal-
culated that the net return on Camden Yards, the baseball stadium
beloved by conservatives, where some $200 million in state funds
were invested, was slightly better than 1 percent. Kurt Schmoke,
one of the most talented leaders to come along in a generation,
hoped his legacy as the city's first African American mayor would
be education. When he took the job in 1988, he tried to rename
Baltimore "the city that reads," though the motto curdled into
"the city that bleeds."

But the bleeding began before that. Who doesn't know by now
that as American cities became blacker in the 1950s and '60s, police departments felt fewer qualms about "cleaning them up" with
deadly force? Like Officer Porter on litter patrol in the Gilmor
Projects, police force was nearly always rationalized for its hygienic
powers, the same way it is explained today. In Baltimore, a broom
wasn't strong enough; sometimes the state needed a hose. When
things seemed to be getting out of hand, such as when two officers were shot in 1964, the police department initiated a practice they called "turn-up"; they mobilized specially armed squads
to conduct hundreds of violent, warrantless searches. In 1966 the
United States Court of Appeals for the Fourth Circuit put an end
to the practice, with an interesting rationale:

Baltimore City has escaped thus far the agony and brutality of the riots experienced in New York City, Los Angeles, Chicago, and other urban centers. Courts cannot shut their eyes to events that have been widely publicized throughout the nation and the world. Lack of respect for the police is conceded to be one of the factors generating violent outbursts in Negro communities. The invasions so graphically depicted in this case "could" happen in prosperous suburban neighborhoods, but the innocent victims know only that wholesale raids do not happen elsewhere and did happen to them. Understandably they feel that such illegal treatment is reserved for those elements who the police believe cannot or will not challenge them. It is of the highest importance to community morale that the courts shall give firm and effective reassurance, especially to those who feel that they have been harassed by reason of their color or their poverty.

The court's thinking ran counter to the minds of law-and-order political men like Spiro Agnew, the Baltimore County executive, and his more openly bigoted rival, George Mahoney. During the 1968 riots, which began in Baltimore two days after Martin Luther King Jr.'s assassination, Agnew—by then Maryland's governor—convened an audience that included Verda F. Welcome, a Maryland state senator; Parren J. Mitchell, the head of Baltimore's Community Action Agency; state delegate Troy Brailey; and black members of the city council. (Walter P. Carter of the Congress of Racial Equality, the black Baltimorean most commonly linked to desegregating housing in the city, was always already off Agnew's list.)

"I did not request your presence to bid for peace with the public dollar," Agnew told them. Then he hectored the officeholders to stop bellyaching when fellow blacks called them Uncle Tom or Mr. Charlie's boy. These city leaders recognized the difference between what the court hoped to preserve and the spiteful might that Agnew represented. Parren Mitchell, on his way to Congress in 1970, walked out of the meeting in disgust. The misalliance was called out in the *Afro:* "Agnew Insults Leaders." Agnew publicly blamed Stokely Carmichael and H. Rap Brown for inciting the arson and looting that would leave six dead, 700 injured, 5,000 arrested, and hundreds of businesses destroyed. If he could have put them both behind bars, he would have. Though he could not do that, he was quite successful in directing national mores toward hard punishment and prison for public disorders carried out by citizens pursuing racial justice.

Today's interracial Baltimore police force stands accused of having a general "turn-up" policy, not just for houses but for people. Fred Moten, a professor at the University of California, Riverside, has said that if urban-success models are linked to Giuliani's New York and broken-windows police tactics, then "we"—meaning black people—"are the broken windows." The horrors suffered by Amadou Diallo and Abner Louima don't have to be recalled to verify the error of criminalizing black citizens. But the strategy prevails in Baltimore, a city of about 620,000 where the Central Booking and Intake Center processes 73,000 people a year and commits 35,000 of them to the City Detention Center.

At a rally in May 2015 the spiritual brother of lost dope boy Freddie Gray (Save a Dope Boy was a local NGO) described the simplicity of being arrested in Sandtown. If the police ask you your name and you refuse to give it, you get locked up. (The Department of Justice found that in Ferguson, Missouri, a black man had been arrested for giving a version of his first name that differed from the one on his driver's license. The crime? Making false statements to a police officer.) Though the police are violating the law, they're not wrong; the young men they encounter on the Baltimore streets who look like they're selling drugs *are* selling drugs. The only way the city police can bring "peace" to Sandtown is by selectively discarding the Bill of Rights and practicing war without end. Because the police department protects the historically white, heavily financed waterfront areas of the city against the others, the war must often be practiced with preemptive strikes. This is really the colonial model, where rule is simply the exercise of power without any law to gussy it. The power here is, fundamentally, to determine who lives and who dies.

> Sandtown, North and P
> Park Heights, R and G
> —Big Ria, "Hey You Knuckleheads" (1996)

As children, we learned to survive bullies and predators, but the other lethality started for me at the end of junior year in high school, puttering around with my neighborhood friends in my dad's Toyota. I had only a slight and vague sense of street-level law enforcement. Once, on the way to the Morgan University radio station for a Kwanzaa program, my cousin, a legendary teacher and activist known in West Baltimore as Brother Charlie, had described some of our relatives as "playing dip-and-dodge with the police." Maybe I thought that was kind of hip, exciting, and strange. Defying and evading the police was distant from my life of algebra and Latin, "Din Daa Daa," Sunday school, and wrestling practice. But my encounter with 5-o in the summer months of 1985 was not an exciting game. When plainclothes officers threatened me with loaded guns at a stoplight and accused me of grand theft auto they seemed absolutely deadly to me. I was surprised to learn that policemen went undercover; I had assumed that the gunmen who took over the car were armed robbers on a spree. I otherwise learned from the encounter that you evacuate your bladder and bowels when you believe that you are going to die.

I didn't know enough then about the nuances of the past to link the police to the slave patrol, but after that incident, shared with lifelong friends who lived in the row houses next to mine, and after being detained over and over in Baltimore, then in New Jersey, in Connecticut, and in California, in a car, on foot, everywhere, I understood. The slave part makes a difference, because slave legacy is a kind of nation, and all of us facing the law's deadly force have this sense about who belongs to that nation and how we need them and what we need them for. The day of the Baltimore riots last April, Sandtown teenagers noted the slavery kinship alive again, the air of amity, respect, concern, and sharing. The tribal roots and metropolitan shoots of this legacy resounded forcefully in Big Ria's B-More anthem, "Hey You Knuckleheads." In the native idiom, the young girl heralded the sovereign land of the street corners and neighborhoods that dominate the black world and that the right-minded among us have been mostly successful in suppressing. The celebration of the open-air drug market, the bloody street corner, and the public-housing project is a reclamation of an ignored black reality, akin to the hidden world that was revealed by slave narratives, such as those written by Frederick Douglass.

The flairful badmen and sad martyrs haunting the landscape of Big Ria's song always remind me of Booker Jones of Stricker

Street, who murdered two white children and was shot by police who said he wouldn't be taken alive. The boy killed at Harlem Park Middle for his starter jacket. Craig Cromwell, my junior-high classmate who went to a rival Catholic high school. The assassin Dontay "Man" Carter, who targeted white men on his killing and kidnapping spree and briefly escaped trial by jumping out the judge's bathroom window. The boy on West Lombard Street who drove over a police car and crushed the officer inside to death, and then got off. My running partner, Donald Bentley. The first guy gunned down at a telephone booth on my street the year I finished college. The dope fiend on Pimlico whom I overheard being leaned on before he was gunned down. The bloody brothers Tariq Malik and Ismael Malik Wilson. Champ and Darius (who rode his Honda Elite scooter in Fila slippers), the hustlers who protected me when I was a teenager. Brian Wolst, dead in police custody. Little Chris, killed by the police in the street. And when I was at home after the recent riot, a guy from my set, Byron Showell, a bishop's son, also gunned down in the street. Of course we can't stop death, but who wouldn't want to know, as we say at home, how to carry that thing? The poet Sterling Brown wrote, "Lemme be wid such like men / When Death takes hol' on me." Our lineages of ghosts and phantoms and spirits help us to manage the chaos.

It's hard not to want our white fellow citizens to share at least this one dimension of our lives more fully. One Baltimore case I think about took place at a new café on Cathedral Street, in Mount Vernon. I was getting breakfast and I could tell that the people running the place were a family from Highlandtown or maybe Hampden, close-knit white enclaves set off by a peculiar accent, the one from the John Waters movies that people use to make believe they know Baltimore. The order was wrong and I sent the food back to the manager in an understated manner, but he was gruff with me in a way that went outside the rules for interracial peace in the city. He then proceeded to outdo his rudeness to me by being curt with the two muscular busboys, who looked to all the world like recent parolees. (We'd say they "just came home.") We weren't in the county, and I was amazed.

One thing that the writer Chester Himes observed during the '60s and that I have noticed to be true for most of my life is that very many black people are willing to die before they will adopt the submissive attitude that they, rightly or wrongly, associate with what was necessary to endure under slavery. (Plenty of people refused to endure it then.) I had simply never heard a white man use an insulting tone that freely with black men who had just come home. On the news a few weeks later I heard that the manager's body was found. Shortly after that the busboys confessed to executing him; their pictures were at the ATM. Dignity is another kind of national sovereignty we live in and protect.

The black neighborhoods of Baltimore—like Sandtown, which kind of runs between Druid Hill Avenue and Payson Street—are like that, too, like countries, defended lands. Sandtown has a historic coherence partly because it runs between Monroe and Pennsylvania, the famous boulevard for black life during a significant portion of the twentieth century, home to the Royal Theater, to musical genius Eubie Blake, to the bandleaders Cab Calloway and Chick Webb, and to Baltimore's siren, Billie Holiday. It has also been for a long time a vibrant crossroads for adult city life, music, culture, religion, food markets, and narcotics. My favorite landmark is Everyone's Place on North Avenue, a thirty-year-old bookstore run by Baba Nati that easily outdistances its early competitors like Liberation Books in Harlem or Pyramid Books in D.C. It is like a black-nationalist-bent mini–Strand Bookstore in a row house at Penn North. Everyone's Place put an intellectual hub in the center of an all-black neighborhood. That is a revolutionary act when you live in neighborhoods where houses are the same price as Detroit's automobiles.

On the other side of Gwynns Falls Parkway from Mondawmin is Frederick Douglass High School, among the first black secondary schools south of the Mason-Dixon Line and the alma mater of the black Supreme Court justice Thurgood Marshall and the sociologist E. Franklin Frazier. Neither Marshall nor Frazier attended this "new" Douglass, relocated in the 1950s as a kind of last gasp of the segregation era, but the school has catered to the needs of the western side of the city and enrolled students from many different neighborhoods, especially those in easy walking distance from Sandtown and Reisterstown Road. Traditionally, Douglass meant to us Westsiders what Paul Laurence Dunbar High School, the home of so many basketball legends, has meant to black Eastsiders. The east–west divide of the black city was weaponized in the 1980s by a guy who came from out of town to popularize a radio show, but it took hold with the same intensity and imagined community conveyed by the names of the Los Angeles street gangs, which warped and fragmented young people in the 1990s. Today there is a deadly gang problem, with roots about as deep as a tweet.

But one of the real boundaries is concrete and steel. At the southernmost edge of Sandtown stands the Highway to Nowhere, a metaphor of the deliberate failure and bad faith of 1960s urban renewal. It is a mile and a half of sunken highway, pitched initially as a part of slum clearance, that stops and crescendos into nothing, a powerful symbol of political inertia because it is meaningless except as a mark of "vertical sovereignty," a bulky three-dimensional underpass reminding the observant of the state's ability not simply to remove and change the past but to control and categorize space, a monument to the imminent splintering that is such a dominant factor in black life.

Of course what is not really possible to understand about Sandtown is that it is, from street to street, an unending series of open-air drug markets and shooting galleries, of catcalls for "boy" or "girl." That means that when the police cruisers move out of sight, highly organized and commercially profitable narcotics exchanges take place. Disputes here are settled violently and fatally. It's embarrassing to admit it, and easier to ignore the confluence of forces that creates something that is more or less unthinkable —that a quadrant of a major city operates precisely like Ciudad Juárez, and has consumed generation after generation, banging a gun for coke or dope, decade after decade. The narco trafficking has outlasted any known employment industry, empowering the ambitious entrepreneurs and chemically numbing the idealists. Prison, death, and impairment are the fate of both groups, as the young dealers become the users.

What was unbelievable about the April Uprising, what made it a genuine uprising, is that eighteen-year-old corner hustlers, dope boys, hoppers, curb servers, parolees, people who've never held a job and don't anticipate holding one, typically don't have enough invested in the state to riot against it—but for some reason now they do. When I visited a high school on McCulloh Street, at the edge of Sandtown, a school that embraced the students dismissed from everywhere else, and asked the teenagers whether they were ready to return to throwing bricks at police cars if there were an acquittal in the trial, two students swiftly piped up: "We is!"

The Porter trial reflected the same extreme views that now fully dominate American life and have failed to halt the cycle of entropy, malaise, and outright disaster. One brother I talked to at the trial was convinced that Officer Porter would receive a guilty verdict for police misconduct, since he repeatedly stated that he had violated circulated guidelines by not buckling Freddie Gray into a seat. Even on television, the police are known to punish people who run away, so on the street everybody believes that Freddie Gray wound up dying from a retaliatory "rough ride" in a police van. But after a day's deliberation, the jury told the judge they were deadlocked. When another two days brought no movement, the judge declared a mistrial. One juror believed that Porter had committed no crimes whatsoever; conversely, another held fast to the idea that Porter was a killer, guilty of manslaughter. The state voiced its determination to retry Porter, and in the meantime went to the Maryland Court of Special Appeals, delaying the trials against the other officers.

The six suspended officers might have been useful on the street during 2015, when 344 people were killed in Baltimore City—a per capita record—66 of them in the Western District where Porter had once been on patrol, the deadliest place in the city. Only one in three of those murders has been cleared from police books.

There seems, really, no way out for Freddie and William and Marvin and Larry, if the economy grows or contracts, if we move beyond the inner city or not. Walking west from the Cold Spring subway stop after the trial, I talked with a Gray family friend, a guy who was now a politico with ties to evangelical ministries but had once run with the late Little Melvin, the drug lord reputed to have called the end to rioting in 1968. As he talked to me about other horrifying cases of wrongful police force, we passed the car wash, and boys raced fat-tired ATVs by us as night came on. We were not far from where crosses had been burned in the late '60s to keep potential black homebuyers away, the teachers, postal workers, and steelworkers. Now I wondered about my mother's block, with its aging homeowners born before World War II, with a house that is already boarded up. Who belongs to the generation prepared to revitalize the modest city neighborhoods that desegregation left behind?

So, in protest against the unjust killing of not just one Freddie Gray but generations of black women and men, and understanding that the remedy here is in the hinterland if it ever appears, a riot makes a lot of fucking sense.

RACHEL KUSHNER

"We Are Orphans Here"

FROM *The New York Times Magazine*

STANDING AT AN intersection in Shuafat Refugee Camp, in East Jerusalem, I watched as a boy, sunk down behind the steering wheel of a beat-up sedan, zoomed through an intersection with his arm out the driver's-side window, signaling like a NASCAR driver pulling in for a pit stop. I was amazed. He looked about twelve.

"No one cares here," my host, Baha Nababta, said, laughing at my astonishment. "Anyone can do anything they want."

As Baha and I walked around Shuafat this spring, teenagers fell in behind us, forming a kind of retinue. Among them were cool kids who looked like cool kids the world over, tuned in to that teenage frequency, a dog whistle with global reach. I noticed that white was a popular color. White slouchy, pegged jeans, white polo shirts, white high-tops. Maybe white has extra status in a place where many roads are unpaved and turn to mud, where garbage is everywhere, literally, and where water shortages make it exceedingly difficult to keep people and clothing clean.

So few nonresidents enter Shuafat that my appearance there seemed to be a highly unusual event, met with warm greetings verging on hysteria, crowds of kids following along. "Hello, America!" they called excitedly. I was a novelty, but also, I was with Baha Nababta, a twenty-nine-year-old Palestinian community organizer beloved by the kids of Shuafat. Those who followed us wanted not just my attention but his. Baha had a rare kind of charisma. Camp-counselor charisma, you might call it. He was a natural leader of boys. Every kid we passed knew him and either waved or stopped to speak to him. Baha founded a community center so that older children would have a place to hang out, because there is no open space in Shuafat Refugee Camp, no park, not a single playground, nowhere for kids to go, not even a street, really, where they can play, because there are no sidewalks, most of the narrow roads barely fitting the cars that ramble down them. Younger kids tapped me on the arms and wanted to show me the mural they painted with Baha. The road they helped to pave with Baha, who supervised its completion. The plants they planted with Baha along a narrow strip. Baha, Baha, Baha.

It was like that with the adults too. They all wanted his attention. His phone was blowing up in his pocket as we walked. He finally answered. There was a dispute between a man whose baby died at a clinic and the doctor who treated the baby. The man whose baby died tried to burn the doctor alive, and now the doctor was in critical condition, in a hospital in Jerusalem. Throughout the two days I spent with Baha, I heard more stories like this that he was asked to help resolve. People relied on him. He had a vision for the Shuafat camp, where he was born and raised, that went beyond what could be imagined from within the very limited confines of the place.

In an area of high-rise apartment buildings clustered around a mosque with spindly, futuristic minarets, a pudgy boy of ten or eleven called over to us. "My dad is trying to reach you," he said to Baha. Baha told me that the buildings in that part of the camp had no water and that everyone was contacting him about it. He had not been answering his phone, he confessed, because he didn't have any good news yet for the residents. I got the impression Baha was something like an informal mayor, on whom people depended to resolve disputes, build roads, put together volunteer committees, and try to make Shuafat safe for children.

The building next to us was twelve stories. Next to it was another twelve-story building. High-rise apartments in the camp are built so close together that if a fire should happen, the results would be devastating. There would be no way to put it out. The buildings were all built of stone blocks that featured, between blocks, wooden wedges that stuck out intermittently, as if the builders had never returned to fill the gaps with mortar. I gazed up at a towering facade, with its strange wooden wedges, which made the building look like a model of a structure, except that it was occupied.

The pudgy boy turned to me as I craned my neck. "This building is stupidly built," he said. "It's junk."

"Do you live here?" I asked him, and he said yes.

Shuafat Refugee Camp is inside Jerusalem proper, according to the municipal boundaries that Israel declared after the Six Day War in 1967. (Though the entire walled area is frequently referred to as the Shuafat Refugee Camp, the actual camp, run by the United Nation's relief agency for Palestinian refugees, is only a small portion. Adjacent to the camp are three neighborhoods that are the responsibility of the city of Jerusalem.) The Palestinian Authority has no jurisdiction there: the camp is, according to Israeli law, inside Israel, and the people who live there are Jerusalem residents, but they are refugees in their own city. Residents pay taxes to Israel, but the camp is barely serviced. There is very little legally supplied water, a scarcely functioning sewage system, essentially no garbage pickup, no road building, no mail service (the streets don't even have names, much less addresses), virtually no infrastructure of any kind. There is no adequate school system. Israeli emergency fire and medical services do not enter the camp. The Israeli police enter only to make arrests; they provide no security for camp residents. There is chaotic land registration. While no one knows how many people really live in the Shuafat camp and its three surrounding neighborhoods, which is roughly one square kilometer, it's estimated that the population is around eighty thousand. They live surrounded by a twenty-five-foot concrete wall, a wall interspersed by guard towers and trapdoors that swing open when Israeli forces raid the camp, with reinforcements in the hundreds, or even, as in December 2015, over a thousand troops.

Effectively, there are no laws in the Shuafat Refugee Camp, despite its geographical location inside Jerusalem. The Shuafat camp's original citizens were moved from the Old City, where they sought asylum in 1948 during the Arab-Israeli War, to the camp's boundaries starting in 1965, when the camp was under the control of the Jordanian government, with more arriving, in need of asylum, during and after the war in 1967. Now, fifty years after Israel's 1967 boundaries were drawn, even Israeli security experts don't quite know why the Shuafat Refugee Camp was placed inside the Jerusalem municipal boundaries. The population was much smaller then and surrounded by beautiful green, open forestland, which stretched to the land on which the Jewish settlement of Pisgat Ze'ev was later built. (The forestland is still there, visible beyond the separation wall, but inaccessible to camp residents, on account of the wall.) Perhaps the Israelis were hoping the camp's residents could be relocated, because they numbered only a few thousand. Instead, the population of the camp exploded in the following decades into the tens of thousands. In 1980 Israel passed a law declaring Jerusalem the "complete and united" capital of Israel. In 2004 Israel began erecting the concrete wall around the camp, cutting inside Israel's own declared boundaries, as if to stanch and cauterize the camp from "united" Jerusalem.

If high-rise buildings are not typically conjured by the term "refugee camp," neither is an indoor shopping mall, but there is one in the Shuafat camp: two floors and a third that was under construction, an escalator up and down, and a store called Fendi, which sells inexpensive women's clothes. The mall owner greeted us with exuberance and pulled Baha aside to ask for advice of some kind. A teenager who worked at a mall ice-cream parlor, a hipster in a hoodie and eyeglass frames without lenses, did a world-class beatbox for me and Moriel Rothman-Zecher, a writer and organizer who had walked me into the camp in order to make introductions between me and Baha and to serve as my Arabic interpreter. Moriel and the teenager from the ice-cream shop took turns. Moriel's own beatbox was good but not quite up to the Shuafat Refugee Camp beatbox standard. We met an accountant named Fahed, who had just opened his shop in the mall to prepare taxes for residents. He was stunned to hear English being spoken and eager to use his own. The tax forms are in Hebrew, he explained, so most people in the camp must hire a bilingual accountant to complete them.

Before the separation wall was constructed, the mall was bulldozed twice by the Israeli authorities, but the owner rebuilt both times. Since the wall has gone up, the Israelis have not tried to demolish any large buildings in Shuafat, though they have destroyed individual homes. Armed Palestinian gangsters could take away someone's land or apartment at any moment. A fire or earthquake would be catastrophic. There are multiple risks to buying property in the Shuafat camp, but the cost of an apartment there can be less than a tenth of what an apartment would cost on the other side of the separation wall, in East Jerusalem. And living in Shuafat is a way to try to hold on to Jerusalem residency status. Jerusalem residents have a coveted blue ID card, meaning they can enter Israel in order to work and support their families, unlike Palestinians with green, or West Bank, ID cards, who need many supporting documents in order to enter Israel—to work or for any other reason, and who also must pass through military checkpoints like Qalandiya, which can require waiting in hours-long lines. Jerusalem residency is, quite simply, a lifeline to employment, a matter of survival.

There are also non-Jerusalemites in the camp. Since the wall went up, it became a sanctuary, a haven. I met people from Gaza, who cannot leave the square kilometer of the camp or they risk arrest, because it is illegal for Gazans to enter Israel or the occupied West Bank except with Israeli permission, which is almost never granted. I met a family of Brazilian Palestinians with long-expired passports who also cannot leave the camp, because they do not have West Bank green IDs or Jerusalem blue IDs.

Shuafat camp is often depicted in the international media as the most dangerous place in Jerusalem, a crucible of crime, jihad, and trash fires. On the day that I arrived, garbage was indeed smoldering in great heaps just inside the checkpoint entrance, against the concrete separation wall, flames jumping thinly in the strong morning sun. I had been to countries that burn their trash; it is a smell you get used to. My main concern, over the weekend I spent in the camp, was not getting my foot run over by a car. If you are seriously hurt in the camp, there isn't much help. Ill or injured people are carried through the checkpoint, on foot or by car, and put in ambulances on the other side of the wall. According to residents of the camp, several people have unnecessarily died in this manner.

As we walked, I began to understand how to face the traffic without flinching, to expect that drivers are experienced at navigating such incredible human density. I asked Baha if people were ever run over by cars, assuming he would say no.

"Yes, all the time," he said. "A child was just killed this way," he added. I hugged the walls of the apartment buildings as we strolled. Later that evening, I watched as a tiny boy riding a grown man's bicycle was bumped by a car. He crashed in the road. I ran to help him. He was crying, holding out his abraded hands. I remembered how painful it is to scrape your palms, how many nerve endings there are in an open hand. A Palestinian man told the little boy he was OK and ruffled his hair.

When I asked Baha if garbage was burned by the separation wall because it was safer—a way to contain a fire, like a giant fireplace —he shook his head. "It's, aah, symbolic." In other words, garbage is burned by the wall because the wall is Israeli. Drugs are sold along the wall by the Israeli checkpoint, not for symbolic reasons. The camp organizers, like Baha, cannot effectively control the drug trade in a zone patrolled by the Israeli police and monitored by security cameras. Dealers are safe there from the means of popular justice exacted inside the camp. The most heavily militarized area of the camp is perhaps its most lawless.

The popular drug the dealers sell is called Mr. Nice Guy, which is sometimes categorized as a "synthetic cannabinoid"—a meaningless nomenclature. It is highly toxic, and its effects are nothing like cannabis. It can bring on psychosis. It damages brains and ruins lives. Baha told me that Mr. Nice Guy is popular with kids as young as eight. Empty packets of it sifted around at our feet as we crossed the large parking lot where buses pick up six thousand children daily and transport them through the checkpoint for school, because the camp has only one public school, for elementary students. Every afternoon, children stream back into camp, passing the dealers and users who cluster near the checkpoint.

I didn't see the dealers, but I doubt Baha would have pointed them out. What I mostly noticed were children working, being industrious, trying to find productive ways to live in a miserable environment and to survive. Across from Baha's house, a group of kids run a car wash. We waved to them from Baha's roof. Baha introduced me to a group of teenage boys who own their own moped-and-scooter-repair service. He took me to a barbershop, where kids in flawless outfits with high-side fades were hanging out, listening to music, while a boy of about thirteen gave a haircut to a boy of about five. A young teenager in a pristine white polo shirt and delicate gold neck chain flexed his baby potato of a biceps and announced his family name: "Alqam!"

The children in the barbershop were all Alqam. They ran the shop. They were ecstatic to see Baha. We were all ecstatic. The language barrier between me and the boys only thickened our collective joy, as my interpreter Moriel was whisked into a barber chair for a playfully coerced beard trim, on the house. The boys and I shouldered up for selfies, put on our sunglasses and posed. Whenever men shook my hand after Baha introduced me, I sensed—especially after Moriel left that afternoon—that men and boys would not get so physically close to a Palestinian woman who was a stranger. But I was an American woman, and I was with Baha, which made me something like an honorary man.

Later I told myself and everyone else how wonderful it was in the Shuafat camp. How safe I felt. How positive Baha was. All of that still feels true to me. But I also insisted, to myself and everyone else, that Baha never expressed any fears for his own safety. In looking at my notes, I see now that my insistence on this point was sheer will. A fiction. It's right there in the notes. He said he was nervous. He said he'd been threatened.

Also in my notes, this:

Baha says, two types

1. Those who want to help make a better life

2. Those who want to destroy everything

And in parentheses: *(Arms trade. Drugs trade. Construction profits. No oversight wanted.)*

"I wanted you to meet the boys because they are nice people," Baha said, after we left the barbershop. "But they do all carry guns." It was only after I returned home to the United States that I learned, in the banal and cowardly way, with a few taps on my computer, that two Alqam boys, cousins who were twelve and fourteen, had been accused of stabbing, with a knife and scissors, an Israeli security guard on a tram in East Jerusalem. I still don't know whether they were related to the boys in the barbershop. Several of the young assailants in what has been called the Knives Intifada have been from the Shuafat camp, which has also been the site of huge and violent protests in which Palestinians have been killed by Israeli forces. In 2015 three children from the Shuafat Refugee Camp lost eyes from sponge bullets shot by Israeli forces.

The other thing I suppressed, besides Baha's admissions of fear, was his desire for police. I didn't write that down. It wasn't part of my hero narrative, because the police are not part of my hero narrative. "Even if they have to bring them from India," he said several times, "we need police here. We cannot handle the disputes on our own. People take revenge. They murder."

A Middle East correspondent I met in the West Bank, hearing that I was going to spend the weekend in the Shuafat camp, asked me if I "planned to visit Shit Lake" while there. Apparently that was his single image of the place. I assumed he was referring to a sewage dump, but Baha never mentioned it, and after seeing Baha's pleasure in showing me the community center, the roads his committee had built, the mall, which was the only open gathering space, all things that, for him, were hopeful, I wasn't going to ask him for Shit Lake.

That correspondent had never stepped foot in the camp. I hadn't expected to, either, until I was invited on an extensive tour of the occupied West Bank, including East Jerusalem, and was asked to choose a subject to write about, for a book to be published next year. With no previous experience in the region, and little knowledge, I gravitated instinctually to Shuafat camp. From my own time there, the sustaining image is shimmering white. The kids, dressed in white. The buildings, a baked tone of dusty, smoke-stained white. The minarets, all white. And there was the 1972 Volkswagen Beetle in gleaming white, meticulously restored. It was on the shop floor of a garage run by Baha's friend Adel. A classic-car enthusiast and owner myself, I wanted to talk to Adel about the car. He showed me his garage, his compressor, his lift. Like the escalator in the mall, these were things you would never expect to find in a place without services.

We sat, and Adel made coffee. He and Baha told me about the troubles with the drug Mr. Nice Guy. They said every family has an addict among its children and sometimes among the older people as well. A third of the population is strung out on it, they said. It makes people crazy, Adel and Baha agreed. Is there a link, I asked, between Mr. Nice Guy and the kids who decide, essentially, to end it all by running at an Israeli soldier with a knife? They each concurred that there was. Two years earlier, Baha said, by way of contrast, there was a man from the Shuafat camp who did a deadly car ramming. The Israelis came and blew up his house. He was older, Baha said, and out of work and he decided that he was finally ready to lose everything. With the kids, Baha said, it's different. It's an act of impulsive courage. The drug helps enormously with that.

Adel kept making reference to his nine-year-old daughter, who is physically disabled and cannot attend school. I asked to meet her or Adel asked if I wanted to meet her. Either way we ended up in Adel's large apartment, and his daughter Mira was wheeled out to the living room. Mira was burned over most of her body and is missing part of one arm and a kneecap. Her face and scalp are disfigured. A school bus filled with children from the Shuafat camp were on a trip to Ramallah when their bus collided with a truck on wet roads. The bus overturned and burst into flames. Five children and a teacher burned to death. Dozens were injured. Emergency services were delayed by confusion over who had jurisdiction. As a result, Mira and other children had to be taken in the cars of bystanders to the closest hospital. The accident took place between the Adam settlement and Qalandiya checkpoints, in what is called Area C of the West Bank, which is entirely under Israeli control. The likelihood of something like this occurring was well known. Later, a report from Ir Amim, an Israeli human rights group, established that the tragedy resulted from the multiple challenges of living beyond the separation barrier. Roads were substandard. There were too many children on the bus, the children had no access to education in their own communities, and there was no oversight.

"When the accident happened, we didn't know how to cope with it," Baha told me. Someone got up on a loading dock in the camp and called out the names of the dead. Afterward, Baha and Adel cried all the time. They felt that the lives of Shuafat's children were disposable. They decided to start their own volunteer emergency team, through WhatsApp, and it has eighty members, who are trained in first aid and in special skills they are ready to employ at a moment's notice. They are saving up to purchase their own Shuafat camp ambulance, whose volunteer drivers will be trained medical professionals, like Baha's wife, Hiba, who is a nurse.

Baha, I noticed, seemed more optimistic about their emergency team, and about the future, than Adel did. At one point, Adel, who has a shattered and frantic but loving, warm energy, turned to me and said, "We are orphans here."

Mira, who had been transferred from her wheelchair to the couch, sat and fidgeted. She understood no English but was forced to quietly pretend she was listening. I kept smiling at her, and she smiled back. I was desperate to give her something, to promise something. It's very difficult to see a child who has suffered so tremendously. It's basically unbearable. I should give her the ring I was wearing, I thought. But then I saw that it would never fit her fingers, which were very swollen and large, despite her young age; her development, after the fire, was thwarted because her bones could not properly grow. I'll give her my earrings, was my next idea, and then I realized that her ears had been burned off in the fire. I felt obscene. I sat and smiled as if my oversize teeth could beam a protective fiction over this poor child, blind us both to the truth, that no shallow gesture or petty generosity would make any lasting difference, and that her life was going to be difficult.

The travel agency in the Shuafat mall is called Hope. There is a toy store in the mall called the Happy Child. The children I met were all Baha's kids, part of his group, on his team, drafting off his energy, which was relentlessly upbeat.

I have to re-create, with all the precision I can manage, to remember what I am able to about Baha. I see Baha in his pink polo shirt, tall and handsome, but with a soft belly that somehow reinforces his integrity, makes him imperfectly, perfectly human. Baha singing "Bella Ciao" in well-keyed Italian, a language he learned at nineteen, on the trip that changed his life, working with Vento di Terra, a community-development and human rights group based in Italy. Later, I sent a video of Baha singing to various Italian friends, leftists who were thrilled that a guy in a Palestinian refugee camp knew the words to "Bella Ciao."

Baha's friends and relatives all hugging me and cheek-kissing me, the women bringing out boxes that contained their hand-embroidered wedding dresses, insisting I try on each dress, whose colors and designs specified where they were from: one in black with white stitching, from Ramallah. Cream with red, Jerusalem. In each case we took a photo, laughing, me in each dress, with the woman it belonged to on my arm.

Everyone imploring me to come back, and to bring Remy, my eight-year-old, and I was sure that I would come back, and bring Remy, because I had fallen in love with these people.

And in the background of the hugs and kisses, in almost every home where we spent time, the TV playing the Islamic channel,

Palestine al-Yawm, a relentless montage of blood, smoke, fire, and
kaffiyeh-wrapped fighters with M16s.

The constant hospitality. Coffee, tea, mint lemonade, ice water,
all the drinks I politely accepted. Drank and then sloshed along,
past faded wheat-pasted posters of jihadist martyrs.

Come back. Bring Remy. I will, I told them, and I meant it.

Late at night, Baha and Hiba decided to show me their digital
wedding photo book. It was midnight, their two young daughters
asleep on couches around us. Hiba propped an iPad on a table
—she was four months pregnant, expecting her third child, a boy
—and we looked at every last image, hundreds of images, of her
and Baha in highly curated poses and stiff wedding clothes, her
fake-pearl-and-rhinestone tiara, her beautiful face neutralized by
heavy makeup; but the makeup is part of the ritual, and the ritual
is part of the glory. The two of them in a lush park in West Jerusalem. Every picture we looked at was, for them watching me see the
images, a new delight: there were more and more and more. For
me, they all started to run together, it was now one in the morning, I was exhausted, but I made myself regard each photograph
as something unique, a vital integer in the stream of these people's
refusal to be reduced.

I slept in what they called their Arabic room, on low cushions, a
barred window above me issuing a cool breeze. I listened to roost-
ers crow and the semiautomatic weapons being fired at a nearby
wedding celebration, and eventually I drifted into the calmest,
heaviest sleep I'd had in months.

The next day, Baha had meetings to attend to try to solve the
water problem. I spoke to Hiba about their kids. She asked me at
what age Remy started his piano lessons. "I want music lessons for
the girls," she said. "I think it's very good for their development."
As she said it, more machine-gun fire erupted from the roof of a
nearby building. "I want them to know the feel, the smells, of a different environment. To be able to imagine other lives."

When I think of Hiba Nababta wanting what I want for my child,
her rightful desire that her kids should have an equal chance, everything feels hopeless and more obscene, even, than my wanting
to give earrings to a child without ears.

I went with Hiba that morning to her mother's house, where
she and Hiba's sisters were preparing an exquisite meal of stuffed
grape leaves and stuffed squashes, the grape leaves and vegetables

grown on her mother's patio. We were all women, eating together in relaxed company. A sister-in-law came downstairs to join us, sleepy, beautiful, with long red nails and hair dyed honey-blond, in her pajamas and slippers. She said that she was leaving for New Jersey with her husband, Hiba's brother, and their new baby. Relatives had arranged for them to immigrate. She would learn English and go to school.

When it was time to say goodbye, a younger sister was appointed to walk me to the checkpoint. Halfway there, I assured her I could walk alone, and we said goodbye. On the main road, shopkeepers came out to wave and smile. Everyone seemed to know who I was: the American who had come to meet with Baha.

At the checkpoint, the Palestinian boy in front of me was detained. I was next, and the soldiers were shocked to see an American, as they would have been shocked to see any non-Palestinian. There was much consternation in the reinforced station. My passport went from hand to hand. The commander approached the scratched window. "You're a Jew, right?" he blurted into the microphone. For the context in which he asked, for its reasoning, I said no. But in fact, I'm ethnically half-Jewish, on my father's side, although I was not raised with any religious or even a cultural connection to Judaism. My mother is a white Protestant from Tennessee. I might have said, "Yes, partly," but I found the question unanswerable, on account of its conflation of Zionism and Jewish identity. My Yiddish-speaking Odessan great-grandfather was a clothing merchant on Orchard Street. My grandfather worked in his shop as a boy. That is classically Jewish, but my sense of self, of what it might mean to inherit some trace of that lineage, was not the kind of patrimony the soldier was asking after. I was eventually waved along.

The day I left Shuafat camp was April 17. Fifteen days later, on May 2, Baha Nababta was murdered in the camp. An unknown person approached on a motorcycle as Baha worked with roughly a hundred fellow camp residents to pave a road. In front of this very large crowd of people, working together, the person on the motorcycle shot at Baha ten times and fled. Seven bullets hit him.

It is now December. Baha's wife, Hiba, has given birth to their son. His father is gone. His mother is widowed. But a baby—a baby can thrive no matter. A baby won't even know, until it is told, that someone is missing.

ALAN LIGHTMAN

What Came Before the Big Bang?

ON WEDNESDAY, FEBRUARY 11, 1931, Albert Einstein met for more than an hour with a small group of American scientists in the cozy library of the Mount Wilson Observatory, near Pasadena, California. The subject was cosmology, and Einstein was poised to make one of the more momentous statements in the history of science.

With his theories of relativity and gravity long confirmed and his Nobel Prize ten years old, he was by far the most famous scientist in the world. "Photographers lunged at me like hungry wolves," he had written in his diary when his ship landed in New York two months earlier.

For years Einstein had insisted, like Aristotle and Newton before him, that the universe was a magnificent and immortal cathedral, fixed for all eternity. In this picture, time runs from the infinite past to the infinite future, and little changes in between. When a prominent Belgian scientist proposed in 1927 that the universe was growing like an expanding balloon, Einstein pronounced the idea "abominable."

By 1931, however, the great physicist had been confronted with telescopic evidence that distant galaxies were in flight. Perhaps even more convincing, his mathematical model for a static universe had been shown to be like a pencil balanced on its point: give it a tiny nudge and it starts to move. When he arrived in Pasadena, Einstein was ready to acknowledge a cosmos in flux. He told the men gathered in the library in their suits and ties that the observed motion of the galaxies "has smashed my old construction like a hammerblow." Then he swung down his hand to emphasize the point.

What arose from the shards of that hammerblow was the cosmology of the Big Bang: the idea that the universe is not static and everlasting—that it "began" some fourteen billion years ago in a state of extremely high density and has been expanding and thinning out ever since. According to current data, our universe will keep expanding forever.

Sean Carroll, a professor of physics at the California Institute of Technology, is a Big Bang cosmologist. He is also one of a small platoon of physicists who call themselves quantum cosmologists. He wants to know what happened at the very first moment of the Big Bang, whether time or anything else existed before it, and how we can tell the future from the past. Such bedrock questions in physics, which have been seriously posed only recently, might be likened to Descartes asking for proof of his existence.

Quantum cosmology is speculative work, but Carroll explained its allure: "It's high risk, high gain." We do not yet possess a full theory of gravity, space, and time in the quantum era. Nevertheless, some of the sharpest minds in physics, including Stephen Hawking, Andrei Linde, and Alexander Vilenkin, have pondered the subject. It is a tiny field, not for the timid. The first difficulty is that the birth of our universe was a one-performance event, and we weren't there in the audience. An understanding of the very beginning of the universe also requires an understanding of so-called quantum gravity: gravity at enormously high densities of matter and energy, which are impossible to replicate. Most physicists believe that in this quantum era, the entire observable universe was roughly a million billion billion times smaller than a single atom. The temperature was nearly a million billion billion billion degrees. Time and space churned like boiling water. Of course, such things are unimaginable. But theoretical physicists try to imagine them in mathematical form, with pencil and paper. Somehow, time as we know it emerged in that fantastically dense nugget. Or perhaps time already existed, and what emerged was the "arrow" of time, pointing toward the future.

Physicists hope that within the next fifty years or so, string theory or other new theoretical work will provide a good understanding of quantum gravity, including an explanation of how the universe began. Until then, the quantum cosmologists will debate their hypotheses, each backed up with pages of calculations.

When I reached Carroll on Skype, he was wearing a hoodie and jeans in the comfortable study of his home, in Los Angeles. I was stationed in an uninhabitable guest room of my house, in Concord, Massachusetts: practically next door, in cosmological terms. Carroll is an articulate explicator of science as well as a highly regarded physicist—he's written scientific papers with titles such as "What If Time Really Exists?"—and he talks about his favorite subject with evident pleasure. He is forty-nine years old and barrel-chested, with puffy cheeks, jowls, a full head of reddish hair, and a mischievous schoolboy glint in his eye.

Carroll is obsessed with the relative smoothness and order of the universe. Order in physics has a concrete meaning. It can be quantified. Furthermore, conditions of disorder are more probable than conditions of order, just as a deck of cards, once shuffled, is more likely to be jumbled up than precisely arranged by number and suit. Applying those considerations to the cosmos at large, physicists have suggested that given the amount of matter that exists we should expect the universe to be far more disordered and lumpy than it is. The observable universe has something like one hundred billion galaxies in it, but when viewed over sufficiently large expanses of space, it looks as uniform as the sand on a beach. Any large volume of space looks about like any other. It would be far more probable, say the physicists, to see that same material concentrated in a much smaller number of ultralarge galaxies, or in large clusters of galaxies, or perhaps even in a single massive black hole—analogous to all the sand on a beach concentrated in a few silicon boulders.

The improbable smoothness of the observable universe, in turn, points toward unusually tidy conditions near the Big Bang. We don't understand why. But the order and smoothness, known to physicists as a state of low entropy, is a clue. "I strongly believe that the low entropy of the early universe is a puzzle that the wider cosmology community doesn't take nearly as seriously as they should," Carroll told me. "Misunderstandings like that offer opportunities for making new breakthroughs."

Carroll and other physicists believe that order is intimately connected to the arrow of time. In particular, the forward direction of time is determined by the movement of order to disorder. For example, a movie of a glass goblet falling off a table and shattering on the floor would look normal to us; if we saw a movie of scattered shards of glass jumping off the floor and gathering themselves into a goblet perched on the edge of a table, we would say that the movie was being played backward. Likewise, clean rooms left unattended become dusty with time, not cleaner. What we call the future is the condition of increasing mess; what we call the past is increasing tidiness. Our ability to easily distinguish between the two shows that time in our world has a clear direction. Time also has a clear direction in the cosmos at large. Stars radiate heat and light, slowly spend their nuclear fuel, and finally turn into cold cinders drifting through space. Never does the reverse happen.

Which brings us back to the unexpected orderliness of our universe. Working with Alan Guth, a pioneering cosmologist at the Massachusetts Institute of Technology, Carroll has developed a not-yet-published theory called two-headed time. In this model of the universe, time has existed forever. But unlike the static cosmos imagined by Aristotle and Newton and Einstein, this universe changes as the eons go by. The evolution of the cosmos is symmetric in time, such that the behavior of the universe before the Big Bang is nearly a mirror image of its behavior after. Until fourteen billion years ago, the universe was contracting. It reached a minimum size at the Big Bang (which we call $t = 0$) and has been expanding ever since. (Other quantum cosmologists have proposed similar models.) It's like a Slinky that falls to the floor, reaches maximum compression on impact, and then bounces back to larger dimensions. Because of the unavoidable random fluctuations required by quantum physics, the contracting universe would not be an exact mirror image of the expanding universe; a physicist named Alan Guth probably did not exist in the contracting phase of our universe.

It is well known in the science of order and disorder that, other things being equal, larger spaces allow for more disorder, essentially because there are more places to scatter things. Smaller spaces therefore tend to have more order. As a consequence, in the Carroll-Guth picture, the order of the universe was at a *maximum* at the Big Bang; disorder increased both before and after. Recall that the forward direction of time is determined by the movement of order to disorder. Thus the future points away from

the Big Bang in two directions. A person living in the contracting
phase of the universe sees the Big Bang in her past, just as we do.
When she dies, the universe is larger than when she was born, just
as it will be for us. "When I came to understand that the reason
I can remember the past but not the future is ultimately related
to conditions at the Big Bang, that was a startling epiphany," said
Carroll.

If you think of time as a long road and the Big Bang as a pothole somewhere in that road, then a sign at the pothole telling
you the direction to the future would have two arrows pointing in
opposite directions. Hence the name "two-headed time." Near the
pothole itself, caught between the two arrows, time would have no
clear direction. Time would be confused. In the subatomic version
of goblets and houses, shards of glass would jump off the floor
to form goblets as often as those goblets would fall and shatter.
Unattended houses would become neater as often as they would
become more cluttered. Both movies would be equally familiar to
any subatomic being living at the Big Bang.

According to Carroll and Guth, the two-headed-time theory
could become even more elaborate and strange. The point of
minimum size and maximum order of the universe might not have
been the Big Bang of *our* universe but the Big Bang of *another* universe, some kind of grand protouniverse. Our universe, and possibly an infinite number of universes, could have been spawned
from this parent universe, and each of the universes could have
its own Big Bang. The process of spawning new universes from a
parent universe is called eternal inflation. The idea was developed
by quantum cosmologists in the early 1980s. In brief, an unusual
energy field (but one permitted by physics) in the protouniverse
acts like antigravity and causes exponentially fast expansion. This
unusual energy field has different strengths in different regions of
space. Each such region expands to cosmic proportions, and the
energy field becomes ordinary matter, forming a new universe that
is closed off and completely out of contact with the protouniverse
that sired it.

A second major hypothesis is that the universe, and time, did
not exist before the Big Bang. The universe materialized literally
out of nothing, at a tiny but finite size, and expanded thereafter.
There were no moments before the moment of smallest size be-

cause there was no "before." Likewise, there was no "creation" of the universe, since that concept implies action in time. Even to say that the universe "materialized" is somewhat misleading. As Hawking describes it, the universe "would be neither created nor destroyed. It would just BE." Such notions as existence and being in the absence of time are not fathomable within our limited human experience. We don't even have language to describe them. Nearly every sentence we utter has some notion of "before" and "after."

One of the first quantum cosmologists to suggest that the universe could appear out of nothing was Alexander Vilenkin, a Ukrainian scientist who came to the United States in 1976, when he was in his midtwenties. He is now a professor of physics at Tufts University. When I visited him in his office on a hot day in July, he was wearing sandals and a loose black shirt. His single window looked out on a dull brick building across the street. "The view from my previous office was better," he said. Boxes of unpacked books littered the floor; on his bookshelf was an Einstein doll given to him by his daughter.

In the Soviet Union, Vilenkin's acceptance to a graduate program in physics was rescinded, possibly at the instigation of the KGB. Before he emigrated, he worked as a night watchman in a zoo, giving him plenty of time to think cosmological thoughts. In the United States, Vilenkin got his PhD in biophysics. "I was doing cosmology on the side," he said. "It was not a reputable field of research at that time." Vilenkin is a serious man who, unlike many physicists, does not much joke around, and he takes his work on the universe at t = 0 extremely seriously. "No cause is required to create a universe from quantum tunneling," he says, "but the laws of physics should be there." Briefly, we chat about what "there" means when time and space do not yet exist. On this score, Vilenkin likes to quote Saint Augustine, who was often asked what God was doing before He created the universe. In his *Confessions*, Augustine replied that since God created time when He created the universe, there was no "before."

When Vilenkin talks about quantum tunneling, he is referring to a spooky phenomenon in quantum physics, in which objects can perform such magic feats as instantly appearing on the far side of a mountain without traveling over the top. That mystifying ability, which has been verified in the laboratory, follows from the fact that subatomic particles behave as though they can be in many places at once. Quantum tunneling is common in the tiny world of the atom but is highly improbable in our human world. It has never been observed at larger scales—which explains why the phenomenon seems so absurd. But in the quantum era of cosmology, very near t = o, the entire universe was the size of a subatomic particle. Thus, the entire universe could have "suddenly" appeared from wherever things originate in the impossible-to-fathom quantum haze of probabilities. (I put "suddenly" in quotation marks because time didn't exist, but I have just now realized that in this very sentence I used the verb "did," which is the past tense of "do" . . .)

What does it mean to say that the entire universe was like a subatomic particle, existing in the twilight world of the quantum? James Hartle, a leading quantum cosmologist at the University of California, Santa Barbara, has, with Hawking, developed one of the most detailed models of the universe "during" the quantum era near the Big Bang. Time appears nowhere in Hartle and Hawking's equations. Instead, they use quantum physics to compute the probability of certain snapshots of the universe.

Although an expert in quantum theory, Hartle admits to being baffled by the application of quantum physics to the universe as a whole. "It is a mystery to me," he said, "why we have quantum mechanics when there is only one state of the universe." In other words, why should there be probabilities that alternative conditions of the universe exist when we inhabit only one? And do those alternative conditions actually exist somewhere?

The quantum cosmologists are aware of the vast philosophical and theological reverberations of their work. As Hawking says in *A Brief History of Time,* many people believe that God, while permitting the universe to evolve according to fixed laws of nature, was uniquely responsible for winding up the clock at the beginning and choosing how to set it in motion. Hawking's own theory provides an explanation for how the universe might have wound itself up—his method of calculating the early snapshots of the universe has no dependence on initial conditions or boundaries or anything outside the universe itself. The icy rules of quantum physics are completely sufficient. "What place, then, for a creator?" asks Hawking. Lawrence Krauss, a physicist, reaches a similar conclusion in his book *A Universe from Nothing,* in which he argues that advances in quantum cosmology show that God is irrelevant at best.

One would expect most quantum cosmologists to be atheists, like the majority of scientists. But Don Page, a leading quantum cosmologist at the University of Alberta, is also an evangelical Christian. Page is a master computationalist. When he and I were fellow graduate students in physics at Caltech, he used to quietly take out a fine-point pen whenever confronted with a difficult physics problem. Without flinching or pausing, he scribbled one equation after another in a dense tangle of mathematics until he arrived at the answer. Although he has collaborated with Hawking on major papers, Page parts ways with him on the subject of God. He recently told me, "As a Christian, I think there is a being outside the universe that created the universe and caused all things. God is the true creator. All of the universe is caused by God." In a guest column on Carroll's blog (which is called *The Preposterous Universe*), Page sounds simultaneously like a scientist and a theist:

> One might think that adding the hypothesis that the world (all that exists) includes God would make the theory for the entire world more complex, but it is not obvious that is the case, since it might be that God is even simpler than the universe, so that one would get a simpler explanation starting with God than starting with just the universe.

Significantly, most quantum cosmologists do not believe that anything *caused* the creation of the universe. As Vilenkin said to me, quantum physics can hypothesize a universe without cause — just as quantum physics can show how electrons can change orbits in an atom without cause. There are no definite cause-and-effect relationships in the quantum world, only probabilities. Carroll put it this way: "In everyday life we talk about cause and effect. But there is no reason to apply that thinking to the universe as a whole. I do not feel in any way unsatisfied by just saying, 'That's the way it is.'"

The notion of an event or state of being without cause drives hard against the grain of science. For centuries, scientists have attempted to explain all events as the logical consequence of prior events. Page argues that at the origin of our universe—whether in the two-headed-time model or in the universe-out-of-nothing model—there was no clear distinction between cause and effect. If causality can dissolve in the quantum haze of the origin of the universe, Page and other physicists note, there is reason to question its solidity even in the world that we live in, long after the Big

Bang, which is surely part of the same reality. "Causality within the universe is not fundamental," said Page. "It is an approximate concept derived from our experience with the world." Strict causality could be an illusion, a way for our brains, and our science, to make sense of the world. But without strict causality, how can we take responsibility for our actions? A crack in the marble foundation of causality could send tremors into philosophy, religion, and ethics.

Quantum cosmology has led us to questions about the fundamental aspects of existence and being, questions that most of us rarely ask. In our short century or less, we generally aim to create a comfortable existence within the tiny rooms of our lives. We eat, we sleep, we get jobs, we pay the bills, we have lovers and children. Some of us build cities or make art. But if we have the luxury of true mental freedom, there are larger concerns to be found. Look at the sky. Does space go on forever, to infinity? Or is it finite but without boundary or edge, like the surface of a sphere? Either answer is disturbing, and unfathomable. Where did we come from? We can follow the lives of our parents and grandparents and their parents backward in time, back and back through the generations, until we come to some ancestor ten thousand years in the past whose DNA remains in our body. We can follow the chain of being even further back in time to the first humans, and the first primates, and the one-celled amoebas swimming about in the primordial seas, and the formation of the atmosphere, and the slow condensation of gases to create Earth. It all happened, whether we think about it or not. We quickly realize how limited we are in our experience of the world. What we see and feel with our bodies, caught midway between atoms and galaxies, is but a small swath of the spectrum, a sliver of reality.

In the 1940s the American psychologist Abraham Maslow developed the concept of a hierarchy of human needs. He started with the most primitive and urgent demands, and ended with the most lofty and advanced. At the bottom of the pyramid are physical needs for survival, like food and water. Next up is safety. Higher up is love and belonging, then self-esteem. The highest of Maslow's proposed needs, self-actualization, is the desire to get the most out of ourselves, to be the best we can be. I would suggest adding one more category at the very top of the pyramid, above even self-actualization: imagination and exploration. Wasn't that the need that propelled Marco Polo and Vasco da Gama and

Einstein? The need to imagine new possibilities, the need to reach out beyond ourselves and understand the world around us. Not to help ourselves with physical survival or personal relationships or self-discovery but to know and comprehend this strange cosmos we find ourselves in. The need to ask the really big questions. How did it all begin? Far beyond our own lives, far beyond our community or our nation or our planet or even our solar system. How did the universe begin? It is a luxury to be able to ask such questions. It is also a human necessity.

EMILY MALONEY

Cost of Living

FROM *The Virginia Quarterly Review*

IN 2008 THE hospital where I worked—a Level II trauma center
just outside Chicago—was $54 million in debt. Everyone seemed
to be aware of this fact; the figure floated beneath the surface of
all our conversations, an unspoken rigidity we seemed to bump up
against everywhere we turned. We were to be careful when we distributed small stuffed animals to unhappy children in the ER, were
told to dispense fewer scrub tops to adolescents with dislocated
shoulders and bloodied shirts, to pay attention to the way that
canes seemed to walk off as if under their own power. Everything
cost money, Helene, our nursing manager, reminded us, even if
the kid was screaming and had to get staples in his scalp. I was an
ER tech then, someone who drew blood, performed EKGs, and set
up suture trays. Most of my knowledge of the world of the ER came
through direct patient care. If a nurse or a doctor needed something for a patient, I'd get it for them. I'd run into the stockroom,
sort through yards of plastic tubing, through dozens of disposable
plastic pieces, acres of gauze. We—the techs—were expected to
guard against the depletion of resources. Helene seemed to remind us at every available opportunity by tacking notes up on the
bulletin board in the staff break room. PLEASE CONSERVE YOUR
RESOURCES. ONLY USE WHAT IS NECESSARY. These notes were
pinned next to our Press Ganey survey results, a form sent to patients upon discharge. Helene blacked out staff names if the feedback wasn't positive. But the question of resources seemed like the
kind of problem that couldn't be solved through gauze or surveys
or suture trays.

When it was quiet—a forbidden word in the emergency depart-

ment—I'd help with the billing. We'd break down charts as fast
as possible: scan them, assign codes, and decide what to charge.
Names I vaguely recognized flew by on the PDF reader. I studied
my handwriting on their medication lists, a form techs weren't supposed to fill out but did anyway. (Nurses were supposed to keep
up with the medication lists, but there was never enough time for
them to actually do it.) Because there were only twenty slots on
these forms, I sometimes had to use two pages.

I was twenty-three at the time, still paying off the cost of the
mental-health-care debt I took on at nineteen, a cost I believed I
would shoulder well into my thirties, a figure that felt more like a
student loan than an appropriate cost for medical care. I didn't understand the nature of my mistake at the time, that I should have
gone somewhere else for treatment—maybe the university hospital, where the state might pick up your bill if you were declared indigent, or nowhere at all. Sitting on a cot in the emergency room,
I filled out paperwork certifying myself as the responsible party for
my own medical care—signed it without looking, anchoring myself to this debt, a stone dropped in the middle of a stream. This
debt was the cost for living, and I accumulated it in the telemetry
unit, fifth floor, at a community hospital in Iowa City, hundreds of
miles from home. There, I spent too much time playing with the
plastic shapes that dangled from my IV line, which dripped potas-
sium ions in carefully meted doses, like dimes from my future life
funneled into a change-counting machine. My health insurance
at the time occupied the space between terrible and nonexistent.
I couldn't imagine the amount of money I'd spent—the debt I'd
incurred—in attempting to end my life. *Suicide should be cheaper,* I
remembered thinking. Probably half the costs were for psychiatry,
for an illness it turned out I never really had. I was depressed, but
a lot of people were depressed in college, it seemed. I only tried
to kill myself after I began taking—and then stopped taking—all
the medications I'd been prescribed, twenty-six in all. All for what
turned out to be a vitamin deficiency, combined with hypothyroid-
ism and a neurologically based developmental disorder.

And then there were the unintentional costs, those involving
loss of work, lost friends, having to ask my father if he would drive
to Iowa City and help me pack up all my belongings and move into
a new apartment, since my roommate, who had also been diagnosed with mental illness, had developed a profound depression

and had moved out. He wanted to drive to Mexico on a motor-cycle. My life did not have space for motorcycles.

When my bill finally reached me, it wasn't itemized, just "bal-ance forwarded" from the hospital to the collection agency, after my paltry insurance covered the initial cost. From then on, I'd get calls requesting that I boost my payments, or I'd call them to switch bank accounts and they'd harass me on the phone. They would call me on my cell phone while I was at work, in the car, at home, in between shifts at the hospital, which I sometimes worked back to back if I could. For a long while I ignored them. I blocked their number, refused to answer when they dialed. My debt was five figures, an immense sum for someone making only $12.50 an hour. My coworkers in the ER were largely sons and daughters of first-generation immigrants. Most of them lived with their parents, and made up for it by driving nice cars. I lived in a third-floor walk-up almost far enough away from Iowa City to forget how much money I owed, and to whom.

At the hospital where I worked, patients returned again and again, a kind of catch-and-release program, we joked, so nobody would pay for these stays. Some insurance plans prevented payment—as a kind of penalty—to hospitals that readmitted patients who'd been discharged inside thirty days. No payment to the hospital to disimpact a cognitively disabled 98-year-old woman, or to start two IVs and admit a woman who, at 108, had explained to the techs in providing her medical history that she had lost one of her older brothers in "the War," in a trench in France in 1917. The government thought that these people should have been cured, explained in hundreds of pages on the Centers for Medicare & Medicaid Services website, then later in the documents that made their way across Helene's desk. How do you explain the cost of a perennially septic patient whose nursing-home status and inconsis-tent care meant we'd see her again next month?

The patients who appeared on my screen flashed in bits and pieces, their visits reduced to minor explanations, to ICD-9 codes used to categorize their illnesses or injuries. I'd use their chart to determine what they should pay. If we were in doubt, we were ex-pected to bill up (though this was never explicitly discussed)—that is, if someone received medical care from a physician assistant or other "midlevel" provider, the patient's care might cost less; but if the physician assistant or a nurse practitioner did more work (sutures, for example), the care could still get bumped up a level.

Suicide attempts were particularly resource-dependent. Patients were admitted to a medical floor—perhaps ICU—to deal with the physical costs of their attempts. Later, they transferred to psychiatry inpatient—nicknamed Fort Knox, as it was locked—after they had stabilized. The attempters came in sporadically, surprises tucked into the low points of our afternoons, beside admissions of women who had inexplicable feminine bleeds, and elderly men who slipped off sidewalks and into the street on sunny days. The attempters were people with conviction, but who lacked the ability to follow through. Who could blame them for their ineptitude, considering they wanted to do it at all?

There were rules in charging patients for emergencies, unique explanations for one billing code instead of another. If someone was discharged from an inpatient floor, she might find a toothbrush marked eight dollars, an IV bag marked twenty-five. In the emergency department, we assigned a level based on the type and duration of care, rather than itemizing each treatment individually, a complex algorithm based on many factors, but usually distilled into a few questions: Was the patient treated on the trauma or medical side of the ER? Sutures or no sutures? Cardiac workups? EKGs? Each level had its own exacting specifications, a way of making sense—at least financial sense—of the labyrinthine mess of billing. There was a surcharge for the physician (it was cheaper if they saw the physician assistant instead), and assorted charges for interventions, for the trappings of emergency—bandages, braces, Ortho-Glass for splinting. There was an expectation that you moved as quickly as you could. Hopefully you did not commit any errors along the way.

How much should it cost to put staples in a child's head? Staples seemed complicated. We weren't supposed to use anesthesia. It sounds like an act of unspeakable cruelty, but the truth of the matter is that people have less sensation in their scalps than other parts of the body. The staple guns were autoclaved or thrown out after use; there were only so many staples available per gun. We stocked the ones that held fifteen or else twenty, and usually two or three or four did the job. Shafiq, the physician assistant I worked with most days, liked to mix a local, topical anesthetic—lidocaine-epinephrine-tetracaine, or LET—for children who came in needing staples. I loved the sharp smell of LET when I mixed it. The chemical reaction meant it started to work immediately after mixing, so I assembled the ingredients in front of the patient, stirred with the wooden end of a long Q-tip, which I then flipped and dipped into the solution to apply the gel. It reminded me of chemistry lab, of the courses in community college I liked best—black tabletops, wooden stools, a type of precision. In the meantime, the patient sat and bled on the cot. And then we waited until the anesthetic had done its job.

In patient charts, the LET sometimes bumped up the level of care. We asked patients' parents if it'd be OK if we used a little numbing gel for the child's scalp, and of course everyone said yes —yes, yes, yes. For us, this was tantamount to asking someone if they'd like elective cough syrup, or an aspirin, or some small gesture.

There were other costs. Dermabond was expensive—it was for open wounds, just superglue used to adhere flaps of skin back into place. We gave small stuffed toys to children who wouldn't stop crying in the ER, and although someone donated those toys, the time we spent stocking them meant that they cost as much as any other type of equipment we might use. Even the inexpensive things could be counted as a potential place to stem waste: sandwiches consumed by diabetics or (more likely) hungry techs, the little packages of cookies we used to placate toddlers whose siblings had been brought in. The boy on the bicycle, hit by a bus, whose blood was drawn twice because it clotted in the lab. A man in a C-spine collar, strapped to a backboard, off to X-ray for expensive films.

Helene told us everything was expensive; to be careful. Not everyone needed an EKG, or blood cultures, though that was usually a physician's problem, not a tech's responsibility. One of our docs only worked weekends and alternating holidays, brought doughnuts for the nurses—sugar placated even the angriest among us, the most difficult—and drew blood cultures on everybody over the age of fifty-five, which felt like just about everyone we ever saw. Helene seemed to speak to him without ever actually speaking to him—this guy who swooped into our hospital on a part-time, just-a-few-shifts-a-month basis, and spent money our hospital didn't have. I saw the waste in the cultures we'd draw on patients who inevitably were septic, others who were going to be discharged and thus would not need blood cultures, which took days to grow in glass bottles. By the time the blood cultures had grown, the patients would be long gone. It was like banding birds, a doc told me once. Still, I'd flick the lids off the bottles with my thumb, stick the patient's vein with a butterfly or straight needle, puncture the lid of the culture bottle with the needle attached to the other end of the tubing, and fill them to the appropriate line. Drawing blood bumped billing up a level. Cultures, even more.

These patient charts, the ones we broke down, were the happy endings in our emergency department. These were the patients who went home, who had some place to go, who left the hospital alive and in good condition. Patients who died flashed up on our screens occasionally, but those were easy to bill: level 5, the most expensive, as we would have performed "heroic measures" to try to save them. The lifesaving stuff was always exorbitant: The techs lined up to do CPR, two large-bore IVs, one in each arm, using what the paramedics called the coffee straw—an enormous needle. An EKG, or two, or three. An X-ray. And sometimes, depending on the nature of the illness, the cardiac cath lab, where a group of physicians, a nurse, and a scrub tech would thread the patient's arteries with a needle.

At nineteen, I needed a Helene for living, a responsible party who could have told me, You don't need to do this. That there were cheaper or better options than ending one's life. Instead, I swallowed 8,000 milligrams of lithium carbonate, received a gastric lavage and activated charcoal, then ended up on a monitoring floor, which added to the expense. From there, I was transferred to the psychiatric ward, where we spent all of our time in the dayroom. When I left, I told everyone how it wasn't every place you could start your day with *The Carol Burnett Show*, but really all I could think about was what this treatment was going to cost me for years to come.

This thought, this recollection of the hospitalization, the subsequent bills, the cost of the ambulance to drive my unconscious body across town, the now-fading first-name basis with the guy who was ultimately assigned to my account, in collections (Jeff? Or was it Ted?), was something that came up—briefly, repeatedly, stunningly—whenever I worked in billing, like a bee sting. There was the prick of remembering, the wash of sudden insight. How responsible, how careful were we? Did I make a mistake in the last chart? Could I go back and revise? There was the guilt of billing a patient for too much—and we knew so many of these bills would never be paid, especially when there was no insurance to bill. Self-pay, we called them. You'd see it on the first page, upper right-hand corner, a mark against their futures. If I had a question, I could ask one of the two dedicated billers for our department. But then I'd start to recognize the handwriting as my own. Had I really put in for that test at the physician's request? And it cost *how much?*

Shafiq seemed to be one of the few in the department aware of the costs we assigned to our patients. He routinely cleaned and returned suture kits to patients and taught them how to remove their own stitches. We'd just throw away the tweezers anyway, and this way we could save the patient a trip back to the ER to get those sutures removed. "Nah, it's not a big deal," he'd say to the patient, handing him the tools. "Just take 'em out. Don't cut yourself." Shafiq had paid fifty dollars per credit hour to finish his degree in physician assistant studies at a community college on Chicago's West Side. He viewed himself as practical. Shafiq spoke endlessly about how basic medical care should be free, how we were "hosing everyone" by charging for LET, for staples, for particular levels of care. What if we were to treat everyone equally? What then?

At some point I started billing differently. I can't say when. It could have been when we had a patient die and I had to bill his family. It could have been when I saw the dizzying costs that were itemized for inpatient bills, or the time the woman I evaluated —my patient, our patient—and then billed was saddled with an amount she could never hope to pay. I remember her: how she came in and explained that things were difficult, that she didn't have insurance, but she needed someone to lance the boil that had erupted at her waistline. It had been causing her incredible pain, to the point where she could no longer dress herself. *Please,* she said. But she had already been registered, been given an ID bracelet, all the apparatuses of the emergency department and its tracking. Her bill popped up later on my screen; I saw the amount. This, somehow, totaled the cost of living. I thought of my own un-paid medical debt, reduced the amount, told no one, and let the next chart flash across my screen.

*

Every December, I buy a cake for my second birthday: another year I'm still alive. Some years it's a cupcake; other years I opt for a grocery-store sheet cake. I invite friends over, or I have dinner with my husband and we sit and talk about work. I say that I've bought a cake. "Great," he says. He loves surprise cake. He doesn't know.

Recently, my bank was bought by another bank. This would not be a notable fact except that I have been banking there since shortly after I was born. Before that, my parents banked there, and in the very early days of the institution, my aunt worked there as a teller. I modeled as a child, and I would endorse the checks from my earnings while lying on the bank floor, whose green carpeting hasn't changed in more than thirty years. When the bank relocated down the street, everything remained the same. I still know all the tellers and the personal bankers, the vice president, the president, Rodney, who works in the basement, reconciling transactions, I swear, with a red pencil. Any of them could look at my account and see that a collection agency had been debiting money on the twenty-fifth of the month, and had been doing so for almost ten years.

But the routing numbers changed with the acquisition, and so I called the collection agency to find out what had to be done. Perhaps I could give them a new routing number over the phone. Perhaps I would have to send them a canceled check. The company had offices in Iowa and Illinois, but the number was from Iowa, where I had been hospitalized. For years, upon seeing an Iowa number flash on my screen, I didn't pick up, just sent the calls to voicemail: my Iowa landlord, my friends, old coworkers, bosses, professors, and once, admission to graduate school. Now, dialing the number felt strange.

The woman on the other end of the phone explained that the call may be recorded, that she was a debt collector and was attempting to collect a debt, the phrasing of federal law. Her voice was Iowa, flat vowels of the Upper Midwest. "You know you've been paying this debt for a long time," she said.

"I know," I said. The conversation usually went something like this. So long, so much money. Usually debt collectors have to harass people on the phone, but not me, not anymore. I had fallen into line, paid the minimum every month on autopay. Twenty-five dollars a month times how many years equaled a bed on a monitoring floor.

"It's beyond the statute of limitations."

"Excuse me?" I was sitting at my father's desk. My husband and I had bought a house nearby, and we had begun to inherit all the stuff of aging parents. I had the new checks in my hand, the new checkbook. I rubbed my thumb on its pleather case. My chest felt full of the sterile strips we used to pack wounds: yards and yards of knit-cotton ribbon crammed into the cavity left by a lanced boil or pustule. The silence pooled larger and larger. I said nothing.

"If you were to stop paying it, nobody would be able to go after you, and it wouldn't show on your credit report."

I waited. "So I can stop paying it?" I asked.

"I'll remove your autopay information from my computer. Have a great weekend," she said, and hung up.

And then I did, too. I held the phone in my hand. It couldn't be right: they would call back in five minutes, or ten, or next week, or next month, when the payment was due, but nobody did.

These days, I work far away from patients, writing up results of clinical trials or else abstracts for scientific congresses. The patients appear to me as raw data, depersonalized ID numbers, or in graphs that depict the efficacy of a particular drug, or as a way to explain value: one drug may cost more than another drug, but it is more useful, or requires fewer doses. The patients are further away —an idea, an endgame, a target hard to reach. All the work I do —the abstracts, the manuscripts, the slide decks—is in support of one drug, the next blockbuster, they call it. We are expensive, us medical writers. When I freelance for an agency, I bill by the quarter hour—like attorneys, or psychiatrists—and I think of Helene, her voice in my head. I try only to use what is necessary. But what, exactly, is necessary?

GREG MARSHALL

If I Only Had a Leg

FROM *Electric Literature*

UP WITH KIDS started as an unofficial offshoot of Up with People, the 1970s show choir now notorious for its ties to an evangelical cult, the Nixon administration, and Halliburton. Our director Bonnie's salad days had been spent touring with the group, which she referred to simply as People. It took a real insider to drop two prepositions. So much projecting over the years had left her vocal cords frayed and full of benign polyps. Now in her forties, an UP WITH KIDS T-shirt plunging from her chest and a wad of nicotine gum in one cheek, she suffered from a permanent case of laryngitis, the kind only characters on Nick at Nite got with any regularity and only then for the better part of an episode.

Looking back, it was probably just the fact that she had been a smoker, but as Bonnie reenacted long-lost Super Bowl halftime shows in the Presbyterian church where we rehearsed, squeezing out notes like the debarked corgi on our block, it was like music itself had worn her out. I couldn't imagine a better life.

Every summer my family took a trip with Up with Kids and patiently watched me scream "Supercalifragilisticexpialidocious" into a microphone on the boardwalk outside Universal Studios or snap and twirl through a Beach Boys medley, a plastic lei flying around my ears. Outside a tank of honking sea lions, we beamed that Sea World (not the more traditional choice, Disneyland) was the happiest place in the U.S.A., and at an America Sings Summit in Washington, D.C., my preemie sister Chelsea and I didn't worry that we weren't good enough for anyone else to hear we just sang, sang a song, like the Carpenters.

Dragged to all of our cheesy performances, my older brother Danny called Up with Kids the Special Olympics of acting, which was fine with me. Sparkling in a loose-fitting gold lamé shirt while my little sister was trapped in a puckering leotard of the same material, I was the actor among social rejects. Bonnie's daughter, for one, had Down syndrome. Most of us Kids were damaged in more minor but no less noticeable ways: chronic pinkeye, deforming acne, facial hair. One girl with the last name Wood insisted we call her Holly Wood even though her real name was something like Sarah. Another boy pushed a walker around stage.

It goes without saying I have mild cerebral palsy, though my family downplayed the condition in my childhood by telling people I had "tight tendons." In Up with Kids I found not just a fun after-school activity but also a place where dragging my right foot and having my right arm frozen at my side were not necessarily to my detriment. It would be an overstatement to say I used my limp to get plum roles, just that, in retrospect, they all fell into a certain pattern. I sat on thrones or made pronouncements from center stage, blowing kisses and doing small claps. No one could stand quite like I could. Pelvis thrust forward, my right foot dangled off my slender ankle so that my legs, in princely tights, formed a jaunty lowercase *k*.

By far my best role with Up with Kids was also, fittingly, my last. In the fifth grade, Bonnie cast me as Scarecrow in *The Wizard of Oz*. It was my best role, I should say, because I had always loved *Oz*. This was my excuse, with the help of the hobby shop in the basement of Cottonwood Mall, to essentially live over the rainbow. Before I'd even highlighted my lines, the merch began pouring in: an Emerald City snow globe, an accent pillow of Scarecrow's face, a Toto stuffed animal. While my brother bought the latest Beckett in the card shop upstairs, tracking the value of his Shaq and Michael Jordan rookie cards like they were blue-chip stocks, I hauled out to the parking lot a life-sized cardboard cutout of Scarecrow, the Wizard, and Tin Man and propped it at the foot of my bed to block out the sports wallpaper. Dolls of what I referred to as the Big Four danced on chunks of yellow brick on my windowsill, blotting out the sun.

For a kid with a limp, it was easy to see Dorothy's plight as orthopedic. Skipping as best I could, I'd struck out on the replica of the

Yellow Brick Road at MGM Grand in Las Vegas. Waiting in line for the Great Movie Ride in Orlando, I'd saluted Dorothy's ruby slippers, which shimmered in a glass case, by trying to click my own battered sneakers. Through my toddler years, I'd preferred, like Dorothy, never to take off my shoes, even when I slept. It felt better to keep my feet encased in a little magic. (This magic did not extend to the ankle-foot orthosis shoved *into* my shoe, but with socks on I could survive the rubbing.) Following surgeries on my tight Achilles tendon and hamstrings in the third grade, I made sure my cast was as close to emerald green as fiberglass could get, like it could have been sticking up from a field of poppies or out from under a house. Even the braces on my teeth at that age were green.

Sure, I knew that if Glinda could have popped onto the pilled carpet of Cottonwood Presbyterian she would have told me, in her airheaded way, I needed look no further than my own two feet. This had never stopped me from daydreaming. Tin Man needed a heart, Cowardly Lion needed some nerve, and I needed a new leg, one that wasn't short and small in circumference around the calf and ankle; one that wasn't zipped up the back with scars; one that didn't need to be taught how to skip.

Whether in a cast or not, I never stopped thinking about my leg. Part of my brain was always sending stray signals to the tips of my toes, making me feel mildly electrocuted. What I loved about the stage was that self-consciousness was a given and it was against the rules to walk and talk at the same time, which I can't do anyway. It wasn't a matter of forgetting about how my knee pointed inward or my right heel floated off the ground. It was about all of us feeling awkward together.

Once we did our vocal warm-ups and tongue twisters, I'd sink into my role, feeling almost ecclesiastical, a golden angel observing some sacred rite. I couldn't walk a straight line, but ask me to shoot bolts of electricity out my fingertips and my hands would tremble with the effort. At the end of each rehearsal, I'd squash Chelsea's Munchkin costume under her coat as we waited beside the glowing Jesus marquee for Mom to pick us up. *Come celebrate His life,* it said, or *Feeling sad?*

As our first show neared, Bonnie crowded the stage with as many farmhands, crows, talking trees, flying monkeys, Winkies, and

Munchkins as there were cleared checks. She threw emerald smocks over the denizens of Oz and a gold tiara on the busty blond giant playing Glinda. Our Toto had rheumatoid arthritis and, though she yelped in pain, we only thought to bring her kneepads once we also thought to make her wear a migraine-inducing headband with floppy ears and draw whiskers on her cheeks. Chelsea and the other Munchkins wore ruffled sleeves and scrunchies that even I had to admit were pretty cute. Being a Munchkin was perfect for my little sister. She leapt around the stage like a replaceable idiot while I carried the show with my natural stage presence.

The same show business philosophy that led Bonnie to book our summer stock at amusement parks led her to schedule our final *Oz* performance in a homeless shelter in downtown Salt Lake City, Bonnie's philosophy being that a captive audience is better than one composed exclusively of parents and relatives. Only those too sick or stoned stayed for the duration, their faces dirty and drawn, a bunch of Aunt Ems and Uncle Henrys doing their best to ignore the spectacle of Bonnie crouched in the center aisle, mouthing along to the action onstage, fleeing an invisible twister.

Sweat rolled down the back of my neck and dripped under my gold lamé as soon as the overture to "If I Only Had a Brain" blasted through the shoddy sound system and I hobbled to my mark, a masking tape X. My leg wouldn't stop shaking as I swung it around. Nerves were a good thing, Mom said. They meant you gave a shit. I was a natural singer. I sang, naturally, all over the house. Sounding good in front of a crowd was an order of magnitude beyond me. And dancing, how to put this? Dancing was, if not my secret power, my secret joy. I wasn't silly enough to think I was actually good at it, but it sure did get a rise out of people. I was only a little worried about what my brother would say.

Since I couldn't hide my chicken leg, no matter how large my quilted poncho from the Costume Closet or how high I pulled my socks, I tried to turn it into part of the act, jerking around like a real-life man of straw, wincing animatedly when my jean shorts rubbed against the incision scar on my tight right hamstring. See-sawing into scenery, my clumsy right foot mashed crows' feet and sent plastic apples spiraling into the first row mere seconds after bitchy trees lobbed them at us. There were genuine gasps when I fell and genuine applause when I got up again. Stuck for ages with a pole up my back, I was finally free to dance.

It wasn't until this last curtain call, when Bonnie presented me, Chelsea, and every other cast member with hollow plastic Oscar statues, that she revealed the big surprise: we were going to meet one of the last surviving Munchkins from *The Wizard of Oz*. It must have been a chore to track down Margaret Pellegrini in those dial-up days of the internet, and I'm not sure how my acting teacher did it. In any case, this chance encounter had the ring of fate as it represented the next logical step in my progression as an actor. I was about to be discovered. Margaret would know agents and producers. All I had to do was sing for her and I'd have it made.

"But I'm a Munchkin," Chelsea said.

"No, you're a weirdo in a gold leotard," Danny said. "Just kidding!"

Margaret is on-screen a lot if you know what to look for, a fly-specked grain of color lost in some patty-cake choreography—as gape-mouthed and adorable as Chelsea had been in the same role. There she is on a footbridge, a flowerpot tipped on her head, as Judy Garland begins to sing "It Really Was No Miracle." Later, as the chorus cheeps, "Wake up you sleepy head," Margaret stretches from an egg in a pink nightgown and bonnet. When I paused the tape we'd rented from Video Vern's, Chelsea squealed and kissed the screen, flying back when a branch of static shocked her.

"You idiot," my sister Tiffany said from the couch.

Mom came over from the kitchen, drying her hands. "Look at that little thing rub her eyes. That woman really knows how to wake up."

Mom wasn't being sarcastic. She saw genuine talent in the Munchkin Pellegrini. Like the pope, a Munchkin didn't have to do anything special to win Mom's affection. She just had to *be*. "I bet she taught Judy a thing or two."

"Look at what she's wearing," Tiffany objected. "A pink nightgown? In the afternoon? And she doesn't even know the steps."

Protest as my siblings might, when the time came we all piled into the Suburban to meet Margaret's plane. Danny sang his version of "The Lollipop Guild," a finger thrumming his small Adam's apple, and Mom kept cackling "I'll get you, my pretty" as I mugged in the mirror up front, practicing my toniest smile for little Margaret. "Brains? I don't have any brains."

"*Brains?*" Mom repeated, emoting to the nth degree. "*I don't have any brains. Only straw.*"

"*Only straw,*" I screamed back.

"This better be the smile I see at the airport," Mom said, leveling a finger at me. "I'm telling you. I want you to be this obnoxious. Ham it up for her, Greg. Ham it up!"

Airport security was considerably more lax in those days and children's musical theater companies could storm the terminal, shouting renditions of "The Munchkinland Song." As I glided along the moving walkway, too tense to bend my spastic knee, Tiffany speed-walked beside me. Even in her baggy pants she moved better than I did. "Don't worry, Googers. You're going to do great."

If I was anxious about our melodic assault, trying not to scratch at the straw stuffed into my jeans, Munchkin Chelsea was downright gleeful, dancing around the terminal with a Tinker Bell wand balled in her fist. Not unlike Bonnie, she had the habit of saying the move she was doing. Leaping and then sashaying over to the gate, she sang, "Leap. Sashay." Once there, she screeched at every stout woman lugging a suitcase. "Is that the Munchkin? Is that the Munchkin?" There's nothing inherently wrong with the term "Munchkin," but like "midget" and "dwarf," it's the kind of word you don't want to say too loudly in an airport.

More than fifty years after the release of the film, a Munchkin's visit was still a big enough deal to attract local news crews and a reporter or two. Passengers began wearily filing out, picking their noses and searching for signs to baggage claim. My mom pulled Chelsea and me to the front of the crowd, beeping, "Scarecrow, coming through," and gave me an encouraging swat on the ass. "You can outsing these spazzes. Make her think you're the only one in the room."

When Margaret stepped off the plane, our ensemble devolved into a rancid cult of celebrity. "The Munchkin!" Chelsea cried. "Munchkin lady!"

We gave Margaret the kind of at-the-gate welcome usually reserved for boys returning from Mormon missions. Kids shook autograph books, snapped pictures, and shook cutesy posters. I DON'T

THINK YOU'RE IN KANSAS ANYMORE!!! In their minds, Margaret hadn't flown coach; she'd fallen from a star. Bonnie's hands flew into motion and we began dinging and donging, singing high and singing low to let *Margaret* know the Wicked Witch was dead.

Even before our song petered out, I noticed how strange Margaret looked, like she really had come from Munchkinland. Her hands were spotted like Tostitos. Her dress was trimmed with feathers where it shouldn't have been and so long she couldn't walk without tripping on it. She'd given up on the war with peach fuzz and the hair on her head looked like it had been dyed with whatever they use to turn cotton candy pink. Parted in the middle, it sat in two fluffy mounds on either side of a very small hat.

"Is she wearing a costume?" I asked as we followed Margaret to the escalator.

"She probably can't find stuff that fits," Tiffany said.

"Not that you can, either, skater girl," Danny said.

"Honestly, you kids," Mom said. "I couldn't even hear you back there and now you won't shut up."

At the luggage carousel, Chelsea weaseled her way to the front of the seething crowd of gold lamé and handed Margaret her Tinker Bell wand. Instead of calling security, Margaret began casting spells. The whole time we pressed around her, and at the talk she gave at a local high school later that day, striding around the apron of the auditorium stage, the microphone Paul Bunyan–sized in her spotted hands, Margaret humored requests to rub her eyes and sing "Wake up you sleepy head." She posed for photos, signed people's crap, and told every child she was beautiful. The word "star" was used liberally. "Maybe you'll be a big star one day, or a little one like me."

It's hard to say exactly when it occurred to me, like the first twinge of a developing cavity, that all this was a little sad. It could have been when Margaret told the auditorium crowd, to an uproar of delight, that Toto made twice as much as she did because the dog had a better agent. It could have been when she projected the promotional poster onstage of Henry Kramer's Hollywood Midgets, the acting company that had given her her big break, or when my mom elbowed me in the middle of Margaret's talk to say she sounded just like a kazoo. "Isn't her little voice just *precious?*"

Most likely, though, the revelation that Margaret was being ex-

ploited for her short stature came months later, on one of those
death-by-senseless-errand summer afternoons, when Bonnie called
my mom to offer me the star role in the new Up with Kids musical.
They were doing *The Hunchback of Notre Dame*. I remember press-
ing the phone hard into my ear, my smile stuck in place as Mom
piloted the Suburban into a parking lot and slapped me high five.
Chelsea, who slept whenever we drove anywhere, yawned awake
from the backseat. "What's going on?"

"Greg's going to be the star," Mom said.

"You don't have to decide right now," Bonnie growled softly. I
thought I could hear her take what must have been two tasteless
chomps of her nicotine gum, trying to keep things light, perhaps
sensing she'd erred. "Just think about it, OK? Like I said, no one
could play it like you. You were born for this."

I went to bed that night with a stomachache, the life-sized cardboard cutout of Scarecrow, the Wizard, and Tin Man a monstrous
silhouette at the foot of my bed. I didn't want to be hired because
of my disability, like Margaret had been. Duct tape a pillow to my
shoulders and add a bell tower and the musical was pretty much
my daily life. I wanted to be a star, not a groveling Hollywood
hunchback. "They'll find another kid to play Quasimodo in two
seconds," Mom sighed the next morning. "But if you don't want to
have fun anymore, you don't want to have fun anymore."

Officially retired from Up with Kids, I got my acting kicks in
school plays. I was the only seventh grader with a speaking part
in *Guys and Dolls*. Honing my gangster accent, I played Joey Bilt-
more, tossing off lines like, "She ain't a horse. She's a doll!" The
next year, my acting career once again became extracurricular as
I got a callback to play a dwarf in City Rep's production of *Snow
White*. I didn't get the part. After reprimanding me for having my
hands in my pockets, my secret way of appearing nonchalant, the
red-haired director tried to wrench my back straight and excused
me as soon as she saw me struggle across the stage, saying I just
wouldn't fit into the show.

A chance for redemption came in the ninth grade, when my
drama teacher announced we would be putting on *The Wizard of
Oz*. I promptly threw my hand into the air and volunteered the
use of my replica 1939 shooting script. I'd sprouted to a gangly
five-ten and badly needed my hamstrings surgically lengthened

once again, this time on both sides. My walk was a crouch and a persistent hammertoe on my left foot bloodied my sock, but I demanded to hold off on the operations until after the play. My school needed me.

At the audition, while my competitors struggled through tepid R & B songs and climbed on chairs à la Britney Spears, I crooned "If I Only Had a Brain" and trilled the scales. Leaving the auditorium that night, a goth kid in the back row slapped me high five. "Dude, you're totally going to get it."

I arrived late for the dancing portion of the audition the next day. A couple of girls walked me through the routine in the aisle and soon I was shambling up onstage to the tune of "Merry Old Land of Oz." With a *ha ha ha, ho ho ho,* and a couple of *tra la la*'s, I was skipping my way to the lead.

The middle-aged choreographer pulled me aside as I came offstage. This woman was not a teacher but one of the industry people my drama teacher had brought in to help with the production. I expected her to tell me I was a shoo-in for Scarecrow but instead she said, "What's wrong with your leg? It looked like you weren't rotating from the hip." She clutched one of her sharp shoulders, wheeling it around to illustrate her point, as if just watching me made her sore.

"Are you talking about my shoulder?" I asked, hopeful.

"No, your leg," she clarified.

I should have been flattered. She thought I was injured.

Ordinarily, I had an arsenal of excuses about my limp. Sometimes I told people it was knee pain from growing so fast, the kind that left Tiffany sobbing on the floor of my parents' room, moaning about the end of her snowboarding career. Sometimes I said my legs were simply different lengths. I'd recently told a substitute tennis instructor at the country club that, yes, my tendons had been operated on but my orthopedic surgeon had screwed up and now it was a big mess. Who can say why the truth—at least the truth as I understood it—popped out of my mouth when a lie about tripping on plastic apples would have suited me better?

"I have tight tendons," I said.

"Oh," the choreographer said, not missing a beat. "Because it looked like your hip wasn't working right." Here again she worked her shoulder. The woman was as lean and elegant as a candlestick with her chignon and ballet flats, her cheekbones set at handsome angles. "Will it be getting better in time for the show?"

"No," I admitted. "It won't."

The woman offered a serenely understanding smile, as if I were a golden retriever, all blond hair and bad hips. "Well, you did really great."

Children are sad creatures, so full of hope and light and judgment. So sure of their place in the world. My first thoughts, as I waited for Mom to pick me up, were ones of anger. Who was this haughty witch to tell me what I could do? If she was so special, why was she volunteering at a junior high instead of choreographing on Broadway?

Of course, such thoughts denigrated the whole enterprise—the school, the play, my meager acting ability. Part of me wanted to tell her how *believable* I could be as Scarecrow. When I fell, the audience would gasp, and when I got up again they would cheer. It wouldn't have mattered. I wasn't in Up with Kids anymore. A kid with a limp didn't have a chance at what my drama teacher had told us to call a "principal."

In the choreographer's gentle rejection lay a deeper truth: I would never be a professional actor. The fantasy was over. Later, I'd call this my Munchkin moment: the moment I realized I was window dressing along the Yellow Brick Road, not the one skipping down it. I was one of the little people some other, more charismatic teenager would pledge not to forget. That night, I took down the glittery star that had hung on my door for years and fondled Margaret's autograph in my replica *Oz* script as if she were a real celebrity. She'd signed it "Munchkin Love."

My drama teacher was clever. Outright shafting the kid with the limp would have been poor form and so, instead, she gave me the title role. It was not lost on me that Professor Marvel prognosticated from a sitting position on a wooden crate and that the Wizard didn't sing or dance and bellowed most of his lines in the wings, behind a curtain. Being upstaged by a dog was one thing. It took a special actor to be upstaged by a plywood head and a member of the stage crew wagging the chin for comedic effect. Great and powerful I was not. Given so little to do, I overacted every scene I was in, shouting so loud the mic cut out, unleashing a low electrical drone as the house lights strobed.

If I came across as apoplectic, if my fingers flew in the face of any-one who came too close, I have my hand-dancing days at Up with Kids to thank. Because my gray tuxedo jacket was much too short, the sleeves rode up my wrists, leaving my cuffs to billow. With every herky-jerky hand motion, threads popped. I was a good man and a bad wizard, handing a diploma to Scarecrow, a medal to Cowardly Lion, and a ceramic heart to Tin Man. Like Dorothy, I knew there wasn't anything in that leather-fringed purse for me. I wouldn't be getting a new leg. I was stuck with the one I had.

During the curtain call of our final performance, I took my bow and retired to a wobbly rainbow platform at the back of the stage. A moment later, the chorus parted and Scarecrow, Tin Man, and Lion skipped in to a standing ovation. There wasn't enough space on the rainbow platform to do anything more than sway to the music, to bob my head and arch my eyebrows to keep the spidery tears of self-pity from crawling down my cheeks. To someone in the audience, it might have looked like nothing at all: a kid worn out with happiness after a fulfilling run, and then, confused, making a premature exit stage left as Scarecrow and Dorothy presented my drama teacher with flowers.

It took a while to compose myself in the dressing room and turn in my costume. No matter how encouraging the rest of my fam-ily would be, my smart-ass brother was sure to put me down for running offstage in tears. When I made it back to the auditorium, covered in flop sweat and runny makeup, they were waiting for me like always, scattered over a few otherwise empty rows. The Wizard of Oz head scowled down at us from the stage, his chin now wag-ging open like he'd suffered a stroke.

"You're right. It was a nothing role. What can I say? You got totally, completely screwed," Mom said, swinging her gold purse on her shoulder.

"I'm proud of you for toughing it out, Greggo," Dad said.

"You certainly made the most of it," Mom went on. "Ask any-body. You were the only one I could hear."

I gave Tiffany a hug and tried to keep a neutral expression on my face as my brother shuffled toward me down the aisle, popping a pretzel into his mouth. To my surprise, he offered the only thing I'd ever really wanted from him: a positive review. "It was way less shitty than Up with Kids," he said, chewing. "You had a real dog play Toto this time and Dorothy was pretty hot." Putting a hand on my soaked head in an odd display of brotherly affection, his eyes lost that joking sparkle. "Seriously, Gregor. You were the best thing in the show."

This, it turned out, was my final bow.

Leg surgeries the next Christmas kept me from auditioning for my high school drama department's one-act play. I can't remember what the play was called, but the gist of the plot was that a monstrously deformed writer was being held prisoner in a closet. As I was spread-eagle in a wheelchair at the time, encased in Ace bandages and knee immobilizers that went from my butt cheeks to my ankles, *Crippled: The Greg Marshall Story* would've been a fitting title. It's not that I couldn't have tried out. It's that I didn't have the balls.

There were other things to fail at in high school: making the tennis team and convincing my friends I was straight. None of them were as fun as belting out "If I Only Had a Brain" to the homeless. Little home-video footage remains from my brief dramatic career. I suppose this is for the best, as it allows me to remember my histrionics as scene stealing, my voice as blunt and captivating. If I didn't limp, I tell myself, I might really have made it.

For the next few weeks of that semester, as I graduated from wheelchair to walker, my teachers let me out five minutes early so I wouldn't be trampled. I think it was tipping through those empty halls that I gained a begrudging respect for Margaret Pellegrini. If the opposite of being typecast for having a disability is not being cast at all, being a Hollywood Midget didn't sound so bad. At a time when nearly everyone who had worked on *The Wizard of Oz* was dead, she was still signing autographs, rubbing sleep from her eyes. Mom was right: the woman knew how to wake up. Every *Oz* anniversary landed Margaret a spot on the local news, where she repeated her famous line (at least it was famous to me) about Toto having a better agent.

*

History isn't told by the winners. It's told by the living. When you're a kid, you're taught success depends on embracing who you are. It's actually much simpler than that: to succeed, you have to stick around. By marching around in a replica costume like the veteran of some whimsical war, Margaret recast herself as an indelible part of the story. Outlive the coroner and you become the grand marshal of all things Over the Rainbow. Sometimes surviving is its own form of stardom.

BERNARD FARAI MATAMBO

Working the City

FROM *Transition*

AFTER WE ARE accepted into college in the U.S., Cato and I meet every day to assess our progress. It's Monday morning in Harare, late May. The morning wind hauls down the streets carrying a sharp chill, nipping at my ankles. I am waiting for Cato outside the Center, watching the sun's rays bounce off the wash of passing cars on Nelson Mandela Avenue, a clamor of voices piercing its way through the sunshine. He is usually here by now, but some days he has other leads on the outskirts of the city. I imagine in the industrial parks, places like Graniteside and Southerton. It's never certain he will show up, but often he does, his bald head bouncing cheerfully in the crowd, catching glints of the sun like an orb of polished metal.

After a while, though, I decide today is not one of those days. So I go on without him, threading my way through the crowded sidewalk, floating into the city like another leaf longing for a sail.

We are trying to raise money to get to America. While I have received a full scholarship, Cato's best bet lies in a partial scholarship with an $8,000 hole in the middle. I have my doubts he will plug it, but Cato seems undeterred. As though the hole was nothing. He already has his passport even, something I have yet to figure out for myself. He hasn't used it yet, and got it expressly for the purpose of this journey, something that could happen once all our things are in order. I have gone as far as getting my headshots done and that's it, haven't had a chance to dread those long lines at the passport office even, protracted horror shows that go on for entire blocks.

Because he is brave Cato often speaks of the things we will do when we get to America, how on slow Ohio weekends we will visit each other. He can picture himself driving down for a visit. He will have gotten his driver's license by then, he says, something we have decided is much easier to get there than in any cardinal direction within this country. Usually I play it safe, say nothing, but once in a while I risk it and imagine myself taking a train three hours across rural Ohio to visit him. In my head it's a version of Cecil John Rhodes's train, complete with the bathtub and meticulous kitchen, my eyes fixed through its windows, watching the easy world slide by.

We still need to figure out the monies for our visa applications, and the costs for a full medical examination, things neither of us has ever had to do, unless of course one includes probable medicals done before either of us was five years old, when every child in this nation had a national Road to Health Card, and had to be dragged to the clinic each month to get weighed and immunized against things in the water and the air stalking Africans. Back then it was mostly the scale that I found most dreadful, a mechanism that always struck me as someone's long-strapped leather shoulder bag forgotten at the clinic and now suspended precariously on something that resembled a meat hook. Always one of the plump nurses had to wrestle you onto its cold pleather seat, angling your feet into the two narrow holes in the bottom through which you could kick at the air while you screamed yourself hoarse, disturbed by all the strangeness. Only after your bum was warm with the injection would the nurses smile at you, throw you some lovely comments of how good you were, all the while the scent of methylated spirit everywhere, cooling down your bum. I can smell it still, feel it pinch high up in my nostrils as I walk past Harvest House, the sun low and loud in my face, making me sneeze. I doubt how the medical will be done given my anxieties about hospitals and their smells, but anxiety or not, a medical must be done, especially the TB test.

We will need pocket money for the first few weeks when we get there, we have been told, but given the way we have lived up till now, Cato and I figure that part is the easiest. We usually go on one meal a day, and if things came to it I am sure we could get by a kind week without food, licking our lips to keep them from chapping. Cato's determined to make do, says we will carry our own soap and toothpaste from here, introduce our new college friends over there to Geisha soap and Close-Up toothpaste, teach them how to hand wash their clothes and save their money. For a while I consider hand washing the clothes of my classmates for money when I get there, but let it pass. The way people speak about getting a job over there it's like picking low-hanging fruit off a ripe tree.

It's mostly the air tickets that have us worried. The monies involved there are frightening things, sums Cato and I have never in our lives been near. Factor the swell of inflation into that and the figures involved are not for the fainthearted. They make even my well-to-do uncle clear his throat then fall silent for hours, like he was actually watching the television.

Like every other thing on a shelf in this country, air ticket prices change so often and upward, costing a little more today than they did yesterday. For Cato and me it's like watching our American Dream move further down the road the harder we work our way toward it. The faster we try to run, the quicker it gallops away.

But Cato and I have a plan. We are approaching everyone and anyone we think may have money to give our way. We have written letters of inquiry to banks, members of Parliament, government ministries, airlines, government ministers, nongovernmental organizations—both domestic and international, private and public corporations, and general citizens known for charitable works or their good economic standing, a list that includes pastors, churchgoing men and women, and the wives of army generals. Cato has even written letters to embassies all over the city, including the African ones, places that I am certain would not help us even if the pope begged them to and Saint Peter promised them the heavens. Places like the Nigerian Embassy located right there on Samora Machel Avenue, the building so quiet a shade of green I had never noticed it until Cato pointed it out to me, stating his intentions.

You never know, he said. And it wasn't my destiny to stop him.

It must have been all that talk of oil wealth that gave him the nerve, that and our desire to leave no stone in this city unturned. We are trying out every rock that may move.

Once in a dark fantasy, strung out by the city and feeling the veins in my temples vibrate with blood, it crossed my mind to write to the college that accepted me asking them to buy my air ticket. Why wouldn't I? That would solve everything.

But my fears overruled me, loud barking credible things inside me that knew better. The way they saw it, the school had given me too much money, every dollar of scholarship I needed, down to the coins. Why burden the college with you again, they wondered. Why stand up and go again forward, hands full of trembling, bowl in hand, ask, *Please, sir, may I have some more?*

The way my paranoia saw it, this was one sure way to lose my scholarship, my ingratitude coercing the school to rescind it. How else would my actions be perceived if not as ingratitude? I knew what had happened to Oliver; the exhaustion was making me think funny, flooding my mind with the filth.

I head up Nelson Mandela Avenue toward First Street, the sun full in my face, pass the TV Sales and Hire store where I try to look at the shop window displays and keep telling my reflection one day I will buy the electronics for my home here. Across the road I catch the warm scent of fresh glazed doughnuts rising from the ovens at Sammy's Bakery. I could plunge into the smell with longing, nest into its crevices and nooks imagining my teeth sinking into the dough. But I have taught myself to redirect the hunger from my stomach, have it leave there, direct it into effort toward working the city.

We handwrite all our letters at the Center, a place we have come to think of as our base, the U.S. Embassy's educational advising office. A dark auditorium separates this section from the rest of the embassy's public library, and the air conditioning in it feels like magic. Sometimes before our scholarships came in, before the winter, I would find my way to this dark space just to escape the bright sounds flooding the landscape of my life. For some reason or the other, Cato was always there, typing away. It must have been how we began. Up till then I had carried a healthy reverence for him, how the clean vowels of his laughter seemed to wither away whatever ache or bruise sat within him.

We prefer to deliver our letters in the mornings, delivery rounds we call them, Monday morning being the exception for me. No one wants an orphan clamoring on their doorstep just then—why would they? So I do my rebooking rounds instead. Somehow I think of it as letting the city breathe, allowing its lungs to fill up, to take in the oxygen it needs to course through the veins of its body, and keep the city's heart beating before I saddle more of my needs on its shoulders again.

It can get tired of you, this city, lose its patience with you and close its fist.

I take a right at the intersection on Second Street, across from Africa Unity Square, and walk toward Eastgate Shopping Mall, where the Air Zimbabwe city offices are located.

For what it's worth, Cato and I have booked seats on flights to America with a number of airlines. It makes the journey feel real, palpable even, like it's something that could actually happen. Neither of us has been on an airplane, but it's a bridge we will cross when we get there, figure what all the talk of bucket seats really is about. For now our bookings have to do. The airline holds your seat for a week at a fixed price, and the best part is you don't need to pay anything. But after that week your booking is canceled and you must start all over again.

Cato and I rebook dutifully. Week in and week out.

Midmorning we do our follow-up rounds, checking if any of our letters have received a response. I trek down from Eastgate and weave my way through the streets from one office to another, walking beneath the cold drawn-out shadows of tall buildings and the city's wide spreads of sunshine. But building to building no luck is coming my way today. Flat noes are rare, but *We cannot help you at the present time* is a familiar line. In a large sunny office overlooking the Centenary Bridge a woman tells me their organization will only give to orphanages and orphans from them, not individuals right from the street. We prefer it that way, the lady says, when I hear myself ask her why. It's our company's policy.

Outside the wind is still sharp but a swell of warmth has gathered in pockets throughout the city, mostly in front of buildings in full glare of the sun. I watch a clutch of street kids on First Street busk lazily against a dustbin, waiting for a target to besiege with begging. Any time now the street preacher will set up, prepare to deliver hours of his sermon, get people born again and collect the tithes. I am reminded how in a way I am no different, we are all working the city in the ways we see fit, the ways we have each been equipped. Given the way things are, I think of it sometimes as searching a large comatose body for vital signs of life each day, every interaction the murmur of a pulse, an imperative cue to something viable: no matter how weak, there is reason to hope here, it seems to say, and I resolve I will write more letters in the day, deliver them on my rounds tomorrow.

We have hand delivered every single one of our letters all over the city, tracking down every address on foot. Easily in a day we can clock ten, fifteen kilometers on our calves, working the city. We have a strategy. I think of it as working the city in concentric circles, all emanating from the Center. All places we deliver to must be in the central business district of the city, or at worst, within walking distance to the Center. It saves us transportation costs. Banks are the easiest to get to in this regard; most of them are stacked up on two stretches of Samora Machel Avenue, their large dark glass façades shiny and pristine like mirrors for elephants. Somebody says this is the Wall Street of Zimbabwe, but I know nothing about it. I imagine instead row upon row of computers, black and green screens, people making money in jackets and ties.

A few more banks are located on or close to First Street, all in walking distance from each other. Luckily for us, more banks have opened for business of late; twenty years after independence and finally indigenously owned banks have gained traction. This is before they all start going broke, when the bank runs hit them. For now one seems to open each week, which translates for Cato and me to one more letter for us to drop, one more point to pin our hopes on.

In the beginning, intimidated by their often barren and austere entrance halls, I would end up leaving my letter downstairs at the entrance reception with the guards, which had not been a part of my ambition, which had been to get to the elevator and find my way to the large air-conditioned offices of the bank executives upstairs, certain meeting them in person would enhance my chances at an air ticket. I could picture myself talking to those men, which they mostly were, baldheaded men in dark suits and neckties that flowed down the ample curvature of their bellies, men that I had seen on television talking about growth and profit margins. They had grown up in Rhodesia, under the same conditions as my father, and rehearsing the scenes in my head I could hear myself make sense. But once in the entrance hall something about me seemed to betray my unease in that space, and wouldn't you know it, the guards just seemed to have the powerful mood detector for it. While I did what I could to keep my cool, they could zero in on my nervousness like it was the epicenter of skunk. I would feel from the back of my head their tall, sinewy frames floating across the hall, coming for me and sending me away, but not before taking my letter and offering to deliver it themselves.

But that was a month ago.

After weeks of no reply I wised up and altered my strategy, had to find a way into the buildings without inviting their attention.

Now when I do my bank rounds, I'm usually assembled in my prom suit, trying not to look hungry and lost. I have all my papers and letters in a large khaki envelope with a U.S. Embassy seal on it, something that dispenses with all manner of questions. Frankly speaking I could have gotten this envelope from anywhere, and I could be armed with the whitest of ill intent, but the seal offers me all the credibility I need. At worst they mistake me for a messenger but after some cheerful small talk, I get access to the elevator and find my way.

We work the edges of the business district past midmorning but before the afternoon. Around 11 a.m. or so is a good time, after the tea break at 10 but before lunch at 1 p.m. It's a window when everyone usually is at their desks or at least somewhere within their office building longing for sunshine, trying to kill the lazy hours before lunch.

To keep the hours productive, I head out to seek the travel clinic Cato mentioned last week. It's somewhere in Avondale, he said, and the TB bubble test is still reasonably priced there. That was the rumor he had heard.

The prospect of carrying a bubble under my skin for three days makes me nervous. With the way I pick at my skin, I could pick at that bubble until I tore it out. I don't mind bloodying my fingers either, and can go hours watching my blood dry. But the test must be done.

Usually I take an emergency taxi out there when I have some money to spare, an old Peugeot 404 or 504 station wagon from

Leopold Takawira Avenue, the seats so worn you can feel the tension in the spring firmly against the bones in your buttocks. Normally, though, I get there the way I am getting there today. I walk from the Center, cutting up along Angwa Street and past Kwame Nkrumah Avenue, onto Julius Nyerere Way, where just before the National Arts Gallery the cool shades of the park, heaps of dry leaves and palm fronds, welcome me in, the kaylite and plastic litter everywhere, the stretches of green lawn so well manicured they could be in an art show.

On the other side of the park the Avenues begin, a well-treed residential neighborhood peppered with street vendors, private hospitals, exotic trees, and clinics. A sign has been hammered into one tree warning of the evils of abortion. Another tree advertises a carpenter, the sign rusting like blood at the edges. Suddenly I wonder why Cato and I haven't raided this neighborhood yet. It's somewhere you can't rule out a wealthy doctor who would understand. I make a mental note of it, and start looking at the signs on doctors' offices, assessing their qualifications, judging every book by its cover. We will have to start with the guys that learned abroad.

Adjacent to the Avenues are Belgravia and Avondale, neighborhoods where Cato's travel clinic should be. By the time I find it, it turns out I am a whole week late: the price has changed beyond what I can afford, beyond what I even value to be reasonable.

It has crossed my mind to sit down somewhere nice and sunny and give myself a clean bill of health on those forms. In other words fake the medical exam, then find a doctor's receptionist who will stamp everything clean. No one will ever know. But this TB thing has me worried. What if I actually end up catching it overseas and end up dying alone in a cold place? What if I end up dying there anyway?

It's close to lunch hour by the time I get back into the city. Had I walked any faster, maybe I would have gone to the Center, hoping to run into the other guys, nourish myself with their good news. I could have sat down even, and watched *The NewsHour with Jim Lehrer* in the auditorium, evading my hunger until we are kicked out of there for lunch.

Lunchtime is key for us. After we are kicked out, the Center is closed for the hour. Usually we mill about downstairs at the entrance for a while, waiting for a variation to our plans, which these days normally end up with us on the grass in Africa Unity Square. I find myself walking toward there anyway, thinking about how I am running low on working capital. Besides my kombi fare I have nothing, and even that can only see me through to the end of next week. I keep calm and in my head note it as an emergency. It doesn't have a capital *E* yet, but it's close.

Two lovers sit in the grass in the park eating popcorn. A sign near them says DO NOT SIT IN THE GRASS but no one pays attention, the park lawns are infested with people as though the law has demanded it. Once in a while a photographer approaches the couples, offering his services. I move about and find a bench.

In the beginning, too anxious for any news that could alter our fates, Cato and I could burn the whole hour just walking about the streets, watching how the light pools onto various surfaces across the city while we waited for businesses to open again for the afternoon. Once, busy with our anxiety, we even walked over to Parliament and asked for a tour just so we could expend our energy. Cato put the argument forward that by studying abroad we were going to be ambassadors for our country, which only meant we had to know it better before we took up our posts. That was before things had changed. It's all cream and maroon in there, the wood a polished shine, warm and rich with the scent of decades-old sweat.

These days, though, the anxiety has sobered us down and we are grateful for the break. When we are in luck and either of us has some money to spare, we head up to Farm & City Bakery, right near the National Railways station. It is not the closest place to the Center, and frankly speaking, given the accumulated ache in our calves we could do with going somewhere closer. But I have convinced Cato that the buns they have there taste like something from a movie; you tear into them with your teeth and so soft is their flesh they practically melt on your tongue. It's like feeling your mouth getting born again. We arrive for the buns just in time, just as they are leaving the oven, before the syrup is glazed on. With the size nose I have, I can smell them in the air all the way from Wayne Street. And if I inhale right and keep my imagination loose, I can get half-full on that scent alone.

*

We share everything we have. On bad days we can split a single bun. On better ones we can gorge on half a dozen each, lean back in the grass, and for a moment watch the city like it was something we owned. We call this a buns party. Once we even bought Cokes, and I could have sworn something else was in it besides all the euphoria of the world. It made us talk funny. I sat there afterward dreaming of whole busloads of Africans on the highway to America, a bridge straddling the ocean, one head lodged somewhere in West Africa, Senegal, following the horizon all the way to the American East Coast. Every single person on it had a visa, his or her medicals, complete and paid for.

But that had been that day.

I file away the loud honks and lunch-hour screeches of traffic somewhere in my head, and head down Kwame Nkrumah Avenue, toward Tendo's workplace.

For years this was Union Avenue, until it wasn't. I can't seem to track when exactly the switch was, but I want to think it must have been in the late 1990s, when farm invasions and land reform became en vogue in the papers.

Tendo and his height are both in. He seems to have acquired more of it since the end of high school six months ago. We joke about that, then step out of his office, and after talking for a bit we figure out my working-capital situation. Maybe next week or so, when he is paid, he says, then right there in the street, folds one of his big arms around me, envelops me in a hug.

The hours seem to slide by much quicker in the afternoons, a single outing and somehow I have burnt a whole hour, usually while waiting for an appointment with someone who never comes, or while I am hovering across from an entrance, trying to stumble into a building with someone important, catch the elevator ride with them, explain my case, then it's 3:30 before I know it, and the cold wind is finding its way down the shaded streets, nesting again where the sun has pulled away, left quietly like a veil. Afternoons are buzzer-beater times, moments to follow up on the leads that are dying out, drop in on places you know nothing will come of, but can't do with the suspense.

In an hour the pavements are thronged in crowds and carts of fruit vendors, the streets crammed with cars, turned alive by the blare of kombis, colorful refrains from the mouths of conductors searching for passengers. I pull my jacket closer to my body, the cold cutting swiftly through my bones.

Once, after one of our days, I caught Cato standing in front of the large maps upstairs at the Center, tracing his finger over northeastern Ohio, whispering the name of his college.

I wander about the city a while, avoiding heading downtown where I am supposed get the kombi. Something about walking the streets alone moves me, something about standing here watching people and their exhaustions pour out of the city, leaving the buildings behind, leaving the streets alone with the litter and street kids. I can feel the livid pain in my knees, how they feel dry and broken behind the kneecaps from all the walking. I could buckle against a doorway and fall asleep for hours. But I walk about for an hour or two instead, my eyes transfixed from time to time at the displays in shop windows. Somewhere in my mind I am purchasing all sorts of furniture, cramming it into the rooms of a small house I have bought somewhere in the future, one of the suburbs I have never been to in this town. It's all just talk up there but I can't help it for a while, until everything in my head is so vivid and alive I can't help but be afraid of my head. Maybe it's the hunger, I want to think, half believing, half watching every streetlight light up against that night's deep blue sky.

Once, beneath it, on a construction block without lights, I saw a beggar woman dressed all in white, wearing my mother's face. Her lower limbs wrapped in bandages inked in blood.

We have never actually discussed what we want of ourselves once we head off, what it is Cato and I want to achieve by leaving. But I assume it's something good. Talking may jinx it. I wonder what he is up to at this hour, what tower light he is staring at in his neighborhood when he daydreams. I wonder too, if tomorrow he will come in. His bald head shining, his large smiling teeth.

KENNETH A. McCLANE

Sparrow Needy

FROM *Kenyon Review*

I had a brother, and that says it all.
— From a conversation overheard on a New York City bus

WHEN I WAS growing up in Harlem, there was a tough neighborhood bully, Lynwood,[1] who had killed someone in a brutal shooting, and he was feared by all of us. Most of us knew other tough kids and many of us had heard rumors about them. Yet no one really knew if John had stabbed the fat boy, or if Frankie had smothered the pink-faced, scarecrow-looking vagabond, Raif; but Lynwood's acts were verifiable: there were bodies.

My neighborhood was usually safe; murders were as uncommon as zebras or cobras on wealthy Park Avenue. On my street, 147th Street, everyone knew *who* did the shooting; it was only the authorities who were perplexed. *Coloreds like to kill each other,* one of New York's finest was overheard confessing in a fit of candor, as he conducted the "rigorous" crime investigation, hauling in suspects who might have easily confessed to kidnapping the Lindbergh baby. One suspect was blind: he couldn't *see* a gun; the other, one of the neighborhood's true griots, had witnessed, just before the murder, "a comet strike a pharaoh's house in the third century."

Unfortunately, my brother, Paul, did witness the murder when he was merely eight years of age. It occurred in front of our brownstone, a few feet from him. Paul seemed preternaturally selected for horrible encounters, and if anyone were to find trouble, it was

1. "Lynwood" is a pseudonym.

he. Paul seemed inevitably to attract the attention of the police, and for that reason, and a host of others, he hated them.

When he was six years old, Paul was held by a policeman for two hours in a dreary police station for stealing money from someone four years his senior—Paul was no saint, but he was not a thug at age six: I doubt if anyone is. At the time, Paul was going to the famous Collegiate School—the oldest independent school in America, where I, too, languished—and he was doing well. And though he never liked the school and felt rightfully that it was the "white boy's kingdom" (his term), he was the usual boyish amalgam—a bit randy on Monday, taciturn on Tuesday, studious on Wednesday and Thursday, and skittish on Friday.

In his early years at the school, Paul easily made friends with the janitors and all the staff—they liked his easygoing camaraderie with them: they saw in his natural reticence a reservoir of respect, something that the other Collegiate boys, used to having their way with princes and kings, rarely evidenced. Paul brought Simeon, the custodian, a book he thought he would like, and Simeon and his friends held a birthday party for my brother—replete with a piñata, which Paul attacked like a prizefighter. Paul was never more delighted.

Paul, too, was very gifted at music—and he played the recorder well, often taking the instrument, after a Sonny Stitt–like daring solo and hitting it tenderly against the music stand, as he would later hit the skins of the drums, touching them lightly, as a feather skims the surface of a pond. Here Paul, characteristically, was acting out: he would be a drummer, not a reed player, but he wouldn't state as much—you had to read his body.

Yet I well recall my brother being brought home by my father after his time at the police station, how much he was shamed by sitting among the dispossessed, envisioning what the world expected of him; my brother that day, moving slowly, vacantly, as if his spine had been infected with a deadly virus. Paul was literally half-stepping, his bones sidling against themselves, as if his locomotion had been eviscerated. It might have been funny if it were not *my* brother. From that moment on, he detested the police.

Paul, in truth, was oddly grafted to my family, as if the providential birth stork had somehow made a mistake and flew to the wrong house. When Paul was three, I recall him packing his bag and heading out of our Harlem residence, with that grim determination that is the hallmark of children. Although the young often anticipate running away from home after some tiff, nothing palpable had occurred to occasion this departure. Paul was simply giving bodily testimony to something ineluctable, although it hurts me now to admit it. Characteristically, Paul did not *belong* to us: He was a night person; my parents and I were morning people. Paul was usually quiet; we were story-rich. Paul *loved* the streets; they terrified us. My parents, of course, did not permit Paul to leave, although they did let him walk a hundred yards from our house, watching him from the window just before he engaged the corner and would become invisible, like Annie, a girl we had all heard about who had, on a bright Sunday morning, simply "disappeared," a notion as unusual and frightening in 1954 Harlem as seeing the giant sinkhole in the Seventy-Seventh Street Riverside Park field—a place where all of us would go to play softball on weekends—a miraculous hole so enterprising that one could witness the water running under the field, like sluicing fingers of quicksilver, as if the world above needed a busy subterranean terrarium. In the three years I watched the hole, it would grow larger and more menacing, brimming with bottles, potato chips bags, broken dolls, condoms, all rising like a demented volcano; and you could hear the water gurgling, the city seemingly alive, the first time that I understood that the city was truly *geologic*, wondrous, nature-rich. Young Filbert—who had six fingers on one hand, five on the other, and had recently arrived from South Carolina, part of the Great Migration—said that even Annie might be in that hole: young Filbert who would later, on a simmering August day, slip into the Hudson River, head out toward the George Washington Bridge, swim farther than any of us could imagine, angle close to the mythic Little Red Lighthouse, and then head back to us, not damaged or deracinated, his body luminescent.

Harlem in the 1950s, in the early spring, was lovely, and my mother, brother, and I would often walk from our house on 147th Street to 116th Street, traipsing down Broadway, welcoming the new bodegas, which seemed, in the glance of an eye, to appear everywhere—the Spanish lofting like a splendid aria; the young men proudly hoisting their children on their shoulders like precious gifts; the zoot-suiters, already beginning the process of growing obsolete, up to less than good, never bothering us; the young men, and the oldsters, who saw my mother as beautiful, tipping their hats; a few of them, with studied decorum, saying, *It's a beautiful morning;* a few of them watching my mother, then thin-hipped, a bit lustily, as she gracefully sauntered away. Harlem was a community of shared values, and I had a legion of family and would-be family. I was never unattended. Should my brother and I misbehave, Aunt Tina or Aunt Alvatine (neither of them blood relatives, though you dare not tell them that!) would whip me—I was a child of 147th Street, and every adult on that street watched over me, and everyone had the right to set me straight.

In truth, it must have been horrible for Paul, being placed among people as otherworldly as his family must have appeared. It wasn't that we didn't love him, or he us. It was simply that we were incomprehensible to one another. Some of it, possibly, was that Paul was a fledgling musician—he would later become a good jazz drummer, playing at times with Carman McCrae; some of it, just as truthfully, was that Paul, by desire and impulse, loved life, although he seemed to be doing everything imaginable to forswear it, be it with alcohol or pills; some of it, quite simply, was human peccadillo, and the realization that our desire to have Paul live might yet require an alembic that we could not discern; and some of it, most powerfully, involves the truism that love—no matter how prodigal—can ill perform every miracle.

Still, whatever the reason, Paul would die of alcoholism in his early thirties, something that even today I find incomprehensible. We often talk about life and its possibilities; for those of us who have lost a brother, there seems a great gash in the universe: there was the world before, when whatever the world's verities, your brother was there participating, at times driving you crazy; at times, making you mute with his daring.

Often, when I am talking with parents at Cornell, the parents will, in an understandable moment of duress, worry that their child may not get accepted to Harvard Business School or get the plum job on Wall Street. Sometimes, without meaning to, I'll stammer, *Is your child alive?* This, of course, is not what parents wish to hear from their child's adviser, and yet it is my most profound ministry.

Make a big noise, my brother used to say, but he was resoundingly silent, moody, imperturbable, and not in the way of a monk or an aesthete—not in a way that was serviceable. Paul was an activist —that is, you knew he loved you because he performed it. His body in its oscillations was his language. If you couldn't comprehend this, Paul was merely a cipher. In fact, if you didn't know this about him—if you didn't understand his inner life, that interiority that was as hard as an uncut diamond and just as murky, you might have even been scared of him, for his solemnity might be perceived as truculence or anger, none of which was true. Yet if you are not easily comprehensible, if you do not fit into our facile categorizations, we stand ready with rocks at the stoning ground, which is why fear can always raise a mob—be it in Harlem or Sioux Falls. And Paul seemed a veritable lightning rod for others—cops, as I've said, always found him irresistible; the headmaster of our school actually wondered if Paul was "possessed." If you are among the elect today, someone must be relegated to the inelect. Paul, like hundreds of others, was not conscious of how his indeterminacy influenced us: he was simply trying to live. But I remember his telling me, he was very young, only five years old, two years after he made his initial pilgrimage to leave our house, *People don't like me.*

And I recall when we visited George Washington's home in Mount Vernon, that lovely mansion that makes me understand why one tenaciously fights for empire, how Paul, at age four, simply became prostrate at the entrance of the slave quarters, which was merely a mound of unadorned stones. I was trying to fathom how Washington might throw a coin across the Potomac; Paul just slumped down, as if he were constitutionally tired, as if the whole magnitude of the Middle Passage had settled upon him, like a death mask. We thought he was sick—he didn't move for ten minutes. It was not a temper tantrum, he was not unconscious —it was simply as if the enormity of the human devastation had entered him.

When I was thinking about going to graduate school, in my usual fit of anxiety, I told my brother that I was considering Brown University in Providence, Rhode Island, a place I knew little about. Paul, at the time, was living in Harlem with my parents, half in college, half in chaos, playing his drums at local joints, drinking and smoking pot—and he was beginning to evidence that detachment that some found troublesome, and others—women especially—found sweet. Paul was then an alcoholic, although I didn't truly understand it, and I would later fail him, calling him at home, instead of visiting, thinking of him, instead of gathering him bodily up. Paul, like all addicts, knew how to outmaneuver us—"I can't visit this weekend, I've got a gig," he'd say, when I asked him to come to Ithaca. He couldn't visit because I would not have let him drink, and he knew that. And, in truth, he wanted to protect me. He knew that I would be overwrought, that whatever his dilapidation, I was even less available. Truth for us, sadly, was a Maginot Line that neither of us dared cross. And he was right: I would never truly make him ante up. I was too self-involved to truly comprehend my brother's life—I was too self-infested. And, even today, I rarely extend myself to others in the flesh: I'll give money for any cause; I'll write a letter to save near any living thing. But I find it impossible to put myself truly on the line—to act. I don't visit people I love. I'm afraid of the telephone so I rarely make calls. I simply can't do it. So my own reticence, coupled with my brother's illness, made us both unapproachable.

"Ken, get in the car," my brother yelled. He was looking fit, well nourished, and happy, as vibrant as when he was seven and chided me for liking Susie, a girl who, charmingly, would wait for me on her stoop, from nine to three, until I returned from school.

"I'm driving you from Ithaca to Providence—get in." Paul has just driven 250 miles from Harlem to Ithaca and now he was attempting to drive to Providence, Rhode Island, another 350 miles. And yet he did it: he drove carefully, said nary a word on the entire trip, and had his friends tell me about Brown. "Tell my bro what this place has?" he said. "Don't dope it down." And then we slept for five hours, and he drove back to Ithaca, driving with the skill of a practiced chauffeur, and once at my driveway, he literally thrust me out of the vehicle, as if staying another minute might turn him into stone. "Bro, you know now what to do." And then he drove back to New York City. He was ill then, but you wouldn't know it.

That was Paul's way.

I knew little of this when the murder occurred in front of our brownstone, within a few feet of our small front yard, when Paul was eight. Paul had watched it through the first-floor window, barely twenty-five feet from the crime. It was horrible, and my brother would never forget it, especially the sight of the victim's attempt at extracting the bullet from his own chest. "It was like he was trying to confirm his own murder," my brother would later say. Yet as the policeman began his interrogation, he admonished my brother, "I know you *didn't* see anything," and Paul—whatever else his demons—was not tone-deaf.

In Harlem, in the 1950s, the police acted like gods, and my brother would never cower. As I was Paul's older sibling by two years, I was supposed to watch over him, which was more than a notion. As you might well imagine, Paul was little interested in my protection. I well recall Paul giving a patrolman "the finger" after the officer stopped his police car and asked him a "minor" question concerning his friends' whereabouts. Paul was merely age ten; the officer was bored. Since the officer was clearly not the least concerned about my brother's friends, three kids who could barely manage a pimple, he quickly returned to his patrol car. And yet Paul—who was then as thin as a car antenna—was itching for a fight. Paul didn't like the police, he didn't like their assumed superiority, and he didn't like to feel as if he were "an ant dancing on a Cadillac," which the police, in their intemperate questioning, always seemed to demand of black people. When Paul's body tilted to the left and his head developed a slight upward inclination, I knew he was no longer interested in "quiet palaver." And yet Paul was still only ten—which meant that he knew everything and nothing. And this was America, and I was his brother.

Suddenly, the officer jumped out of his vehicle, and I was certain that he had somehow intuited my brother's distaste. If I was worried, my brother was boisterous. Paul stood up, looked the officer in the eye, and said, "Did *you* forget something? Your gun, maybe?"

I was aghast. The cop looked at my brother, as if he had finally *seen* him, and yet things were still unfixed, gauzy. This is a very dangerous moment for anyone, but especially for blacks and whites who know so little about each other—especially, that is, when one of them has a gun. "You're crazy," the officer said, shaking his head as he walked away, with that hip-strutting swagger, which is someone's idea of manliness. Undeterred, Paul just pointed at his head and slowly rotated his long fingers counterclockwise. "Yeah, *I'm* crazy, asshole," he said.

Lynwood, who was only sixteen when he shot that boy in our yard, was given a wide berth by everyone in my neighborhood, and my friends would try to hide, slinking into the alleys when he appeared. Lynwood had an odd way of simply becoming present: there was a pause in the scenery, one of the tenants might be yelling a belated welcome to a passerby, and Lynwood would materialize like an apparition, mayhem and horror trailing in his wake.

Lynwood was malevolent, truculent, and brittle, and it seemed as if one were always in midsentence with him, as if the subject had been lost but the verb was firing like a crazed piston so that one might perceive the action but not the context. One time he brutally hit a boy for simply looking as if the boy had a question: *Don't look stupid,* Lynwood yelled and popped him in the head, the young boy's face appearing like a symbol of twentieth-century torment, as the blood flowed down his chest.

And yet I also remember that Lynwood presented my mother with a beautiful rose one Sunday morning. The rose was big, "skyscraper tall," as Fred, the neighborhood floriculturist, termed it, although Fred was known for his hyperbole. Lynwood never explained this lovely gesture; my mother was simply undone by his generosity. Like so much that happened in those years, it did not make much sense to me, or at least I did not try to understand it. My friends thought that Lynwood had gone crazy; I simply thought that he liked my mother, which was not difficult, since she took everyone seriously, often bringing them a sweet, or praising some act of unheralded civic responsibility. My mother, for example, began a neighborhood preschool, with mixed results. For a few weeks the children came, but then a few of them discovered basketball; then a few others, the local movie theater; in a few weeks, it was just my brother and I, learning about the "hidden treasures" of Harlem. Yet people valued my mother's high-principled affirmations, even if they found sustenance elsewhere. And my mother, somehow, saw something precarious and incandescent in Lynwood: "There's something sweet in him," she often said.

After the rose incident, I was determined to say hello to Lynwood, thinking that my acknowledgment might limit his possible scenarios for havoc. If you are constitutionally cowardly, it is best to take whatever little fight you have immediately to the confrontation; retreat will hasten soon enough. Yet Lynwood never truly threatened me—in my case, thank goodness, it was merely all mouth; he was even gentle, in his own peculiar way.

One day, with a solemnity reserved for a parish priest, Lynwood told me that he wanted "someone to get out of Harlem. I'm going to die," he said. "I'm going to continue to hurt people," he continued, his last statement as precisely enunciated as Julie Andrews's thrilling elocution in *Camelot.* "I want *you* out of here!" Lynwood

commanded, his entire body suddenly yawing between anticipation and dread, with a new, evangelizing insistence that might even
smash the ghetto it so frightened both of us. A wish, I now realized, could be a dangerous thing.

Then, Lynwood smiled—his face seeming to gather where his
eyes were narrowing—and seeing how frightened I looked, he became contrite: "Shit, I'm not going to kill you—you'll piss yourself
to death." And so Lynwood, though sixteen, began to "father me,"
a ritual where he would "adopt me," which was his term, and make
certain that I made something out of myself, go to college. Never
mind that I had my own quite wonderful father and mother, this
was immaterial. Lynwood had made his decision: I was going to
get out of Harlem—I was his one good thing, his one good act.
During May and in December, Lynwood would appear, ask to see
my grade report, and I'd hand it over, trying to make it look as if
this was the most natural act in the world. Luckily, I was a good
student. In all honesty, in the early years, the school I attended
rarely gave you grades—they provided long, written responses—
two paragraphs for each class. Lynwood, as I recall, didn't read
them: he'd simply tell me that I was "doing well." And so he didn't
need to give me an "ass whipping." In retrospect, it is even possible
that Lynwood had "consulted the stars," he remained so ethereal.

In my self-involvement, I really did not comprehend how much
Lynwood's gesture meant for him and for me. I did do well in
school—my parents would not have otherwise—and I went on to
graduate school and teaching at Cornell. And I didn't see Lynwood until I learned that he had been sent to prison. Hearing
that he was at Sing Sing, I decided to visit him, a drive of three
hours from bucolic Ithaca. I hadn't seen him in twenty years—he
was thin, wiry, and unusually meditative—and he had that sharp-
boned figure that one immediately wants to feed, to fatten up, that
look that my aunt Josie used to call "sparrow needy." For a moment, I couldn't conceive that he would have frightened anyone
—I saw, I guess, what my mother had gleaned in him, his unsullied
sweetness.

"Ken, good to see you," Lynwood said. "But why did you come,
did you miss your ass whipping?"

Immediately, I recalled the old Lynwood: the body may change
but the mind does not. His remembering the one thing that I too

well connected with him surprised me, and his elation reminded me that he was mercurial—that things could easily move from good to bad, from commonplace to perilous.

"I wanted to see you and thank you for helping me," I told him.

He looked at me rather quizzically. "I heard you're teaching at college, that you're married and doing good. That's something," he said.

I wanted to say more, to explain how his investment in me suggested that there was something in him of great provender, something worthy, possibly even Augustinian in his bountiful complexity, but it was merely romantic, and it would have sounded hollow, paternalistic. Before I could even become more self-reproachably odious, he began to shuffle in his chair, looking as if he must have somewhere to go—this was not good for either of us.

Then he stood up, and I saw how painfully thin he was. I had been there for merely five minutes. I hadn't even had time to contemplate the banal surroundings or compare the walls to the other prisons I had visited, often giving poetry readings, where the inmates, if they didn't like the poems, at least liked that I took the time to visit with them—in such places, the gift of the unusual, even a dubious college teacher, was often life itself. Sing Sing, of course, was famous for its closeness to New York City, thirty miles up the Hudson, and its illustrious prisoners, Willie Sutton and Julius and Ethel Rosenberg, and the fact that the same inmates who would later be housed within its walls constructed it. I found myself quickly looking about the table, seeing the gum tabs on the wall and the floor, the furious pencil markings on the desktop, a few ill-conceived numbers, possibly of a lawyer, or a friend, fitfully etched into the Formica, the listing of a wife or girlfriend who, more often than not, if not today or tomorrow, would refuse to return. I thought, too, of how many people I knew who had been sent "up the river," a term first fashioned in Sing Sing. There were more black people in prison than in college, and the numbers kept growing. The prison, sadly, had become America's true growth industry—today we make fast food and prisons: things that we can eat and things that eat us up, I recall a prisoner pundit stating.

"This is too much good news," Lynwood told me. "I didn't think anyone from the neighborhood would look me up, especially one who escaped." The word "escape" seemed to hover misshapen in the air, like a leaking helium balloon, bulbous, and addled. Suddenly, finding himself in a place where his language and experience had rarely taken him, I saw Lynwood begin to stammer. The world seemed as stolid and indecorous as if it were made of plasterboard. I wanted language, an entreaty; Lynwood, now, was simply a prisoner, waiting to die. "Have a good life," he said.

I watched as he walked through the gates and remembered how much he had frightened us, he, merely ten years our senior. People had often said that Lynwood would kill for kicks, that he acted for no worldly reason, that he had no feeling for anybody. My brother, Paul, years after seeing the killing, once tried to tell me that it wasn't Lynwood who had done it—I don't think Paul was willfully misremembering. He was simply older; he, too, had found his future torturous; things that had once made sense to him were oddly inchoate, disconsolate. And people in Harlem as elsewhere were full of contradictions. Yes, there were easy calls in my community. There was Larry, who, from age three, always wanted to play house and wore dresses and would later be seen adorned with Vera Wang. He'd now be called a cross-dresser, but from the moment we first knew Larry, he was simply Larry, and all of us accepted him. Surprisingly, whatever else we didn't know about ourselves—and we were a veritable congress of commencements—Larry seemed oddly integrated, and he would often stand as a beacon of discernment for us when things grew choppy. If suffering rarely makes one generous, it can make one wise—and it may be wrong for me to say Larry suffered—he, in fact, seemed self-assured, the only person in my community, paradoxically, who knew who he was. The rest of us were simply struck by the hammer. Larry, for example, told my brother that it was OK for him to drop out of college. It was OK simply to be a musician. "Look at me," he said to my brother. "Do you think I asked anyone for permission?"

"Bro," Paul said, "when I was younger, I once went to a bar on 138th Street—one of those funky places that scare people, the kind of place you writers like to imagine but would never be caught in—the kind of place that even frightened me." He was silent for a moment, talking, I think here, for once truthfully to his brother. Speaking, that is, in the way my parents had hoped he would have talked when they were alive—when he was most vulnerable. "In the bar I bought a bag of grass, and this big dude took my money and then said it wasn't enough, that I owed him for six bags. I wasn't a saint—I had purchased from him before—but I didn't owe him anything. That I knew.

"The guy was getting more anxious, he had a gun, and he wasn't interested in the money—he wanted to make a scene—he wanted to . . ." Paul found himself scavenging for the word, looking toward the sky, as if the answer were present there. The word Paul compromised on was "humiliate," a word that seemed oddly grandiose, but he employed it. "He wanted to humiliate me.

"I wasn't into much, but I wasn't going to let that happen," my brother continued. "And so I began to think about how I would hurt him, what I could do—I was looking at the bar, going through scenarios, most of them useless.

"Suddenly, Lynwood appeared, in that way he always did, seemingly coming from nowhere. 'Let me handle this,' he said. And he took the pusher and rushed him out the door and I never saw him again. I don't know why I said it, but I told Lynwood, 'Please don't hurt him.'"

Paul suddenly stopped talking, and I hoped he would continue, but for someone who had rarely offered the slightest intimacy in speech, I knew that this was merely the first tentative voicing. Paul might say more; he might, just as easily, return to his vaulted privacy.

Paul and I never returned to that moment, so his short foray into speech seems like a sacrament. When he died from septicemia after a very short stay in the intensive care unit of Roosevelt Hospital, where he never truly regained consciousness, my distraught parents asked me to gather up his few personal articles. Paul had placed the things that he would wear once he got well in a yellow plastic milk carton, everything neatly packed and folded, as if they were to be presented to someone of inestimable value. There were two pairs of jeans, three pairs of socks, five pairs of undershirts, two T-shirts, a pair of beaten-up Converse sneakers, none of which, of course, was ever used, so I had little to do. On the top of this haphazard congress, looming like an epiphany, was the only article that was not clothing, a copy of my book of poems, *To Hear the River,* which I had dedicated to Paul. The poems interestingly alluded to James Baldwin's novel *Another Country,* which centers on the death of Rufus, a black jazz musician who would, in a fit of rage and self-hate, hurl himself off the George Washington

Bridge, and how his death implicated us all. My title celebrated the twenty-four times the Hudson River called like a siren to Rufus, presaging his demise: how Rufus, death-tainted, could not elude his fate. The novel asks: Has any one of us ever been truly present at our lives?

When I had given my book to Paul, he simply nodded. In the two years he had it, Paul had never said a word. I thought he hadn't read the book or liked it. Like so much between us, it seemed simply to have fallen through the universe, like something useless or inconsequential. But there it stood on the top of that hodgepodge, like the earth's irrepressible language. What if I had never seen it? What if I had never looked at that haphazard totem of Paul's things? What if neither one of us had been born or had the other, if we, however fitfully and messily, had not loved one another? My parents now are dead, both of them taken by Alzheimer's disease. I'm happily married and loved by a woman far better than I could ever imagine or deserve. I've taught a number of very fine students and helped a few of them to go far farther than they or I ever thought possible. I've had wonderfully supportive friends and colleagues. It's been a good life.

You're my brother, Paul often said. *You're my brother.* And both of us—in good and bad—whatever can be said about us, tried desperately to understand what that implied, to take on the risk of presence, as Baldwin would term it, to bear witness to what we did or did not do. Life is a chain of unalterable dalliances and failings, and it is also, just as powerfully, the tale of drives to Providence and Ithaca, forays into dangerous clubs by ones who truly ventured there and by ones who could only venture there as an act of the imagination; and it is, just as ineluctably, a tale of grace, of happenstance. What is, is.

The last poem I published was about Paul; it was written twenty-six years ago. I haven't composed a poem since, and even there, no matter how much I wished it otherwise, he seemed to vanish.

CATHERINE VENABLE MOORE

The Book of the Dead

FROM *Oxford American*

*These are roads to take when you think of your country / and interested bring
down the maps again*

I WAS THREE years old when the Killer Floods hit West Virginia.
We were spared, my family and I. My parents had recently bought
a stone cottage in a hilly Charleston neighborhood with great
schools. Dad had just graduated from law school. We lost nothing,
while thousands of our neighbors were ejected from their homes
into the icy November waters that claimed sixty-two lives; the 1985
storms still sit on the short list of the most costly in U.S. history.
In the aftermath, newspapers accumulated the miracles and spec-
tacles. An organ caked with mud, drying before a church. The
body of a drowned deer woven into the under-girders of a bridge.
Two nineteenth-century mummies that had floated away from a
museum of curiosities in Philippi, recovered from the river.

None of this suffering was ours. "Ours." My mom—a ginger
from the low country whose freckles I was born to—packed me
up for a week of relief work in a hangar at the National Guard ar-
mory. Her task was to deal with the hills of black trash bags, sent to
Appalachia from abroad, stuffed with clothing that recalled dank
basements and dead people's closets. For endless hours she sorted
it into piles by age, size, sex, and degree of suitability. Meanwhile,
I dressed up in the gifts of the well-meaning and the careless. Stiletto heels. Crumbling antique hats. Tuxedos, gowns, belts, and
bikinis. "Nobody wants to wear your sweaty old bra, lady," my mom
muttered to one of these imagined do-gooders, tossing it aside. On
the contrary—I did, very much! I modeled the torn, the stained,

and the unusable, cracking up the other volunteers. Mom saw how little of the clothing was functional, how much time was being wasted in the sorting, but she was desperate to be of use.

Disaster binds our people to this place and each other, or so the story goes. Think of the 118 mine disasters our state has suffered since 1894, the fires, explosions, and roof falls. Or the floods, whether "natural"—like the one this June that killed at least twenty-three people (as I write this, my friends come home from recovery work, stinking of contaminated mud)—or those induced by humans, like the coal waste dam that burst at Buffalo Creek in 1972, when 125 people drowned in a tsunami of slurry. (Pittston Coal called it an "act of God.") Other disasters are less visible, inside our bodies even: the rolling crisis that is black lung disease claims a thousand lives every year, while an addiction epidemic seems to be robbing entire generations of our children. West Virginia's drug overdose death rate is the highest in the nation. Then there is the toxic discharge: from the 2014 Elk River chemical spill that poisoned the water of 300,000 residents to the microreleases leaking daily from the sediment ponds that serve mountaintop removal sites.

Appalachian fatalism wasn't invented out of thin air. If your list of tragedies gets long enough, you start to think you're fated for disaster. And maybe the rest of the country starts to see you that way, too. I watched a documentary last year about the outsized influence of extractive industries here. It was a well-rehearsed narrative, this litany of disaster—land grab, labor war, boom, bang, roar —on and on in the dark theater. I admired the film in some ways —the bravery of naming each and every pain, the courage of its makers to pass into the tunnel of it, to point fingers along the way. But as I sat through this latest iteration of Appalachian grief writ large, I began to seethe—not at some alleged oppressors, but at the narrative itself. *I cannot live inside the story of this film,* I remember repeating to myself, like a chant. *That can't be my story because nothing lives there.*

Admittedly, there's a spellbinding allure to disaster, close cousin of the sublime. Hypnotic and wordless, the disaster repulses even as it propels one's attention toward it. I know, because I'm victim to its seduction, too. I live five miles from where the Hawk's Nest Tunnel tragedy unfolded, along the New River Gorge in Fayette County. Hawk's Nest is an extreme in a class of extremes—the

disaster where truly *nothing* seemed to survive, even in memory
—and I have made a home in its catacombs. The historical record
is disgracefully neglectful of the event, and only a handful of the
workers' names were ever made known. What's more, any understanding of Hawk's Nest involves the discomfort of the acute race
divide in West Virginia, seldom acknowledged or discussed. Indeed, race is still downplayed in official accounts. Disaster binds
our people, maybe. But what if you're one of those deemed unworthy of memory?

Here's what we know: Beginning in June of 1930, three thousand
men dug a three-mile hole through a sandstone mountain near
the town of Gauley Bridge for the Union Carbide and Carbon Cor-
poration. The company was building an electrometallurgical plant
nearby, which needed an unlimited supply of power and silica, and
the tunnel was determined to be the cheapest and most efficient
source of both. A dam would be built to divert a powerful column
of the New River underground and down a gradually sloping tunnel to four electrical generators; the ground-up silica rock har-
vested during excavation would be fed into the furnace in Alloy.

Three-quarters of the workers were migratory blacks from the
South who lived in temporary work camps, with no local connec-
tions or advocates. Turnover on the job was rapid. By some reports, conditions were so dusty that the workers' drinking water
turned white as milk, and the glassy air sliced at their eyes. Some
of the men's lungs filled with silica in a matter of weeks, forming scar tissue that would eventually cut off their oxygen supply;
others wheezed with silicosis for decades. When stricken, the migrant workers either fled West Virginia for wherever home was, or
they were buried as paupers in mass graves in the fields and woods
around Fayette County. The death toll was an estimated, though
impossible to confirm, 764 persons, making it the worst industrial
disaster in U.S. history.

If the company had wet the sandstone while drilling, or if the
workers had been given respirators, most deaths would likely have
been avoided. Yet through two major trials, a congressional labor
subcommittee hearing in Washington, and eighty-six years of silence, neither Union Carbide nor its contractor—Rinehart & Dennis Company out of Charlottesville, Virginia—has ever admitted
wrongdoing. Calling the whole affair a "racket," in 1933 the com-

pany issued settlements between $30 and $1,600 to only a fraction of the affected workers and their families. The black workers received substantially less than their white counterparts.

Soon after the project wrapped, the workers' shacks were torn down and a country club built to serve Union Carbide's employees. A state park was established at the site in the mid-1930s, and the Civilian Conservation Corps built a charming stone overlook at what has become one of the most misunderstood and most photographed vistas in the state: the New River, dammed and pooling above the Hawk's Nest Tunnel. Historical memory of the event has since then constituted nothing short of amnesia. Despite its status as the country's "greatest" industrial disaster, it remains relatively unknown outside of West Virginia, and even here the incident is barely understood and seldom examined. It took fifty years for the state to mark the deaths at the site. The governor who presided over the disaster's aftermath, Homer Adams Holt, who went on to serve as Union Carbide's general counsel, excised the story from the WPA's narrative *West Virginia: A Guide to the Mountain State*. Many also believe that when a novel based on Hawk's Nest was published in 1941, Union Carbide convinced Doubleday to pull and destroy all copies.

The word "disaster" emerged from an era when people often aligned fortunes with positions of planetary bodies. It joins the reversing force, "dis-," with the noun for "star." As in, an "ill-fated" misfortune. If a disaster is an imploding star, then the rebirth of a star is its antonym. Recovery is a process of reconstitution—of worldly possessions, of wits. It is never complete. Not today, in the aftermath of June's floods, and not in 1930. Eight decades on, West Virginia hasn't recovered from Hawk's Nest. How could it? —when so much of what was lost still hasn't been named.

Now the photographer unpacks camera and case, / surveying the deep country, follows discovery / viewing on groundglass an inverted image.

I'll admit I've got a thing about falling in love with dead women writers and chasing their ghosts around West Virginia. So when I found out Muriel Rukeyser, an American poet well known for both her activism and her documentary instincts, had visited and written a famous poem about Hawk's Nest, I had to know more. Rukeyser was born on the eve of World War I to a well-to-do Jewish family whose heroes, she wrote, were "the Yankee baseball team, the Republican party, and the men who build New York City." Her father co-owned a sand quarry but lost his wealth in the 1929 stock market crash. Until then, it had been a life of brownstones, boardwalks, and chauffeurs. As a girl, she had collected rare stamps with the heads of Bolsheviks and read like mad; slowly, over the course of her childhood, she awakened to what the comforts of her life may have signified in the world.

At twenty-three, Rukeyser found out about the nightmare unfolding in Fayette County from the radical magazines she read, and for which she wrote. After *New Masses* broke the Hawk's Nest story nationally in 1935, it became the cause célèbre of the New York left. The House labor subcommittee began a hearing on the incident the following January. For a couple of weeks, the country absorbed the event's gruesome details in mainstream media, but the federal government never took up a full investigation, despite the subcommittee's urging. So early in the spring of 1936, Rukeyser and her photographer friend, a petite blonde named Nancy Naumburg, loaded up a car with their equipment and drove from New York to Gauley Bridge to conduct an investigation of their own. I imagine Muriel, fresh from winning the Yale Younger Poets Prize for her first book, *Theory of Flight*, in a smart, fitted blazer and a sensible skirt, glad to take the wheel from Nancy, especially on those curvy roads through the mountains. Their trip would form the foundation of Rukeyser's poem cycle "The Book of the Dead," included in her groundbreaking 1938 collection of documentary poems of witness, *U.S. 1*.

The women originally planned to publish their photographs and text side by side, but for unknown reasons their collaboration never materialized. The method was in vogue at the time, as writers and artists across the country—mostly white—dispatched themselves to document the social ills of the Great Depression in language and film. That same summer of 1936, Margaret Bourke-White and Erskine Caldwell traveled from South Carolina to Arkansas, bearing witness to the Depression's effects on rural communities for what would become *You Have Seen Their Faces*. James Agee and Walker Evans were also traveling, witnessing sharecropper poverty in Alabama for what would become the most famous of these texts, *Let Us Now Praise Famous Men*. The American road guide, as a genre, was also coming into its own. The federal gov-

ernment assigned teams of unemployed writers to turn their eth-
nographic gaze to the country's landscape and social history, pro-
ducing the American Guide Series, which aspired to become "the
complete, standard, authoritative work on the United States as a
whole and of every part of it." The Federal Writers' Project published its first in the Highway Route Guide series, *U.S. One: Maine
to Florida,* the same year that Rukeyser released her own *U.S. 1.*
"Local images have one kind of reality," she wrote in the endnotes
to "The Book of the Dead." "*U.S. 1* will, I hope, have that kind and
another too. Poetry can extend the document."

Much of what I know about Rukeyser's life during this period
comes, strangely enough, from a 118-page redacted chronicle
of her activities, composed by the FBI. In 1943, J. Edgar Hoover
authorized his agency to spy on the poet as part of a probe to
uncover Russian spies; her "Communistic tendencies" placed her
under suspicion of being a "concealed Communist." When the
investigation began, she was noted as thirty, "dark," "heavy," with
"gray" eyes. In 1933, the report reads, she and some friends drove
from New York to Alabama to witness the Scottsboro trial. When
local police found them talking to black reporters and holding fly-
ers for a "negro student conference," the police accused the group
of "inciting the negroes to insurrections." Then, in the summer of
1936, after her trip to Gauley Bridge, Rukeyser traveled to Spain
to report on Barcelona's antifascist People's Olympiad. In the process, she observed the first days of the Spanish Civil War from a
train, before evacuating by ship. Her suspicious activities in the
1950s included her appeal for world peace and her civil rights
zeal. The FBI mentions "The Book of the Dead" only once, in passing, as a work that dealt with "the industrial disintegration of the
peoples in a West Virginia village riddled with silicosis."

Its twenty poems recount the events at Hawk's Nest through
slightly edited fragments of victims' congressional testimony, lyric
verse, and flashes from Rukeyser's trip south. She lifted her title
from a collection of spells assembled to assist the ancient Egyptian
dead as they overcame the chaos of the netherworld—"that which
does not exist"—so they could be reborn. One of these texts,
which concerns the survival of the heart after death, was carved
onto the back of an amulet called the Heart Scarab of Hatnefer, a
gold-chained stone beetle pendant that the Metropolitan Museum
of Art excavated from a tomb and put on display in New York in

1936, the same year Rukeyser began her version of "The Book of the Dead."

Curious to learn more about Rukeyser's time in West Virginia, I called up a scholar named Tim Dayton, who had searched the poet's papers for clues about the poem's composition. He told me that Naumburg's glass plate negatives of Gauley Bridge have since been lost, and that Rukeyser's research notes are missing. The only evidence of their journey, I learned, consisted of a letter, a map, and Rukeyser's treatment for a film called *Gauley Bridge,* published in the summer 1940 issue of *Films,* but never produced.

In the letter dated April 6, 1937, Naumburg offered Rukeyser her "personal reactions to Gauley Bridge" and suggested a general outline for the piece. The document provides some clues about whom the women spoke to and what they saw—a few names, a vignette or two, and a description of the "miserable conditions" of those living with silicosis. "Show how the tunnel itself is a splendid thing to look at, but a terrible thing to contemplate," Nancy wrote to her friend. Show "how the whole thing is a terrible indictment of capitalism." She signed off, "Are you going to the modern museum showing tomorrow nite?"

The map of "Gauley Bridge & Environs" is signed by Rukeyser and drawn in her hand. At the center is the confluence of the New and Gauley Rivers, where they form the Kanawha. Off to the side she sketched their little car, its headlights beaming forward. In cartoonish simplicity, she outlined the shapes that I recognize from my daily life: the trees, the bridge, Route 60. But some of her markings held greater mystery: a long, winding road jutting back into the mountains labeled, as best I could make out, "Nincompoop's Road"; a house that was "Mrs. Jones'." Rukeyser marked a big X on the town of Gauley Bridge, and an X over Alloy, rendered as a boxy factory belching smoke. She drew clusters of Xs next to two towns I'd never heard of on the Gauley River: Vanetta and Gamoca. This tracing of my home in her hand held the promise of a new way of knowing Hawk's Nest.

I gradually came to see that "The Book of the Dead" is itself a kind of map. (So much so that a literary critic, Catherine Gander, convincingly argues for the text to be read as a rhizomatic map in the spirit of Deleuze and Guattari's *A Thousand Plateaus.*) Not only do the poems' titles quite literally refer to people's names and elements of the landscape—"The Road" or "The Face of the Dam:

Vivian Jones"—the sequence also sketches out a crucial yet missing piece of the official Hawk's Nest story, a narrative thread usually so common in the media's treatment of disaster that it's become a trope: the "pulling together of community." Six poems in, we meet the Gauley Bridge Committee, an organized group of ten tunnel victims, their family members, and witnesses, whose caretaking and advocacy role had been totally absent from anything I'd read about the crisis up to that point.

Rukeyser introduces them in "Praise of the Committee." They sit around a stove under a single bare bulb, in the back of a shoe repair shop in Gauley Bridge, amid the din of machine belts. They are: Mrs. Leek (*cook for the bus cafeteria*); Mrs. Jones (*three lost sons, husband sick*); George Robinson (*leader and voice*); four other black workers (*three drills, one camp-boy*); Mearl Blankenship (*the thin friendly man*); Peyton (*the engineer*); Juanita (*absent, the one outsider member*).

The room is packed with tunnel workers and their wives, waiting. The committee's purpose is to feed and clothe the sick and lobby for legislation. George Robinson calls the meeting to order. They discuss the ongoing lawsuits, a bill under consideration, the relief situation. They talk about Fayette County Sheriff C. A. Conley, owner of the hotel in town, who heads up "the town ring." Rumor has it that he's intercepting parcels of money and clothing at the post office, sent by well-meaning New Yorkers to tunnel victims. At the end of the poem, their spectral voices rise up like the chorus from a classical tragedy, asking: *Who runs through electric wires? Who speaks down every road?*

This scene played over and over in my head like the beginning of a film I wanted to believe existed about Hawk's Nest. A film like the one Muriel meant to make, a story of dignity and resistance that was yet to be told.

Touch West Virginia where // the Midland Trail leaves the Virginia furnace, / iron Clifton Forge, Covington iron, goes down / into the wealthy valley, resorts, the chalk hotel. // Pillars and fairway; spa; White Sulphur Springs.

In the early Appalachian spring of this year—what proved to be the wet eve of June's storms I found myself barreling down Route 60 with "The Book of the Dead" in the passenger's seat. The rivers swelled brown and bristled with snags of trees beneath color-

drained mountains capped with a dusting of snow. I was following Rukeyser's map, becoming a tourist in my own home. Along
the road I saw metal buildings printed with soda pop logos and
heard the shrieks of peepers in their vernal ponds. Easter loomed,
and a church's sign assured me: DEATH IS DEFEATED. VICTORY
IS WON.

First stop: the "wealthy valley" from the cycle's opening poem,
"White Sulphur Springs." It began as a resort hotel, marketing the
area's geothermal springs and relative freedom from insect-borne
disease to slaveholding autocrats across the South, who evacu-
ated their families from the lowlands each summer. The hotel was
known then as the Old White—a string of cottages encircling a
bathhouse, where the South's antebellum politics and fashions
played out around a burble of sulfurous waters with allegedly cura-
tive properties. Later, the owners of the C&O Railway changed the
name to the Greenbrier. Though the sickly smelling spring was
capped in the 1980s, the hotel is still run as a resort with a casino
by West Virginia's current Democratic governor, the coal operator
Jim Justice.

Whenever I catch sight of the Greenbrier, there's an initial moment of nausea. Like standing in the center of a vast array of radio
telescopes or driving up a holler surrounded by a massive but out-
of-sight surface mine. When Rukeyser drove through, the hotel's
stark white façade had just been redone, but the inside was still
Edwardian and dim, draped in the depressing purples and greens
of a deep bruise. Global merchant powerhouses like the du Ponts
and the Astors would have been flying into the brand-new airport
for the hotel's famous Easter celebration, where princesses, movie
stars, and politicians performed their circus of white gentility.

I parked beside a utility van brimming with roses and entered
the building's interior galleries, which glowed like Jell-O–colored jewels. A dramatically lit hallway displayed busts of what
appeared to be the same white man carved over and over in
alabaster. I watched as workers prepared for daily tea service by
putting out plates of sweets, around which tourists swarmed like
wasps. A cheeky pianist played the theme song to *Downton Abbey*
as I grabbed a cookie and made my way back outside. I wandered
down Main Street to Route 60 American Grill and Bar, where a
man from Jamaica was beating a man from Egypt at pool. The bartender answered the ringing phone: "Route 60, may I help you?"

Some chunks of something slid into the fryer. I played "I Saw the Light" on the jukebox and drank by myself, before heading off to sleep in my car at the Amtrak station, a redbrick cottage perpetually decorated for Christmas. The entire town of White Sulphur Springs would in a few months be under floodwaters; three bodies would be pulled from the resort grounds, where the five golf courses had, in a handful of hours, become a lake.

The next morning, I continued along the path Rukeyser laid out in her poem "The Road," rolling westward through the Little Levels of the Greenbrier Valley, passing limestone quarries and white farmhouses drifting in pools of new, raw grass. In Rainelle, I stopped at Alfredo's to eat an eggplant sandwich in a room full of steelworkers talking about ramps, the garlicky onion that heralds our spring. After, I skirted the mangled guardrails of Sewell Mountain, a 3,200-foot summit that today is clear-cut by loggers, where General Robert E. Lee once headquartered himself under a sugar maple in the fall of 1861. I passed Spy Rock, where Native Americans sent up signal fires, watched for their enemies. New beech leaves glistered like barely hardened films.

In the afternoon I arrived at the Reconstruction-era courthouse in Fayetteville, less than a mile from my home, and climbed its entrance of pink sandstone. Most tunnel-related court documents were turned over to Rinehart & Dennis as part of the 1933 settlement deal. Even so, I found overlooked summonses, pleas, and depositions scattered throughout the county's hundreds of case files. Soon, I held a blueprint of the tunnel in my hands, apparently entered as an exhibit in the first case to go to trial. It suggested the elegance of a graphic musical score, yet filled me with that stony disaster dread. At the time of the trial, some of the plaintiff's witnesses were actively dying. Still, the jury deadlocked, and accusations of jury tampering arose when one juror was observed traveling to and from the courthouse in a company car. In time, the plaintiff's lawyers were on record for having accepted a secret payment of $20,000 from Rinehart & Dennis to grease the wheels for a settlement. (In a turn of unexpected, though slight, justice, half the money was later distributed among their clients, by judge's order.)

As I sat in the clerk's office trying to put the pieces together, Fayette County Circuit Judge John Hatcher walked in. We traded wisecracks back and forth for a while, and then I showed him what

I was looking at. "Awful what happened," Hatcher said. "They killed a lot of blacks." Then he launched into a story from World War II in which the American GIs give out chocolate bars to the survivors of a concentration camp, but the richness of the sweets makes their starving bodies sick. I wasn't sure what the point of his story was until he looked me square in the eyes and said: "Nazis."

I am a Married Man and have a family.   God / knows if they can do anything for me / it will be appreciated / if you can do anything for me / let me know soon

I left Fayetteville and followed Route 60 over Gauley Mountain, crossing the tunnel's path three times. I came into Gauley Bridge, the first community off the mountain and the first one you come to on Rukeyser's map. It's equal parts bucolic river town and postindustrial shell. I stopped at a thrift store, one of the only open businesses in the downtown core, and bought a copy of Conley and Stutler's *West Virginia Yesterday and Today* for thirty-five cents. Adopted officially into the public school curriculum in 1958 but used widely in classrooms since its publication in 1931, it's literally a textbook case of white people's amnesia. The index does not list "Slavery." The existence of "Negroes" is acknowledged six times, most often in relation to their "education." It's mute on the lost lives at Hawk's Nest, offering instead a description of an engineering marvel and a scenic overlook.

Back out on the street, I heard a sweet voice call out: "Diamond, are you working today?" I looked up and saw a frail man with pale blue eyes, rubbing his nose with a tissue. I told him I was Catherine but that I wished my name were Diamond, and he said, "You favor her. She just started working down at the nursing home."

He turned out to be Pastor Charles Blankenship, the preacher at Brownsville Holiness Church and the proprietor of the New River Lodge, formerly the Conley Hotel, where I planned to stay the night. What looked to me now like three shabby stories of grayish-yellow brick was a swanky stop for travelers when it was built in 1932, something I could imagine on the backstreets of Miami Beach. I believed Charles when he told me that Hank Williams had stayed at the Conley on many occasions. There's strong evidence that Rukeyser had stayed here too; her son Bill remembers a black-and-white postcard of it among her keepsakes.

In 2016 I found the lobby a friendly clutter of dusty MoonPies, hurricane lamps, and old panoramic photos that lit up for me the Gauley Bridge of 1936: its busy bus station and café, its theater and filling stations, the scenes of prior floods. A bulletin board displayed one of those optical illusions of Jesus with his eyes closed —stare at it long enough (i.e., *believe*) and his eyes are supposed to open. Most of the hotel's residents today are long-term tenants, elderly or on housing assistance, but this lobby used to hum, Charles told me, recalling the thick steaks that fried on the grill at the restaurant. The Conley filled up most nights when Charles's dad worked here as a porter, hauling luggage to the rooms of rich people passing through on their way to the East Coast. "I can picture them coming through the door," Charles said. "He used to get calls all night."

Charles was born in 1939 and grew up in a company house in a nearby coal camp called Big Creek, located about where Rukeyser drew "Nincompoop's Road" on her map. Like everyone I would meet, he wanted to know what I was doing in Gauley Bridge, so I told him I was looking into Hawk's Nest and Rukeyser's poem. He said he preached a funeral a few years ago for a woman whose daddy died of silicosis in the tunnel. He mentioned this fact in his sermon, and after the service, some of the woman's relatives came up and thanked him. They hadn't known.

I suddenly thought of the cycle's poem titled "Mearl Blankenship," about a "thin friendly man" who worked on the tunnel and served on the Gauley Bridge Committee. I asked Charles whether he had any relatives by that name. "That was my daddy," he said. I told him about Nancy's letter to Muriel, in which she wrote, "Stress, through the stor[y] of Blankenship . . . the necessity of a thorough investigation in order to indict the Co., its lawyers and doctors and undertaker, how the company cheated these menout [*sic*] of their lives."

"Well, what about that?" said Charles with wonder. "He possibly did . . ." He told me that his dad, whose nickname was Windy, had died at the age of forty-one. "He took that heart attack right over there," Charles said, gesturing toward some couches in the lobby. That night his father had told Sheriff Conley, the hotel owner, over and over: "I'm hurting so bad in my chest." Through the night, Conley fed him an entire bottle of aspirin pills. By the time he was rushed to a medical clinic around 2 a.m., Mearl had just hours to live.

I read "Mearl Blankenship" to Charles. Most of it consists of a letter that "Mearl," a steel nipper who laid track in the tunnel, wrote to a newspaper in the city about his condition. At that point, he was losing weight and feared the worst. When I got through reading the poem, Charles said: "That wouldn't be my dad. He never worked like that over there." I asked him who he thought the guy in the poem was, and he said he didn't have a clue. "It's very unusual because all the Blankenships I knew." He asked me for a photocopy, and then we discussed the brand-new aorta he got for free from a hospital in Cleveland.

That evening, I attended Charles's church with a friend. The sanctuary of Brownsville Holiness, perched on a pitched hillside along the Gauley River, is adorned with red wall-to-wall carpet and a single, simple wooden cross. Services kicked off with an hour's worth of live karaoke for the Lord, as congregants took turns singing at the altar, backed by members of a band who arrived late and casually set up around them. Then they all prayed in tongues. After, Charles shouted, "To know Christ is like coming out of a dark tunnel into the light! There is power in the blood of the Lamb! In the city where the Lamb is the light, you won't need no electric there!" On multiple occasions, he stopped the service cold and asked both my Jewish companion and myself to approach the altar and give witness. I smiled with a Presbyterian's customary politeness and declined. "Maybe next time," said my good-natured friend.

Brother Nathan, with his thin, tawny hair and slow, easy voice, rose to read a scene from scripture. Simon and the other disciples were gathering up their fishing nets after nary a nibble all night, just as Jesus told them to throw the nets back out again, for no apparent reason. "Nevertheless," said Simon, "at thy word I will let down the net." Brother Nathan told us, "The facts will scare you. We need to put aside the facts. It's time to say, 'Nevertheless.' I don't care what the enemy throws at me. The devil can come at me every which way, but nevertheless, I'm going on with God, I'm going on with God, and I'm going all the way . . . Nevertheless, nevertheless, nevertheless . . ."

Weeks later, I still wished I'd gone to the altar, that I'd known the right words about the tunnel to take there. Instead, I pieced together a Mearl Blankenship from census records—a white baby born "Orin M" in 1908 in the lumber company camp called Swiss.

Ten years later, the family was farming; in 1930, "Murrell" was twenty-one and literate, living with his parents in the Falls district of Fayette among coal miners, dam construction laborers, painters, lumber ticks, and dairy farmers. By 1940, ten years after tunnel construction began, "Myal" was an unemployed cement mixer, married to Clara, with whom he had three children, including an infant, Charles. He worked only twenty weeks in 1939 and earned $800. He died of a heart attack on February 3, 1950, and was buried at Line Creek. Charles was ten years old.

I brought a copy of "Mearl Blankenship" back to the Conley on a cold spring day several weeks after my initial visit to Gauley Bridge—"a rough old day," as Pastor Charles put it. I found him eating cheese puffs out of a coffee filter in the dim hotel lobby. He welcomed me back, took the poem, and this time read it to himself silently. He finally looked up, tearful, and said, "I'd say that was my dad. I had no idea. It stands to reason he worked there, because there was no other work back then."

What Charles remembered of his father was his sleeping body glimpsed through the doorway of their coal camp house. Light filtered through some kind of sheer curtain. Once, Charles watched a black snake slither out of the ceiling and dangle in midair over Mearl as he slept. Charles repeated the story about Sheriff Conley and the bottle of aspirin. He repeated the story about the family who didn't know that their kin worked at Hawk's Nest. When I finally got up to leave, he held my hand tight, locked into my gaze, and told me that he loved me. I told him I loved him back.

George Robinson holds all their strength together: / To fight the companies   to make somehow a future. // "At any rate, it is inadvisable to keep a community of dying / persons intact."

While reporting this story, I learned that two of Nancy Naumburg's photos from Gauley Bridge had resurfaced at the Metropolitan Museum of Art. The first is a shot of a town where black tunnel workers lived, Vanetta, which Rukeyser had marked with a cluster of Xs on her map. Raw wood structures line a thin strip of land between the railroad and the Gauley River. The air holds fog—or is it smoke? A scatter of people sits waiting for a train in the distance, where the tracks vanish into perspective.

After my first night at the Conley, I woke early and started down the abandoned rail line toward Vanetta. The cool, misty air sang with the frenzy of mating frogs and feeding birds. A dripping rock wall rose up on my right; wild blue phlox, oyster mushrooms, and sandy beaches spread down to the river on my left. After crossing a trestle, I began to pass into the frame of Nancy's photograph.

It was the same bend in the track that Leon Brewer, a statistician with the Federal Emergency Relief Administration, rounded in 1934. The apocalyptic dispatch he filed in confidence soon afterward counted 101 residents of Vanetta, occupying "41 tumble-down hovels, [with] 14 children, 44 adult females, and 43 adult males." All but ten of the men were sick. "Support for the community comes from the earnings of 15 of the males, 14 of whom suffer from silicosis. Thirteen are engaged on a road construction project 18 miles away and are forced to walk to and from work, leaving them but 5 hours a day for labor. Moreover many . . . are frequently too weak to lift a sledge hammer."

According to Brewer, these black families froze through the winter, starved and begged for both food and work. (One white local told me that he used to hunt for duck in the area where some of the sick, hungry workers camped on flat rocks next to the river; once, they asked him to bring them back a duck, and instead he returned with crow as a joke.) Brewer called for direct relief, "despite the protests of the white people," and an immediate improvement in housing and sanitation. He declared that anyone who wanted to return home should be given passage and assistance with reconnecting to his or her home community. "At any rate," he wrote, "it is inadvisable socially to keep a community of dying persons intact. Every means should be exerted to move these families, so that they may be in communities where they will be accepted, and where the wives and children will find adjustment easier."

The other Naumburg image that resurfaced depicts the interior of a worker's home in Vanetta: George Robinson's kitchen. Robinson, who came from Georgia, was the closest thing to a media spokesperson that the black tunnel worker ever had. In the frame of the photo, light falls onto a cookstove with kettles at the ready, the papered-over wall of Robinson's board-and-batten home arrayed with essential cooking implements: a whisk, a muffin tin, a roasting pan. A white rag dries on a line in the light.

I conjure the scene in the shack. I see George sitting, reciting what he told Congress and the juries, almost rote by now. His breathing is labored. I see his wife, Mary—is she distracted by thoughts of dinner, whether she should offer these women something to eat? Has a white lady ever been in her kitchen? Maybe they reminded her of the social workers who came from Gauley Bridge. Maybe Nancy is setting up her camera, her head ducking under the black cloth, as she peers through the ground glass, trying to get the focus right. Why, Mary wonders, had she chosen that wall? What did she read there? Did Mary want it to be read? Muriel sits, jotting down what George tells her in a notebook, wanting to capture it all, but also attempting to maintain eye contact—aware at every moment of the discomfort her privilege brings into the room. Was theirs a welcome visit, I wonder, or did the presence of these two white women disrupt the family's hard-won and precarious sense of sanctuary?

Muriel and Nancy made this visit in the spring that followed Robinson's congressional testimony; by June he was in the hospital, and by July 1 he was dead of "heart trouble" at fifty-one. On July 12, they buried him at Vanetta. I never found George Robinson on any census, nor do I know if he had children, or where I might begin to search for any surviving relatives. The only picture of him I ever came across was an Acme press photo from the D.C. hearing in which he is misidentified in the caption as "Arthur" (for that matter, his last name was misspelled in the congressional record). He sits at a table with papers spread around him, wearing a plaid woolen coat and button-up shirt. His arm is raised midgesture and his mouth paused midspeech as he describes to the labor subcommittee chair the conditions under which he worked and contracted silicosis.

Robinson testified that he ran a sinker drill straight down into the rock, that it was operated dry, and that he wasn't given any protective gear. He witnessed two men crushed by falling rock. "The boss was always telling us to 'hurry, hurry, hurry.'" He described the dusty trees in the labor camps where black workers lived around the tunnel mouth, the shack rousters paid by the company to physically coerce the sick men to work. Sheriff Conley came around and ran off those who couldn't continue, he said, men so weak they had to "stand up at the sides of trees to hold themselves up." He remembered one who died under a rock. Robinson knew of 118 who perished, had personally helped bury

35, and estimated a total death toll of 500. He said the company burned down the camps when the project was completed, so the workers would scatter. They even "put some of the men in jail because they wouldn't vacate the houses."

Bernard Jones—a white man who lost his father, uncle, and three brothers to silicosis—gave new context to this exodus story in a 1984 oral history with occupational health specialist Dr. Martin Cherniack. The white merchants at Gauley Bridge had liked the idea of the tunnel workers at first, said Jones, because they thought money was to be made from them. But eventually, they got "irritated" and accused them of "thieving," stockpiling stolen goods under a nearby railroad bridge. The merchants and professionals wrote an open letter denouncing the media for printing "propaganda" about their town, decrying the "undesirables, mainly Negroes" who had taken up residence there. Still, some of the black workers who lacked either the health or the means to go elsewhere attempted to stay at Vanetta. "Who it was I do not know," said Bernard, "but somebody in Gauley Bridge went across the river in Vanetta, and they put a big cross up there on the hillside and wrapped it with rags and soaked it with gasoline and set it on fire. Well, these black people, when they seen that cross burning, that scared them. And the next morning one group right after another came down that railroad track headed for the bus station, going back home to the South."

And now here I was, the latest white witness-invader, tromping in the opposite direction, back into Vanetta, where not a single structure was left. I saw a path that led from the tracks up the hillside and into the woods. Rukeyser's poem "George Robinson: Blues" tells me to look to the hills for the graveyard, and so I followed its lines into what was becoming a warm, cloudless spring day. I found it: a cemetery covering the whole mountain. I saw a corroded gravestone from 1865 and the fresh grave of an infant buried the day before, but I never found George Robinson's.

He shall not be diminished, never; / I shall give a mouth to my son.

In press photos and newsreels from 1936, Emma Jones appeared white, beautiful, and hungry. Sometimes she wore a little fur around her neck. She—who had lost three sons and was soon to lose both her brother and her husband—had become the white face of the tunnel's suffering in the American mind, the media's "Migrant Mother" of this particular disaster.

When construction began, she and her husband, Charley, lived at Gamoca (jah-MO-kah), a little town with a company store and a swinging bridge over the river, just down the tracks from Vanetta. She had nine children at the time and would go on to have two more. Charley and her sons worked in the coal mines, when there *was* work (which there wasn't). That is to say, they bootlegged. It was one of Charley's customers, a foreman at the tunnel, who convinced them to look for jobs at Hawk's Nest. Charley became a water boy. Cecil, the oldest son, was a driller. The youngest, Shirley, a nipper. And Owen, the middle son, had a mean streak and disliked blacks, so the company supervisors made him a foreman and gave him a ball bat.

The brothers got sick around the same time; their father held out a few years longer. Emma went out to Route 60 and begged for money to buy them chest X-rays. Before Shirley died—so skeletal Emma could lift and move him around the house like a lamp—he made his mother promise to have the family doctor perform an autopsy on his body. The doctor, in fact, preserved the lungs of all three brothers, hardened like cement, in jars as proof of their disease. *The Jones Boys.* That's what the doctor's son and his wife called the disembodied lungs after the old doctor died, I guess to make the whole thing feel less atrocious. The lungs sat in the couple's basement for years like forgotten pickles—until they loaded them into the back of their pickup truck, drove them up to the dump at the top of Cotton Hill Mountain, and chucked them over the side. "They sure made a racket when they went down over the mountain," the woman said later in an oral history, "but it sounded like just one jar broke." I used to live on the back side of Cotton Hill and spent long summer afternoons searching for them, to no avail. I imagined the ghost lungs fluttering through the forest at night like little sets of wings, surrounded by halations of shimmering silica dust.

I learned that many of the Jones family's descendants still lived in the area. People like Anita Jones Cecil, one of Charley and Emma's grandchildren. I hesitated before contacting her, worried that I would disrupt her grieving process, or that she wouldn't want to talk to me; worse yet, that she'd want me to stop talking. But when

I found her on Facebook one day, it seemed like maybe she'd been waiting awhile to tell this story. "My family is chained to that place by ghosts," she wrote in the message box. "Hawk's Nest chained my grandmother and my father to Fayette County through generational poverty . . . I have three sisters and two brothers, and I am the only one that went to college. We didn't have a chance."

Anita agreed to meet up at the library in downtown Charleston, where we settled next to a window in a dim, empty meeting room. She struck me as graceful and strong, with long brown hair and brown eyes, deep dimples, and a gaze that felt like a steady hand. She said, "This is what my dad told me, and what I actually think: they actively sought people who were poor, who were desperate and uneducated, and shipped them up here. Expendable people. People that nobody would miss."

Together, we looked at Rukeyser's map. I pointed out the house labeled "Mrs. Jones'." Anita told me it was the small farm that Emma and Charley bought for $1,700 with their settlement money, near present-day Brownsville Holiness. They received roughly twice the compensation that a black family would have received, but there was still nothing left over to live on, and Charley had to go back to work in the coal mines to pay off their debts. For a short time, while she was pregnant with Wilford (Anita's father), Emma worked at a WPA sewing factory in Gauley Bridge to support the family. Her oldest surviving son later said that she gave away bags of potatoes and flour to needy neighbors until the money ran out, and the family was right back where they started.

Charley died in 1941, leaving Emma a single mother with three children under eighteen. Then their house burned down. Emma turned to the Holy Spirit to get her through those times —she prayed and spoke in tongues. Eventually, she remarried and settled in a four-room coal camp house in Jodie, and life got a little easier. She had one of the nicest homes in town, with red tar shingles, a little fishpond, and a colony of elephant ears that she grew and shared with her neighbors. Anita may have never met her grandmother, but she grew up in that house, raised by her grandmother's ghost.

Anita said her father used to warn her not to depend on anybody else, not even a man, for anything. "You have to make it on your own"—that's what the tunnel taught Wilford Jones. But Anita thought it taught him something else too. "My dad was always going on and on about how you should treat everybody the same, everybody's equal no matter what the race, religion, any of that kind of stuff. And I think that was directly related to his experiences as a little child." Anita said her father was clever, could do math in his head. He started college but couldn't figure out a way to pay for it, so he came home to help support the family. The only work he could find was in the coal mines, and by the time Anita was a child, he was sick with black lung. She told me it didn't hold him back. Once, while he healed from heart surgery, "The miners went on strike, and he wanted to go out and picket with staples in his chest," she said. "That's the kind of people we're dealing with when you talk about my family." Near the end, perhaps delirious from lack of oxygen, Wilford got the idea that he was the actual son of Mother Jones, the union organizer who radicalized after she lost her four sons and husband to yellow fever. Some people had a theory that she had given her children up instead, to shield them from the dangers of her work. It became part of Wilford's truth that he was one of those sacrificed sons. Before he died at the age of fifty-six, he told his family to open his chest when he was gone, just as they'd done to his brothers, to perform an autopsy and prove he had black lung. He told them to seek compensation. "I think he dwelled on the past and thought about how things should have been and was sad over it," said Anita. "I personally, I'm a little bit mad."

Anita channeled that rage into a career in social services—she became an economic service worker at the West Virginia Division of Rehabilitation Services, processing relief applications and determining eligibility for Social Security and SSI. When Anita drives past the Alloy plant today, she thinks, "That's who killed my family. That's where our lives went . . . . I watch it happen over and over again in West Virginia, where families of coal miners, families of Hawk's Nest, will lose their primary breadwinner and they just struggle and struggle and struggle until they die." After all the death, after all the wealth was shipped out of the tunnel, she said, nothing was ever given back to Gauley Bridge—no investment in education or infrastructure. "Instead of being developed, it died with those men."

We read Rukeyser's poem "Absalom" together, facing each other in two chairs before a window overlooking the main intersection of Charleston's modest downtown. Somewhere in the shadows of the room, I like to think, Muriel was there—her wavy hair pushed back from her wide forehead, a dimple marking her soft chin. Anita held a photocopy of the poem in her hands, while I held the recorder. She leaned forward, reading half silently and half out loud lines from her grandmother's congressional testimony, jump-cut with fragments of spells from *The Egyptian Book of the Dead*. When Anita got to lines that interested her, she stopped and free-associated.

One of these was a passage that Rukeyser appropriated from the ancient text, meant to ensure that the hearts of the deceased were given back to them before rebirth. Then the deceased get their mouths back, and their limbs stretch out with an electrical charge. They are reembodied, with the power to move between portals of worlds freely. "I will be in the sky . . ." the dead chant.

I asked Anita where she found hope in this story—her story, any of them—because sometimes I simply could not. She said, "Have you ever really looked at Gauley Mountain, how beautiful it is? That's where I find my hope, yes. You think to yourself, God's here. He's here. He's not forgotten any one of those souls that died." She handed me a Bible verse she'd written out: "Fear not, therefore, for there is nothing covered that shall not be revealed; nothing hidden that shall not be known."

"That's what I think of when I think of Hawk's Nest," Anita said. "I'm not afraid. 'Cause I know everything will come out eventually."

I take her to mean, "God knows what that company did."

A few weeks later, I walked three-abreast on the train tracks with Anita and Rita Jones Hanshaw, Anita's sister, toward Gamoca Cemetery, where most of the Jones family is buried. The day threatened rain; the Gauley flowed deep and brown in flood, though we were still months from the June storms that would bury Belva in water. The sisters debated the way up to the graves. Anita tore through the thickening understory in one direction, while Rita and I started up a rugged logging path. Both women found it at once: the array of bathtub-size depressions in the earth, clusters of metal markers nestled among saplings, with blank spaces where the names once were. Tree roots heaved up and twisted the iron fences encircling the burial plots. We came to a slight clearing, shaded by giant hemlock and carpeted in Easter lilies—there in a row, Shirley, Cecil, Owen, and Charley lay buried. A family member with money had recently invested in flat stone markers, engraved with their names. Emma's body rests with her second family in nearby London, West Virginia.

Rita, the spitting image of her grandmother, spoke of her thirst for justice; of Shirley, who was working in the tunnel to save money for college; the thrill she felt a few years ago when she first heard the sound of her grandfather's voice, caught in an old newsreel someone posted on YouTube. Around that time, she and her sister Tammy began digging in the archives for the death certificates of tunnel workers, as a kind of self-fashioned therapy. "We just feel that us doing the research, and finding out what happened, it helps us heal. I know it was before we were born, but we still have feelings about this. It's our grandparents, people we didn't get to know. And through this we feel like we're growing to know them."

For those given to voyages : these roads / discover gullies, invade, Where does it go now? / Now turn upstream twenty-five yards. Now road again. / Ask the man on the road. Saying, That cornfield?

The white cemeteries wouldn't accept the growing number of black dead, and the slave graveyard at Summersville was already full. So Union Carbide paid an undertaker named H. C. White $55 for each tunnel worker he buried in a field on his mother's farm in neighboring Nicholas County. In 1935 a photo of cornstalks and mass graves on the White Farm made its way into the mainstream press and eventually caught the concern of a congressman from New York, who called for an inquiry into the accusations of corporate criminality at Hawk's Nest. Members of the Gauley Bridge Committee and others gave nine days' worth of official testimony, but Congress never took up the labor subcommittee's recommendation to investigate. (The West Virginia legislature passed a weak silicosis statute in 1935, essentially set up to protect employers from similar future disasters.) Nevertheless, a trove of eyewitness and victims' accounts, which would have otherwise gone missing, had been put down on record. And without that, it's hard to imagine Rukeyser's "Book of the Dead"—or much of any memory at all.

The White family sold their farm in 1954, and the record remained more or less as it was until 1972. That year, the state surveyed for a new four-lane road and found human remains in its path, sixty-three possible graves. A state contractor sifted through the soil for bones and placed them in three-foot boxes, reburying them adjacent to the highway, along the towering pink sandstone cliffs that edge Summersville Lake. H. C. White's son, the local undertaker of record, signed off on the whole thing. And there they remained, forgotten again, until 2012.

Thirty miles from Gamoca, at a highway exit called Whippoorwill, I met up with Charlotte Yeager, who played a role in the recent rediscovery of the Hawk's Nest burials. I parked next to a guardrail strewn with the Weed-Eaten heads of wild daisies. Charlotte, the publisher of the *Nicholas Chronicle*, emerged from a gray minivan with a pin on her chest in the shape of a ramp. It was April, and Richwood (another town hit hard by the June floods) had just hosted its big feed.

Charlotte heard the rumors about the bodies of black workers buried in the hills when she moved from Charleston to Summersville twenty years ago. "Everybody knew it, you know. It was just kept hush-hush because they were embarrassed." She tried a few times to locate them but with no luck. Then one day, she read a story in the Charleston paper about two guys—likewise haunted by the missing men—who had led a reporter to this site, claiming it held some of the workers' graves. One of them, Richard Hartman, later told me that the first time he went to Whippoorwill, he had to pick his way over rusting appliances and piles of roadkill that the highway department had been tossing over the side of the road for years. The sun's glint on a metal grave marker between the trees and trash was all that gave it away.

After that newspaper story, word got out, and a group of community members arose around a common desire to rededicate the cemetery. They included not only Charlotte, but local high school students, religious leaders, filmmakers, government officials, and descendants of white tunnel victims—like the Joneses. They cleared the area around the graves; the state came out and did a radar survey of the site. Rita Jones Hanshaw, a schoolteacher, and her sister Tammy began digging into vital records for names of workers. Plans for a memorial park were drawn up and then realized at a 2012 ceremony honoring the dead. A white barefoot preacher from Summersville joined with a black minister from Beckley to anoint the site with water from the New River; local youth lit a candle for each departed soul. It had taken eighty-two years, but hopes ran high that the workers' families might be reunited with their loved ones across death.

Charlotte led me through an elegant archway, past a stone engraved with the story of Hawk's Nest, and up a short path to several neat rows of depressions, each marked with a wooden cross and an orange surveyor's flag. After days of rain, the depressions held clear, still water that reminded me of baptismal fonts in a church sanctuary. Hemlock, beech, and red maple saplings grew among and inside them; moss and ferns cushioned lichen-draped boulders forming natural benches around the burials. Sunlight dappled the glossy leaves of rhododendrons. It would have been almost peaceful if not for the rushing traffic above our heads. But it was beautiful, in spite of itself.

Later, as I sat in my car next to the creek that drained Whippoorwill into the lake, I thought with disgust: I swim here in the summer. Then I got a random call from a friend who had lost the hard drive that contained her life's digital history, who sought my advice for its recovery. I told her that the thing about data is it's not invisible; it's there, in traces. Every byte has its physical form. Poetry, I remember thinking, fills in the gaps.

Defense is sight; widen the lens and see / standing over the land myths of identity, new signals, processes:

The Gauley Bridge Historical Society is headquartered in some shambles in a narrow green building on Route 60, next to a bridge that burned twice in the Civil War. I had heard that the old museum held documents relating to Hawk's Nest, so I'd made an appointment to visit. It was raining when I walked in, and Nancy Taylor sat at a desk among empty display cases and stacks of files. She looked at me like the public school teacher she is and said, "How can I help you?" in a tone that sounded like, "Impress me." I told her I'd come to see the material she mentioned on the phone, and she started handing me bundles of papers.

I took them to a table and began flipping through one of the stacks. I saw typewritten lists of names, mortality tables, narratives, and I felt the quickening of adrenaline through my blood. I started urgently taking photos for later study, but it soon became clear that the pages—which appeared to be multiple sections of a single text—were in jumbled disarray: faded legal-size photocopies

of names, some barely legible, and hopelessly out of order. Under
the tin roof in the rain, I spent hours of the afternoon reconstruct-
ing the document. Nancy seemed into it and said she didn't have
anything else to do. The chief of police even dropped by to add his
two cents. What he said, I don't remember. All I could think about
was the sorting. Finally, I put the last of its 227 sheets into place,
which turned out to be the title page: *Accident and Mortality Data
on Rinehart and Dennis Company Employees and Miscellaneous Data on
Silicosis,* Copy No. 2, March 10, 1936. Nancy and I cheered. She
let me borrow the manuscript (I think she was grateful for the new
order). I felt its preciousness in my hands, its presence in my car
on the way to the copy shop.

When I finally read it, I could see it was the company's version
of everything—their racially segregated tallies of employees who
died in West Virginia from 1930 to 1935 (110 total); their count
of "alleged" silicosis victims (14); their estimation of the number
of men they admit actually died of the disease (basically none).
Line by line, they rebutted the testimony of the Gauley Bridge
Committee's members, tearing into them with audaciously racist
and belittling commentary, blaming the victims and "radical agita-
tors" for all the trouble. Of their leader, George Robinson, they
wrote that he was faking it all, in order to enjoy "notoriety, travel
without cost to himself, and the pleasure of making an impression
on white people for probably the first time." One section included
a list of the deceased for whom H. C. White had served as undertaker: sixty-one employees (fifty-six black, five white) and five
camp followers, including three women. Thirty-six he buried at
the White Farm; the remainder were placed in other local cemeteries or shipped out of state to towns like Syria, Virginia; Union,
South Carolina; Knoxville, Tennessee . . . This list was flawed and,
like the congressional hearing, not enough, but it was a beginning.

It was the beginning of more than memory. I'd found the company's narrative, yes, but it held the names, each one the beginning of a spell against the narrative of disaster. And against shame.
Each one, a link to descendants for whom this list likely mattered
a whole lot more than it did even to me. Here was the evidence
one could intone. Like Rukeyser's poem, the list ran counter to
the version of events where we all crawl off and die quietly. It held
the potential to move that story, and it had been sitting here this
whole time.

How had it made its way into this halfway shut-down museum? Nancy casually mentioned the name of a mutual acquaintance of ours who might know more about its origins, so I called him up. "I got [those materials] in a way that I probably shouldn't have," he told me. "I'll be real cryptic here. I was able to get into the rooms at the power station where they stored all the records, and I borrowed a lot of stuff one night, and I shared that with a number of folks . . . And then I put the originals back." This was back in the 1980s. Apparently, he said, the company gathered every scrap of information they could find about the disaster and put it all in a room that "looked like a jail cell," under the power house.

and this our region, // desire, field, beginning.   Name and road, / communication to these many men, / as epilogue, seeds of unending love.

I used to be able to walk so close to the dam that I could practically climb across it. At its edge sat a creepy beige trailer with a single light that could be seen from the gorge's rim at night. On a wet day in April, I set out for it; I wanted to see the dam as it strained against the spring rains. The river ran wicked under the bridge where I parked and then started down a gravel road thronged with red warning signs: EXTREME DANGER — IF YOU NOTICE CHANGING CONDITIONS, GET OUT!

I had pushed levers called questions and the story had opened. How unqualified, how unprepared I felt for what I had found. Until that day at the Gauley Bridge Historical Society, few words had adhered to the uncounted dead, so I could abstract them in the "supposed" or "alleged" past. Suddenly their scale had become specific, and therefore vast. I knew their families were out there, in my mind always somewhere south of here, living—either in full knowledge of their family's inheritance, or in ignorance of it. Their trauma, I presumed, could be traced down through the generations. Yet none of this suffering was mine, was it? "Mine." I feared I was reinforcing some kind of savior narrative I had about my own white self—a middle-class woman who just wanted to "do the right thing," not embarrass anybody, most especially herself. I worried that, instead of resurrecting, I had desecrated the resting dead—ghosts who had never elected me their spokesperson. The names of the Hawk's Nest dead gave me powers I wasn't sure I deserved.

Birds of prey called from the Appalachian jungle, the purple bells of the paulownia trees rang out as I walked, listening for the dead. I turned to look behind me. I rattled my keys. What was I afraid of? The dam of history, bursting. I felt it cracking open, an inner chamber of the disaster that I hadn't known existed. I was afraid—of the woods, of the story, of the names.

I saw that a new barbed-wire gate had gone up to stop public access to the top of the dam, so I headed down a trail toward the river's edge, where waves dashed boulders like the starry backs of breaching whales. *These are roads to take,* Rukeyser wrote. I believed her. I took the roads. I thought of my country. And it had taken me to this terrible June, still looking to name what I'd found in the tunnel, for some cathartic shudder of light. The document *has* expanded, but into a longer list of undervalued, erased lives, as the rivers in West Virginia run their banks, as #WeAreOrlando and #BlackLivesMatter shout over and over to #SayTheirNames. Soon I will wake to #AltonSterling and #PhilandoCastile. Soon I will wake to Donald Trump's nomination for president. The same white supremacy that allowed, condoned, and covered up the mass killing at Hawk's Nest still asserts its dominance. The road of history is flooded with all of this, and so am I. But this is the road I must go down. It's the only one we have.

I drew closer to the water's rush and caught a view of the dam through the trees. I stopped and stared, and as I lifted my camera to record, I swear I heard the dam's steel gates groan. Those red signs flashed in my mind: KEEP AWAY! KEEP ALIVE! I ran scurrying back up the path. Circular clusters of fallen paulownia blossoms lit the way like lavender spotlights. With relief, I reached my car, and then I heard and felt a thunderous thump in the gorge behind me—something geological in scale fell. I thought of the blast from a surface mine, and then of my own beating heart.

EMPLOYEES OF RINEHART & DENNIS COMPANY AND
CAMP FOLLOWERS WHO DIED IN WEST VIRGINIA,
APRIL 1, 1930–DECEMBER 31, 1935

This is a fraction of the Hawk's Nest dead—almost certainly, other victims' names were never recorded by the company, either because they died elsewhere or because their race meant they were written off. If disaster is the undoing of a star, then each of these names is a star being born. For more information, visit HawksNestNames.org.

Name	Age	Race	Place of burial
Abraham, Eugene	21	B	White Farm, Summersville, WV
Adams, Winfred		B	Clairmont, NC
Alexander, James	32	B	Logan, WV
Allison, Robert	39	B	White Farm, Summersville, WV
Andrews, Sidney	22	B	Lewis Cemetery, Summersville, WV
Bales, Alonzo	24	B	Lewis Cemetery, Summersville, WV
Barrot, Nathan	45	B	White Farm, Summersville, WV
Blakley, Thomas		B	Diamond, WV
Blankenship, Ballard	30	W	Lindsey, WV
Blankenship, Oran Mearl	41	W	Line Creek, WV
Bostic, Marshall	22	W	Elk View, WV
Bostic, (Mooney) Willie	16	B	Vanetta, WV
Bostic, Ray Ernest	28	W	Elk View, WV
Brown, James	26	B	White Farm, Summersville, WV
Brown, Parker	38	B	Potters Field, Fayetteville, WV
Brown, Walter Burley	21	W	Syria, VA
Browning, Fred	30	B	White Farm, Summersville, WV
Burdette, Rufus	51	W	Poe, WV
Caldwell, Henry	30	B	Vanetta, WV
Cashion, Richard Wesley	48	W	Ansted, WV
Chambers, Benny	23	B	Lewis Cemetery, Summersville, WV
Chatfield, Fred	30	B	Vanetta, WV
Childers, Lewis B.	18	W	Dixie, WV
Clark, Nelson	30	B	White Farm, Summersville, WV

Cole, Lonnie C.	34	W	Jumping Branch, WV
Cooper, Mack	35	B	Lewis Cemetery, Summersville, WV
Cox, Milton	32	B	County Poor Farm
Daniel, A. L.	40	W	Atlanta, GA
Daugherty, George	35	B	White Farm, Summersville, WV
Devine, Henry	61	B	White Farm, Summersville, WV
Dickinson, Frans	42	W	Mt. Carbon, WV
Dixon, James	46	B	White Farm, Summersville, WV
Elders, Sylvia	35	B	White Farm, Summersville, WV
Euill, Gaston	36	B	Amherst, VA
Evans, H. C.	26	B	White Farm, Summersville, WV
Flack, Dewey	21	B	White Farm, Summersville, WV
German, Ben	38	B	Beckley, WV
Goines, Marvin	24	B	Not Noted
Green, Clemon	28	B	White Farm, Summersville, WV
Haines, D. W.	34	W	Sunset Memorial Park, Charleston, WV
Hancock, Bennie H.	47	B	Hunter Cemetery, WV
Harvey, Calvin	38	B	White Farm, Summersville, WV
Hendrick, Henry (Harry)	42	W	Hendrick, WV
Hicks, James	42	B	Union, SC
Hockens/ Hawkins, Richard		B	White Farm, Summersville, WV
Hunt, Thomas	45	B	White Farm, Summersville, WV
Inabinet, (S) Walter	27	W	St. Mathews, SC
Jackson, Whirley	24	B	Not Noted
Jackson, Wm.	40	B	White Farm, Summersville, WV
Johnson, Golden Allen	59	W	Gamoca, WV

Johnson, John	57	B	Boomer, WV
Johnson, Luther		B	White Farm, Summersville, WV
Johnson, Raymond	38	W	On Gauley, WV
Johnson, Robert	30	B	Vanetta, WV
Johnson, Walter	42	B	Prince, WV
Johnson, William	42	B	Montgomery, WV
Jones, Cecil L.	23	W	Gamoca, WV
Jones, Charley	52	W	Gamoca, WV
Jones, Charlie	52	B	Glen Ferris, WV
Jones, Lindsey	36	B	Vanetta, WV
Jones, Owen	22	W	Vanetta, WV
Jones, Robert	37	B	Not Noted
Jones, Shirley	18	W	Gamoca, WV
Kincaid, Walter	59	W	Terry Cemetery, Victor, WV
Kube, A. L.	52	W	Roadsville, VA
Lane, Henry	26	B	Knoxville, TN
Lee, Sydney	33	B	Denmar, WV
Littlejohn, Mary	40	B	White Farm, Summersville, WV
Lyles, Ernest	23	B	Diamond, WV
McCalphin (McCalton), John	30	B	White Farm, Summersville, WV
McCrorey, George	31	B	Chester, SC
McDaniel, Clara	23	B	Glen Ferris, WV
McDaniel, Robert	50	B	Spring Hill, WV
McKeever, Grover		B	White Farm, Summersville, WV
McKission, James	30	B	White Farm, Summersville, WV
Means, Charles	21	B	Vanetta, WV
Miller, J. H.		B	White Farm, Summersville, WV
Mitchell, Fred	40	B	Rock Hill, SC
Monagan, John	35	B	Lewis Cemetery, Summersville, WV

Name	Age	Race	Location
Moore, James	47	B	White Farm, Summersville, WV
Morgan, Ellwood	42	B	Clanton, AL
Morrison, John	24	B	Summerlee, WV
Moses, Lona	25	B	Lancaster, SC
Murphy, Robert	46	B	Camden, SC
Murphy, Sam (Sim)	24	B	White Farm, Summersville, WV
Nelson, Alex	44	B	White Farm, Summersville, WV
Nelson, George	44	B	Fayetteville, WV
Patterson, Charlie	25	B	Lewis Cemetery, Summersville, WV
		W	Not noted
Pickett, Willie T.	45	B	County Poor Farm
Potts, Jesse	73	B	Diamond, WV
Powell, Will	36	B	Mt. Holly, SC
Reed, Ernest	23	B	Lancaster, SC
Reed, W. M.	55	B	White Farm, Summersville, WV
Robinson, George	51	B	Vanetta, WV
Robinson, Will	60	B	Bayes Cemetery, Fayetteville, WV
Robinson, Willie	29	B	Summerlee, WV
Saunders, Walter	40	B	Diamond, WV
Sendusky, Albert	49	B	Vanetta, WV
Scott, Joe	45	B	Knoxville, TN
Shepherd, Howard	21	W	Gamoca, WV
Sherrod, John		B	White Farm, Summersville, WV
Singleton, Roosevelt	31	B	White Farm, Summersville, WV
Skinner, C. M.	47	W	Thurmond, WV
Slaughter, Hudson	25	B	Pierce's Cemetery, Fayetteville, WV
Sloan, Mat	31	B	Vanetta, WV

Smith, Bee	29	B	Vanetta, WV
Smith, Frank	45	B	White Farm, Summersville, WV
Smith, H. L.	60	W	Mt. Holly, NC
Smith, John	28	B	Hot Springs, FL
Smoke, Emanuel	50	B	White Farm, Summersville, WV
Stokes, Willis	40	B	White Farm, Summersville, WV
Street, Lewis Walter	46	W	Swiss, WV
Stringer, Ralph	33	W	Cleveland, OH
Strong, John	37	B	White Farm, Summersville, WV
Sykes, Walter P.	24	W	Peachland, NC
Thompson, Enoch		B	White Farm, Summersville, WV
Ward, John	26	B	Kings Mt., NC
Ward, Sam	30	B	Vanetta, WV
Watkins, Sam	38	B	Vanetta, WV
Watts, W. A.	42	W	Not Noted
White, James		B	Diamond, WV
Williams, Joe	30	B	Lewis Cemetery, Summersville, WV
Williams, Willie		B	White Farm, Summersville, WV
Wilson, James	32	B	Summerlee, WV
Woodard, Calvin		B	White Farm, Summersville, WV
Woods, Frank	23	B	White Farm, Summersville, WV
Woodward, Will	40	B	Lewis Cemetery, Summersville, WV
Yarber, George	18	W	Beckwith, WV

Last Taboo

FROM *The New York Times Magazine*

THESE ARE BANNER times for penises on-screen. In the last eighteen months or so, I've seen casually naked men on *The Affair* and on *Girls,* plus casually naked robots on *Westworld.* Penises have appeared on *Game of Thrones* (where one was once violently disappeared) and been simulated by a killer drill on *American Horror Story: Hotel.* They were in movies like *Get Hard* and *Unfinished Business;* one was there-ish on John Cena in *Trainwreck;* they showed up in stunt form on a meek Adam Scott in *The Overnight* and through the boxer briefs of a smugly sunny Chris Hemsworth in *Vacation.* Ralph Fiennes spent some of this spring's *A Bigger Splash* having a glorious time wearing nothing. And then there was *Weiner,* a hit documentary about the scandal started by the disseminated bulge in a politician's underwear. Once upon a time, just seeing a man's rear on television might cause a scandal; now you don't have to go too far out of your way to encounter his front. Our cultural standards have relaxed just enough to show a man in full.

And why not? Women have long been asked to take off their clothes, out of both artistic necessity and rank gratuitousness. Isn't it men's turn? Even when the nudity veers into homophobia (and boy, can it), there is an "at last" quality to all of this bareness: it's so matter-of-fact, so casual. (We're not, to be clear, talking about erections; there's still a line between a flaccid, out-of-focus penis attached to what's probably a stunt double on *The Affair* and, say, a European troublemaker like Gaspar Noé filming aroused, ejaculating ones.) We've gotten more gender-neutral, more feminist, more comfortable with our various bodies, more used to seeing dudes in gym locker rooms, better at Instagram and Snapchat and Tumblr—and so, too, have we gotten more OK with penises.

Some penises, anyway.

A vast majority of these penises are funny, casual, unserious. Their unceremonious appearance—as naturalism, comedy, symbolism, provocation—is new, and maybe progressive. But that progress is exclusive, because these penises almost always belong to white men. As commonplace as it has recently become to see black men on television and at the heart of films, and as normal as it's becoming to see male nudity in general, it has been a lot more difficult to see those two changes expressed in the same body. A black penis, even the idea of one, is still too disturbingly bound up in how America sees—or refuses to see—itself. I enjoyed HBO's summer crime thriller, *The Night Of,* but it offered some odd food for thought: the most lovingly photographed black penis I've ever seen on TV belonged to a corpse in the show's morgue. Meanwhile, the series' most sexual black character was a rapist inmate.

The black penis is imagined more than it's seen, which isn't surprising. This newly relaxed standard for showing penises feels like a triumph of juvenile phallocentrism—it's dudes peeking over a urinal divider and, as often as not, giggling at what they see. Not all of that peeking is harmless; some of those dudes are scared of what they've seen. And knowing that—knowing even a whiff of the American history of white men's perception of the black penis —leaves you vulnerable to attack, even when all you think you're doing is going to see, I don't know, *Ted 2.*

Officially, there are no penises in *Ted 2,* the comedy written by, directed by, and starring Seth MacFarlane that was a hit last summer. And yet they're everywhere—scary black ones. Mark Wahlberg plays a New England knucklehead named John, who swears that you can't use the internet without running into one. When a mishap at a fertility clinic leaves him covered in semen, a staff member tells him not to worry; it's just the sperm of men with sickle-cell anemia, a disease that, in the United States, overwhelmingly afflicts African Americans. John's best friend, Ted—a nasty animated teddy bear—gets a huge kick out of this: "You hear that? You're covered in rejected black-guy sperm," it says. "You look like a Kardashian!"

The sperm bank is the pair's Plan B. Plan A entails Wahlberg and the bear breaking into Tom Brady's house and stealing some of his spunk as he sleeps. When they lift the sheets, staring at his crotch, they're bathed in the golden light of video game treasure. In another movie, this might be a clever conceit. Here it feels like paranoid propaganda, a deluxe version of what entertainment and politics have been doing for more than two hundred years: inventing new ways to assert black inferiority. Now a teddy bear has a greater claim to humanity than the black people it mocks.

This is what's been playing out in our culture all along: a curiosity about black sexuality, tempered by both guilt over its demonization and a conscious wish to see it degraded. It's as old as America, and as old as our movies.

The national terror of black sexuality is a central pillar of the American blockbuster. In 1915 D. W. Griffith's *The Birth of a Nation* envisioned a post–Civil War country run by feckless white abolitionists, nearly ruined by haughty blacks and then saved by the Ku Klux Klan—a mob whose energies are largely focused on rescuing a white woman from a half-black, half-white lieutenant governor's attempt to force her into marriage. That's just the plot; Griffith's genius was at its most flagrant in the feverish surrounding details. The country isn't even done being rebuilt in *The Birth of a Nation,* and here comes the KKK, already determined to make America great again. The movie crackles with sensationalist moral profanity. Many of the black characters, for starters, are played by white actors, all having a grand time making randy savages out of their roles.

This was American cinema's first feature-length masterpiece. A full century later, it has lost none of its hypnotic toxicity. Even now, to see this movie is to consider cheering for the Klan, to surmise that every black man is a lusty darkie unworthy of elected office, his libido, his life. Its biases are explicit and electric. Griffith established a permanent template with this movie, not just for filmed action but for American popular and political culture—a fantasia of white supremacy, black inhumanity, and the tremendous racial anger that's still with us today.

Look at Governor Paul LePage of Maine, who, speaking at a town hall meeting in January, blamed invading dealers for the state's drug problem—men with such cartoonishly "black" street names as "D-Money, Smoothie, Shifty." They come north for business, he said, and "half the time, they impregnate a young, white girl."

LePage might have been channeling Griffith—or cockamamie pseudoscience like "The Negro as a Distinct Ethnic Factor in Civilization," a 1903 article in which the Baltimore doctor William Lee Howard argued that integration was impossible, not simply because black people were savages but because they were savages who hungered to rape white women. "When education will reduce the large size of the Negro's penis," he surmised, "as well as bring about the sensitiveness of the terminal fibers which exist in the Caucasian, then will it also be able to prevent the African's birthright to sexual madness and excess."

Finding the source of this fear isn't difficult. You can read the history of the black penis in this country as a matter of eminent domain: if a slave master owned you, he also owned your body. Slaves were livestock, and their duties included propagating the labor pool. Sex wasn't pleasure; it was work. Pleasure remained the prerogative of white owners and overseers, who put their penises where they pleased among the bodies they owned. Sex, for them, was power expressed through rape. And one side effect of that power was paranoia: Wouldn't black revenge include rape? Won't *they* want to do this to *our* women?

So from the time of slavery to the civil rights era, with intermarriage illegal, black men faced every possible violence, including castration and far worse, as both punishment and prevention against even presumed sexual insult. An exchange as common as eye contact, as simple as salutation, could be construed as an assault. Black men were bludgeoned and lynched for so little as speaking to white women. In 1955, while visiting Mississippi from Chicago, Emmett Till was kidnapped, tortured, and shot for supposedly whistling at a white woman. As a boy, I was told that story the way you warn a child about traffic lights, seat belts, and talking to strangers. Till's age ensured that you never missed the point: he was fourteen.

Claude Neal was twenty-three—a farmhand in Jackson County, Florida, who in 1934 was accused of raping and killing his white boss's twenty-year-old daughter, Lola Cannady. He was moved from jail to jail so white lynch mobs wouldn't find him before the trial. But eventually they tracked him down in Alabama, holding the jailer at gunpoint and absconding with Neal. The news of his capture attracted a bloodthirsty crowd of as many as three thousand. Lest a riot ensue and someone get hurt—someone besides Neal —he was lynched by a group of six, who then dragged him behind a car to the Cannadys' farm, where Lola's family members took turns slashing and shooting his corpse. Onlookers stabbed at it, spit on it, ran their cars over it. His body was then driven back to town and strung up in an oak so that the full mob could have its way. People skinned him. His fingers were cut off and, eventually, jarred. He was set on fire.

In 2011 Ben Montgomery rereported Neal's murder for the *Tampa Bay Times*. His article contains a passage in which one of those first six assailants recalls what happened that day: "Well, I guess we was pretty liquored up, and I ain't like that no more, but we cut off his balls and made him eat them and say they was good. Then we cut off his pecker and made him eat it and say it was good." The nadir might have been castration, but the bottom was reached well before Claude Neal was turned into a string of just-married cans, before his humanness was mistaken for a knife block, a sheet of shooting-range paper, kindling. Maybe he did take that poor girl's life, but we'll never know: he never went near a courtroom. There's no unremembering that his own life ended as a chew toy for hellhounds.

The warning in these stories is obvious: be careful near white people. The warning between the lines isn't hard to spot, either: be careful because your sexuality, to them, is hazardous.

It's funny how often we're forced to remember that. This year, the second season of Lifetime's *UnREAL*, a juicy scripted drama set behind the scenes of a *Bachelor*-like reality show, introduced a black bachelor in order to toy with America's dubious assumptions about the sexual prowess of black men. (The real show turned out to be as self-incriminating as the fictional one.) In September, Lena Dunham made an irritating paradox of those assumptions when she took public umbrage after the football player Odell Beckham Jr. paid her insufficient attention at this year's Met Gala, a perceived slight that seemingly devalued her worth as a white woman. It was a twenty-first-century offense that seems as if it could have been taken in the nineteenth.

The nation's subconscious was forged in a violent mess of fear, fantasy, and the forbidden that still affects the most trivial things.

A century after Griffith, you're free to go to a theater and watch Chris Hemsworth throw his legs open and parade his fictional endowment, while sparing a thought for what it would mean if a black star who goes by the Rock were to do the same. By the end of the 1960s, some black people were wondering that about Sidney Poitier: How much longer would a forty-year-old man have to stay a movie virgin? How many more times could he be made a mannequin of palatable innocuousness? In 1967, after black neighborhoods across the country burned in race riots, Poitier slapped the face of a haughty racist at the emotional apex of *In the Heat of the Night,* when he was just about the biggest star in Hollywood and at the peak of his talent. By the end of the year, though, in *Guess Who's Coming to Dinner,* he was back to his serene, tolerable self, playing the only kind of Negro a liberal white family could imagine as worthy of its young daughter: Johns Hopkins– and Yale-educated, excruciatingly well-mannered, neutered.

In his cultural history of the penis, *A Mind of Its Own,* David M. Friedman includes part of a letter that a Pennsylvania lieutenant named William Feltman wrote in 1781 after a dinner on a Virginia plantation, during which he was served by teenage boys whose penises were visible beneath their clothes. The plantation's owners seemed to assume the casualness now reserved for all those white movie and TV penises, but Feltman was agog: "I am surprized this does not hurt the feelings of the fair Sex to see those young boys of Fourteen and Fifteen years old to Attend them, [their] whole nakedness Expos'd, and I can Assure you It would Surprize a person to see those damn black boys how well they are hung." Abolitionists and others loosely sympathetic to black people were equally enthralled, writing stories that made heroes of slaves with names like Selico, Itanoko, and Zami—men who were excellent lovers and, also, immodestly well-hung.

Reading about yourself in this way—reduced—is disorienting. I don't feel that way, like a savage, a Selico, a walking schlong. I know the fantasy exists. It renders black men desired on one hand and feared on the other. But that's a script for somebody else's movie, one that blaxploitation films began to flip not long after Poitier showed up for dinner and, arguably, *because* he did.

The ingenuity of the blaxploitation era, with all its flamboyant, do-it-yourself carnality, was its belief in black women and men and its conflation of danger and desire. The movies—self-consciously, hyperkinetically black—were at full strength from the very end of the 1960s through the first half of the 1970s, and more or less kicked off with a literal bang: Melvin Van Peebles directing himself doing the nasty in *Sweet Sweetback's Baadasssss Song*. If the movies are ridiculous, they're ridiculous in the way bell-bottoms, platforms, and hair the circumference of a disco ball can now seem like camp. But back then, that was simply the way things were: *baad.* You went to *Slaves, Super Fly, Dolemite,* and *Blacula* because you wanted to see yourself, but also because these movies were the political repossession of toxic myths. *Shaft* named a detective while winking at his anatomy. Black men were swinging their dicks for black audiences. The films wanted not just to master the myth but also to throw it headfirst out the window.

But the myth has wings, and they've since attached themselves to white writers and directors—one or two of whom even know how to fly with them. For every couple of Seth MacFarlanes, there's a Quentin Tarantino: someone who would consider himself an Enlightenment figure, an abolitionist, woke.

The Hateful Eight, Tarantino's Reconstruction western from last winter, is another of his blaxploitation remixes. This one gathers a group of barely acquainted people—all positioned on negligibly opposite sides of morality, history, and the law—and traps them, Agatha Christie–style, in a shack during a blizzard. A lot of them get to spinning yarns, but only one of those stories earns a flashback: the one told by Major Marquis Warren (Samuel L. Jackson), a cavalryman turned bounty hunter. At just about the movie's halfway point, he tells a grizzled Confederate general named Sanford Smithers (Bruce Dern) a tale about the general's dead son. Warren says he happened upon the younger Smithers and, recognizing him, staged an act of racial retribution, which the flashback shows us. The son crawls naked through snow toward Warren's midsection and puts his head in front of the major's genitals. Then the score goes horror-film crazy and cuts back to Jackson, who gives the narration all the Zeusian jive that you pay Jackson to summon. With the old Confederate officer shuddering in disbelief, Warren boasts that this shivering white boy sucked his "*warm. Black. Dingus!*"

In the world of this film, Tarantino is playing with the truth. He's playing with math (I at least found more than eight hateful people). But most important, he's playing with fire. His movie runs along the third rail of race in America: that black dingus. Who knows if Warren made this story up. Courtesy of Tarantino, he knows that nothing turns a white man red faster than a black penis. The story's probable falseness only makes it more devastating, because falseness is what the story messes with: the fear of black male sexuality; how it's chasing your white wives, mothers, and daughters; that the black penis can be a vengeful weapon. Opening up the threat to sons laughs at the ludicrousness of it all. That dingus is coming for everybody.

This flamboyance is partly how Tarantino's films have come to understand black people—as mighty movie types rather than as human beings. *The Hateful Eight* made its defiant appearance during the centennial of *The Birth of a Nation,* and the movies share the same post–Civil War era. Watching Jackson stand over that bobbing white head, you feel the inversion of Griffith's template. Tarantino orchestrated lurid, white-on-black sexual violations for *Pulp Fiction* and *Django Unchained,* so you notice the inversion of his own template, too. This time it's black power dominating white that's presented both as a kind of rape and a mode of justice. Tarantino revises the social parameters of the Hollywood western so that racism and misogyny are its villains. Most of that revision, though, still hangs from a black penis.

Even if you're Tarantino and learned from blaxploitation, why propagate these myths—what the Depression-era journalist W. J. Cash, late explicator of the Confederate psyche, once called the "Southern rape complex"? Why continue to frame black power as a genital threat? For white artists concerned with black life, the myth matters, and it should: it's a white invention. But attempts to dispel that myth tend to reinforce it, sometimes because the mythbusters' love for black men seems indistinguishable from what's supposedly despicable about them. Hence those cartoon heroslaves, Selico, Itanoko, and Zami. It can be a peculiar thing being black in this country. Even the people who claim to love you are capable of these little accidents of hate—the social equivalent of finding hair in your food.

This is it, isn't it? Here's our original sin metastasized into a perverted sticking point: the white dick means nothing, while, whether out of revulsion or lust, the black dick means too much.

One night, when I was twenty-four and living in San Francisco, I met a handsome white guy visiting from Germany. We stood near a window in a crowded bar and talked about an art show he'd just seen. Eventually I brought him to my apartment, where, after removing some of his clothes, he eagerly started to undo my pants. But then he stood there for a moment and gave my crotch a long, perplexed look, like Geraldo Rivera did when, after months of buildup, he opened what turned out to be Al Capone's empty vault. He replaced his clothes and, before exiting, explained himself: "That's not what I expected."

I knew what he meant. He was expecting a *Guinness Book of World Records* penis. He wasn't the only one—just the last to do it with such efficiently rendered disappointment. That hurt, but I remember being amused that, for him, all our attraction came down to was what someone had told him my dick should look like. I remember standing there, half dressed in my living room, and actually saying out loud, "Why does he know that?"

But everybody knows. Anytime a pair of pants is prematurely rezipped or the line goes dead in a sex app's chat window, I always know: He was expecting a banana, a cucumber, an eggplant, something that belongs to either a farm animal or NASA. He was expecting the mythical Big Black Dick (which, online, people just call BBD). That presumption is something you tend to prepare for with interracial sex—that your dick could either render the rest of you disposable or put your humanity on a pedestal, out of reach. That it could make you a Mapplethorpe.

Last year marked the thirtieth anniversary of Robert Mapplethorpe's *Black Book:* ninety-seven black-and-white photographs taken between 1977 and 1986, before and during the AIDS crisis. In the photos, black men sit and stand and contort themselves for portraits, from entirely nude to fully clothed. There are looks of defiance, happiness, and rapture; in a few, there's no "look" at all, just a man in profile, say, his eyes closed, his skin emitting something lunar. There are photos of backs. There's one of two feet, where the light makes the striations in the toes seem like a glacial landmass. There's a bare rear that looks like ripe fruit, another that evokes a Rorschach blot, and one more, taking up the entire lower half of the frame, that looks like a hippopotamus.

Some of the photos are meant to be erotic, and all are meant to seem worthy of being looked at. They're born of the same curiosity and fascination as the black characters in Tarantino's movies. Sometimes what's in the frame can seem hard to work out, almost intentionally miscomposed; in some early pictures I'm not sure Mapplethorpe always knew the difference. In many, though, he obviously did. With *Man in Polyester Suit,* he nailed it. Taken in 1980, the photo is still the star of the *Black Book* group. A gentleman stands in a matching blazer, vest, and trousers, filling the frame from midchest to just above the knee. The image has the basic cheesiness of a department-store catalogue photo—a headless person, not quite facing the camera, arms at his side, his brown hands open. His zipper is open, too, and out of it hangs his penis. It's veiny, uncut, positioned almost equidistant between the hands and bigger than both. Its droop brings it close to Dalí's melting clocks. My favorite detail is the bit of white shirt coming through the zipper. It makes the penis look as if it were getting out of bed. An everyday object—the male power suit—gets a scandalous comic assist.

Man in Polyester Suit is one of the great jokes on American racism, one misconstrued as pornography and therefore as exploitation. Is that America's problem or Mapplethorpe's? (Or, for that matter, Tarantino's?) Are these guys doing social politics or fetishization? The difference between fetishization and romance is that only romance really cares what its object wants. Mapplethorpe and Tarantino both have complicated relationships with that difference.

To spend time with Mapplethorpe's work now is to find in it a kind of distorted love—what that German guy came all the way to America to discover. Mapplethorpe found most bodies beautiful and otherworldly, but especially black ones. He lit dark skin so it looked like wet paint and arranged subjects until they became furniture or evoked slave auctions. That naive, dehumanizing wonder complicates what, at the time, was the radical, defiant feat of inscribing black men—black *gay* men—into portraiture. It strikes a peculiarly foundational American note: this was another white man looking at black men, with effrontery but also with want. You can locate a sense of ownership, of possession, in many of the images. Two of Mapplethorpe's last relationships were with black men. Any eroticism in the photos might have come from the possibility that, sexually, he himself was possessed.

These pictures made Mapplethorpe, who died in 1989, one of the country's most notorious men. Among his most hostile adversaries was the race-baiting Senator Jesse Helms of North Carolina, who called Mapplethorpe's work "sickening obscenity." Whatever we mean when we talk about the culture wars of the 1980s and 1990s culminates with this—Mapplethorpe's pictures of black men, S and M scenarios, and fisting, and the 1990 retrospective at Cincinnati's Contemporary Arts Center that led to an obscenity trial. In its defiance and its awkward ideology, that fellatio shot in *The Hateful Eight* is the opposite of a Mapplethorpe: Tarantino luxuriates in its antieroticism.

The artist Glenn Ligon waged his own museum-ready critique in *Notes on the Margin of the Black Book (1991–93),* in which he dismantled Mapplethorpe's collection and captioned each image with quotes from scholars, from Mapplethorpe's subjects, from people he interviewed in bars. You could find James Baldwin, but you also had some lady named Rita Burke, who worried that these pictures would give you AIDS. Ligon, whose own sly, emotional work investigates the psychological contours of black ontology, doesn't condemn his source material; he opens it out, argues with it. In the end, what he asserts is that a black penis is mysterious only to those who don't have one. He's right: black male sexuality is of interest in American popular culture only when the people experiencing it are white.

There is no paradigmatic white penis. To each man his own. But there is a paradigmatic black one, and how do you stunt-cast for that? When people are turning down sex with a perfectly good black penis to look for a perfectly better one, how do you determine what an authentic-seeming black penis even is? What does the Kevin Hart of black dicks look like? What about the Denzel? And how would a white casting director know?

There's a more pernicious problem at work here, too. The underrepresentation of the black penis bespeaks a larger discomfort with depicting black male sexuality with the same range of seriousness, cheek, and romance that's afforded white sexuality. The history of American popular culture is an immersion in, if not loving white people, then knowing that white people can love. There's been no comparably robust black equivalent. But there is a recent history of black people daring to create one.

So much is going on in the video for Cameo's 1986 hit "Candy" that it makes you dizzy. The song is the happiest sort of funk number—hard-edged and insinuating yet bright. (They sing "candy" so that it rhymes with "today.") In the video, which Zbigniew Rybczyński directed, the surfaces of a cityscape are composited and layered so that figures—musicians, models—keep leaping in and out of them. At some point the women are made to seem as if they're floating upward, like fizz in a champagne flute. The clothes are by Jean Paul Gaultier, who really has a gift for boldly dressing black people. But the most dizzying thing of all is the red codpiece Cameo's frontman, Larry Blackmon, wears over his black tights. It looks like a piece of hard candy.

The same codpiece appears in the video for Cameo's biggest hit, "Word Up," and in "You Make Me Work." Blackmon's boiled-egg eyes and caterpillar mustache give him an out-of-left-field look, even for an R & B artist near the start of the video era, and in Gaultier's comically erotic costumes—form-fitting everything, breastplates, cutout chain-mail tops, big polka-dotted hats—he looks like a trainer at a cartoon sex gym. In the opening shot for "Back and Forth," the codpiece zooms toward the screen, then acts as a pendulum that, in swinging, wipes one scene into the next. The band was contemporaneous with Mapplethorpe, but it controls its own organ. And it's not as though Blackmon had to do a lot of gesticulating or gyrating. The piece spoke for itself. It never said anything all that dirty, but it let Blackmon mess with presumptions and curiosities about his penis. (And about his orientation—that sex gym seemed pretty gay.)

You didn't have to see an actual penis to know when one was speaking to you. Around the time that Cameo was hitting its peak, so was Bo Jackson. He declared himself bi-athletic, playing football for the Raiders and baseball for the Royals. Nike made him the star of a classic campaign—"Bo Knows"—whose crowning image was a black-and-white Richard Noble photograph of Jackson holding a bat behind his head, wearing white baseball pants and football pads over his bare chest. Your eye almost doesn't know where to look. His arms? His stomach? His perfectly symmetrical face?

There's no real threat in that picture. His hands don't hold the bat; his shoulders do. The pads cover his chest in a way that, as a teenager, I found modest. But in the original photo you can see the tops of his thighs—twin sequoias—and the substantial bulge between them. With Larry Blackmon, I figured I was supposed to look at his crotch and probably laugh. Jackson's was paralyzing —in a way that would have further appalled Lieutenant Feltman at that plantation dinner. But I was amazed. Jackson's cockiness was comprehensive. He wasn't coming after anybody. We were supposed to come to him. The slight lean of the legs alone had a gravitational pull. I mean, what else was that ad selling? There weren't even any sneakers in it! Just that man, his black body, its power, his crotch. Just sex. It wasn't an accidental picture, either. Bo knew. Apparently so did Nike, because many reproductions of that image covered up his crotch with ad copy or started at his midsection.

The late 1980s and early 1990s might have been the nuttiest time for black male sexuality. It was a height of the culture wars and of identity politics, which pitted creative people against moralists and artists against one another. Black men were often the crux. On one hand, they were the antagonists of news reports and America's nightmares: rapists, muggers, criminals, gangstas, kids liable to "wild out," sometimes guilty, a lot of times not. On the other hand, hip-hop, African American comedy, and sports were moving them to the center of the culture, making stars of rappers, stand-up comedians, and athletes, men like LL Cool J, Eddie Murphy, and Michael Jordan. Prince was the 1980s' greatest erotic adventurer. Madonna made a coffee-table scrapbook called *Sex* that featured the priapic rapper Big Daddy Kane in a three-way with her and Naomi Campbell. It was the Kim Kardashian's *Selfish* of its day, except much further out there.

America loved famous black men and feared the rest of them. Then someone murdered Nicole Brown Simpson and Ron Goldman, and the prime suspect was her black ex-husband, O.J. After that, the pride certain white people took in letting someone like O.J. be one of them must have seemed like a cruel, postlapsarian joke. Two recent major projects about Simpson, a drama and a documentary, made the whole tragedy seem inevitable, essential to our natures and the races' relationship to each other, all bound up in the original sin of slavery and the racism it manufactured. No one can ever quite agree on who's the sinner and who has been sinned against, whether it's 1994 or right now.

But at least now it's easier to find more of the kind of sexual black imagery that was so freighted a few decades ago. The internet contains bottomless warrens of black men starring in their own pornos. There are pictorials of old celebrities and viral images of current celebrities' wardrobe mishaps. The pride in some of these websites counteracts the fetishizing that sends some people hunting for BBD and the self-reducing that leads other people to offer it up. Mainstream American culture is still ambivalent about what to do with black men's sexuality, but you can find unequivocal comfort on shows like *House of Cards, Broad City,* and *Jessica Jones,* in which white women are convincingly, inoffensively attracted to black men who aren't the shows' stars but are permitted to be sexual.

But needing to be permitted is part of the problem.

We have a strong, ever-proliferating sense of how white people see the sexuality of black men, but we are estranged from how black men see themselves. Post-blaxploitation, that connection was primarily confined to the art world. The queer film essays of Marlon Riggs and Isaac Julien, from the late 1980s and early 1990s, remain different but intellectually conjoined odysseys of the male gaze, aimed at himself—two black mirrors. Otherwise, there was virtually no television and very few movies that were seriously interested in normal black desire, straight or otherwise. That's changing. The Starz crime drama *Power* is about an unfaithful black crime boss (Omari Hardwick), and a few months ago, it made room for a casual cameo by the rapper 50 Cent's penis. And that bartender who slept with Jessica Jones happens to be Luke Cage (Mike Colter), who now has his own show, a so-so blaxploitation-minded superhero drama that presents Colter as the sexiest man on television (or any streaming service). The record-industry soap opera *Empire* doesn't even seem to know there ever *was* a white gaze; it's the least self-consciously black show I've ever seen. The only people the power family at the show's core won't sleep with are one another, but we're only two and a half seasons in. Give them time.

There is still something missing from our picture of black male sexuality, though, regardless of who's looking: romance. We know black men can grind, but rarely do we see them love—as though

we'd have to upend too many stereotypes, shed too much pathol-
ogy, making it impossible to get there.

There's a magnificent new movie called *Moonlight* that knows
how hard that is. It's the story of a young Miami man named Chiron (it's pronounced "shy-RONE"), who is portrayed, over about
twenty years, by three different actors. His mother's a junkie. A
drug dealer becomes a father figure. Chiron flees bullies who
suspect—as he does himself—that he might be gay. ("What's a
faggot?" he has to ask, at one point.) Barry Jenkins wrote and directed the movie and fights it past the clichés in Chiron's biography, which are clichés only in the movies. For one thing, *Moonlight* is surpassingly gorgeous. The depth-of-field camera work and
luscious soundtrack give the movie atmosphere. You can feel the
humidity. You can also feel the hormones roiling this kid, who is
desperate to connect them to someone, then desperate to bury
them. But he can't. And that's because—and this is important to
say because it's *so rare*—Jenkins knows Chiron is a human being.
Not because he's a sex machine.

It's as if Jenkins has seen the punks and thugs and clowns
who've popped up in so many movies, as if he knows about the
fetishes and the gazing, about imperfect allies like Mapplethorpe
and Tarantino, about all the gawking that's done at black men and
their penises without ever truly seeing. It's as if he knows all of
this and is determined to strip it all away. There's nothing inherently wrong with black men's sexuality—only the ways it has been
distorted, demonized, and denied. Blackmon had his codpiece for
protection. Jenkins is certain that Chiron needs something even
stronger: affection.

When I was nine or ten, I spent the summer at a camp at my school.
One day, after swimming, I was showering, zoned out but dialed
in. I snapped out of it when I heard two older boys talking. "Yo,
he's looking at your dick!" "What going on, man? What are you
doing?" They were talking to me. One of them was lean, very fit, a
shade darker than I am and, incredibly enough, named David. His
eyes were small but bright. And I had been looking at his penis.

I didn't know what to say, so I told the truth. "Yours is so much
handsomer than mine!" They almost fell over laughing. The wonder with which I said it probably was funny. "You a faggot!" David
said. I stayed a "faggot" for the rest of my school life.

The only penises I'd ever seen at that point were as black as David's. But I noticed his. He was twelve or thirteen and more developed. Admiring it got me cast out of our little Eden—but only because that's how boys are. We didn't know about sexual myths or racial threats, about the taboos that we would discover are our particular birthright. I didn't, anyway. Not yet. I just saw a penis. And it was beautiful.

CHRISTOPHER NOTARNICOLA

Indigent Disposition

FROM *North American Review*

IF YOUR BODY dies in Broward County, Florida, and nobody
claims your body as the body of their next of kin, your body will
be burned and disposed of by the Broward County Indigent Cremation and Disposition Program. The Broward County Indigent
Cremation and Disposition Program will tend to your body's final
disposition in accordance with the law. According to the law, your
body is an indigent body—a body in need, a body lacking, defi-
cient, wanting. Your body is a destitute body, a body which requires
aid. Your body is a poor body, an impecunious, penniless, down-
and-out, derelict, bum body. Your body is now, and henceforth,
the body of a pauper, until such time as your body is burned, and
thus, no longer a body. After your body is sufficiently burned, Broward County will box what is left, your cremains, and store this box
for 120 days. If your cremains are not claimed by a next of kin in
120 days' time, Broward County will scatter your cremains in the
Atlantic Ocean. If at this time, or at any time following the date of
the scattering, your next of kin should wish to acquire the coordinates of the spot from which your cremains were scattered, they
may submit a request in writing to the Broward County Medical
Examiner records custodian via fax at 954-327-6581.

The indigent body of Jonathan Welker calls upon Michael Pazin
for help. Michael Pazin is not an indigent body. Mike has a job. His
job is cutting grass, and in South Florida, that job is a year-round
occupation. Mike started his job alone, going house to house with
a push mower, finding work where work was needed, and he cut
out a name for himself in the landscape of Pompano Beach. Over
no small amount of time, he built himself a rather large client

base. One large enough, Mike thinks, for a two-man crew. Mike runs his crew out of his pickup truck, to which he attaches an open-air, flatbed trailer every morning in order to transport the equipment he needs to mow, blow, and go. And he goes every day, all day, so long as there's green to be cut and money to be made. The American Dream.

The indigent body of Jonathan Welker calls upon the American Dream for help. Mike tells me that Jon's body is in bad shape. Jon's body is afflicted with some type of diabetes and uses this affliction as an excuse to frequently visit hospitals. During these visits, Mike tells me, Jon's body receives fluids, nutrients, and temporary shelter against the South Florida elements. During these visits Jon's indigent body is at rest. These visits typically do not last longer than hours, although sometimes they last for days, for the medical professionals at the hospital care for the functioning of Jon's body, and they sometimes determine that it will not function for long. Even so, Jon's body finds a way out of the hospital and onto the streets, into the hospital and back out again, over and over, in a cycle that pauses only when somebody else intervenes. Mike and I intervene.

The indigent body of Jonathan Welker is not alone. Mike and I arrive at a motel to find Jon's body accompanied by somebody, a girl's body. The pair appear as though they have been treated quite badly, and both bodies seem to be frail, visibly broken bodies. Two of the same kind of body, as if sculpted of the same earth, grown from the same tree. Overripe and dangling bodies, refusing to fall bodies. Bodies abandoned, or bodies ignored, but for the attention of the American Dream and me.

The indigent body of Jonathan Welker speaks softly. Softer, I think, than looks allow. Mike tells me that Jon's body is without a single mean bone, and I think it shows. I think Jon's body sounds like somebody I could have known from high school, like the guys I used to skip class with, like the anybodies I run into at the gas station near the neighborhood where I grew up. It's hard for me to hear Jon's body take on gracious tones, to thank and show appreciation toward me and toward Mike. We just showed up. We're nothing but additional company for Jon's body.

The indigent body of Jonathan Welker speaks of friends and of an evaporating pool of resources. Jon's body, Mike says, is afflicted with a lack of domicile. There is no neighborhood for Jon's body to gravitate toward. There is no home base to run to. It is difficult for me to imagine an existence without the fail-safe of patronage, without a house I know I can return to no matter how bad my situation is, without anyone to call upon with any certainty. A zero-consistency life. Mike tells me this disease has been attacking Jon's body for as long as he can recall.

The indigent body of Jonathan Welker bargains in desperation. The American Dream and I have only so much to give and the motel is charging more than we, even combined, can afford. Jon's body confers with this somebody, and the two clash over differences. The pair discuss, body to body, just what a body is worth. The comfort of a hotel bed. A kindness for a kindness. A moment apart for a night alone. A pound of flesh. Jon's body breaks from the conference and the girl's body is put forth. A payment for a payment. Jon's body agrees that this is the best option, the only option left on the table. The girl's body shudders and then accepts. Mike and I intervene.

The indigent body of Jonathan Welker watches the American Dream drop twenty dollars U.S. currency, and turn around. Mike picks up his feet and reaches a full sprint before he rounds the corner. He runs all the way home. I stay with Jon's dejected body for only a short time before I, too, reach into my pocket and hand him what little money I have in my possession. Jon's body is grateful, more grateful than I think natural, considering the sum does not add up to enough for even half a night in the worst motel in Pompano. Still, Jon's body is upright and cordial as it latches onto that somebody, and the two turn to walk away without direction.

The indigent body of Jonathan Welker does not call upon Michael Pazin for help. Mike continues to cut grass and his business continues to grow. He rents a warehouse near Dixie Highway where he stores his ever-increasing stockpile of equipment and spare parts. Like the owners of some of the neighboring warehouses, Mike has installed an air-conditioning unit and brought in a couch, turning the former sweatshop into an effective home away from home. A clubhouse, of sorts. A place for work and a place to relax after a long summer day in the sun. The perfect mix of business and pleasure. The American Dream.

The indigent body of Jonathan Welker sits on a couch in a warehouse near the warehouse where Michael Pazin loads his equipment onto his lawn trailer. A friend of a friend calls upon Mike for help. Jon's body called this friend of a friend looking for a place to spend the night, and the only place this friend of a friend could think of, Mike tells me, the only place he could spare, was his home away from home. His warehouse. Mike understands, and relates to this friend of a friend. Mike agrees to check on Jon's body in the warehouse nearby, to see if Jon's body is where this friend of a friend remembers leaving it.

The indigent body of Jonathan Welker becomes the property of Broward County, Florida. Jon's body was naked, Mike tells me, and stiff like a caught fish pulled from the icy water at the bottom of the cooler. Naked, he says, and embarrassing. An awkward kind of body, like a body caught in the act. A body frozen in the actions performed in the presence of nobody. An echoing body, bouncing laughs and uncomfortable wakeup calls off the concrete walls and ceilings and out the bay door of the air-conditioned storage unit. Calls that degenerate, to drift off and find their way to police officers as somber and respectful phone calls. The American Dream calls upon Broward County for help.

The indigent body of Jonathan Welker does not call upon Broward County for help. Jon's body does not call upon anybody, and never will again. Nobody receives a call from Jon's body and nobody minds the absence of that call. A calm acceptance overcomes Jon's body, as if there were no difference in the body of the willing and the body of the willed. The indigent body of Jonathan Welker does not disagree with Broward County, or the American Dream, or the idea that something must be done with the indigent body of Jonathan Welker. Jon's body is in no position to disagree with anybody, anymore.

If your body is a part of the American Dream in Broward County, Florida, and nobody can claim that your body has acquired a body of worth, worthy of commemoration, your body will be burned and disposed of by the Broward County Indigent Cremation and Disposition Program. The Broward County Indigent Cremation and Disposition Program. The Broward County American Dreamation and Disposition Program. The Broward County Program for the Cremation and Disposition of the American Dream. The Program for the American Dream in Broward County, Cremated and Disposed. Dream Program. Disposition. Cremation. American. Broward County, Florida. Fax 954-327-6581 for the coordinates.

MEGHAN O'GIEBLYN

Dispatch from Flyover Country

FROM *The Threepenny Review*

THE AUGUST BEFORE last, my husband and I moved to Muskegon, a town on the scenic and economically depressed west coast of Michigan. I grew up in the state, but most of my friends have left it, or else are too beleaguered by children to answer their phones. We live in a trailer in the woods, one paneled with oak-grained laminate and beneath which a family of raccoons have made their home. There is a small screened-in porch and a large deck that extends over the side of a sand dune. We work there in the mornings beneath the ceiling of broadleaves, teaching our online classes and completing whatever freelance projects we've managed to scrape together that week. Occasionally, I'll try to amuse him by pitching my latest idea for a screenplay. "An out-of-work stuntman leaves Hollywood and becomes an Uber driver," I'll say. "It's about second chances in the sharing economy." We write the kinds of things that return few material rewards; there is no harm in fantasizing. After dinner, we take the trail that runs from the back of the trailer through an aisle of high pines, down the side of the dune to Lake Michigan.

Evenings have been strange this year: hazy, surreal. Ordinarily, Michigan sunsets are like a preview of the apocalypse, a celestial fury of reds and tangerines. But since we moved here, each day expires in white gauze. The evening air grows thick with fog, and as the sun descends toward the water, it grows perfectly round and blood-colored, lingering on the horizon like an evil planet. If a paddleboarder happens to cross the lake, the vista looks exactly like one of those old oil paintings of Hanoi. For a long time, we assumed the haze was smog wafting in from Chicago, or perhaps Milwaukee. But one night, as we walked along the beach, we bumped into a friend of my mother's who told us it was from the California wildfires. She'd heard all about it on the news: smoke from the hills of the Sierra Nevada had apparently been carried on an eastern jet stream thousands of miles across the country, all the way to our beach.

"That seems impossible," I said.

"It does seem impossible," she agreed, and the three of us stood there on the shore, staring at the horizon as though if we looked hard enough, we might glimpse whatever was burning on the far side of the country.

The Midwest is a somewhat slippery notion. It is a region whose existence—whose very name—has always been contingent upon the more fixed and concrete notion of the West. Historically, these interior states were less a destination than a corridor, a gateway that funneled travelers from the East into the vast expanse of the frontier. The great industrial cities of this region—Chicago, Detroit, and St. Louis—were built as "hubs," places where the rivers and the railroads met, where all the goods of the prairie accumulated before being shipped to the exterior states. Today, coastal residents stop here only to change planes, a fact that has solidified our identity as a place to be passed over. To be fair, people who live here seem to prefer it this way. Gift shops along the shores of the Great Lakes sell T-shirts bearing the logo FLYOVER LIVING. For a long time, the unofficial nickname for the state of Indiana was Crossroads of America. Each time my family passed the state line, my sisters and I would mock its odd, anti-touristic logic ("Nothing to see here, folks!").

When I was young, my family moved across the borders of these interior states—from Illinois to Michigan to Wisconsin. My father sold industrial lubricant, an occupation that took us to the kinds of cities that had been built for manufacturing and by the end of the century lay mostly abandoned, covered, like Pompeii, in layers of ash. We lived on the outskirts of these cities, in midcentury bedroom communities, or else beyond them, in subdivisions built atop decimated cornfields. On winter evenings, when the last flush of daylight stretched across the prairie, the only sight for miles was the green and white lights of airport runways blinking in the distance like lodestars. We were never far from a freeway, and at night the whistle of trains passing through was as much a part of the soundscape as the wind or the rain. It is like this anywhere you go in the Midwest. It is the sound of transit, of things passing through. People who grew up here tend to tune it out, but if you stop and actually listen, it can be disarming. On some nights, it's easy to imagine that it is the sound of a more profound shifting, as though the entire landscape of this region—the North Woods, the tallgrass prairies, the sand dunes, and the glacial moraines—is itself fluid and impermanent.

It's difficult to live here without developing an existential dizziness, a sense that the rest of the world is moving while you remain still. I spent most of my twenties in South Chicago, in an apartment across from a hellscape of coal-burning plants that ran on grandfather clauses and churned out smoke blacker than the night sky. To live there during the digital revolution was like existing in an anachronism. When I opened my windows in summer, soot blew in with the breeze; I swept piles of it off my floor, which left my hands blackened like a scullery maid's. I often thought that Dickens's descriptions of industrial England might have aptly described twenty-first-century Chicago. "It was a town of machinery and tall chimneys, out of which interminable serpents of smoke trailed themselves for ever and ever, and never got uncoiled." Far from the blat of the city, there was another world, one depicted on television and in the pages of magazines—a nirvana of sprawling green parks and the distant silence of wind turbines. Billboards glowed above the streets like portals into another world, one where everything was reduced to clean and essential lines. YOU ARE BEAUTIFUL, said one of them, its product unmentioned or unclear. Another featured a blue sky marked with cumulus clouds and the words: IMAGINE PEACE.

I still believed during those years that I would end up in New York, or perhaps in California. I never had any plans for how to get there. I truly believed I would "end up" there, swept by that force of nature that funneled each harvest to the exterior states and carried young people off along with it. Instead, I found work as a cocktail waitress at a bar downtown, across from the state prison. The regulars were graying men who sat impassively at the bar each night, reading the *Tribune* in silence. The nature of my job, according to my boss, was to be an envoy of feminine cheer in that dark place, and so I occasionally wandered over to offer some chipper comment on the headlines—"Looks like the stimulus package is going to pass"—a task that was invariably met with a cascade of fatalism.

"You think any of that money's going to make it to Chicago?"

"They should make Wall Street pay for it," someone quipped.

"Nah, that would be too much like right."

Any news of emerging technology was roundly dismissed as unlikely. If I mentioned self-driving cars, or 3-D printers, one of the men would hold up his cell phone and say, "They can't even figure out how to get us service south of Van Buren."

For a long time, I mistook this for cynicism. In reality, it is something more like stoicism, a resistance to excitement that is native to this region. The longer I live here, the more I detect it in myself. It is less disposition than habit, one that comes from tuning out the fashions and revelations of the coastal cities, which have nothing to do with you, just as you learned as a child to ignore those local boosters who proclaimed, year after year, that your wasted Rust Belt town was on the cusp of revival. Some years ago, the Detroit Museum of Modern Art installed on its western exterior a neon sign that read EVERYTHING IS GOING TO BE ALRIGHT. For several months, this message brightened the surrounding blight and everyone spoke of it as a symbol of hope. Then the installation was changed to read: NOTHING IS GOING TO BE ALRIGHT. They couldn't help themselves, I guess. To live here is to develop a wariness toward all forms of unqualified optimism; it is to know that progress comes in fits and starts, that whatever promise the future holds, its fruits may very well pass on by, on their way to somewhere else.

My husband and I live just up the hill from the grounds of a Bible camp where I spent the summers of my childhood, a place called Maranatha. People in town assume the name is Native American, but it is in fact an Aramaic word that means "Come, Lord," and which appears in the closing sentences of the New Testament. The apostolic fathers once spoke the word as a prayer, and it was repeated by people of faith throughout the centuries, a mantra to fill God's millennia-long silence. When the camp was built in the early years of the last century, a more ominous English formulation—"The Lord is Coming"—was carved into the cedar walls of the Tabernacle. Everyone is still waiting.

From Memorial Day to Labor Day, the grounds are overrun with evangelical families who come from all over the Midwest to spend their summer vacations on the beach. They stay for weeks at a time in the main lodge, and some stay for the whole summer in cottages built on stilts atop what is the largest collection of freshwater dunes in the world. My parents own one of these cottages; so do my grandparents. Each year, a representative from the DNR comes out to warn them that the dunes are eroding and the houses will one day slide into the lake—prophecies that go unheeded. Everyone plants more dune grass and prays for a few more years. I once pointed out to my mother that there is, in fact, a biblical parable about the foolish man who builds his house on sand, but she chided me for my pedantic literalism. "That parable," she said, "is about having a foundational faith."

We moved here because we love this part of Michigan and because I have family here. Also, because it's cheap to live here and we're poor. We've lost track of the true reason. Or rather, the foremost reasons and the incidental ones are easy to confuse. Before, we were in Madison, Wisconsin, where we were teaching college writing and juggling other part-time jobs. As more of this work migrated online, location became negotiable. We have the kind of career people like to call "flexible," meaning we buy our own health insurance, work in our underwear, and are taxed like a small business. Sometimes we fool ourselves into believing that we've outsmarted the system, that we've harnessed the plucky spirit of those DIY blogs that applaud young couples for turning a toolshed or a teardrop camper into a studio apartment, as though economic instability were the great crucible of American creativity.

On Saturday nights, the camp hosts a concert, and my husband and I occasionally walk down to the Tabernacle to listen to whatever band has been bused in from Nashville. Neither of us is a believer, but we enjoy the music. The bands favor gospel standards, a blend of highlands ballads and Gaither-style revivalism. The older generation here includes a contingent of retired missionaries. Many of them are widows, women who spent their youth carrying the gospel to the Philippines or the interior of Ecuador, and after the service they smile faintly at me as they pass by our pew, perhaps sensing a family resemblance. Occasionally, one of them will grip my forearm and say, "Tell me who you are." The response to this question is "I'm Colleen's daughter." Or, if that fails to register: "I'm Paul and Marilyn's granddaughter." It is unnerving to identify oneself in this way. My husband once noted that it harks back to the origins of surnames, to the clans of feudal times who identified villagers by patronymic epithets. John's son became Johnson, et cetera. To do so now is to see all the things that constitute a modern identity—all your quirks and accomplishments —rendered obsolete.

This is among the many reasons why young people leave these states. When you live in close proximity to your parents and aging relatives, it's impossible to forget that you too will grow old and die. It's the same reason, I suspect, that people are made uncomfortable by the specter of open landscapes, why the cornfields and empty highways of the heartland inspire so much angst. There was a time when people spoke of such vistas as metaphors for opportunity—"expand your horizons"—a convention, I suppose, that goes back to the days of the frontier. Today, opportunity is the province of cities, and the view here signals not possibility but visible constraints. To look out at the expanse of earth, scraped clean of novelty and distraction, is to remember in a very real sense what lies at the end of your own horizon.

Many of our friends who grew up here now live in Brooklyn, where they are at work on "book-length narratives." Another contingent has moved to the Bay Area and made a fortune there. Every year or so, these West Coasters travel back to Michigan and call us up for dinner or drinks, occasions they use to educate us on the inner workings of the tech industry. They refer to the companies they work for in the first person plural, a habit I have yet to acculturate to. Occasionally they lapse into the utopian, speaking of robotics ordinances and brain–computer interfaces and the mystical, labyrinthine channels of capital, conveying it all with the fervency of pioneers on a civilizing mission. Being lectured quickly becomes dull, and so my husband and I, to amuse ourselves, will sometimes play the rube. "So what, exactly, is a venture capitalist?" we'll say. Or: "Gosh, it sounds like science fiction." I suppose we could tell them the truth—that nothing they're proclaiming is news; that the boom and bustle of the coastal cities, like the smoke from those California wildfires, liberally wafts over the rest of the country. But that seems a bit rude. We are, after all, Midwesterners.

Here, work is work and money is money, and nobody speaks of these things as though they were spiritual movements or expressions of one's identity. In college, I waitressed at a chain restaurant, the kind of place that played Smashmouth on satellite and cycled through twenty gallons of ranch dressing a week. One day, it was announced that all employees, from management to dish crew, would hereafter be referred to as "partners." It was a diktat from corporate. Everyone found this so absurd that all of us, including the assistant managers, refused to say the word without a cartoonish, cowboy twang ("howdy, pardner"), robbing it of its intended purpose, which was, of course, to erase the appearance of hierarchy. This has always struck me as indicative of a local political disposition, one that cannot be hoodwinked into euphemism. When you live at the center of the American machine, it's impossible to avoid speaking of mechanics.

Winters here are dark and brutal. On weekends, my husband and I will drive into town, where there are five or six restaurants that have different names but identical menus. Each serves fried perch and whitefish sandwiches, plus a salad section that boasts an Epcot-like *tour du monde:* Chinese salad, taco salad, Thai chicken salad, Southwest salad. In Michigan, they still—thankfully—believe in iceberg lettuce, or, as one menu has it, "crisp, cold iceberg lettuce." At the more high-end Muskegon restaurants, you can order something called a wedge salad, which is a quarter-head of iceberg covered in tomatoes, bacon bits, and what appears to be—but is not, actually—a profane amount of blue cheese *and* French dressings. "Oh, shit," my husband said the first time I ordered one in his presence, "they forgot your dressing." Of course, anyone familiar with iceberg heads knows that they are baroquely layered and dense; you truly do need all that dressing. People in Michigan understand these things.

But even here, in Muskegon, there are headwinds of change. At the farmers' market, there is now one stand that sells organic whole-bean coffee and makes pour-overs—the only place in town —while you wait. The owner, Dave, wears white Oakleys and speaks as though he learned about the artisanal revolution at a corporate convention. "The best places are those that have five things on the menu," he tells us. "Don't make it complicated, man. Just make it good." Across the street from the market is a farm-to-table restaurant where you can order sous-vide octopus and duck tortellini. A sister restaurant recently opened next door, Whistlepunk Pizza, a sparse, stone-oven joint whose ingredients list, scrawled on brown paper, includes maque choux and Swiss chard sourced from local farms. "Whistlepunk," reads the restaurant's website, "is an affectionate term given to the newest member of a logging camp."

Muskegon is, in fact, an old logging hub, a mill town once known as the Lumber Queen of the World. It's tempting to see in such gestures evidence of the hinterland becoming conscious, an entire region rising up to lay claim to its roots. It would be easier to believe this if the coveted look in *Brooklyn Magazine,* about ten years ago, were not called "the lumberjack."

There are places in the Midwest that are considered oases — cities that lie within the coordinates of the region but do not technically belong there. The model in this mode is Madison, Wisconsin, the so-called Berkeley of the Midwest. The comparison stems from the 1960s, when students stormed the campus to protest the Vietnam War. The campus mall is still guarded by foreboding Brutalist structures that were built during that era as an intimidation tactic. I taught in one of these buildings when I was in graduate school. The other TAs complained about them, claiming they got headaches from the lack of sunlight and the maze of asymmetrical halls. I found them beautiful, despite their politics. During my first day of class, I would walk my students outside to show them the exterior. I noted how the walls canted away from the street, evoking a fortress. I pointed out the narrow windows, impossible to smash with rocks. "Buildings," I told them, "can be arguments. Everything you see is an argument." The students were first-semester freshmen, bright and bashful farm kids who had come to this great metropolis — this Athens of the prairie — with the wholesome desire to learn.

Those buildings, like all the old buildings in town, were constantly under threat of demolition. Many of the heavy masonry structures had already been torn down to make way for condo high-rises, built to house the young employees of Epic — a healthcare software company that bills itself as the "Google of the Midwest." The corporate headquarters, located just outside town, was a legendary place that boasted all the hallmarks of Menlo Park excess: a gourmet cafeteria with chefs poached from five-star restaurants, an entire wing decorated to resemble Hogwarts. During the years I lived in Madison, the city was flush with new money. A rash of artisanal shops and restaurants broke out across town, each of them channeling the spirit of the prairie and its hardworking, industrial ethos. The old warehouses were refurbished into posh restaurants whose names evoked the surrounding countryside (Graze, Harvest). They were the kinds of places where ryes were served on bars made of reclaimed barn wood, and veal was cooked by chefs whose forearms were tattooed with Holsteins. Most of the factories in town had been turned into breweries, or the kind of coffee shops that resembled an eighteenth-century workshop—all the baristas in butcher aprons and engaged in what appeared to be chemistry experiments with espresso.

Meanwhile, the actual industry, unhidden in the middle of the downtown, looked as though it had never been used. There were gleaming aluminum silos and emissionless brick chimneys. In the prairie stockyards near my apartment, blue railroad cars were lined up like children's toys. Beyond the fences, giant coils of yellow industrial hose glimmered in the early morning light, as beautiful as Monet's haystacks. I doubt that any visitor would see in such artifacts the signs of progress, but when you live for any period in the Midwest, you become sensitive to the subtle process by which industry gives way to commerce, and utility to aesthetics.

Each spring arrived with the effulgent bloom of the farmers' market. The sidewalks around the capitol became flush with white flowers, heirloom eggs, and little pots of honey, and all the city came out in linen and distressed denim. There were food carts parked on the sidewalk, and a string quartet playing "Don't Stop Believin'," and my husband and I, newly in love, smoking on the steps of the capitol. We kept our distance from the crowds, preferring to watch from afar. He pointed out that the Amish men selling cherry pies were indistinguishable from the students busking in straw hats and suspenders. It was strange, all these paeans to the pastoral. In the coastal cities, throwbacks of this sort are regarded as a romantic reaction against the sterile exigencies of urban life. But Madison was smack in the middle of the heartland. You could, in theory, drive five miles out of town and find yourself in the great oblivion of corn.

In the early days of our relationship, we were always driving out to those parts, spurred by some vague desire to see the limits of the land—or perhaps to distinguish the simulacrum from the real. We would download albums from our teen years—*Night on the Sun, Either/Or*—and drive east on the expressway until the sprawl of subdivisions gave way to open land. If there was a storm in the forecast, we'd head out to the farmland of Black Earth, flying through the cropfields with all the windows down, the backseat fluttering with unread newspapers as lightning forked across the horizon.

Madison was utopia for a certain kind of Midwesterner: the Baptist boy who grew up reading Wittgenstein, the farm lass who secretly dreamed about the girl next door. It should have been such a place for me as well. Instead, I came to find the live bluegrass outside the co-op insufferable. I developed a physical allergy to NPR. Sitting in a bakery one morning, I heard the opening theme of *Morning Edition* drift in from the kitchen and started scratching my arms as though contracting a rash. My husband tried to get me to articulate what it was that bothered me, but I could never come up with the right adjective. Self-satisfied? Self-congratulatory? I could never get past aesthetics. On the way home from teaching my night class, I would unwind by listening to a fundamentalist preacher who delivered exegeses on the Pentateuch and occasionally lapsed into fire and brimstone. The drive was long, and I would slip into something like a trance state, failing to register the import of the message but calmed nonetheless by the familiar rhythm of conviction.

Over time, I came to dread the parties and potlucks. Most of the people we knew had spent time on the coasts, or had come from there, or were frequently traveling from one to the other, and the conversation was always about what was happening elsewhere: what people were listening to in Williamsburg, or what everyone was wearing at Coachella. A sizable portion of the evening was devoted to the plots of premium TV dramas. Occasionally there were long arguments about actual ideas, but they always crumbled into semantics. What do you mean by "duty"? someone would say. Or: It all depends on your definition of "morality." At the end of these nights, I would get into the car with the first throb of a migraine, saying that we didn't have any business discussing anything until we could, all of us, articulate a coherent ideology. It seemed to me then that we suffered from the fundamental delusion that we had elevated ourselves above the rubble of hinterland ignorance —that fair-trade coffee and Orange You Glad It's Vegan? cake had somehow redeemed us of our sins. All of us had, like the man in the parable, built our houses on sand.

A couple of weeks ago, there was a mass baptism in Lake Michigan. There is one at the end of each summer, though I haven't attended one in years. It was a warm night, and so my husband and I walked down to watch, along with my mother and my sister and her two-year-old daughter. The haze was thick that evening, and it wasn't until we were nearly upon the crowd that we could see it in its entirety: hundreds of people standing along the shore, barefoot like refugees in the sand. Out in the water, a pastor stood waist-deep with a line of congregants waiting their turn in the shallows. Farther down, there was another pastor standing in the lake with another line of congregants, and even farther down, near the rocks of the channel, a third stood with yet another line of people. The water was so gray and still, the evening air so windless, that you could hear the pastors' voices as they recited the sacramental formula: "Buried with Christ in baptism, raised to walk in the fullness of life." Whenever someone emerged from the water, everyone on the beach cheered and clapped as the congregant waded back through the mist like a ghost, his clothes suddenly thin and weighed down with water.

My mother saw someone she knew in the crowd and walked over to say hello. A small drone flew over the water, hovering over each of the pastors, and then darted along the shoreline. My sister pointed it out. "It must be filming," we decided. The beach was clean from a recent storm, empty except for some stray pieces of driftwood, bleached white and hewn smooth as whale bones. The seagulls were circling in frantic patterns, as though trying to warn us. Usually they glide over the beach in elegant arabesques, but there was no wind on this night, and they flapped like bats, trying to stay afloat.

The whole scene seemed to me like a Bruegel painting, a sweeping portrait of community life already distilled by time. I imagined scholars examining it many years in the future, trying to decipher its rituals and iconography. There was something beautiful in how the pastor laid his hands over each congregant's face, covering her hand with his own, something beautiful in the bewildered look on the congregant's face when she emerged from the water. Although I no longer espouse this faith, it's hard to deny the mark it has left on me. It is a conviction that lies beneath the doctrine and theology, a kind of bone-marrow knowledge that the Lord is coming; that He has always been coming, which is the same as saying that He will never come; that each of us must find a way to live with this absence and our own, earthly limitations.

The crowd erupted again in cheers. I was watching my niece run through the surf, watching my sister pretend to chase her. Each time the crowd cheered, she threw her hands above her head, as though it were for her. The drone made its way toward us, descended and hovered there, just above the water.

"That's unsettling," I said. The machine was idling above the water, appearing to stare us down. It was close enough that I could see the lens of its camera, a red light going on and off, as though winking at us.

"It knows we're not believers," my husband whispered.

"Let's go," I said. We made our way into the crowd, hoping to disappear within it. Everyone was dressed in brightly colored shirts and smelled of damp cotton. We passed my mother, who was laughing. The voices of the pastors carried irregularly across the water, and once we were deep in the crowd, their incantations seemed to overlap, as though it were one voice, rippling in a series of echoes. "Buried with Christ . . . Raised to walk in the fullness . . ." Things were ending and beginning again, just as everything is always ending and always beginning, and standing there amid the sea of people, I was reminded that it might not go on like this forever. We made our way to the shore, where the crowd thinned out and the sand was firm with water, and beyond the fog there appeared, on the horizon, the faintest trace of a sunset.

KAREN PALMER

The Reader Is the Protagonist

FROM *The Virginia Quarterly Review*

THE SUMMER OF 1989, shortly after my second husband and I married, we buckled my two daughters, who were seven and three, into the rear seat of a used car purchased for cash. We'd already sold most of our belongings and walked away from the rest, and packed the car's trunk with what remained: clothing and toys, pillows and blankets, four place settings, one pot, one pan. We told no one where we were going. We meant to disappear. Driving east out of California, we decided on our new names. If we hadn't been so shell-shocked, it might have been fun, the idea of starting over, starting fresh, in a place where we were unknown. But this was do-it-yourself witness protection. Hidden under the driver's seat was a book on how to create new identities, but it couldn't tell us who we'd *be*.

We stopped in Boulder, Colorado. My new husband had once spent a day in the town, and he remembered it as a friendly place. We drove around for a while. The brick downtown seemed quaint, the neighborhoods leafy and safe. A park with a fast-running creek appealed to the girls. I liked the idea of living near a university, with a tranquil campus, the prospect of lectures and music, young people everywhere.

From a phone booth outside a supermarket, we called a number we found in a real estate magazine. My new husband spoke to the realtor on duty, and within minutes he'd arranged a trade: a month's rent for painting a condo that was for sale. We were worried about money, about making what we had last. The realtor met us at the property. He opened up the garage, which was empty but for a few rollers and pans on a shelf, and five-gallon buckets of paint. The condo had two bedrooms, two baths. A concrete patio on the other side of sliding glass doors. The high-ceilinged living room echoed. Such a melancholy sound. The realtor handed over the key.

For a week it rained every day. The storms kept us inside, but also, we were afraid to go out much, afraid to be seen. My new husband and I rolled white paint onto the walls. The girls colored or watched television on a black-and-white set we'd picked up at Goodwill.

My three-year-old tugged at my legs. She had her blanket over her shoulders and a book in her arms: she wanted a story. For more than a year now, the demands of everyday life had required all my attention. I'd trusted only what I could touch, what I could see or hear or feel. I had two daughters to protect, and things I'd once believed essential had fallen away. Books were among the abandoned; one day, halfway through a beloved novel, I set it face-down, and that was the end of that. I couldn't read nonfiction, either, or newspapers, or magazines; that is, nothing meant for adults. My little daughter leaned against my legs. The older girl had joined us, her anticipation charging the air. Reading to my children—that, I could manage.

My mother read to me a lot when I was young. Our family life was often fraught: my father uncommunicative, physically absent, and emotionally cool; Mom either at his throat or steeped in hostile despair. Reading was her lifelong escape. One effect this had on me was that I believed that books were alive, not just the tales within them but the objects themselves. When I was seated in my mother's lap with a story, the stiffness of the cover told me what it was to have a spine. The words in their regular rows were like heartbeats; the pages, turning, fluttered like wings.

The story my daughters wanted was Jon Stone's *The Monster at the End of This Book*.

Grover, one of the characters from *Sesame Street*, is the narrator. Frightened by the monster that he imagines awaits him on the last page, he speaks directly to the reader: "Listen, I have an idea. If you do not turn any pages, we will never get to the end of this book."

Grinning, my daughters turned the page.

Grover ties the next page down with a rope. *Turn.* "You do not know what you are doing to me!" *Turn.* He nails the next page into place. He builds a brick wall. *Turn, turn.*

By the end the girls were giggling, breathless from the tension. It didn't matter that they'd heard this story so many times. Fall. Winter. Spring. "Please do not turn the page," Grover pleads. "Please please please."

Turn.

On the last page Grover cries: "Well, look at that! The only one here is . . . ME. I . . . am the Monster at the end of this book."

The real protagonist of the story is, of course, the reader. The subject is existential dread. Who is the monster, and what does it want, and how will it end?

In the living room, we sat cross-legged on the floor and watched rain fall onto the concrete patio. After a while, the clouds blew away, and we ventured out for a walk to a nearby drugstore. The sun dropped into the Rockies, bats flew through the tops of cottonwood trees. The wet grass looked electrified.

Longs Drugs, hunkered at the corner of Iris and Twenty-Eighth, was a beacon, cheerful, full of color and light. You could live out of that store, if you had to; it sold anything you might want in one place. We wandered the aisles. The girls played with makeup samples and inspected the display of discounted summer gear: boogie boards, sand pails and shovels, aluminum beach chairs.

For what beach? I wondered. The ocean was twelve hundred miles away. So was my ex-husband, my daughters' father. He was the reason we ran. I'd fallen in love with another man and left him, and he went off the rails. He stalked and threatened us. Months after the separation, he kidnapped our younger child.

California was still a year away from passing the nation's first antistalking law, written after a series of high-profile murders, including those of four women in Orange County who were killed by former lovers or former husbands or aspiring suitors. The new law would go beyond the limits of a temporary restraining order to prohibit persistent following and harassment, the threats of bodily harm that sometimes precede devastating violence. By 1993, all fifty states would have such statutes on the books.

But during the period it took to finalize my divorce, the authorities could do nothing to help. Even if they had, my ex-husband was unafraid of cops or courts, and I believe now, as I did then, that the threat of jail time would not have deterred him but rather inflamed his desire for revenge. I got my daughter back only by promising to give up someone else I loved, the man for whom I'd left him. That promise was a lie.

At Longs, my new husband parked himself by the magazines, a newspaper rolled under one arm. I stared down the rows of paperbacks. Romances, westerns, science fiction. A rack of *New York Times* best sellers. *Oh,* I thought. *Books.* Since childhood, they'd seen me through everything, been my teachers and companions, my family. Standing there, I felt the shape of their absence, but I was unmoved.

By the end of that first week in Boulder, I'd secured an interview for a position as a proofreader. The company was an "independent publisher," unnamed in the classified ad. I didn't recognize what a rarity the listing was. Colorado had just come out of a recession and the jobs section of the local paper was thin, most of the ads for food service and minimum-wage retail. In my former life I'd worked as a typesetter, or a secretary, and I felt qualified to proofread, but I was worried about being asked for references. On the phone, however, all I had to say was "English major," and the interviewer cut things short and requested that I come in.

The publisher was in a nondescript two-story building a few blocks north of Boulder's downtown mall. No signage out front, only a street number. The front door was locked. I rang the bell but no one came. I knocked but there was no answer. I loitered on the sidewalk. It was raining again but fitfully, the moisture disappearing in patches, like footprints erasing themselves. I rang the bell again. This time a shiny-haired young woman in jeans and a button-down shirt answered. "Hello, Karen," she said decisively. For a moment my mind went blank. She was, I realized, the first person ever to address me by that name.

She led me up a flight of stairs, into a room furnished with a conference table and chairs. We chatted briefly about the weather. "It's late in the summer for the monsoon," she said. I associated that word with the tropics, with flooding and disaster; surely that didn't happen here. The young woman said, "But everything changes after Labor Day." Her manner wasn't unfriendly, exactly, but it wasn't friendly, either. "What do you publish?" I asked.

Without answering, she lifted a typescript from a stack on the table and passed it over to me, along with a sharp red pencil. "We can get into that later," she said. "For now, I'd like you to go through this and mark it up for errors. Shouldn't take long."

When she was gone I skimmed the text, relieved to see that it was nothing technical. But when I returned to the opening sentence, the letters suddenly blurred. I couldn't make them cohere. And I panicked, thinking, *I really can't read.*

Calm yourself—I may have said it aloud. *Look at the spelling.* I ran a hand over the paper; it felt lightly furred, dry. I read the sentence again, concentrating, decided it was fine, and moved on to the next. I saw a mistake and marked the correction. In this way I worked through the pages. Finished, I set them aside. A preternatural quiet had descended, no sounds of conversation, no hum of office machinery. My mind emptied; the words from the pages were gone. Finally, the young woman returned. She collected the test and whisked it away.

Some minutes later, she came back in smiling. She led me into a second, smaller room. The walls here were lined with bookcases, the shelves packed tightly with softcovers, some workbook-sized and brightly colored, like study guides.

We sat in facing armchairs. Again, we chatted. The vibe now coming off her felt affable and benign. "Yes, we're new to Boulder," I said. "No, I don't ski." "Two kids—mostly, I've been home with them." I expected her to press me about my lack of work history, my inability to provide references, my nonexistent degree, everything I'd left back in California with my old name. But the young woman shrugged. "You passed the test. That's all we care about." She herself was a PhD candidate in classics. "We hire a lot of grad students," she said. "It's a nice group. If you have time today, I'd like you to meet Peder. He's the publisher."

Was it really going to be this easy? I couldn't believe my luck.

She handed me a pamphlet. The cover said PALADIN PRESS. "Have you heard of us?" she asked.

I had not.

"I'll leave you alone again for a while," she said. "You can browse through our catalogue. Have a look at the shelves. You'll get a sense of what we do here. If you're OK with it, we'll take the next step."

When she was gone, I opened the pamphlet. I don't know what

I expected, some dull corner of academia, or pornography, maybe; that would explain the building's security and the air of secrecy. In fact, most of Paladin's books were instructional. Some of the subjects seemed quirky, even fanciful: smuggling, soldiering, locksmithing, espionage. Others were devoted to life off the grid. How to hunt your own food, how to survive in the cold. How to disappear.

This last one forced me from my seat. We'd been here a week, and that guide to creating new identities was still in the car. My new husband had purchased it before we left California, from a survivalists' store in L.A., but we hadn't read it—at first because we were consumed with fear, and with getting away, and then because we were paralyzed by the enormity of what we'd done. That Paladin had published such a book was, I realized, only a bizarre coincidence, but it felt like a message to me.

I walked along the shelves, titles jumping out from the books' spines. *Get Even: The Complete Book of Dirty Tricks. 21 Techniques of Silent Killing. Black Medicine: The Dark Art of Death. Deadly Brew: Advanced Improvised Explosives. How to Kill Someone with Your Bare Hands.* My legs shook, a muscle in my cheek throbbed. *Hit Man,* I read: *A Technical Manual for Independent Contractors,* and pulled the book from its place.

When we were dating, my ex-husband used to say to me, "Baby, my life is an open book." He'd offer up candid stories about his difficult childhood in New York, his time in the army, his various jobs, some of which weren't entirely legal. My father was someone who was busy in the world but silent at home, and I grew up hungry for a man's words. My ex-husband, I believed, spoke the truth. After we married, however, things changed between us. If I complained about his anger or his drinking, his resentments or what I eventually realized were lies, he'd say, "Never judge a book by its cover." This shift in aphorisms was, I think, meant to undermine my feelings about his behavior, and to hint at unacknowledged "depths." And then one night he told me, "I once killed a man."

We were still living together then, though I'd begun the affair that would end us. He doled out the story of the murder at the tail end of a hellishly surreal fight that began with a dropped plate but soon enough was about everything. I started the fight, or he did;

I don't remember anymore. What I do remember is my desperate need to get away from what he was telling me, running from kitchen to living room to bedroom.

The man he claimed to have killed was someone he'd known back in New York who'd raped a neighborhood girl. The rape was, he said, common knowledge. The man had gotten away with it, the crime either unreported or investigated improperly. This, too, was also common knowledge, a story related in bars.

My ex-husband was then twenty-six, only a few weeks out of the army, unemployed and at loose ends. He ran into the rapist at a downtown drinking hole. The man was older but he'd been in the army, too, and he was also unemployed: they had things to talk about, and together shut the place down. Afterward, out on the sidewalk at 2:00 a.m., my ex-husband suggested a walk. They wound up at the East River. Staring into the water, feeling confidential, or avuncular, the rapist bragged about having "dated" the neighborhood girl. "Ugly women," he said, "they need love, too." My husband nodded, steering the man to the river's edge. Then he shot him and pushed the body in.

"It was easy," he told me. "Like tossing a piece of trash. No one saw. No one knew. No one ever even missed him."

He had me trapped in a corner of the bedroom.

"I don't believe you," I said defiantly.

He pincered my biceps until it burned. "*What you've done to me.*"

"You're a monster," I said.

The look on his face: he was astonished.

The change in him was instantaneous, remarkable. The whole *point,* he explained, ignoring my terrified moans, was that he'd killed the guy *for* the girl. He was a *hero.* Why couldn't I see it? "That fuck," he said, "got what he deserved."

In the light of the following day—making the girls their breakfast; overseeing tooth-brushing, and dressing; belongings collected, everybody into the car; a numbing drop down into our family routine—the story struck me as impossible in every detail, even laughable. Except for one thing: I knew he carried a gun. Was the murder true? In the years since, I've never been able to verify it. Maybe it happened by some other means, at some other time. Maybe the story was invented in every detail. Either way, it meant something to him. A killer, that's how he saw himself. It's how he wanted me to see him, as someone to be mortally feared. He was instructing me, in the clearest possible way, as to what he was capable of.

In March 1993 three people were murdered in Silver Spring, Maryland: Mildred Horn, a forty-three-year-old flight attendant; her quadriplegic eight-year-old son, Trevor; and Trevor's night nurse, Janice Saunders. Mildred and Janice were both shot through the eye with a .22 caliber rifle. The boy was killed in his bed, his tracheostomy opening blocked, his nose and mouth pinched off by a gloved hand.

Mildred Horn had told her family that if anything ever happened to her, they should look to her ex-husband, Lawrence T. Horn. Horn, a former Motown producer and recording engineer, had already tried to kill her, she claimed, and although he now lived three thousand miles away, in Hollywood, California, she feared he might yet manage it. Horn, floundering professionally and in serious debt, had become fixated on a $1.7 million medical settlement that was made on behalf of his son. He felt it manifestly unfair that Mildred controlled this money. He boasted to her about being the sort of man who could and would kill. He'd done it before. While in the service, he said, he'd pushed a fellow sailor off the deck of a ship and made it look like an accident.

But Lawrence Horn didn't shoot Mildred, or Janice, nor did he suffocate his disabled son. Instead, he hired out the deeds to James Edward Perry, a former street preacher and ex-con who, upon his release from prison, decided to become a hit man. At home in California at the time the murders were committed, Horn videotaped himself as he watched television, the camera lingering over a particular program's timestamp. Rather than exonerating him, this ham-handed tactic strengthened the argument for his guilt.

When Perry, the actual killer, was arrested, the police found in his possession a 130-page how-to guide published by Paladin Press: *Hit Man: A Technical Manual for Independent Contractors.*

On the book's cover, a man in a yellow suit and fedora holds a gun fitted with a silencer, his action stance superimposed over the outline of a downed body colored in red. The author is "Rex Feral." Long after I first heard of the case, I discovered that this was a pseudonym for a divorced mother of two who'd written the book because she needed money to pay her property taxes. *Hit Man* initially came in to Paladin as a novel, but the publisher convinced her to turn it into a handbook.

Some of the text is addressed directly to the reader:

> You are working. This is your job and you are a professional . . . When the time is right, make your move. Quietly. Efficiently . . . The kill is the easiest part . . . You made it! Your first job was a piece of cake! Taking all that money was almost like robbery. Here you are, finally a *real* hit man with *real* hard cash in your pockets and that first notch on your pistol.

Perry followed the book's instructions almost to the letter. The two bits of advice he ignored were what brought him down: he used his real name, rather than a false identity, to check into a Days Inn near Mildred Horn's home, and he made a traceable long-distance call.

Once Horn and Perry were convicted, the victims' families sued Paladin Press and its publisher, Peder C. Lund. Plaintiffs' attorneys outlined twenty-two specific similarities between *Hit Man* and the murders, arguing that the publisher's "speech," usually protected under the First Amendment, was in this case equivalent to aiding and abetting in the commission of a crime. Eventually, Paladin settled. The book was pulled in 1999 and Lund agreed to pay the families millions of dollars in compensation.

I am of two minds about this. Philosophically, I would fight to the bitterest of bitter ends for free speech, because if you love words, your only choice is to defend them. People with evil intent will always find a way to do what they want. Horn wanted to rid himself of his ex-wife and claim his son's settlement. Perry wanted a new criminal vocation. Neither required the information in *Hit Man* to fulfill their desires. Lund, I presume, wanted only the sales. But siding with Paladin Press feels like a betrayal of what I know to be true, that words can be dangerous; one way or another, there are always consequences. More pressingly, it feels like a betrayal of Mildred Horn. I might have been her, if I hadn't run.

But I'm mixing things up—that's part of the story, too, a certain confusion that has never been resolved. Because on the day I interviewed for the proofreading job, these murders were still four years in the future.

In that book-lined room at Paladin Press, I clutched *Hit Man* to my chest. Well, I held some book close. It's possible it was another title. I don't think it matters. My apprehension of the work Paladin was sending into the world, the ugliness of it, and how close to home, made me drop the book to the floor: the pages might have burst into flames. I ran out of the room, a matter of self-preservation. I rushed along the deserted hallway, down the stairs, out the front door, and onto the street.

My daughters' delight in *The Monster at the End of This Book* lasted for years, long past when it should have grown stale. There is such pleasure in fear, the thrill of being alive. In Jon Stone's story, the reader becomes the means by which poor Grover moves ever nearer his fate as well as the actual protagonist, the monster at the end of the book. Repeating the journey makes for another kind of pleasure, the ending always the same and therefore utterly, harmlessly known.

After the interview at Paladin Press, I picked up a pizza and returned to the condo. "How did it go?" my new husband asked. "I didn't get it," I said. He took the white box from me and set it on the kitchen counter and folded me up in his arms. The girls, drawn by the sound of my voice, buzzed around us. In that moment I felt so safe. My loved ones were right there. Later, after the girls went to bed, my husband and I would talk about Paladin. I'd tell him how suited I might have been for a job I could never do, because of that room where instruction on how to perpetrate violence kept company with guides on how to escape.

But now it was time to eat.

I cut up the pizza, my husband got out the dinner plates, the four of us sat cross-legged on the living room floor. Through the sliding glass doors we watched rain fall onto the concrete patio. When the clouds blew away, we walked the by-now-familiar blocks to Longs. In the periodicals aisle, my husband flipped through a magazine, the girls curled at his feet, absorbed in comics.

I stared down the display of paperbacks. Science fiction, westerns, romance. A countdown of *New York Times* best sellers. The books wanted only for someone to open them, that they might live.

We disappeared, I thought. I felt hollowed out, but also as if I might fill that empty space with anything.

I don't know what I pulled from the rack. Maybe *Cat's Eye*—I remember reading the novel that year. Maybe it was *Love in the*

Time of Cholera, or *Riding the Iron Rooster.* Or maybe it was one of those family sagas I'd liked so much as a teen, the cover fussy with cutouts and gold-embossed lettering.

I opened the pages and started to read.

When it was full dark, it was time to leave. We stood in line at the register, paid cash for ice-cream bars and an *Atlantic Monthly* and my paperback. Out on the street we all held hands. At the corner we stopped for a light. Cars came and went all around us, headlights and taillights shining white, shining red. We were out in the open, fully exposed, and I shivered, though it was summertime still. I dug in the bag for my paperback book, tucked it under one arm. The light changed and we crossed.

SARAH RESNICK

H.

FROM *n+1*

THERE IS A photo of you standing outside the house in Borough Park, grin wide, head back, laughing. Slender in faded blue jeans against the brick and white stucco, your hair a mass of thick black curls, a little unkempt. This was you: "the fun one." On our summer visits to New York, after the long drive south from Ontario, it is you I want to see most of all.

When your daughter was born, I was five. As I grew older I envied her for having you as a father. We rode the F train to Coney Island, surveying the city through painted windows; ate frankfurters on the boardwalk.

When I was twelve, your mother, my grandmother, passed. We stopped visiting New York. I didn't see or speak to you for fifteen years. By the time I went to college, it was apparent that no one knew where you were.

Suddenly in 2007 you call.

I am living in New York now. You tell your brother, my father, that you are living at a shelter on the Bowery. He comes to town soon after, and the three of us go out to dinner. We don't speak much of the past. You say you are doing well, and we agree to meet again soon. Your hair is cropped short and you are thin, very thin.

What surprises me most: you have no teeth.

You are not there when I stop by after work. The man at the desk gives me this news, not for the first time. I am tired of relying on luck in order to see you. On my next visit I bring you a prepaid cell phone so we can make plans in advance. This makes you happy.

We walk to B&H Dairy, where I order cold borscht and you cherry blintzes. I show you how to use the phone.

My father calls, tells me he has urgent news to share. *I always thought it was cocaine,* he says. *But it was heroin.* He repeats the last word, drawing out the first two syllables. He is wounded, disbelieving. The way his sibling foundered was worse than he had believed. Cocaine is nefarious, sure, but heroin is depraved. He is waiting for me to interrupt—to affirm that I, too, am appalled.

The first time we meet just the two of us, you tell me you have been diagnosed with bipolar disorder. I hardly believe it. You do not conform to any idea I have of a person with bipolar disorder, though the ideas I do have are received, not based on experience. It's just that you seem to me all right, not terribly different from the way I remember you, though your affect is flatter, hollowed. You wear your defeat.

You complain of ceaseless fatigue, a haze in your head. You list your medications: lithium, Topamax, prazosin, Thorazine, lorazepam, also methadone, more I am forgetting, they are always changing. Frankly I am astonished at, worried by, the number of medications you are taking. The lithium concerns me most. I know that it has dangerous side effects. I know that it is used in batteries. Never once does it occur to me that you seem all right because of the meds and not despite them. You are impressionable and take what I say seriously. The only people you talk to are social workers, counselors, medical doctors, psychiatrists, and you do not seek to inform yourself about your own condition. You are not a skeptic. You do not read. You trust what others tell you. The source is of no relevance.

Within weeks—or is it months?—your behavior seems to me more erratic. You are quick to anger. You demand things of me in your text messages. Usually money. I put fifty dollars' worth of minutes on your phone; the next day you've run out, ask for more. Three, four times in a week, you run out of minutes. I tell you it's too expensive to be using the phone in this way, and who are you talking to all of a sudden in any case? You say it is your friend Lenny. He is agoraphobic, you add. He rarely leaves the house. By now you think that I am trying to control you, to do you harm, and you begin making accusations. I get you a better phone plan, and for a few weeks, we do not speak.

Later you explain that you adjusted the dosage of your lithium without first telling your doctor. That was you in a manic phase.

I know better now.

Mostly we talk about your daughter, Sophie. She is twenty-one now and the mother of a boy, eighteen months. The father is a young naval officer with whom she has parted ways, but his parents take care of the baby often. You have not seen or spoken to Sophie since long before her son was born. She wants nothing to do with you. You have tried phoning her, you tell me, but she will not take your calls.

You know of her whereabouts, though, because you are in touch with the naval officer's parents. You call them regularly, hear the latest on Sophie and the baby. They must empathize with you, perceive good intentions. One day they allow you to visit when Sophie is not around. You meet your grandson and you are ecstatic. You talk about it for weeks.

Then one day you phone and they say they will no longer take your calls. They ask you not to call again, hang up.

I am optimistic. This phase will pass; Sophie will come to see that you have changed. I think I know you will be reunited.

We like eating at B&H Dairy and return there often. Today I bring you *Tompkins Square Park,* a recent book of black-and-white photographs by Q. Sakamaki. In 1986 Sakamaki moved from Osaka, Japan, to the East Village. Throughout the 1980s and '90s, he documented the park and its surrounding streets, then a gathering place for the city's marginalized and homeless and a stronghold of the antigentrification movement.

We turn the pages, examine the pictures. I ask you what it was like. You tell me about when you loitered outside an abandoned building turned shooting gallery, waiting in line to buy your next fix. Police officers approached you, but you were neither questioned nor arrested. Instead, they emptied your pockets, took your money. They took everyone's money. Then they left.

It is difficult to know whether your memory is reliable, whether you can be relied on. But I have no reason not to believe you.

*

Today is a good day for you. You get new teeth. You are more confident.

July 2013. My eye lands on a headline in the *New York Times:* "Heroin in New England, More Abundant and Deadly." I can't recall
the last time I saw heroin in the news. Media coverage of drug use
had shifted, or so it seemed to me, to meth.

Officials in Maine, New Hampshire, and Vermont, from "quaint
fishing villages" to "the interior of the Great North Woods," are
reporting an "alarming comeback" of "one of the most addictive
drugs in the world." What's remarkable about the story, according
to its authors, is where the comeback is taking place: not in urban
centers, but in the smaller cities and rural towns of New England.
Experts offer observations. A police captain in Rutland, Vermont,
states that heroin is the department's "biggest problem right now."
A doctor, an addiction specialist, says, "It's easier to get heroin in
some of these places than it is to get a UPS delivery."

Most of the heroin reaching New England originates in Colom-
bia and comes over the U.S.-Mexico border. Between 2005 and
2011 the number of seizures jumped sixfold—presumably in part
because of increased border security—but plenty of heroin still
got through. In May 2013 six people were arrested in connection
with a $3.3 million heroin ring in Springfield and Holyoke, Mas-
sachusetts.

The article describes two addicts in particular, both young
women. They sell sex for drug money. One overdosed and died
after injecting some very pure heroin. The addiction specialist tells
us that he is "treating 21-, 22-year-old pregnant women with intravenous heroin addiction." The lone man identified is the companion of one of the women. Beyond his name and age, nothing
about him or his circumstances is mentioned. All three are white.

I stop when I read, "Maine is the first state that has limited access to specific medications, including buprenorphine and methadone." I open a new tab, search for what the writers mean by the
vague phrase "has limited access to." Earlier that year, the state
enacted legislation to limit how long recovering addicts could stay
on methadone, or similar drug-replacement therapies, before they
had to start paying out of pocket. Medicaid patients will receive
coverage for a maximum of two years. I know that for some people, like you, this is not enough time.

Moving to the United States from Canada was, for me, eight years earlier, an easy enough transition. Much is shared between the two countries, and the culture shock was minimal. Yet even after all this time, I still find that certain ideas I'd taken for granted throughout adolescence and early adulthood—ideas about what a good society tries to make available for its citizens—are here not to be taken for granted at all.

At the Bowery shelter you are a model resident. You participate in group. You see a counselor. You follow the methadone program. You are friendly with others. It is on account of this that you are recommended for Section 8 housing, and before long you are moved into a two-hundred-square-foot studio with a single bed, a private bathroom, a tiny kitchen. The facility, a four-story building, is designated for people living with psychiatric disabilities. Your share of the rent is $260. You are also responsible for your own utilities. These are subsidized based on your income.

For a time you find yourself in a vexing predicament. The state has deemed you "unfit to work." But each of your applications for disability benefits is denied. It is not at all clear how you are meant to survive.

November 2013. The front page of the Saturday paper features a story on buprenorphine under the headline "Addiction Treatment with a Dark Side." Buprenorphine is an opioid used for maintenance therapy like methadone, but is available by prescription. This is new. Since the 1970s, methadone has been distributed through clinics. People participating in methadone programs must go to the clinic at least once a week, and in some cases every day. This is obstructive, even oppressive. A similar drug that can be had by prescription seems like an improvement. But doctors must receive federal certification to be able to prescribe buprenorphine. Federal law limits how many patients a physician can help with the drug at one time. This means that only people with good insurance, or the ability to pay high fees out of pocket, can access it. "The rich man's methadone," the article calls it.

But this—the part that interests me—isn't what the article is about. The article is about how the drug gets "diverted, misused and abused"; how, since 2003, the drug has led to 420 deaths. (By comparison, there are more than 15,500 deaths from opioid

overdose each year.) The article is not about the drug's demonstrated efficacy at helping people with opioid dependencies that
negatively impact their lives. Or about how restricted access to the
drug is likely contributing to its diversion and misuse in the first
place. Studies report that at least some people are self-treating
their dependencies and withdrawal symptoms. I read elsewhere
that medication-assisted treatment with an opioid agonist, such as
buprenorphine, is the most effective treatment available for opioid dependencies.

This is what you tell me: From the time you were young, you possessed an antiauthoritarian streak. This disposition did not emerge
from any particular maltreatment, by family members, say, or teachers; it was your natural orientation toward the world. You were enthralled by the neighborhood kids who attracted trouble even as
you yourself did not act out. You desired proximity to danger and
rebelliousness. Unlike your brother, you attempted to differenti-
ate yourself from your family not by transcending your class, but
by assuming a posture of nonconformity. You liked drugs because
you weren't supposed to like them. For a long time—more than
a decade—you were able to manage your use, to keep it, for the
most part, recreational.

One time your father found your needle and other supplies for
shooting up. He was furious. You wouldn't hear it. When he died
years later his heart was still broken.

I have difficulty reconciling all this with what else you have told
me of your past. I know that you worked for the police as a 911 dis-
patcher. You were good at your job, liked and respected, and soon
you found yourself in a supervisory position. You enjoyed the night
shift, especially, and for a long stretch the Bronx was your district.
The position is notoriously stressful, but you were sharp, capable,
levelheaded, and you excelled.

You were fired when your fidelity to heroin was stronger than it
was to your job.

You love your new apartment, can't believe your good fortune.
When I stop to consider it, neither can I.

Sometimes I imagine what you will do with your time. I picture you
as a volunteer—with other people who use drugs, maybe, or at a

food kitchen or shelter. I feel certain that you will want to do this, that you will do something good, in the way that others did good for you. That maybe we will do something good together. Once, when I am volunteering on American Thanksgiving, I invite you to come along. I know that you have nowhere else to go. You tell me you'd prefer to stay home. A few months later, I make the suggestion once more. Again you decline.

Later I come to recognize this as my own bizarre fantasy, a projection of my savior complex, perhaps. I laugh, not for the first time, at the naïveté of my younger self.

December 2013. Two articles command my attention. The first, a few weeks old, is about a radical clinical trial in Canada comparing the effectiveness of diacetylmorphine — prescription heroin — and the oral painkiller hydromorphone, i.e., Dilaudid, in treating severe heroin dependency in people for whom other therapies have failed. An earlier study in Canada had demonstrated that both diacetylmorphine and hydromorphone are better than methadone at improving the health and quality of life of longtime opiate users. An unexpected finding was that many participants couldn't tell the difference between the effects of diacetylmorphine and hydromorphone. But the sample group receiving hydromorphone wasn't large enough to draw scientifically valid conclusions. So the study investigators created a new trial to test this finding. If hydromorphone were to be found as effective as diacetylmorphine, it could mean offering people the benefits of prescription heroin without the legal barriers and associated stigma. The study results have yet to be published.

Larry Love, sixty-two, a longtime dependent: "My health and well-being improved vastly" during the trial. Love's doctor applied to Health Canada for permission to continue prescribing heroin to Love and twenty other patients after their year in the trial was up. The applications were approved, although renewal was required after ninety days. The federal health minister responded by creating new regulations to prevent such approvals. He insisted Ottawa would not "give illicit drugs to drug addicts." Love, four additional patients, and the health-care center that runs the hospital that oversaw the trial are suing the government in turn. The doctor who submitted the applications, Scott MacDonald: "As a human being, as a Canadian, as a doctor, I want to be able to offer this treatment to the people who need it . . . It is effective, it is safe, and it works . . . I do not know what they are thinking."

The second is an editorial about a Canadian bill that, if passed, would set new guidelines for opening supervised-injection facilities. Like syringe-distribution programs, supervised-injection facilities act as a frontline service for people who use drugs intravenously, giving out sterile needles and other paraphernalia. But they go one step further: users may bring in drugs procured elsewhere and inject them under the watchful eye of trained nurses. Staff members offer instruction on safer technique ("Wash your hands," "Remove the tourniquet before pushing the plunger," "Insert the needle bevel up") and monitor for overdose, which they counteract with naloxone. They do not directly administer injections.

The new law would erect application hurdles so onerous it would effectively prevent the establishment of any new sites. The columnist attacks the government for acting on ideological rather than scientific grounds. "Supervised injection sites are places where horrible things take place." I cringe a little. "The fact is, however, that these activities are even more horrifying when they take place in the streets, and strict prohibition has never been even remotely successful."

There is, I know, only one such facility in all of North America. It's called Insite, and it's in Vancouver.

It is a fall evening and we are on our way to a movie. We pass a small group of Chabad men on the street. It is Sukkot and they are trying to identify secular Jews by sight, inviting them to perform the ritual with the date-tree fronds (*lulav*) and lemonlike fruit (*etrog*), shaking them together three times in six different directions. They have a small truck nearby (the Sukkahmobile). You tell me how a Chabad man befriended you once, how you almost became religious. He wanted to help you, and you had no one else. You went to dinners at his house. He would call to ask how you were. You say that he and his family were some of the kindest people you had ever met. But you couldn't stick with it, and one day you stopped responding.

I take you to see *Ballast,* that film of austere, understated realism about a drifter boy and a grieving man in the Mississippi Delta. It's more about tone than narrative, and I am moved by the beauty and sadness of its barren landscapes. I worry that you are bored, you nod in and out; but afterward you tell me how much you liked it. I decide I will take you to movies often.

Within weeks of Philip Seymour Hoffman's death, a surfeit of reporting:

> Why Heroin Is Spreading in America's Suburbs
> How Did Idyllic Vermont Become America's Heroin Capital?
> New England Town Ripped Apart by Heroin
> Today's Heroin Addict Is Young, White and Suburban
> Heroin's New Hometown: On Staten Island, Rising Tide of Heroin Takes Hold
> When Heroin Use Hit the Suburbs, Everything Changed
> Heroin in the Suburbs: A Rising Trend in Teens
> Heroin Reaching into the Suburbs
> Heroin Scourge Overtakes a "Quaint" Vermont Town
> Heroin-Gone-Wild in Central New York Causes Jumps in Overdoses, Deaths
> Actor's Heroin Death Underscores Scourge Closer to Home
> Heroin Scourge Begs for Answers
> New Wisconsin Laws Fight Scourge of Heroin
> The Scourge of Heroin Addiction
> Heroin Scourge Cuts Across Cultural and Economic Barriers
> Colombian, Mexican Cartels Drive LI Heroin Scourge
> Senate Task Force Hears from Rockland on Heroin Scourge
> Report Shows Heroin Use Reaching Epidemic Proportions in NH
> America's Heroin Epidemic: A St. Louis Story
> Heroin: Has Virginia Reached an Epidemic?
> United States in the Grips of a Heroin Epidemic
> Cheap, Plentiful, Deadly: Police See Heroin "Epidemic" in Region
> How Staten Island Is Fighting a Raging Heroin and Prescription-Pill Epidemic
> A Call to Arms on a Vermont Heroin Epidemic
> Fighting Back Against the Heroin Epidemic
> Ohio Struggles with "Epidemic" of Heroin Overdoses
> Cuomo Adds 100 Officers to Units Fighting Heroin
> Governors Unite to Fight Heroin in New England
> Police Struggle to Fight America's Growing Heroin Epidemic
> DuPage Officials Suggest Laws to Fight Heroin
> Taunton Launches Plan to Fight Heroin After Dozens of Overdoses

There are many more I don't write down.

*

Your disability application is finally approved. You will receive monthly Social Security payments of $780. You are also entitled to the disability that has accrued from the time of your first denied application, which, because it was several years ago, now amounts to several thousand dollars.

There is one condition, however. The state has decided that, given your history, you are unfit to oversee your own finances. You will need someone who can demonstrate gainful employment, preferably a family member, to tend to the money on your behalf.

On a winter morning, early, I take the bus from Prospect Heights to the Social Security office in Bushwick. We have an appointment but we wait a long time. I sign where I am asked to. I attest to my reliability. I assume responsibility.

Soon after I set up a bank account where I am your "representative payee." Your money is deposited to it on the first of each month. From this account I pay your rent, your utilities. We meet every week or two, for food, for a movie, but always so that I can provide you with cash for provisions.

This works for a while.

On the phone one day you tell me you hurt your arm, a man on the street walked right into you, knocked you down to the ground. When I call a few days later to see how you are feeling, you tell me how strange it is, nearly every guy you pass on the street is eyeing you as if he wants to start a fight. These men, they are always brushing up against you on purpose.

Within a week, maybe two, you begin to ramble about the lock on your door, how it's broken, and how you're sure someone is breaking into your apartment to spy on you. You tell me that one day you came home to find a syringe on the floor. Someone planted it there for a supervisor to find, you're certain of it, other residents want your apartment, they want you gone.

I suggest various ways you might resolve these issues. You have excuses, explanations for why each of my recommendations won't work. I ask a lot of questions. Your paranoia does not involve state secrets, the CIA or FBI, tinfoil hats or aliens, the twin towers or global-government conspiracy theories, but the elevation of small anxieties and fears to delusions of persecution. I try reasoning with you, but sometimes, in order to empathize, I must suspend my desire to be rational and take part in your fantasy world. I learn there is nothing I can do for you; you are autonomous in overseeing your own health care. I encourage you to see your psychiatrist and wait. Once your medication is adjusted, you are no longer afraid.

Not long after your disability payments kick in, the debt collectors send notices to my apartment. One is on behalf of an old landlord who, years ago, sued you for rent payments you never made. It has been more than a decade, but this debt has not been forgotten. I mail a check.

Here are some things you might do on a given day: Walk to the methadone clinic to pick up your dose (you are required to go three times a week). Wait in line. Take one bus to the Medicaid office (when your pension kicked in, your monthly benefits went up, pushing you just slightly over the minimum-income requirement). Wait in line. Take one bus to see your psychiatrist (you live in Bushwick; your psychiatrist is in Crown Heights). Wait. Take one bus to the Supplemental Assistance Program office (you lost your EBT card and need to request a new one). Wait in line. Take two trains to see your hepatologist at NYU Langone Medical Center. Wait. Walk to the post office (to pick up the check my father has sent you). Wait in line. Walk to the nearest Western Union (where you would cash checks before you had a bank account). Wait in line. Take the bus and two trains to Maimonides Medical Center in Borough Park (you need a colonoscopy). Wait.

I write down statistics, try to make sense of what I'm reading. In 2012 U.S. physicians wrote 240.9 million prescriptions for painkillers, an increase of 33 percent since 2001. The growth can be attributed to a few related factors: patient-advocacy groups calling for better pain treatment; patients, perhaps influenced by pharmaceutical marketing, requesting drugs from their doctors; doctors, some with questionable ethics, overprescribing drugs.

The U.S. government responded in a predictable way. It introduced more stringent prescription guidelines, authorized DEA investigations and closures of "pill mills." State governments began to use databases to track "doctor shoppers," patients who sought out prescriptions from multiple physicians.

In 2010 Purdue Pharma, the producer and patent holder of OxyContin, introduced an abuse-deterrent version of the drug ostensibly impervious to crushing, breaking, chewing, and dissolving, and therefore more difficult to inhale or inject.

That same year, the number of U.S. drug poisoning deaths involving any opioid analgesic (oxycodone, methadone, or hydrocodone) accounted for 43 percent of the 38,329 drug poisoning deaths, a fourfold increase from 1999, when opioid analgesics were involved in 24 percent of the 16,849 drug poisoning deaths.

Following the government crackdown, supply of pharmaceutical opioids decreased sharply. Demand did not. The street price of prescription painkillers inflated, and many pharmaceutical opioid users opted instead for heroin. A rising supply of heroin kept prices low.

According to one study, more than 81 percent of recent heroin users say they switched after first trying prescription painkillers.

You say that one day, out of the blue, you decided to give it up. Just like that.

You call at around eleven on a weeknight to tell me you are going to call an ambulance—you are in pain. Ten days earlier you had surgery on an abdominal hernia. The procedure was supposed to have been minimally invasive, performed with a scope, a few hours all told, and I waited to take you home. But there were complications. They had to cut you open. You were admitted to the hospital, stayed seven nights. Now you are home again but certain that you are not healing properly. When I arrive at your place in Bushwick, the paramedics are helping you into the back of the ambulance. I get in with you. We sit opposite each other. I ask you questions. You are lucid. I expected you to be doubled over, but you are not. The paramedics confirm that your vitals are good. You have no fever. At this point, I am confident that this trip is unnecessary; that there is nothing to worry about except that you are alone, and you understand what that means. But I stay silent as you tell the paramedics to take you to where you want to go.

When we arrive at the emergency room, the triage nurse evaluates you. You tell her about your pain, your recent surgery. Soon you are wearing a bracelet and gown, sound asleep in a bed. It is past midnight. I sit in the vinyl sled-base chair to read, but am more interested in the ER nurses shuffling through the ward, the gurneys wheeling by, bodies and machines, the perverse game of observation and diagnosis. Who among the patients holds the fate worse than all the others? I know that if you're asleep the pain is not as bad as you said it was.

Not far from your bed, just outside the curtain, a young man in a wheelchair, his neck slackened, his chin drooping close to the chest, vomits. It's viscous, like cake batter. It pours out of his mouth and covers the front of his gown. He is unconscious and makes barely any sound. Now is a good time for a walk. I head outside, buy some chips from the gas station.

When I return, the young man has been moved to the center of the ward, where, shuddering now, he continues to vomit. The former contents of his abdomen pool and spread on the floor. A nurse approaches. I point to the man and ask whether something might be done for him. The nurse frowns, tells me that the man is getting what he deserves; he has done this to himself. She walks away. Several nurses pass the gurney, but no one looks at the man.

It is 4:00 a.m. by the time the doctor sees you. Everything is fine, he tells us. By now the chaos of the ER has quieted. You slept right through it.

Tomorrow, I will get up early and go into work at an office.

For the first time, I resent you.

The morning I visit Insite I awake to a winter sun, a rare reprieve from Vancouver rain. It is still early when I take the bus downtown. The buildings glimmer gold and red under the warming light.

I decided to come here, to make the long trip to Vancouver, because I wanted to see Insite for myself. I wanted to see the place where people who use drugs intravenously can go to inject more safely, the place where, according even to the supportive editorial I'd read earlier, "horrible things take place." By then I had read enough about supervised injection to know that I thought it less horrible than humane. There is much else for which I would reserve the word "horrible," including the treatment by law enforcement of people who use drugs.

Between 1992 and 2000 more than 1,200 fatal overdoses were recorded in Vancouver. Many of these took place in the Downtown Eastside, a neighborhood of ten or so square blocks where more than 4,600 people who inject drugs intravenously were known to live. The HIV conversion rate was the highest in the Western world. (This was due in part to the popularity in Vancouver of using cocaine intravenously: cocaine has a very short half-life, and people injecting the drug habitually might do so as many as forty times a day, as compared with heroin, which tends to be injected one to four times a day.) The city, recognizing that American-style prohibition had failed to bring about any improvement, undertook a kind of crash course on drug policy. A succession of public forums, meetings, demonstrations, and conferences with experts from all over the world brought together drug users and their families, service providers, academic researchers, police, and policymakers to examine alternative approaches—heroin-prescription programs, supervised-injection sites, decriminalization.

In 2003 Insite opened as a pilot research program, exempt from the criminal code. It was not the only new service offered in the city, and it was "no silver-bullet solution," a disclaimer Canadian policymakers, activists, and other supporters used often to describe its alternative approaches. But because it seemed to stand at the threshold of what progressive-minded people deemed acceptable—because, for many, it seemed intuitively *wrong*—it received the most attention, and was widely discussed both province- and nationwide. This, too, interested me. Most Vancouver residents initially opposed the facility but came to support it; this took a lot of convincing, and a shift in the way people understand illegal drugs and those who use them. I wanted to know how this had happened.

In 2006 the Conservative Party in Canada won the national election, ousting the Liberals. For the first time since 1993, Canada had a Conservative prime minister; from the start, he began dismantling the country's social programs. Early on, Insite became a battleground for drug policy across the country. The government tried to shut it down, but the Portland Hotel Society (now PHS Community Services Society), the nonprofit group that runs Insite, mounted a human rights case and took it to the Supreme Court. In 2011 Insite won the right to stay open.

Still, I wondered how long it could last. I wanted to know, too, if something like it could ever exist in the United States.

At 9:00 a.m. five men and women sit on the sidewalk on flattened cardboard boxes, first in line to enter when the doors open in an hour. Outside I meet Russ Maynard, Insite's program coordinator. He's with several college students from a health-administration program, there on a class visit.

As a group, we walk through the reception area into the injection room. At first glance, it reminds me of a hair salon. The room is wide and bright, lined on one side by mirrors and a row of numbered bays, thirteen in all. Each has a stainless-steel counter, a sink for hand washing, a sharps container, a plastic chair, and an extraction hood to collect smoke and vapors.

A platform with a curvilinear counter, the kind you see in hospitals, is raised behind the booths. Lining the countertop are bins that contain all the supplies a person would need to inject drugs —a syringe, a cooker for mixing the drug with water, a sterilized-water capsule for flushing the needle, a tourniquet to tie off a vein. There is, too, a tool for crushing pills.

In the injection room, we arrange our chairs in a loose semi-circle around Russ, who stands. Russ begins his introduction. Insite is operated by Vancouver Coastal Health, the regional health authority, and PHS Community Services Society, a neighborhood nonprofit that focuses on the hard-to-house. PHS started in 1991, after a residents association converted a hotel into housing for the homeless. Today it provides residences for 1,200 people across sixteen buildings.

PHS also provides a range of community-based programs, including a credit union, a community drop-in center, medical and dental services, a syringe exchange, and an art gallery. Users of Insite can access all this simply by coming in, and to get them to come in is Insite's goal. Making contact is the first step toward connecting people, at their request, to vital services they might need. They call the people who use their services "clients."

Russ presents the group with a moral dilemma. "Imagine you're working at the front desk and a woman walks in and she's eight months pregnant, and she wants to come in and inject. You have to make a quick decision. If the line starts getting backed up, there's going to be an argument, or maybe worse. So what's going to happen?"

The room is silent.

I try to visualize the scenario, but it tests the limits of my open-mindedness. It is difficult to imagine supporting a pregnant woman's injection-drug habit.

"Is she going to leave and the clouds will part and the sunshine will hit her face and she'll see the error of her ways and never use again? Or is she going to take some equipment and go use in an alley or a doorway or a hotel room or something like that? If you do take her in, you can connect her with the nursing staff. You can have her housed by the end of the day. You can connect her with food, with services, all kinds of things. And you forgo all of that if you turn her away."

Someone asks about the mirrors. They are a critical design feature, says Russ. Staff use them to monitor clients while maintaining a respectful distance. Clients use them to ensure a certain amount of caution when injecting—to pay more attention to doing it properly. Russ: "You want it in your veins. Because there's a big wash —imagine a wave coming to hit you—and you won't feel anything for a little while. And if you make a mistake, it means that you have to go back out and perform sex work, or beg, or steal, or whatever it is you do to get the ten dollars you need. And that is stressful."

Since 2007 the staff at Insite has been able to refer visitors to Onsite, a detox center on the building's second floor. There are twelve private rooms, each with its own bathroom. Insite connects between 400 and 450 people each year to detox, which, Russ claims, is more than any other project in Canada.

The students leave. One at a time, men and women, young, old, homeless, ordinary, are called in from the waiting room. As they enter, they announce the drug they will be injecting: "down," "dillies," "crystal" (heroin, Dilaudid, methamphetamine). The receptionist records their answers in a database, in case of emergency or overdose.

I watch the mirrors from across the room. A stately man in a wool sweater, navy with white snowflakes, drags a fine-tooth comb through his silvery hair, from the top of his forehead back to his nape. He does this twenty or thirty times before tending to his mustache with the same fastidiousness, never breaking focus. Then he pulls a woolen cap over his head and walks out into the sun.

A young nurse examines the arms of a fiftysomething woman. The woman looks afraid. The nurse speaks in soft tones as she runs her hands along the woman's forearms, helps her to locate a vein that isn't damaged, scarred, or collapsed. The nurse ties a tourniquet around her biceps. They both pause. The woman, hand trembling, inserts the needle. The nurse removes the tourniquet. The woman pushes the plunger.

Hours later, I see the same woman on the bus, traveling along Hastings Street. I want to speak to her, consider doing so, even as I know it's not right (privacy). But the woman is with a friend. Instead I watch her, imagine where she's going, how she will spend her time, what her home is like. If anyone awaits her there.

The woman gets off the bus.

I ask Russ whether he knows any clients who might be willing to speak with me. He hesitates. Donovan Mahoney is doing well, he says. He puts me in touch. Now I am in Donovan's living room. We sit opposite each other, on separate couches. A series of photographs he has taken hangs on the wall above his head. Today Donovan is a talented photographer. His apartment, the garden level of a house in a middle-class neighborhood, is spacious, with a chef's kitchen and newly laid blond hardwood floors. He wears khaki pants and a gray sweater, slim-fitting with an overlapping V-neck. A baseball cap covers his partially shaved head of thick black hair.

Donovan tells me the story of his twenties: he followed a girl to Vancouver, fell into coke, then rock cocaine, then heroin. He'd always thought heroin was dirty, but after trying it for the first time he felt its reputation was undeserved.

For a while he made money as a dealer. When he wanted to binge, he would go to the Downtown Eastside, stay in an SRO hotel where no one would find him. Then one time he didn't go home. He let his monthly rent payments pass, grew paranoid. He left behind all his belongings, including his car. This was in 2001. He lived on the streets, mostly. He didn't like to feel closed in by walls, especially when he was high. He shoplifted, was caught often, spent many nights in jail.

He was wary of Insite when he first heard about it. On the street, he knew that everyone was working an angle. There's a forthrightness to interactions that doesn't exist elsewhere. He found it freeing. But he couldn't understand what would motivate the staff at Insite.

Now he credits them for helping him to achieve all that he has.

Donovan: "They're inadvertently showing you that there's another way of life. You start to have normal conversations. You say
to them, 'What do you do?' They reply, 'I don't know, I'm in a
band.' Of course they are. And then they tell you stuff about what
they do with their girlfriend. Or how they went away for the weekend and saw their parents. To me, to an addict, they're showing
me something. There's a whole other world out there that I don't
even understand. They're showing you what it looks like to be a
normal human being. Which is incredible, because if I'm shooting
dope in an alley, I may bump into somebody who's been through
recovery, and they may be able to guide me. But they're not going
to be around when you need them.

"Addiction isn't nine to five. It's not like, 'OK, tomorrow at ten
o'clock I'm going to go into recovery.' It happens and you don't
really see it coming. It's like, *I think right now, if you guys got me in,
I think I could go.*"

You want to be in charge of your own money. It is frustrating to
have to travel to me every time you run out of cash. Together we
visit your social worker, talk about how this could work. He needs
to make a recommendation to your psychiatrist, to the state, before this can happen. We review your history. For the first time it is
affirmed to me that you are likely to take methadone all your life.
The social worker mentions your dose—120 mg—says it's high,
that you haven't decreased it since beginning the therapy. You acknowledge as much. Still, it has been stabilizing, and the social
worker is not concerned.

I tell the social worker that I will share the bank account with
you, monitor your spending. Satisfied, he makes the recommendation. We open a joint account. Your monthly checks will be deposited and you will be responsible for paying your bills, for making
sure you have enough to get through the month. I will check on
the account through online banking. I keep your savings, a few
thousand dollars left over from the disability back payments, in a
separate account in your name.

For a year, at least, you manage all right.

I know that, in the late '80s and '90s, the rapid spread of HIV
through needle sharing galvanized U.S. activists to challenge state

laws and distribute hypodermic syringes for free, without a prescription; that the rate of new HIV cases in Vancouver among intravenous drug users persuaded even conservative politicians to
consider opening a supervised-injection site; that were it not for
the HIV epidemic, many drug-policy reforms in the U.S. and elsewhere might not have occurred.

I find it curious how few articles on the emerging "epidemics"
—heroin, opioid—mention the disease. I wonder whether it is
because, with antiretrovirals so widely available, HIV is perceived
to be less threatening than it once was. I chase the question for
a time. I print out medical papers, underline findings. I call an
epidemiologist at a prestigious university, who answers my questions patiently. He tells me that some of the best research is being
done by an epidemiologist in Kentucky, who has been following
a cohort of intravenous drug users since 2008. (Appalachia has
disproportionately high rates of nonmedical prescription-opioid
use and overdose-related deaths.) No one in the cohort had yet
been diagnosed HIV positive, but 70 percent have hepatitis C. I
ask why this matters, and he says that rising hepatitis C rates often
forecast HIV outbreaks, because the viruses spread through the
same behaviors—unprotected sexual intercourse and needle sharing—and both require a certain density of drug users to sustain
transmission. But hep C is ten times more infectious, can live outside the body longer, and is extremely difficult to kill; it spreads
more easily. A hepatitis C outbreak indicates that all the factors are
present for an HIV outbreak.

In many ways, it's a ticking time bomb, the epidemiologist says,
especially since, in rural Appalachian communities, knowledge
about HIV tends to be minimal; these populations have not previously had to deal with the disease.

I hang up the phone, look up the data set that tracks syringe-
distribution programs by state. Kentucky, 0; Tennessee, 0; Georgia,
1; South Carolina, 0; North Carolina, 6; Alabama, 0; Mississippi, 0;
Ohio, 2; Virginia, 0; West Virginia, 0; Pennsylvania, 2; New York,
22; Maryland, 1.

You are weak and exhausted, have been for months. Every time we
make plans, you cancel. Months pass and I don't see you. When
by routine appointment you see your hepatologist, he sends you

to the emergency room. You will need a blood transfusion to give you the hemoglobin that you need. By the time I arrive, the blood has been ordered from the bank, is being warmed. We wait for hours. The transfusion itself will take hours, too. I leave you there alone.

Before I go, the doctor tells me that what you are experiencing is a complication from hepatitis C.

We sit at your kitchen table beside the four-drawer wooden dresser, its surface lined with pill vials and bottles of methadone. I tell you about Insite. You appear bewildered, shocked even. "How can that possibly help anyone get off drugs?"

Your first reaction resembles most people's, but it's not what I want you to say. I want you to argue that getting people off drugs need not be the primary goal. I want you to be critical of the status quo—of the morass of law and policy in which you and millions of others are entangled. But you are not. You have only ever been exposed to one idea, one approach: abstinence.

I explain it to you this way: that the most serious harms that arise from drug use—HIV, endocarditis, tetanus, septicemia, thrombosis—come not from the drugs but from external factors. Of all the ways to administer drugs, injecting carries the most risks. The drug solution bypasses the body's natural filtering mechanisms against disease and bacteria. Access to sterile equipment and hygienic injection conditions can mean the difference between living and dying.

I say, thinking you might relate, that policing has an especially devastating effect on people who use drugs intravenously and are entrenched in street life. When they fear the police, they don't stop using, they just move elsewhere—to neighboring areas, where they may create new syringe-sharing networks, or to hidden or indoor locations. In such places, needle sharing is more common, because access to clean needles is cut off. When police are around, users avoid carrying clean needles, for fear of being identified as addicts and harassed. Overdoses increase. Precarious witnesses, fearful that police will follow medical personnel to the scene, fail to seek help.

I have stats at the ready. Nearly 500,000 Americans are incarcerated on drug charges. Another 1.2 million are supervised on probation or parole. Overwhelmingly, those affected are black, and not because they use and sell drugs at higher rates—on the contrary. I say that prison is no place for people who use drugs, help does not await them there. Maintenance therapies using methadone and buprenorphine are not available for people with opioid dependencies. Often an incarcerated person will continue to use drugs throughout a prison stay, and the clandestine nature of his use means that he is now more at risk than he might otherwise have been, using unsterile needles and sharing syringes among multiple inmates. Overdose rates peak in the first few weeks after release from prison, with mortality rates higher than what would be expected in similar demographic groups in the general population.

You begin to understand. You agree none of this is good. But still you are uneasy. You maintain it would be better to encourage people to stop using altogether.

A year has passed since I spoke with the epidemiologist. I read in the newspaper that more than eighty people in Scott County, Indiana, have tested positive for HIV, most of them from a small town called Austin. The outbreak can be traced to intravenous use of the drug Opana, an opioid analgesic. The transmission rate has been around 80 percent.

Meanwhile a woman in Austin buys a license to carry a handgun because she fears for her young children. The woman takes pictures of "all this stuff going on" and calls the tip line. "I do nothing but," she says. On her lawn is a sign: NO LOITERING OR PROSTITUTING IS ALLOWED IN FRONT OF THESE PREMISES.

You resent me now. I am trying to help you budget your money. You are spending your entire monthly payment within the first week. When your next deposit comes, I transfer it into the account you cannot access. Every week, I allow you one quarter of your stipend, after deducting your bills and rent. But you won't stop texting me, asking for more money. I try to reason with you, explain why you need the budget. I try putting my foot down, which amounts to ignoring your texts. You say you are buying a lot of five-dollar bootleg DVDs (Hitchcock is your favorite), but you forget that I know how to do math. And you are not interested in any of the solutions I come up with—a cheap computer, an internet connection, Netflix.

Every time I say no, I know I am passing judgment on you, on the things you desire for yourself (your collection of Adidas sneakers is by now substantial), what you prioritize. I am measuring you against an ethic of responsibility, a conception of the good life, that I do not want to force you to share. I can recognize this, but I can't hew my way out of the irony that accepting your irresponsibility only shifts the burden onto me, and this too seems unjust.

You were lucky once. You and my father sold your childhood home for $300,000. You never risked going to prison to support yourself. But before long, your half was gone, and you started spending my father's share. He cut you off, begged you to stop, but you said no, you had never felt so alive, you were having the time of your life.

We go to the bank and close the joint account, transfer your savings. You have total control.

I feel light.

Your savings vanish within a month.

You show up to an appointment with your psychiatrist, but it is the wrong day. You are confused, delirious. You travel by ambulance to the psychiatric emergency room at a nearby hospital. Your social worker calls to report what has happened. He says you may be showing signs of early-onset dementia. He says you may be abusing your methadone. I tell him about our recent conversation, the one where you told me you were taking Klonopin to sleep at night; the one where you guardedly suggested you may not be taking it as directed.

Two weeks later the social worker calls me again. You have terminated your services with their facility. You are within your rights to do so, and by phoning to let me know, the social worker is breaking protocol. But he is worried, thinks you lied when you said you found a psychiatrist closer to home. He believes you may no longer be fit to take care of yourself. He wants to call Adult Protective Services, would I be all right with that, and might he provide them with my phone number? He says to me, Please, you are the only person H. has.

*

It takes a few days, but I reach you. I come over with pastries from the Doughnut Plant. You seem all right—lucid, lively. You want to know how I know about it all. You are annoyed that someone would call me. You tell me that you like your new facility, that you are happy not to travel to Crown Heights to see your psychiatrist. Getting around the city is hard now. Scoliosis has you bent in two. You are not lying about the existence of this new facility. But when I ask whether you have a new social worker, someone who can help manage your various appointments, who knows what services you are eligible for, who can connect you with the things you need, who you can talk to about your private thoughts, it occurs to you, for the first time, that you do not. I tell you to look into it.

A few weeks later, I hear from my father that you have started traveling to Crown Heights again.

I met R. through a dating app. Now I am sitting with him in a wooden booth in a dark bar drinking Campari with soda and lime. We talk, and it's clear he knows a lot of things. He refuses to say much about it, but for years he studied Kabbalah. He also lived in India, studied Buddhism. Now he works as a professor. We share some ideas about politics, enough to make him stand out among the other dates. We seem to be getting along all right.

Recently he has been to Vancouver. I tell him that I've also been there. We talk about the Downtown Eastside, and he tells me he knows and respects the work of Gabor Maté, whom I interviewed on my trip. Maté is a physician and harm-reduction advocate, a proponent of safe injection sites, who worked in the Downtown Eastside for twelve years. He's also a proponent of the healing powers of ayahuasca, which is how R. knows of him. I enjoy this conversation, the overlaps in our knowledge. I tell him about *Da Vinci's Inquest,* the Canadian television program based on Vancouver's chief coroner turned mayor, the same mayor who was in office when Insite opened. R. tells me that he has done, still sometimes does do, heroin. A casual user.

It's like a test. I can recall the many times I have pointed out, in abstract conversations, that heroin's reputation does not align with scientific evidence; that although it can be devastating for some, it is not, in itself, any more dangerous than a lot of other drugs, and people who use heroin are unduly stigmatized. But here it is no longer abstract. Will I hold it against R.?

Later, when I mention this detail to a friend, she frowns. "I like the other guy better."

You are cured of your hepatitis after a course of Sovaldi, a new pill that clears the disease in 95 percent of cases. The price of this near-certain cure: $84,000. Each pill costs $1,000. You are fortunate to live in New York, the state where Medicaid coverage of the drug is the most generous. Many states pay for only the sickest patients. You are, relatively speaking, not that sick.

For the first time I come across an article in the popular press that challenges the accepted narrative. A professor of psychology and psychiatry named Carl Hart says the heroin public-health crisis is a myth. He claims the attorney general is overstating the problem. The commonly cited metrics are insufficient and misleading: the number of people who have tried heroin doesn't tell you how many people have dependency issues.

Weeks later, I underline a sentence in *Drug War Heresies,* a book that attempts to project and evaluate the consequences of various legalization regimes and drug-policy reforms: "One million occasional drug users may pose fewer crime and health problems than 100,000 frequent users."

There are more interviews to transcribe. I've been procrastinating. Today I am listening to my conversation with Gabor Maté. My friends have been trying ayahuasca, going on retreats, and they all seem to know of him, to hold him in high regard.

I know the quote I want, am waiting for him to say it, fast-forward through my own voice.

He says: "Abstinence is just not a model you can force on everybody. There's nothing wrong with it for those for whom it works. But when it comes to drug treatment there's an assumption that one size fits all. And if you're going to wash your hands of people who can't go the abstinence route, then you're giving up."

He says: "Harm reduction means you give out clean needles, you give out sterile water, you resuscitate people if they overdose. You help people inject more safely. You're not treating the addiction. You're not intending to. You're just reducing the harm."

We decide to see a movie in Williamsburg. In the back of a livery car, you tell me that one thing you really miss, one thing you think you should try to do, is find a female companion. I agree that this would be ideal, but I'm not sure how to help. I say that maybe you should go online. I show you the dating app on my phone and we laugh at its absurdity. I say there must be sites for older people. But you don't have a computer, and you don't have a smartphone. I'm certain you could count the times you've used the internet on one hand.

You tell me about the woman in the apartment below you. Whenever you try to shower, she immediately turns on all her faucets and uses up the hot water before you even have time to undress.

I explain the unlikelihood of this—hot-water distribution in a multiunit building just doesn't work that way. You seem reassured, but the next time we speak, you complain that the problem continues.

Weeks later, you call in a panic. Con Edison is threatening to cut off your service, and you can't afford to pay. The bill is several hundred dollars, despite the subsidy you receive. You tell me you had been running your space heater all day, every day, for weeks —the building had kept the heat on low. You either underestimate my intelligence or the shame is too great.

I call Con Edison, take care of your bill. You haven't sent a payment in six months. When I confront you with this, you insist on your version of the story.

You call a car and ride over to my place because you don't have money to get you through the month. My father says that if I lend it to you, he'll pay me back.

"You know what happened?"

You are sitting at my dining table. You are smiling, and you tell me that when you finally met the hot-water villain, you found her beautiful and fell in love.

You gave her a holiday gift: a note and $30. You stuffed it under her door. She kept the money, of course, but she never acknowledged you.

When you leave I give you extra cash for your car ride home.

A week later, you call to apologize for lying to me about the Con Ed bill. This is a first.

The Canadian government releases details of a damning audit. The audit alleges that PHS Services, which runs Insite and in 2013 received provincial-government funding worth approximately $18 million, misused corporate credit cards and reimbursed improper expenses:

> $8,600 for limousine rides in 2013
> almost $900 per night for a stay in a British hotel
> more than $2,600 for a stay in a Disneyland resort for two adults and two children
> $5,832 for a Danube cruise

The article reveals many other missteps.

I wince. I know how hard these people have worked, how much they've done for the hard-to-house in Vancouver. I know this scandal will taint them forever. To open a facility like Insite, to set up crack-pipe vending machines (as they have also done)—to challenge the status quo in this way—you can't make mistakes. It's like being a politician. Someone will always want to drag you down.

Even as the media narrative continues to focus on heroin use among middle-class youth in suburban neighborhoods and rural towns, I know that other populations are in need of resources and services. A study by the Centers for Disease Control and Prevention shows that rates of heroin use remain highest among males, eighteen- to twenty-five-year-olds, people with household incomes below $20,000, people living in urban areas, and people with no health insurance or on Medicaid.

I take the subway up to the Bronx to BOOM!Health, a peer-run harm-reduction organization. With a small grant from the Drug Policy Alliance, BOOM! is trying to open the first legal supervised-injection facility in the U.S. They've even set up a model site, a single injection booth fashioned after those at Insite. I meet with the organization's president and chief programming officer. He tells me that they want to create a pilot study, much like the one in Vancouver. I know that when advocates in San Francisco tried to set up a facility, the opposition was too great. But BOOM! is optimistic; having Bill de Blasio in the mayor's office presents an opportunity.

I speak with a lawyer specializing in public-health law who argues that a pilot study is not the best strategy. "The people who are moved by evidence are not necessarily legislators. Insite was evaluated every which way. There were so many papers. Most of them are some variation on the theme that it did pretty much what we thought it would do, and it didn't do anything that its detractors thought it might do. Has that proven very persuasive, either in Canada or the U.S.? Not really!"

Framing the facility as an incremental extension of services already available, he suggests, could prove more effective. "Almost do it under the radar." He is not sure that he is correct, but claims that, at least to his knowledge, the federal government never busted a single syringe-exchange program; it was always the local cops and sheriffs.

He adds, hesitantly: "But then the question is: Is that model" —i.e., an unsanctioned facility—"exportable to other cities and states?"

When I began to follow the media coverage of the new "heroin scourge," I didn't have strong ideas about "addiction," except that I knew it when I saw it. I believed it was a disease, and that it should be treated as such. But the more I read, the more people I speak with, the more I begin to question this framework. It is clear that no one—no neuroscientist, psychologist, psychiatrist, or physician —can explain what addiction is or account for its contradictions. Tobacco, cocaine, heroin, alcohol, MDMA, amphetamines—are they inherently addictive? Common knowledge suggests they are. But all around me I see exceptions more than the rule, my friends who use, have used, some or all of these drugs, including heroin, casually. I, too, am one of the exceptions.

I conclude that my own point of view is now best represented by the more radical strands of the harm-reduction movement and by legalization; I can argue, morally, intellectually, why these alternatives are better than what we have now.

Following the lead of those in harm-reduction and drug-users' rights groups, I decide to scrub the word "addict" from my vocabulary, to avoid using the term "drug abuser." The alternatives can be awkward on the page, in a sentence, but it is more important not to reduce a person to this one aspect of her life, not to ascribe all the negative valences carried by these words.

> person with a substance-misuse disorder
> person experiencing a drug problem

person who uses drugs habitually
person committed to drug use

I try carrying these over into speech. This, too, is challenging.

I meet Judith in her studio. She is seventy-five, a painter of Indian peafowl, roseate spoonbills, reddish egrets, and other birds of refined plumage and delicate bills. Earlier in the winter, her son, Spencer, died of a methadone overdose. We face each other, seated in chairs, a small table and a glass of water between us. Judith looks the part of a painter. She is poised, like her subjects, and speaks of her son's death with surprising ease.

"Having a son die this way is not the absolute worst thing a mother can experience. I can think of circumstances far worse."

Her stoicism is not an act. Despite countless visits to detox programs and rehab centers, a frightening prison stay, longtime family support, and the benefit of resources unavailable to most, Spencer was unable to stop using drugs in a dangerous way. Judith understands that she's not to blame.

I examine a framed photograph of Spencer that Judith has pulled out on my behalf. He's tall and fit-looking, blue-eyed, sensitive.

Spencer binged. Methadone maintenance never worked for him. Taking anything at all, including methadone, triggered a dangerous cycle. When Spencer overdosed, it was with methadone he received through a program. He had been trying to give up drugs. Judith believes that Spencer was torn between the life he wanted for himself and the life he seemed fated to have. "He had the right to let himself go if he couldn't be happy."

Judith tells me that methadone-maintenance therapy is without a doubt a terrible thing. I want to say: Maybe for some people, like your son, but it has also helped many others. But I can't say it.

Judith says that a person on methadone still has that "all about me" attitude. What she means is that there is a kind of heroin mind, a way of behaving particular to a habitual drug user. The person may prioritize access to heroin above all else, including relationships with loved ones. Lying and stealing are constants in the repertoire of behavior. A person on methadone, Judith is saying, is still in heroin mind.

I make an intellectual case for methadone, say that for some people it can help to stabilize their lives. But Judith stares at me blankly. She is not interested. I want to appeal with a personal example, but I find it hard to come up with one.

She compares those who rely on methadone with those who seek help, and support others, through Narcotics Anonymous, as her son did. The people who commit to these programs, she explains, commit to a life of service. Spencer may have given up on his own life, but he helped save innumerable others. Judith claims the people she met through NA are among the saintliest she knows.

"You should disconnect from your uncle, leave him behind, drop him. He is taking from you without ever giving back."

I feel defensive, uncomfortable, on your behalf and my own. I feel I'm being perceived as weak for deciding that you, while difficult, are still a person worth knowing.

I say I appreciate the advice.

Judith apologizes, tells me what I really need to do is to find a boyfriend who will treat me like a queen.

I am mistaken. Sophie never does come around. I can't remember the last time you mentioned her name. Two years, maybe more. By now your grandson must be eight or nine.

With the right login credentials and some basic biographical information—first and last name, an approximate age, a residential state past or present, a relative's given name—there's a lot you can find out about a person, even when Google and Facebook turn up little. When I decide, finally, that I will look for Sophie this way, through databases I can access through my job as a fact-checker, it takes me no more than sixty seconds to locate where she is living.

A trail of email addresses with varying domain names (aol.com, comcast.com, yahoo.com) reveals a few of the websites she's created accounts on: a daily-horoscope generator, a payday-loan provider (cash4thanksgiving.com). Presumably these sites have lax privacy policies. My heart sinks a little when I think of her needing a payday loan; it suggests her life has not been an easy one.

I will write to her, I think.

Haywire

FROM *Tin House*

MY FATHER WORE, under his work shirts, a sturdy white bras-
siere. I hated to hug him, hated to feel that elastic strap across his
back, hated having to make myself concave to avoid contact with
the empty cups on his chest.

He painted his nails with clear gloss nail polish. He shaved his
face and his chest, arms, and legs. In his bathroom medicine cabi-
net, tubes of lipstick and mascara and compacts of powder lived
among Preparation H, Brut, and an ancient bottle of Old Spice.

Behind the louvered folding doors of his closet, behind stiff
suits he never wore, hung a collection of women's dresses, wide
cotton shifts, large paisley patio dresses. The floor was an orgy of
heels and brogans, strappy gold sandals and steel-toe boots. *Hus-
tler, Playboy, Genesis, Club,* and *Oui* stacked on the kitchen counters,
in the bathroom, on the blue shag carpeting in the hallway.

When I was an adolescent, my confusion about my father was
a frightening and distracting presence that never went away. *What
was he?*

This was the late 1970s in the American South. If someone used
the word "gay" in my world, he meant effeminate and wrong. He
meant faggot, homo, fairy, sick, or stupid. He meant a joke or an
insult. My father drank Bud, smoked Marlboros, yelled at football,
dated brassy blondes and divorced women, a different gal every
week. *What was he?*

I didn't know what gay was or wasn't, not exactly. Sometimes
men loved men and women loved women—that made sense to
me, but that was not what I was seeing in my house. I was some
two decades away from hearing the terms "transsexual," "transves-

tite," and "transvestic fetishist," and profoundly distant from any understanding of my father, far from even being able to put into thoughtful sentences any of my questions about why and how one's father might date women, watch porn videos at breakfast with his daughter at the table, and wear panty hose and a bra every day under men's clothes. My father seemed to live out a large, dark, and shameful secret that no one was supposed to know about. It never occurred to me that my father could be unaware that other people—including his daughter—saw all this. It never occurred to me until quite recently that he might have felt there was actually nothing to hide.

The two of us shared a household on the south side of Orlando, a brown concrete block ranch with a sagging roof line. Rangy gardenia sprawled in the sunny doorway, obscuring the front door. Faded plastic flowers lined the front walk. In many ways, with its mixture of beauty, tawdriness, neglect, feminine touches, and strangeness, the dark, low house looked a lot like my father.

Sometimes I would wake up in the middle of the night to my dad sitting on the sofa in the living room, where I slept. He chain-smoked; it was always the smoke that woke me.

"What?" I would say, sensing him there on the far end of the sofa before my eyes adjusted to the dark. "What's wrong?" How long had he been sitting there? What did he want? Why were tears streaming down his cheeks?

I didn't call him Dad or Father or even Pop. I called him by his given name, Fred.

To look directly at Fred was almost always difficult. He cried not only when he was sitting on my sofa late at night. He regularly wept driving down Orange Avenue to the ABC. He sobbed during our weeknight dinners. I'd come upon him in the backyard, where I was managing a small garden, and find him standing by the clothesline, smoking, and in tears. Fred's internal weather was an unpredictable mix of energized intelligence, vibrant humor, despair, and tangled sexuality. I sensed he was not bipolar but multipolar; something inside him pulled his core self in every direction available to a man.

Curled up tight under my layers of bedsheets, my knees drawn to my chest, I'd ask him again, "What is it?" He'd shake his head, wipe his face with the sleeve of his white Fruit of the Loom tee, light another cigarette, and lean back on the sofa. "Go back to sleep, girl child."

I went back to sleep.

But in photos of my father as a young man, he is bright-eyed and appears completely, beautifully *normal*. His sparky energy surges out of the frame, but he's neatly groomed, suited, 1950s clean-cut, square corners. In some photos, he looks more than a little like Elvis, with his cowlick swooping into a thick shock of black hair, T-shirt, and jeans. Riding a horse, holding a fish, or laying concrete, his grin, fiercely sweet, is always lit by a flash of wild.

I remember him leaving the house for work when I was little —he worked as an accountant at a missile company in central Florida—wearing a brown suit and starched white shirt, looking like all the other dads in skinny ties, folding into their sedans with cigarettes and briefcases. I remember him sitting in our side yard in a lounge chair on the patio, listening to the Saturday-night ball game on a transistor radio, yelling, *Go, go, go, you've got it! Oh god-damn it.* Jeans, work boots. Buddy Holly glasses. Drinking long-necks. *Hey, baby. Hey now, girl child.* Beer and cigarette in one hand, he'd scoop me up with the other. *Come listen to your old daddy.*

There's a photograph of one of these moments. I'm four or five. I have his dark eyes, dark hair. I'm barefoot in my white nightie, madly in love with my dad. But instead of wild in my eyes, there's sorry, there's worry.

In the 1970s he was gone most of the time. When I saw him, on occasional weekends, I began to notice he'd started perming his hair, wearing floral-patterned shirts, and somehow he seemed both foggy and shiny.

My parents divorced when I was eleven. My mother turned to wax. She was barely able to leave the house. Always edgy, now she nailed shut the windows, tacked thick bedspreads over the cur-tains. She decided *I* really shouldn't leave the house, either, some-times not even for school. She had always believed we were be-ing watched. Now that we were alone, the dangers were too great —peril awaited us in the grocery store parking lot, at the bank, on every bridge. Don't answer the phone. Never give out information.

Great care was taken to vary our route. I had seen the caravan that followed us home from the grocery store, had I not? And I'd seen the foot of the man in the side yard—that foot exposed to the light, his body in the shadows—hadn't I?

Yes. I had seen these things. I had different interpretations than she did and I shared them freely, which increased her fear—this careless spiteful daughter who didn't really see, didn't really know how serious it all was.

My diagnosis of my mother? Super strict. Unreasonably strict. We fought. But I loved my mother and wanted to please her. And when she heard breathing in the house, I heard it too. When she said to crawl on my hands and knees through the house, I did as she asked.

My father's visits trickled to nothing and there was a year or so that I didn't see him at all. Late spring, the year I was fourteen, I finally tracked him down by telephone. I told him my mother was ruining my life—I wasn't allowed to have friends, talk to boys on the phone, shave my legs. He seemed shocked, curious. He'd gotten out, best move he ever made, and now he said he was mystified by his actions. What had he been thinking, leaving me behind to deal with a mentally disturbed woman?

I held my breath, waiting for the answer.

Yeah, he said. He'd come get me as soon as he could and I could be his boarder, pay rent.

Rent? Was he kidding or serious?

In the weeks I waited for my father, I envisioned my new bedroom, maybe decorated with a peacock theme. Or fans. I loved Japanese fans.

And with this move, I knew, there'd be restaurants, and maybe a wardrobe of Jordache jeans, Candies high-heel platform slides in hot pink, friends, parties, one of those makeup sets with one hundred eye shadows and a spectrum of lipsticks and glosses with brushes, all in one giant box that you could haul anywhere.

My own stereo. A curling iron.

I remembered my dad well. I thought about him all the time. I knew exactly what I was getting into: fun. A lot of fun and, at last, a normal life.

In late March he picked me up at the end of the street—we wanted to avoid a scene with my mother. I slid my suitcase into the backseat and climbed into the brown Olds Delta 88, a ship of a car.

I reached to hug him. This was when I first felt the straps under his shirt, going over his shoulders. I assumed it was something medical. Did he have a bad back? A recent surgery?

His eyes were vague, watery, sad. The whole man had drifted, hard, to the left, and it was as if he'd sunk to the bottom of a swamp and come up completely transformed. His hair, permed and gold, looked like pale seaweed. His arms were shaved. I cried out when I saw them—I couldn't help myself. *What?* He looked at me when I yelped, raised an eyebrow, and returned his gaze to the road. I saw his hands on the steering wheel: his fingernails were painted with clear nail polish. *Why?* Panty hose peeked out from under the hems of his pants.

I wanted my other father, the one who looked like a dad.

But I couldn't go back to my mother's house. I was moving in with an alcoholic man who wore women's panty hose under polyester Sansabelts but I knew in my heart that however horrible this was going to be, it would be an improvement over life with my mother.

When we pulled up to his house, which I'd never seen before, he asked me what I thought.

I was quiet for a moment. "It has a number of sad features," I said. I'm sure I grimaced. The place looked as if it was sinking into Florida and the mixture of abandonment and decorations—dead grass and wild vines in the trees and a brightly painted Dutch placard by the garage that said WELKOM!—was hard to understand.

"What are you saying?" He gazed at the low bungalow as though it were a beloved palace.

Every night when I went to sleep I believed that when I woke up, I would find him back to normal. And every day I worked hard to figure him out. What was he, what category did my father go into?

Saturday afternoons, when we went down to the Pine Castle Winn-Dixie and he ordered Lebanon baloney and reached across the counter for the packet of meat with his painted nails and a little bit of makeup on, acting all friendly, talking as though no one could see how totally bizarre he was, I pretended that if *I* didn't see, *no one* saw.

What else did I want from the deli?

I pretended we were normal.

What else did we need? he asked impatiently.

What did we need? I wondered.

I had no idea. To not be in the grocery store, out in public. To not be the people we were. To be completely, utterly, not us.

As I followed him through the grocery store, I felt such shame over being ashamed of my father. I wanted him to think I loved him. I did love him.

In the evening, it was my job to make dinner for us. This life was not quite the amazing teen bedroom and delicious restaurant future I'd had in mind, but at least we could eat normally, my father and I, whereas my mother had complicated rituals around food. Tampering was a constant theme for her, and her diet (and so mine) was restricted to toast, plain chicken, applesauce, grapes, and occasionally baked potatoes.

My father's fridge spilled over with bottles of papaya juice, coconut milk, packets of liverwurst, smoked herring, coleslaw in white plastic towers, banana peppers, a garden of fresh vegetables, and packet after packet of meat. He had two books side by side on the kitchen island: *The Joy of Cooking* and the joy of the other thing. I covered the second book with mail and studied recipes. As I prepared buttered almond rice pilaf for my father, or salad dressing, or set tiny jalapeño slices on carefully laid-out nacho chips for Mexican night, Fred, wearing a Hawaiian shirt and beaded macramé necklace, his ankles weirdly uniform beige with panty hose, would roll into the kitchen, grab me by the shoulders, and insist I invite a friend over for dinner. He'd hand me the phone receiver. Call Karen. Call Sally. Call Miriam next door. Call anyone. My father seemed both to expect normal friendships and not to have any idea how bizarre he was, in equal measure.

"No one can come," I'd demur. "Everyone's busy."

"How do you know? You don't know that." Tears rimmed his eyes. "Oh, come on now. Don't be like your mother."

At my mother's house, I wasn't allowed to invite anyone. At my father's house, he wanted everyone to come. I couldn't bear to tell him the truth: *You're too strange.*

His pleas—phone receiver extended, me vrooming olive oil and vinegar and mustard in the blender or turning the pieces of steak in the iron skillet—were inevitably uttered over the porn movie playing on the television/VCR that sat on our dining room table. A pulsing *mmm mmm mm* in the background as the couples did what they did to the dull tuneless music.

How could he possibly ask me to ask someone over?

But he did. Every night.

Strangers showed up, ringing the bell or just walking in. Men he'd met at the Moose or the VFW, women from the Amber Keg and the Starlight Lounge. Sometimes, with a house full of drunken strangers, I slipped out the back door, returning late at night, when I was certain he and his guests had passed out.

Other nights, the two of us sat alone at the table. I silenced the television, ejected the porn cassette, placed it on the stack on the floor.

He read the paper. Or we played cards or chess. His nails always looked better than mine. He'd grab my hands as I cleared the plates.

"You will never marry," he'd say, suddenly tearful. "You'll never leave me. Because you'll never meet a man like your ole daddy."

I cringed at the words, which seemed both a blessing and curse.

"Let's go jookin'," he'd say after dinner, once a month or so. "What do you say?" His face marbled with hope and gin.

And so instead of going to a friend's house on the weekends (I had none), or going out with a boyfriend, as my classmates did, I went to the bars with my father—my father wearing makeup and a bra and panty hose under his polo and jeans. I was the designated driver, happy enough to be out of the house, happy to drive down seedy Orange Avenue to the Amber Keg, to go inside that dark, cool, musty room and sit at the bar writing in my notebook while he talked and talked to everyone there. Hours later, I steered him to the Oldsmobile, always one of the last cars in the lot. Pressed him into the passenger seat. Drove home. I felt old, odd, confident, superior, doomed, and desolate.

As often as not after dinner, he passed out on the sofa, which was my bed. I turned the television to face the other end of the dining room table, made a tiny sofa-ette out of two dining room chairs, and clicked through the channels for a Clint Eastwood movie.

Other nights, a woman showed up—rarely one I'd seen before. The women were always tall, big-breasted, slim-hipped, wearing lots of makeup, shiny party clothes, and white or silver or black patent high-heel sandals. They draped themselves on my father, who wore what he wore, and was whatever he was, who took them out into the night.

Sometimes in the morning, leaving for school, I'd come down the hallway and if his bedroom door was open, I'd see a woman in his bed.

I could not imagine.

Was this life better than the one I'd had at my mother's house? Hard to say. I constantly regretted my decision to live with him. But when my mother called on weekends to check on me, because she asked lightly how we were doing, I answered lightly, "He's a handful!"

Her edged pause. "Are you safe?"

Long silence. I didn't know if I was safe or not. I'm not sure I knew what safety was. I knew my mother meant something different than most people when she talked about safety. I knew she wanted me to say yes. I was surprised my mother wasn't trying to get me back. And I didn't want to go back. Always, I felt as if I were playing along when I assured her that yes, yes, I was safe.

When I spoke to my mother on the telephone, I stared out the window over the kitchen sink, toward a palm tree, broken-down patio furniture, and perfect blue silk sky. I didn't see the piles of porn magazines, my father's bras on the floor with a heap of laundry, the empty gin bottles sitting on the counter by the sink. I saw a fridge filled with food that was edible, open windows with light streaming in, a little world that was my little world—a journal, a pen, my gold sofa, my neatly folded sheets, my nest.

When it was time for me to go to college, Fred refused to disclose any of his finances so that I could apply for financial aid. He wanted me to stay with him, get a job as a secretary. *If you leave, you're on your own.* So I was on my own. I rode a Trailways bus to the university five hours north, used babysitting savings, worked three jobs.

On breaks, when the school closed, I arranged for special permission to stay in the dorm. I was one of only a few people there. A smattering of students from China and the Middle East walked across the empty campus. We never spoke.

When I graduated, my friends married or moved in with their lovers but I did not. Instead, I worked on a PhD and the much more difficult tasks of how to be less anxious around a man and how to relax inside someone's house, how to love and be loved. I spoke with my father on the phone infrequently. I sensed that I needed to lay down all new wiring in my body and mind so I could choose whom to let in, and whom to keep at bay. I sensed this renovation had to occur at the cellular level and would take many years. Didn't we get all new cells every seven years?

One Friday afternoon, when I was a first-year doctoral student, Fred called out of the blue. He'd be at my house for dinner Saturday, a quick stopover on his way to Four Corners, Arizona, a place he'd always wanted to see.

I was thrilled and nervous. I was delighted to tell my friends he was coming, but of course did not invite them. I scrambled to assemble his favorite from *The Joy of Cooking*: chicken cordon bleu. I bought a bottle of Sancerre, chilled it, and made a salad using tomatoes from my little city lot garden. I set the table on the porch. Cloth napkins. Candles.

He never showed.

I threw the dinner in the trash.

When I finally tracked him down by telephone later that week, he had no memory of any of it.

Wrapped tightly inside my disappointment and despair about his not showing up, there was a tiny nut of relief. It was so hard to be around him. My father was unreliable, not just in terms of behavior, but in terms of identity. I suspected my father was not knowable, not even to himself. Would he even know if I loved him or not?

And always I wondered, *What is Fred?* Gay? Bi? A transvestite? Did he want to be a woman? What was he?

In the library, I slipped into the dimly lit stacks on the second floor, far in the rear of the building, where the psychology texts were located. I'd read, secretly, flooded with shame at the photos of diseased genitals and countless descriptions of sexual deviation. Among the sex with corpses and unspeakable unspeakables, I quietly searched for any book, an article, a paragraph—something that would explain to me what my father was, what he was not, and why. I never found anything that fit him, which underscored the fact that I'd come from unclassifiable, impossible oddness, weirdness so profound that if anyone knew, I'd be ruled out as someone you might want to love.

Did he want to be perceived as a member of the opposite sex? I thought (feared) so when I was young but I don't think so now.

I don't know how my father felt about his genitals, or his gender; now I doubt he had the kind of cognitive organization that allows for such thinking. Fred operated in a different realm: how others perceived him wasn't on the table, much less in the dressing room.

Over the years, I talked to several therapists about my father. One urged me to see the humor in men in dresses and suggested I watch *Tootsie* and *Some Like It Hot*. No thanks. I'd seen the covers on the videotapes at the rental store: men in dresses dressed for a caper with a purpose. I couldn't imagine enjoying those films; I was a girl with a dad who was not amusing and people weren't watching a movie when they watched my dad—it was our lives, no joke.

The woman-dressed men in the movies made sense for the story. My dad did not make sense. Men in women's clothes didn't bother me at all in movies or in life. Typically, they wore clothes well; makeup, carefully applied, made them beautiful. They were clearly *home* in a way my father never was. But coarse hetero men in ill-fitting, frumpy dresses were unbearable to me.

Another therapist told me, "Women can wear men's clothes —suits, ties, pants—and we see nothing wrong with that kind of cross-dressing. Widen your perspective."

I could not widen my perspective. My perspective had been long since overdilated.

Besides, my father didn't really cross-dress. He didn't cross *over*, he crossed *out*. He never seemed comfortable or happy in his skin. He always seemed about to leap out of it.

I knew from my stealth reading that most cross-dressers were straight and married and that most cross-dressed for erotic pleasure, some for self-soothing. I'm not sure that my dad loved women's clothes. Maybe. Maybe he loved what binds a woman. Maybe he loved our softness, our tears, our allowed-for, count-on-it, sanctioned tenderness, our very pliable weakness, our ability to melt and flutter and still be loved. Maybe my dad wasn't anything trans- or cross-. Maybe Fred's cross-dressing was what some psychologists call an "erotic target error": he assigned meaning to gender that was so far from reality, it's incomprehensible to us.

For example, now, across the street from my house, there's a family who hangs a white Christmas wreath on their door—in

March and April. And then in June, the white wreath is exchanged for a green Christmas wreath, complete with balls and bells. Christmas decorations don't mean to this family what they mean to most of the rest of us.

Maybe parts of my father's sexuality and meaning-making map were scrambled in his early cognitive development. Maybe some part of his personality remained a tiny child for whom sex isn't sex; it's something else altogether, like a wreath in July. In this scenario, sexuality is assigned meaning that has no words, but in adult life exhibits powerful energy. Strange urgent sexuality and desire pulse and spin constantly, but never line up in actions or relationships in ways we would normally expect.

Put another way, maybe my father was haywire.

When he had colon cancer the first time, I was in my late twenties and I flew home to Orlando to help him. In the hospital bed the morning of the operation, he dozed as a nurse came in to prep him.

"Oh," she said. "He's already been shaved." She was clearly confused—her chart showed he was to be shaved for the surgery. She had the little kit at the ready.

I looked up at her, anxiously. His nails were painted. Did she see?

"Did he just have another surgery? I didn't see that in the chart." She was touching my father's chest, which was covered with black stubble.

I looked down at the floor. I wanted to say, *Yes, another surgery,* but I didn't want to be caught in a lie. What could I say that would make sense?

She was looking at his legs now. The hair was starting to grow out, black metal filings that covered his pale skin. She looked almost angry with confusion. I realized I'd been editing out the parts of my father that didn't make sense for so long, I no longer saw him how others saw him and perhaps could not.

During the colon cancer treatments, my fiancé offered to come to Orlando to help me with my father. I couldn't imagine the two men in the same world much less the same room.

I had to be with my father on my own.

The fiancé was long distance and then just distance. *Alone* felt safest, the best I could do. By my midthirties, I still hadn't married. I dreamed of a family, children, but it didn't seem possible to pull it off.

PhD in hand, I landed a good job at a small private college in a postcard-perfect town in Michigan, some thousand miles from home. In spring in this village, the streets were ritually washed with buckets of sudsy water by women with brooms. Most people went to church. In the hyperconformity, I thrived. On the surface, no one was weird. Because they had no fluency in weirdness, they would never detect my history. If it was unknowable to them, it didn't exist. Here, only here, I could pass. I had friends. I wrote books. I was a respected teacher. At last, I had a steady boyfriend who lived in the same town I did, a lifelong bachelor who'd had a difficult time growing up in a wealthy family. I felt we were a good match, both so different from regular citizens—his extreme wealth had isolated him as poverty of normal experience had isolated me.

I called my parents on holidays. Over the past two decades, they'd somehow become friends. My mother helped my father, who'd survived a massive cerebral hemorrhage, kept him company on Sunday afternoons. He was wheelchair-bound, paralyzed on his right side. She seemed to love bringing him groceries, arranging aspects of home health care on his behalf.

Sometimes I spoke to the two of them together.

When you coming home? Come on home.

Honey, we'd so love to see you. Can you come down?

Months and months passed between phone calls. I wanted to see them, badly, before it was too late, and yet I couldn't bear to go back to those rooms, those shadows, that story.

One late afternoon I was reading students' stories at my kitchen table when the phone rang.

"It's your aunt Ruthie," a woman said out of the blue. It took me a moment to figure out who she was. My father's sister. We hadn't talked in—years? She sounded angry when she said, "I'm bringing your dad by to see you."

I told her this was not a good time. I was swamped with schoolwork. And summer was sadly already booked—teaching, Ireland. Maybe September?

"We're in Indiana," she said hoarsely. "'Bout two hours away. My God. How long has he been this bad? Did you know he drinks in the morning?"

My father was with her? Two hours away?

She'd driven to Florida and gathered up my dad. Our reunion was her mission. I was just hearing about all this now.

I felt my head fill with something like wet smoke. I couldn't have my father hurtling into my pretty little bungalow, my carefully wrought life, these small, tidy rooms, the orderly village of Holland, Michigan, populated by conservative, religious Dutch Reformers.

I asked my aunt if they could postpone. Maybe I could come to see them . . . later? As I spoke, something happened behind my forehead. An apocalyptic headache was brewing, the likes of which I'd never experienced before.

My aunt grew more insistent. She was only staying one night, dropping my father off at my house for the week, as she was heading north.

I suggested a motel.

A motel was out of the question. They were planning to stay with me, she said. And Fred would be with me until she got back from her trip up north.

"I'm not set up for company," I told my aunt firmly if shakily. I tried to imagine my father, his extravagantly permed long golden hair and makeup, careening past the tidy tulip beds, accosting my teetotaling neighbors with questions. *What the hell with all these churches? Where are the bars? The good-looking women?*

My aunt said they were on their way and she hung up the phone. I wanted to slip out the back door, as I had as a teenager, and run.

And yet, he was my father, whose eyes visibly brightened when I entered the room.

Hey baby, where you been? I've been wanting to talk to you about many things.

No one else's eyes did that for me.

No one else wanted to talk to me, urgently.

After Ruthie said goodbye, a time bomb started ticking. I took three aspirin, but the monstrous headache only intensified. It felt as if my skull was going to divide into two pieces, then shatter. I drove downtown in sunglasses and ordered a double espresso from the coffee shop.

My aunt and my father were in the gas station parking lot when

I pulled up—I'd insisted on meeting them out by the highway. She stood by the hood of the car, arms crossed over her chest, and he was in his wheelchair, smoking by the trunk. The doors to my aunt's station wagon were open, and the two of them seemed flung out of wreckage. It had been a terrible drive. They both looked miserable.

My father cried as he came toward me in his wheelchair with his arms open. We hugged. I touched his soft face. He smelled like home: cigarette smoke and sour, lemony soap and perfume. His hair was pulled back in a long white ponytail. He wore stained khakis, socks, beaten-down work shoes. His fingernails were un-painted. No traces of makeup. Age and poverty and the stroke had all taken their toll.

"He's yours," Ruthie said, looking at me and simultaneously flicking my father on the shoulder.

Fred wanted to hug more. I pressed one hand on his chest, holding him down in his chair.

"He's driving me crazy," my aunt said loudly. "Out of my effing mind."

"What the hell you talking about!" He turned in a half circle, jerked back toward his sister. "You're not listening. You hear but you aren't listening!" my father shouted at her.

My aunt said I had to keep my dad with me for a few days while she went on her vacation.

I explained that I didn't have a guest room and my house couldn't accommodate a wheelchair. There were steps—five or six —just to enter, narrow stairs inside.

She seemed furious. My father couldn't be left alone, she said. He needed care. I needed to care more. Plans for his future needed to be made: Where was I?

Why did you bring him from Florida to Michigan? I wondered si-lently.

Okay, she said, at last, a motel, but that was very expensive. And she desperately needed a break from my dad. She wanted me to stay in the motel with him so she could get on with her trip.

He looked so hurt when she said this.

Why are you here? Why did you bring him here? I couldn't speak these words. I didn't know what to say. I wasn't going to stay in a motel room with my father but I didn't want to say this in front of him. My headache made me wonder if I should go to the ER. It felt as if something were about to burst. I went home.

They shared a room at the Days Inn. The next morning, I came by and helped my father into my car. He grabbed my thigh, hard, and then from his pants pocket pulled out two vials of gin. "Hit?" he said.

I looked at his brown eyes, soft as a llama's. "Hit me."

He wasn't wearing a bra under his pale green, somewhat misshapen polo. His arms were bone-smooth, but not shaved—he was seventy years old now, simply too old for arm hair.

I drove him around the postcard-perfect town, sliding by my house without saying a word, showing him all the churches, taking him past the college, wondering what it had been like for him since the stroke, no longer being able to shave his legs or put on lipstick. In front of the English department building, he put his hand on the door handle. He insisted on seeing my office and meeting my colleagues.

"I'd rather not," I said flatly. "I'm supposed to be working."

"No," he said. "Let's do that." He wanted to meet my colleagues, talk to students.

"No," I said. "It's not a good time."

A group of students, prim in polar fleece vests and pressed jeans, walked their bicycles down the sidewalk. I pointed to the library and the chapel, a great Gothic ship stranded on the lawn, and he pleaded with me to go inside. I ignored his pulling on my arm and, perky addled tour guide, I explained when things were built, and who built these buildings, and why. Blinded by my migraine, I wanted desperately to get an espresso, but I dared not stop. I could not risk my father unleashed. It wasn't just the women's clothes, I realized, that had made it so hard to be in public, my public, with Fred. It was his radical impulsive striding, his need to talk and touch and point and engage, with person, with pillar, parishioner, dog, cashier—he'd say anything to anyone. He was capable of touching a woman's bottom in any situation, or a breast. I'd seen him touch his fingers to a waitress's crotch at a Chinese restaurant.

My father pulled at the car door. "Let's go meet them. I want to hear what they have to say about you!"

"They're not there now," I said. I paused in the loading zone in front of my building.

Students came pouring out the front doors.

"Are too!" He spoke in the chiding tones of someone who would not be fooled. He grabbed my shoulder. "Come on now." He was puzzled, hurt, insistent.

I pressed my head to the steering wheel. He sucked back another little mini gin, produced from where I did not know—his diaper? He was tapping on the passenger window glass. "They're huge," he said. "These gals are huge. The Dutch. They look Dutch." He seemed astonished, impressed, fascinated. "Look at that one! Look at her. Enormous! Look at the size of the buttocks on that one." He gaped in genuine astonishment. "The thighs alone could take out a sober man."

So strong was my desire to please my father, to show him how far I'd come, and to impersonate a normal-daughter life, that I was on the verge of walking around my car, letting him out, taking him into the English department. Walking him down the halls, showing him my office, where I had his photo framed and posed beside the one of my beloved corgi, Cubby. I imagined walking down the hall, holding my father's hand so he wouldn't barge into colleagues' offices, introducing him to my department chair, a slender man who would be dwarfed by my father, who'd never met anyone like my father, never even conceived of personhood taking such a form. Could we do it?

Kathy Vanderveen, the medievalist, walked past my car, and waved, looking curious.

"We just can't, sweetie," I whispered. "Please." I felt the migraine pulsing into my cells.

"Why not?" His mouth was open. He had his palms pressed on the window. "I want to see it."

As a girl, I'd been so focused on the strangeness of his appearance, I hadn't realized how hard it was just to *be* around my father.

We had dinner, just the two of us, at Russ's Diner, where the special was split pea soup, patty melts, and pumpkin pie. Afterward, I drove him to my house. We stood in the driveway together. I was, in this moment, under the fading blue Michigan sky, extremely happy to be next to my father, showing him the house I bought all on my own. He pointed, listed, and as I held his arm, he talked about the pitch of the gables, the impressive thickness of the original timber. We looked in the basement windows. In the backyard, he smoked. I thought about the day he'd taken me to his house in Florida, proud of his purchase, low and damp and dark.

I drove him back to the Days Inn. I refused to stay at the motel with my dad, and he could not stay in my house. Ruthie was pissed. The two of them squabbled while I stood in the doorway trying to think of how to leave. By the time I left the room, my father was not speaking to me or to his sister.

That night, the headache worsened. The room spun. I couldn't see properly. I vomited onto the floor.

In the morning, I took my father to breakfast, just the two of us. He was obsessed with pointing out how the Dutch people were so extremely Dutch-looking in their largeness, and in their plainness. He acted as though he wasn't in a Bob Evans but in a zoo. I felt as if I was with a developmentally disabled adult—then, eating bacon, I realized: I was.

After breakfast, I drove him up Highway 31 to see the blueberry fields. He told me stories about being young, working as an accountant in the next town up—driving this exact stretch of road.

"You were here? In Michigan?"

"You knew that."

"No. You never told me."

"Well, I did, too."

I looked at the man next to me in the car, my father. I'd never thought much about him as a man in his late twenties, building a career, running around the lakeshore. Who was he then? Did he have true friends? Bizarre behavior? A thing for women's panties? Did he have affairs with men? When did the cross-dressing begin? Was it cross-dressing? How did he think about it? But I didn't ask. Some years before, I'd asked my mother when it had started. There was a long pause. She didn't look upset, just surprised, as though I'd found something she hadn't seen in a long, long time and brought it to her.

I never thought we would ever in a million years have this conversation, she said. *How did you know?*

I found her response so unnerving—*how did I know?*—and her subsequent revelations about their intimate life so dark and so shocking, I backed out of the conversation in a blur of confusion and regret.

Now, as we drove up the empty highway, past the blue-red fields,

I thought it might be the last time I ever saw him. I wanted to tell him, *Dad, it's been so hard. You haven't tried to blend in at all. I could never have people over. You haven't tried.* But it felt both mean to say that and also like speaking in a language he didn't know—what was the point?

We pulled into the Lake Shore Antiques mall, where he lit up with excitement. We trolled up and down the aisles. Nearly every object spoke to him and there was a story; he knew even the strangest tools and old farm implements.

People wedged past us, me and this wild-looking, loud-voiced man smelling of gin, clothes stained, gait permanently damaged by cerebral hemorrhage and years of pickling. I didn't care about the stares. My father and I fit in here, perfectly, in this giant pole barn crammed with stuff ripped from its context and heaped in bizarre vignettes: a birdcage on a settee, draped with a fur coat, surrounded by china and toys and three pitchforks. Here, for maybe the first time ever since I'd known him, Fred looked at home, this great glorious odd bird of a man grabbing objects from a crazy chaotic collection, insisting that I listen. I listened. I thought, *He should live here.* My father would fit right into this museum of wayward artifacts, items damaged, loved, given away, this wabi-sabi world of things whose purpose was lost to time, but whose beauty and tenderness still somehow shone through. There, in the junk store, at last, my father and I were together out in the world. For the first time, we held hands in public. I was relaxed. He wasn't pulling me under. I wasn't willing him to be other than he was. We were happy.

Once, when I was in high school, we were at the American Legion, and a man fell off his barstool. It was my father, Fred Sellers, who leapt up and helped the man to his feet. I watched that man clock my dad hard on the jaw. My dad said, reeling, "Just trying to help ya, brother," as he fell. I helped him up. "I'm mystified," he said.

He loved his dogs. He cried when his girlfriends came over and screamed at him for forgetting to show up for their date, or for having another woman in the house. He seemed sincerely puzzled that life wasn't going his way, and terrifically overjoyed at the things he loved: Zellwood corn season; the prospect of our making dinner together, him telling me what to do and me doing it and cleaning up; growing roses. He *loved* roses, most especially, the hybrid called Dolly Parton, those over-the-top huge fragrant copper-red tea roses.

Fred Sellers. My father.

Another decade passed. I hired helpers to care for my dad. When he inherited an enormous sum from his father, a real estate tycoon, he gave the helpers gobs of his money and unscrupulous folks took the rest. I asked him to think about me. But since I'd stayed away, at arm's length from my father, I felt I didn't have much claim and in the end he gave me nothing.

When he was at the end of his life—lung cancer—I went to see him often. Sober, with dementia, he lit up when I came around the corner, beamed over to me in his scooter, and never failed to ask a pertinent question about some recent topic of conversation: Did I go with the ceramic tile or the slate in my bathroom renovation? Did the guy put in heaters so my gutters wouldn't ice over? Why not? How much had that driveway repair cost? What about Obama, what did I think of that man? What books was I teaching? Anything he'd read? Was I teaching Mark Twain? What about Mencken? Then he'd launch into a well-memorized section of one of Twain's works—how could I have a PhD in English, he'd complain, and not know this material by heart? He'd shake his head in disappointment.

On one of these visits, I found my father asleep in his bed, crookedly arranged. I could see his diaper was twisted. He didn't have long to live. I wanted to ask everything. I wanted to have no regrets, no unanswered questions.

My heart was beating so hard, I felt as if a bird were inside me when I leaned over his bed that day.

"Fred," I said. "Fred."

"Yah," he said. He smiled. He gripped my hand hard.

"I want to ask you something."

"No," he said. But since his stroke, no usually meant yes and yes meant no.

"This is a little difficult."

"No," he said, in an encouraging way.

"Why did you wear women's clothes? What was that about

for you?" I imagined I was a kind reporter. Just asking questions.

He looked away, up at the ceiling. He took his hand back. There was a long pause. His roommate's television blared a game show. And then my father, looking me in the eye with his usual curiosity, said, softly, in a tone I'd never heard before, "You knew about that?"

ANDREA STUART

Travels in Pornland

FROM *Granta*

I CAN EASILY recall my first brush with porn, I was seven. My brother and I had set off to see a friend, a boy around our age. When we arrived he asked if we wanted to "see something." We knew it would be good because he was whispering even though his parents were outside, talking over next door's fence. We followed him to his parents' room and watched as he pulled up a chair in front of his father's wardrobe. He had to stand on tiptoe to reach the top shelf. When he clambered down he presented us with a magazine with a pair of bunny ears stenciled upon the cover. It fell open to the center, and there before us was a technicolor image of a topless woman, her strawberry-blond hair flowing in the wind, with large pinky-brown nipples. My brother and I looked at one another. We knew that being naked was naughty; but we had also seen our mother's breasts so we weren't quite sure why this picture was worth all this secrecy and effort. But we stared attentively nonetheless.

Of course as a child I didn't understand this image as pornography any more than our friend did. Nor did I know anything about Hugh Hefner's infamous magazine, created in 1953, long before I was born. We hid the magazine and dispatched it from our minds, dismissing it as yet another one of those mysteries that belong to the adult world.

A decade or so later as a teenager in the late 1970s and '80s, porn seemed the province of sad old men in raincoats who visited barred and grubby shops in London's seedy Soho. Or it was the stuff that boys at my brother's school hid under their mattresses. But attitudes toward sex were changing: intellectual people like my parents proudly kept a copy of Alex Comfort's *The Joy of Sex* on their shelves, which taught a new generation how to have a good time.

Inevitably of course this loosening of mores meant that representations of the nude body and sex were more commonplace. But it was only at university several years later that erotica, such as Anaïs Nin's *Delta of Venus* or Nancy Friday's *My Secret Garden,* became part of my friends' reading repertoire. But porn per se, in magazines or films, had little or no place in my life.

The new libertarianism, however, was having a profound influence on the representation of sex, even if I was too naive to notice it. In the 1970s, the hard-core film *Deep Throat,* in which a doctor encounters a woman with no gag reflex, became a huge hit. Its success ushered in a golden age of porn and erotic mainstream films, like Bertolucci's *Last Tango in Paris* starring Marlon Brando.

By the late '80s, I was working at the feminist magazine *Spare Rib.* I was delightfully out of my depth, but my consciousness was expanding daily. In our Clerkenwell office loft, I was exposed to the debates about women's sexuality, and the images made of them, that raged across the women's movement. Theorists like Andrea Dworkin and Catherine MacKinnon, anxious about the misogyny associated with the porn industry, developed a vociferous antiporn narrative embodied by their slogan: "Porn is the theory, rape is the practice."

Meanwhile, sex-positive feminists argued that porn was an opportunity for sexual self-expression. It was, they argued, a potentially radical act of self-revelation that allowed many women an independent income, access to an empowering political discourse, and the chance to create a sex-positive identity that would enrich their erotic lives. This conflict became known as the sex (or porn) wars, and divides feminist debates on the subject to this day.

By the '90s I was an archetypal third-wave feminist, transfixed by the pleasure-loving, sex-positive model of feminism that the third-wavers espoused. Women, we believed, deserved stimulating material and new sexual narratives. Erotic images circulated around the office, some of them evolving from the material disseminated by American sex educators like Susie Bright and Tristan Taormino. *On Our Backs,* the first erotic magazine created for women by women, was published in San Francisco. Lulu Belliveau, its art director, was surprised at the furor that broke out as a result of its queer-chic images. "I just wanted to make images that I found hot." Soon *On Our Backs* and its British counterpart *Quim* were a must-read for cool queer girls, and one of my friends was featured, bare-breasted and dressed as an angel, with white widely spread wings.

Feminist erotica was a growing industry, and it became de rigueur to be cool about it. In the mid-'90s a friend suggested we get together and watch a film by Candida Royale, a feminist pornographer who aspired to make porn for couples to enjoy. The screening was held at my flat. I bought some wine and nibbles. The invitees arrived and we settled down to watch the video. The event was not a success. The couple on the screen were white, heterosexual, and conventional looking, a cast that in no way represented my multicultural group of friends. The director's approach to sex was so predictable and PC that it seemed almost antiseptic. So it was no surprise that before anyone had a chance to get even a bit aroused the evening fell apart. My partner felt that it excluded lesbian sexuality and stormed off to the bedroom. The black girls felt invisible, the straight girls were embarrassed, and all of us were disappointed. I don't know what would have happened if we had had a chance to watch the whole thing; but I do remember thinking at the time that the sexiest thing about the event was not the film, but the clandestine nature of the gathering.

In those days my feelings about pornography remained largely indifferent, and I watched it only coincidentally, for example dancing in a lesbian club in New York's Meatpacking District, where X-rated images of leather-clad dykes playing with fire and wax flickered around the room, or in my television job, watching clips of *Suburban Dykes,* in which a rakish butch teaches heterosexual women how to do lesbian sex. It was so funny and sexy that I had to rethink porn.

By the noughties, Madonna, with her perpetual play on the motifs of paid sex and porno images, was my generation's mascot. We blithely believed in a new sexual dawn. And we were all flirting with porn. My then lover presented me with a copy of Madonna's coffee-table book, *Sex,* for my birthday. (It is still the fastest-selling coffee table of all time.) In retrospect, the book was a case of style over substance; but I can still remember the excitement of tearing open the silver Mylar sheath that covered the huge book. As I turned its heavy pages I felt cool and edgy. The pictures, taken by the fashion photographer Steven Meisel, were achingly fashionable; if not at all sexy—it was essentially soft-core porn that simulated S and M, bondage, and anilingus. As a gesture toward authenticity it also featured real-life porn stars like Joey Stefano, as well as mainstream actresses like Isabella Rossellini and lesser luminaries like the rapper Vanilla Ice.

Not long after this I was commissioned to write a piece about Annie Sprinkle, one of the great doyennes of U.S. porn, who had come over to England to present her new show at the Institute of Contemporary Arts. I was excited to meet her: she engaged with feminist issues, and to make the evening more interesting still, there had been a controversy about part of her act. In New York, members of the audience were allowed, if they so chose, to examine her cervix through a speculum, but the British establishment banned this, deeming it obscene. The inevitable controversy that followed about censorship, obscenity, and art reverberated through the cultural community and the event sold out.

My partner and I slipped into our seats, beside a man shivering with excitement. He told us that Annie Sprinkle was his favorite porn star. As soon as Sprinkle and her partner, a champion of eco issues, got onstage, hugging and dancing around the faux trees, this man, overwhelmed perhaps by the illicit atmosphere of porn, or the lesbian couple holding hands beside him, began to masturbate. We moved seats quickly, feeling sullied and intruded upon. The incident reinforced the seedy, objectifying image of porn, which this event was meant to belie.

I returned home that night to research the piece I had agreed to write. But when I watched the videos that made up Sprinkle's back catalogue, they were of the same old formula, replete with all the typical tropes of hard-core porn: vaginal and anal fistings, double penetrations, and gang bangs in dirty rooms and urine-stained pissoirs. The material grew darker: Sprinkle was being penetrated by the stumps of amputees. This was completely different from anything I had ever seen, imagined, or thought of as sex. Clearly the porn industry was engaging in practices that had previously been beyond the pale. I remember breathing in but not being able to breathe out.

What was any of this to do with the erotic, I wondered? Of the sweet, fleshy tumbles with my partner? It was the aesthetics of the freak show. Come, it said, let us watch women's flesh be poked and prodded, stretched and spread to the limits of what is bearable; a hideous, awful circus that used spurious theories to excuse its profound hatred and abuse of women. When I stopped watching all I wanted was to somehow un-see this material, mercifully wipe it from my mind. But the flashbacks went on for months.

Despite these abominations, pornography, among many feminists, was still seen not as a problem but an opportunity. And third-wave feminists like myself dreamed of establishing a utopia where we would be as free as men about our sexuality. It was a vision that entranced my generation; and a feminist porn industry emerged to make it true. Our porn would not be like the mainstream industry that abused and exploited women like Linda Lovelace, star of *Deep Throat*. Instead this was porn for women by women; a pornographic utopia, where the performers were treated well; and the representation of sex challenged the tedious images that had evolved in La La Land where women's bodies were merely the landscape, and men's pleasure the real goal.

I recently traveled to San Francisco, commissioned to explore the city's feminist porn scene. It is one of the most significant hubs of the contemporary American feminist porn industry, and has produced porn for over a hundred years, ranging from one-reel silent classics, such as *A Free Ride*, where a man picks up a girl in his Ford Model T automobile, to adult productions like smokers, blue movies, and stag films.

The city's alternative porn scene is an industry within an industry, a subset of L.A.'s dominant porn-valley scene, the biggest porn hub in the world. The San Franciscans specialize in BDSM (bondage, domination, sadomasochism) just as other locations specialize in couples' porn or other genres.

I am staying at the Geary Street Hotel, popular with fashionable gay men. The furnishings are minimalist and the broadband is super fast. I am going to a feminist porn shoot in the morning, so I decide to watch some mainstream porn, to explore the contrast between the two worlds. I choose a generic but well-known porn provider. The content is classified into numerous categories: ebony, lesbian, gang bang, anal, as well as a couple that I have to decipher by watching, for example, POV, which means "point of view," and DP, which stands for "double penetration." I start soft

with the lesbian category, and open up a tab randomly. I am confronted by a group of three women with dyed blond hair extensions, matching pink leotards, and white fishnet tights, attacking
each other with pink dildos. Their nails are long and white and
I cannot help but worry as they insert them into each other. The
women moan loudly, and I wonder who is fooled by this display,
especially since there has been virtually no contact with a clitoris.
Mainstream porn's egregious indifference to women's pleasure is
obvious; it is effectively a middle finger up to women and their
needs.

I click again. As a black woman, I'm curious about the "ebony"
category. I am presented with a series of black women being penetrated by black and white men. The ubiquitous porn aesthetic
continues. Almost all of the women have the same hair and nail
extensions, the same massive implants and terrible makeup. I click
again, disconsolately. The next image is a woman trying to insert a
supersized dildo into her own anus. The dildo is hard and inflexi-
ble. The pain she is experiencing is evident for all to see. And then
surreptitiously, she looks swiftly to the right, and I see a moment
of fear pass over her face. I wonder if she is looking at someone,
someone whom she is frightened of displeasing, and I wonder suddenly if this is a trafficked woman, deprived of all choice.

The next click and I am in the gang bang section. This is particularly harrowing: the configuration of one woman and four men
looks like an attack. The girl tries to accommodate every organ and
hand, manipulating her body so as to avoid as much discomfort
and pain as possible, while unconvincingly feigning pleasure. The
misogyny of mainstream porn has created a sexual narrative that is
irrelevant to how women really achieve pleasure. It has enshrined
practices like anal sex and shaving pubic hair as de rigueur even
though many women do not want to do them. The clip concludes
with a predictable close-up of traumatized anuses and semen dripping from faces. It breaks my heart that we are breeding a generation of men who will see this dispiriting spectacle, even before they
have enjoyed their first kiss.

I promise myself that I can stop soon. I click again. A tired-
looking woman in her late forties is ranged across a bed, while a
hideous man inserts the handle of a rake into her vagina. I rub my
eyes—I am reaching the end of my tether. I click again. This time I
am confronted by a woman lying on the ground with a man fisting

her while another is pissing on her face. I shut my computer down abruptly, truly shaken. I understand now why some women don't watch mainstream porn for fear of what they will find. And I recall a quote from a well-known porn director, who once said to the writer David Foster Wallace, "Nobody ever goes broke overestimating the rage and misogyny of the average American male."

It is largely in response to this pernicious industry that feminist porn has evolved. Feminist pornographers emphasize the importance of practicing safe sex, as well as issues of consent, and stress the right of performers to negotiate how they present themselves and what they will or will not do. On a more theoretical level, feminist porn asserts that sexual minorities (for example, black, trans, or older subjects) should take an equal place in queer porn's erotic panoply. More profoundly still, feminist porn is an attempt to decolonize women's imaginations, reminding us that we are more than just the object of desire, more than just abject victims of a misogynist culture, but active, yearning seekers after sexual pleasure, who deserve erotic satisfaction. Feminist porn urges us to create new sexual scripts and build new imageries that focus less on pleasing men, and how women should look, and more on what truly fulfills us.

I am on my way to my first porn shoot, chauffeured by my cab driver, a young Nepalese man who has won his green card through the lottery, and is struggling to come to terms with this unfamiliar city.

He asks me what I am doing in San Francisco and I tell him that I am writing a piece on feminist porn. He looks at me carefully through the rearview mirror, and says, "No, no, no, we are not involved with that." I don't know what he means by this, but smile politely back, and we both tactfully change the topic.

There is someone else already at the entrance: a young work-experience girl of Ethiopian descent, who wants to know more about working in alternative film. She is the only other interloper on this shoot and we get close over the day. My contact buzzes the formidable spiked gate open and comes to escort us into the Pink & White Productions studio, where filming is to take place. We walk into an unruly cul-de-sac that houses a series of alternative business. Pink & White is situated opposite a music company, beside a Harley-Davidson repair shop.

I am here to see the filming of *The Crash Pad* series: an ongoing online sequence inspired by Shine Houston's award-winning film, of the same name, released in 2005. Houston, who has become a formidable figure in the feminist porn industry, evolved the Crash Pad model. Undoubtedly it is genius: born out of the reality-TV era, it features an apartment where couples, whether of long standing or recent hookups, go to have sex. The space is rigged with cameras, and we, the voyeurs, get a chance to watch.

I am distracted by two women sitting together at a table eating hummus and fruit. I am not sure initially who they are, but suspect that they are the performers (otherwise known as the "talent" or "models") who are scheduled for that morning's shoot. My suspicion is confirmed when they start on the paperwork demanded by the studio. This may seem dull, but the rigor with which feminist porn producers both inform and legislate their relationship with their workers is one of the most significant differences from the mainstream porn industry, whose exploitation and abuse of their "talent" has been a major complaint of the antiporn lobby. The team here is very much a family, young and fun and multicultural, but still scrupulous about documenting their relationship with their performers.

Anyone who wants to perform at Pink & White must present their driver's license or passport showing their date of birth and legal name. They must sign waivers that give up their right for approval of the finished product, and present a medical certificate of their HIV status. There is another questionnaire, optional this time, which is a sort of getting-to-know-you list with a hippy twist, asking for the performer's stage name, nickname, and zodiac sign. It asks whether they are "tops or bottoms"; that is, whether they prefer to be the active or passive sexual partner. It asks whether or not they are in a relationship, and for details such as "Turn ons!" and "Who I'd like to meet!" Finally, there's a query about "tags, nicknames, and pronouns," asking performers whether they prefer to be called he, she, we, or they; and whether they identify as trans, queer, feminist, polyamorous, butch, or femme.

It seems to me that the working conditions at Pink & White represent the best intentions of feminist porn. Most of the staff work on both sides of the camera, and understand the particular challenges of shooting porn. They collaborate with their performers on the choreography of the scenes, as well as dress, makeup, and accessories. Indeed, the performers are consulted all the way, including how they want to be photographed for marketing material like the DVD covers. It is no surprise that Shine Houston is widely known in the business as "the ethical pornographer."

But it is the wide variety of body types represented in *The Crash Pad* series that, according to my contact Jiz Lee, most appeals to Crash Pad customers. Pink & White productions include young bodies and old ones, black bodies and white ones, fat ones and thin ones, trans ones and tattooed ones, as well as the disabled. It is an aesthetic that is very different from both the mainstream porn universe and the wider media in general. It is no surprise that this sublime variety is what provokes the most feedback and gratitude. For if you are one of those people—most of us—whose body style is rarely represented anywhere in the media, it is thrilling to be represented as beautiful and sexy.

The intern and I go outside so she can have a smoke. We are joined by the two performers who have driven all the way from Wisconsin for this. River Stark is a petite dark-haired girl in a wheat-colored sweater and green jeggings. Her partner is taller, with an equally beautiful face, and dark hair with a strip of pink. It is only her arms, strong and defined, that make me wonder if she might be trans. Her nom de plume (or rather, nom du porno) is Viviane Rex. I ask her why she got into porn. Sucking voraciously on an e-cigarette she replies, "I am a feminist. And doing porn is a way of saying 'fuck you' to everybody who believes that a trans woman shouldn't be allowed to live."

Viviane has a solid porn CV, and works in the mainstream industry as well as in feminist porn. She also runs her own studio. They both talk big, but behind the bravado there is a sweetness about them. They show me their tattoos and tell me what else they want done. And when they discover that I am from London they are thrilled: they love *Doctor Who* and have a huge crush on Peter Capaldi. Watching their shining faces I realize how young they are, and thus of course how vulnerable.

*

The performers go to the bathroom and prepare for the shoot. Makeup and fake tan are not compulsory in feminist porn, but this pair prefer to use both. Meanwhile the intern and I are allowed into the set—a bedroom with olive walls and cream curtains over faux windows. The double bed sheet is rust-colored, one pillow orange, the other yellow. It's a generic bedroom—but around the bed is the camera equipment to record the sex that will soon follow.

We return to the main part of the studio since we are not allowed to be in the crash pad while Shine and her team are filming. I tell the intern that I'm a bit nervous. She agrees. Both of us are familiar with the more extreme BDSM that sometimes is part of the studio's repertoire, including caning, electric play, and bondage.

The feed starts, and the pair begin to kiss, like they really mean it, a kiss that promises real lovemaking, people in search of real pleasure. They are a beautiful couple and it is a pleasure to watch them. I have seen River's body earlier when she dashed onto the set, and it is not a porn body, more a dancer's body with perfect champagne-cup breasts and a thin landing strip of hair on her pudenda. They undress and get into bed. I knew that Viviane was trans but I had assumed she was post-op. I was wrong: she has a penis, and not a modest one, either. This is a really impressive schlong.

For a second I am not sure how things will work, until the pair really begin to get it on. The real penis competes with a variety of sex toys, whose use is encouraged by the studio, perhaps because of sponsorship deals. They are confident in this scenario, especially Viviane, who works a lot for the big mainstream porn studios. River reaches for her partner's surgically enhanced breasts. (She will later tell us, to our amazement, that the mainstream porn merchants have encouraged her to have more surgery, because apparently her DD cups aren't big enough.) It is easy to tell that they are comfortable with each other; there is enough affection between them to make the sex feel genuinely passionate. Certainly watching this is much more enjoyable than watching the mainstream fodder on the internet. But I can't help but notice that there are tropes from the parent industry that I wish weren't there: the over-speedy thud thud thud of penetration (whether with pe-

nis or dildo), the random face- and bottom-slapping. I get a sense
that the San Francisco producers are worried that lesbian sex is
too soft and girlie to be cool; and that it needs to be roughed up
and sped up.

All of a sudden the sex talk is interrupted by the sound of rev-
ving engines from the bike shop, but the two concerns have lived
beside each other for a long time and happily work around each
other. Someone is sent to ask them to desist, for the time being
anyway. Filming is resumed and the sex heats up. Then all of a
sudden the feed goes down and we can no longer see the action.
All we can hear is River's ululating cries. They rise up and down
like scales on a piano, and I realize, as the crescendo of the oh, oh,
oh, oohs of her pleasure reverberate in my head, that for me this
sound bereft of images is the most exciting moment of all.

The afternoon shoot is very different. Two French girls, Moriah
and Riley Saint, arrive. There is a lot of whispering in corners and
strained voices. One of the girls keeps disappearing and there are
numerous outbursts of tears. I wonder if one of them, or both,
has cold feet. Inevitably some of those who agree to do a porn
shoot as a sort of pair-bonding exercise find that they cannot go
through with it. This does not surprise me. It is a brave—perhaps
even a foolish—act to enshrine an image of your passion on the
web. Once uploaded, it is virtually impossible to erase. So in the
end one of the girls pulls out and the other, makeup-free and hair
pulled into an unglamorous topknot, diligently masturbates for
the required time, and gets paid the standard fee: $400. Her part-
ner, meanwhile, is sobbing outside.

I feel wrung out by the day, particularly this last scene. Despite
the porn industry's assertion that sex is a spree, something to
merely bring us off, I am aware that porn plays with dangerous
toys, not just dildos and whips, but love and desire, fidelity and
betrayal. I can imagine myself in that girl's position, feeling, in
a moment of bravado, that I could do this thing, and then real-
izing that I couldn't; that this very private act was now to become a
product completely out of your control, something anyone could
share, buy, watch, and judge. What might a transient act like this
do to one's relationship, to others who love you? Would it break
the spell of love, or cement it?

*

How and why does a woman get into the business? As much as it seems a cliché, a lot of them still seem to be recruited from the vast number of females who, like the wannabe starlets of old, migrate from small towns attracted by the beacon of Tinseltown; hoping to be dancers, singers, or other kinds of performers. A much smaller number actively seek out the porn industry hoping to become famous—but there are no stars in porn anymore.

In order to understand the decision to work in porn, I interview the gender-fluid performer Jiz Lee, who prefers to be referred to as "they." Jiz is described on the Pink & White roster as a production assistant, but this modest title belies the significant position in San Francisco's porn scene that Lee has occupied: ten years of work, and more than two hundred projects across six countries, winning numerous awards. As well as working in L.A.'s mainstream porn industry, including hard-core gonzo productions, Jiz has worked extensively in queer and independent porn.

We grab a chance to talk whenever there is a rare break in Lee's duties:

"How did you get into the porn industry?" I ask.

"I was a dancer in L.A. and I needed to make money. And it seemed as if it was a chance to use my body and support myself."

"You started in L.A.'s mainstream porn industry. Did you have any bad experiences?"

Jiz hesitates for a moment and replies: "Well there were some not so awesome moments."

There is a long pause. I am not surprised. Reticence regarding the ugly side of the mainstream porn business is something that I experience again and again when I talk with porn actresses who have worked in L.A.'s porn valley. I cannot help but wonder if there is a desire to play down the bad stuff, so that civilians won't blame them for being involved in the business in the first place.

Our discussion continues the following afternoon at a bar near San Francisco's LGBT center, a building in the Mission District of the city. Emboldened by mojitos, I ask the question that I am most curious about: "Are you out as a porn star to your family?"

The pause is prolonged, before Lee responds: ". . . not all of them."

My next interview is intriguing. It is with a female academic I shall call "B," who has been interested in porn, as an intellectual issue, for some years. After much thought she decided that she wanted to do a porn shoot, but her partner was not happy about her doing it without him. They decided that they would do the porn shoot together, and chose a well-established filmmaker who prefers to work directly with couples; or would matchmake those who didn't know each other, making sure that they genuinely fancied each other.

B was reassured by how collaborative the process was. The couple discussed what they would or wouldn't do. An attractive house was rented. There was good catering and champagne. Silly porn names were chosen. Discussions were held with the director about how they wanted to do it. A minimal crew was used to make the pair comfortable. "At first it was awkward," she said. "I thought about everyone and everything. But very soon I forgot and got into the situation . . . I am very good at focusing on my own pleasure. It was fun. We felt like naughty kids, doing something rude and kinky."

The result was something of a surprise. The film was a revelation: "To see our sexuality onscreen—the rapport that we had built together—made me proud; we were beautiful. And the dance that our bodies made on film was lovely." Watching herself was a surprise, she said. "I always wondered about how I looked when I was having sex, but my body was fine." And like most people she was curious to see what her face looked like when she came. She was reassured. "In a film you can see yourself being desired. Best of all, looking back at the rushes, I could see the way that he looked at me, how truly he desired and loved me." I asked her if she would do it again.

"Maybe a couple of times but no more than that," she said, almost to herself. "Then it might become routine; and our actions self-conscious." She hesitated again, shook her head, and added, "No—I have got what I wanted."

B's experience fascinated me. It illustrated that it was not that she had been filmed having sex that was the issue—indeed, for her that was liberating. It was that she didn't rely on the porn business for her bread and butter, that she was already a financially independent, professional woman who could chose to do this or not. She could remain largely anonymous, and thus avoid the taint (however unfair) associated with sex work. It illustrated, in other words, that a woman can only be sexually free if she is also in control of the means of production.

It made me wonder whether, in these, the best of circumstances, it is more rewarding to be the performer than the voyeur; doing, living, and touching, rather than merely passively watching. In an age where more and more of us conflate doing with watching, it is important to remember that porn is not sex; it is merely its fleshless representation.

San Francisco, the metropolis that once nurtured the feminist porn industry, and previously one of my favorite cities, is changing. Once the mecca to which gay, lesbian, and trans folks flocked to find their queer tribe, San Francisco is now one of the most expensive cities in the United States. Queer seekers are priced out of the market, and go elsewhere, to Oakland across the bay, for example, or to other American cities like Seattle or Austin; their place in the city taken by young people with more prosaic goals. In this newly gentrified and increasingly conservative city, it is no surprise that San Francisco's last lesbian bar closed down in 2015.

Despite feminist porn's influence on the media, art world, and academia, it has never been a financially viable undertaking; not least because women are not interested in buying porn in large quantities. The free products available on sites like Porn Hub are a disincentive, too, to pay for porn of any variety. And so the huge and thriving alternative porn product that the San Franciscans dreamed of generating simply has not come to pass. Piracy, too, which is rife online, has had a hand in undercutting the monetary stream that should fill the coffers of feminist pornographers. A sign of the industry's stagnation is the fate of the Feminist Porn Award, designed to recognize the talent of the sector—it has not been put on for a few years now. A number of notable feminist porn producers, too, who once aspired to make a living in this milieu, have moved on to other professions.

The great black feminist poet Audre Lorde once wrote that "the master's tools will never dismantle the master's house." But feminist porn director Shine Houston countered this by saying: "What I've learned in this business is that you absolutely can dismantle the master's house using the master's tools." Houston's retort was made in the hopeful days of the San Franciscan feminist porn scene, when practitioners believed that they could establish a thriving feminist porn industry. But this has not proved to be the case. The master's tools have not dismantled the master's house. And the dominion of the mainstream porn industry is unassailed.

JUNE THUNDERSTORM

Revenge of the Mouthbreathers:
A Smoker's Manifesto

FROM *The Baffler*

THE POWERS THAT be say antismoking legislation is for our own well-being. Nothing could be further from the truth. The attack on cigarette smoking does not improve the lives of those it claims to protect, be they the "self-destructive" workers who smoke or the moralizing professionals who complain about having to smell them. Antismoking legislation is, and always has been, about social control. It is about ratcheting up worker productivity and fostering class hatred, to keep us looking for the enemy in each other instead of in those who are making a killing off cigarettes and antismoking campaigns alike. It legitimates the privatization of public space, limits popular assembly, and forces the working class out of political life into private isolation via the social technology of shame. It whitewashes the violence exacted on the poor by the rich to make it all seem like the worker's own doing. It is, in short, class war by another name.

It is easy to charge hypocrisy on the part of supposedly benevolent governments concerned with "public health." Alcohol and sugar damage the consumer to an extent comparable to cigarettes, and hurt "nondrinkers" as well—ask any woman familiar with drunk men, or the cane cutters of Latin America. But the class character of the war on smoking is so pronounced that one begins to wonder just who the "public" in "public health" is anyway. It certainly does not include Nicaraguan plantation workers, nor most black Americans—unless we can call police murdering

Eric Garner for selling single cigarettes some sort of "pro-life" operation. Of course, cops in the United States also kill black men simply for walking around and breathing, so maybe cigarette packs should read: "Smoking Is a Leading Cause of Death Unless You Are a Black Man, in Which Case SMOKE 'EM IF YOU GOT 'EM."

Neither does the "public" protected by public-health initiatives include people of the working class, no matter what color they are. If it did, initiatives would be directed first and foremost at the process of production, not consumption. And I mean production of everything. After all, anyone who works for minimum wage already expects organ damage, physical pain, a reduced quality of life, and an untimely death. And that, no doubt, is why the "If You Smoke You'll Get Sick" warnings on packs aren't working very well to inspire this particular group to quit: working shit jobs for shit pay is making the working class sicker, faster. And yet the promoter of "public health" does not concern herself with how the workers must soon enter the building to demolish rotten fiberboard all day. She is interested only in what they consume outside the door on their brief ten-minute breaks. Why should this be?

The Polluting Poor

This apparent contradiction clears up once we understand that the public-health campaigns of modern government have never been about protecting everyone. They are, rather, about protecting the most privileged citizens from the dangerously contaminating poor. "Health and safety" provided the rationale for corralling dispossessed peasants into England's workhouses and slave-trading navy, just as "health and safety" was the slogan of British imperialists working to justify colonialism and the slave ships themselves. In fact, it seems when civilized governments discuss "health and safety," what often follows is "sickness and death," so we are wise to stay on guard.

From early modern times, the emerging capitalist bourgeoisie worked to articulate its particular value in contrast to the "hedonistic" aristocrats and the "irrational" underclass, both imagined as grotesque. The masses, in particular, came to be defined by a supposed excessive enjoyment of bodily pleasures. This was in pointed contrast to the new self-denying entrepreneur, who pretended not

to have any bodily functions. Orgasms, eating, sweating, and shit-
ting were impolite, dirty things, which anxious bourgeois moralists
projected onto others in a fit of collective neurosis.

Indeed, women, the poor, and "primitive" colonial subjects were
all conveniently constructed as porous and leaking "mouthbreathers" driven by primal desires, while elites were rational, well contained, and ultimately decoupled from the body and its practical
functioning. The poor or racialized woman, imagined as spread-
ing disease with her unbridled sexuality and infecting touch, was
of particular concern to the new social hygienists. Hence the trope
of dangerous servant women such as Typhoid Mary, the New York
cook who was quarantined for more than two decades after being
apprehended in 1915 as a "symptomless carrier."

This social imaginary persists today in many guises, one of which
is the dehumanization of the polluting smoker via her depiction
as a series of dismembered rotting body parts (such as the nasty
impaired lungs we keep seeing in antismoking propaganda), all in
the interest of public health. Car emissions, soda pop, pharmaceutical medications, and nano-weaponized drones all have the potential to disturb the healthful existence of the young white bourgeois
child, yet her mother supports these ventures with her taxes and
consumer choices while spitting insults at the smoker waiting at a
bus stop: she's just a toxic bag of body parts, after all.

I recently saw a woman brandishing the Mercedes-Benz of stroll-
ers walk through a sea of idling traffic toward a smoker only to say
the smoker was "murdering her baby" by polluting the air. Such an
act has nothing to do with protecting children, and everything to
do with venting bourgeois malaise by attacking powerless people
whom state authorities have constructed as abject and undeserving of respect. These same state authorities allow corporations to
poison our food and water supply—so of course they don't mind
if we lose our shit over some smoking neighbors instead. Indeed,
the mouthbreathing neighbor with nasty black lungs is apparently
more threatening than cigarette smoke itself: although the smoky
wisp that has not yet been inhaled is more toxic, the great danger
to nonsmokers, according to public-health authorities, is secondhand smoke. Ultimately, the cigarette stands in for what bourgeois
bystanders have always been most afraid of—the notion that they,
too, have bodies, and that these bodies materially coexist with, and
indeed create, the "vile" working class.

Public Space, Reclassified

I am not suggesting any sinister conspiracy of technocrats here, but rather a confluence of vested interests. The push to ban smoking in the workplace in the 1980s did indeed stem from research on "Increasing Productivity Through On-Site Smoking Control"—but of course not everyone concerned about tobacco was a profit-seeking vampire, nor were foes of workplace smoking specifically targeting the poor. Smokers at the time were still considered "classy."

This is why the 1980s campaign to vilify smoking was one and the same with a bid to de-class it. Much as women were sold sophistication by way of Benson & Hedges, Holiday, and Parliament, with men offered similar (simulations of) power and mobility in Marlboro Country, cigarettes were to be made unappealing through new associations with foulness, odor, dirt, depravity, uncontrollable desire, and the inescapability of body parts—concepts that the bourgeoisie, in their efforts at distinction, had long projected onto the racialized working poor. In other words, cigarettes were symbolically associated with the lower classes *before* the poor were the majority of those (still) smoking, this being part and parcel of constructing the act of smoking as unhealthy. Smoking was consistently depicted as both unhealthy and an emerging professional-life taboo that might derail an eager yuppie's career advancement. "Cigarettes May Burn Holes in Your Career" was the alarm sounded in a 1985 magazine feature in *Career World,* with other savvy works of eighties career counseling echoing the same theme.

Now, in 2016, cigarette smoking in North America is indeed more common among people living in poverty. They smoke because they do not have the time or money to eat properly, because other, more respectable mind-altering drugs are not available to them, because it is something to enjoy. They do it because their jobs (when they still exist) are so boring and physically painful that they would rather die. Yet professionals in the wellness industry routinely describe their smoking social inferiors as "stupid" and "irrational" on the basis of their supposedly self-undermining lifestyle choices.

It's by now an iron law that whenever the poor are discussed, so are their "bad life choices." If professionals can't do something properly or fast enough, they can readily avail themselves of a diagnosis of one or another "health problem"—even something as vague and generic as "stress" or "burnout." These are conditions that are imagined to have stricken them randomly—as opposed to a malignant, self-inflicted malady tied to their lifestyle, upbringing, or that sketchy antidepressant they stupidly decided to take. Even though so many children of the professional class clearly have asthma due in part to the persistent bourgeois hygiene neurosis (the antibacterial hand gel all but mandated by this neurosis being a proven contributing factor), they and their germophobe parents deserve empathy, time off, and specific disability rights. By contrast, working-class smokers deserve only reproach and are asked to tiptoe around the expansive sociomoral and self-induced sensitivities of the rich.

This wildly differential diagnostic treatment, which draws on age-old caricatures of the poor as case studies in lapsed self-control, parallels the entirely differential structure of empathy in the working-class workplace: whenever low-income workers can't do something properly or fast enough, they are simply fired, and anything that would otherwise qualify as a health problem or disability is chalked up to "personal failure." After all, this is someone who made the "bad choice" to live in poverty in the first place.

It is no coincidence that these same workers are widely perceived to deserve the exemptions of "health" as little as they deserve proper pay. "Public health" has always reinforced class divisions through such unequal attributions of "choice" versus "constraint." As a university student, I could not get a proper note from the Office of Students with Disabilities prescribing some time off to quit smoking because, as the nurse said, "Starting smoking is something you *chose* to do." My peer with back problems also chose to get into the car that crashed during her European holiday, yet it seems to be taken for granted that professionals simply "need" vast cosmopolitan mobility. (One can almost hear a public-health flunky confronted with this counterexample gasping at the suggestion that this health outcome was also, in some deep sense of things, an earned one: *You can't suggest that was her own doing! . . . One needs to get around somehow!*)

No equivalent concept of structural "constraint" is applied to the working-class smoker, who is rather imagined to enjoy (but mishandle) infinite power and choice. This is so even though the smoker in question is brought up to smoke just as the jetsetter is

to fly, and continues to do so largely because state and capital consider her undeserving of food. In fact, the smoker needs nicotine
to function just as the suburban professional needs his car, and
if *she* can't perform at work for even just two days, it will actually
matter. She may lose what little food access she has. Furthermore,
this smoker's daily activities, paid and otherwise, which would be
curtailed by the pains of nicotine withdrawal, are generally important for the greater social good. An obvious early casualty is the
caregiving labor involved in the "second shift" duties of working
mothers in the domestic sphere. *Huffington Post* writer Linda Ti-
rado says it all:

> When I am too tired to walk one more step, I can smoke and go for
> another hour. When I am enraged and beaten down and incapable of
> accomplishing one more thing, I can smoke and I feel a little better,
> just for a minute. It is the only relaxation I am allowed. It is not a good
> decision, but it is the only one that I have access to. It is the only thing I
> have found that keeps me from collapsing or exploding.

And so the lowest-paid workers continue to smoke, with public
smoking restrictions serving only to inspire working-class shame
and ruling-class belligerence. Whether because workers smoke or
their friends do, the traditional places of working-class congrega-
tion are now closed to them—the pub, the diner, the park, and
even the sidewalk. It is no coincidence that fifteen feet from the
door stands the gutter. And how convenient for the boss that shoo-
ing smoking workers from the door downstairs makes it less likely
for them to bond in conversation.

Today's student left is unfortunately complicit. Its adherents
implement "scent-free spaces" prohibiting perfume, tobacco, and
industrial odors in their organizing meetings, because it is apparently more important that the fraction of bourgeois professionals with allergies participates in their "anticapitalist" social movements than the majority of all people living below the poverty line.
They call these maneuvers "accessibility policies."

Once, at an Occupy Wall Street assembly, standing six feet beyond the last concentric circle in the parking lot, I lit up a cigarette. In short order, I was asked to leave. I insisted on Occupying. Such are the grinding wars of public accommodation in the
United States—a country whose people are so poorly entitled to
any public space that simply occupying a park is a big deal. In

other countries around the world, workers do that sort of thing all the time. Maybe the American resistance could go and do likewise —if, that is, its leaders would welcome workers to their meetings, cigarettes and all.

Smokers of the World, Exhale!

If the lifestyle lords of the ruling class want us to quit smoking, they can provide us with the resources required to spend a quarter of our waking hours drinking kale smoothies, doing yoga, and attending trauma therapy just like them. As long as they fail to meet such elementary demands of mutual social obligation, they deserve much worse than a little secondhand smoke. Meanwhile, we members of the smoking class might consider using bourgeois paranoia to our advantage. We might start organizing "smoke-ins" fifteen feet away from high-end daycares, exhaling in their general direction until all kitchen and cleaning staff are paid five times the minimum wage plus full health and dental coverage. Persons of the educated class may suggest this is "mean" or "violent," of course, at which point we may direct them to the reputable oeuvres of Frantz Fanon and Walter Benjamin.

If the government really cared about working-class smokers' health, our political elites could easily fund our well-paid vacations, free therapy, and other support services by slashing corporate subsidies. Instead, they direct bourgeois unhappiness our way. Instead, they blame the poor for contaminating the world, while funding paramilitary offensives in defense of filthy transnational mining projects and neocolonial oil-and-resource wars –conflicts that will make the world much less safe for their children than a smoldering cigarette ever could. Indeed, even if government did offer smoking citizens the most tempting of Golden Handshakes, we might nonetheless exercise our prerogative to refuse their dirty money and blow smoke in their faces instead.

In the meantime, my last words for the smokers are simply: Never let anyone make you feel ashamed. You should be able to smoke precisely as much as you want. This is not because mass-produced cigarettes or "Big Tobacco" are beautiful things. They are not. It is, rather, because *we* are beautiful and precious. Our *lives* are beautiful and precious. Our lives, despite what the bosses say, are actually for our own enjoyment, not to make others' lives easier, cleaner, and lazier. As long as the value of professionals' lives is not measured primarily in terms of their effects on *others,* but according to their pleasure, so shall our own lives and value be measured.

Like them, we shall pursue our own desires for pleasure no matter how whimsical, and if our desire is to smoke, then offended professionals can just hold their breath for once—perhaps using this blessed interval of silence to meditate on their thieving class and its own grotesquely swollen "carbon footprint." If state and capital are going to steal our precious energies and vast hours of our lives to line their pockets with profit, leaving us with poor sleep, insufficient rent money, and a diet of 7-Eleven specials as we provide the country's most basic services, the very least we deserve is to enjoy our cigarettes in peace. So if anyone asks, it's not that smoking should be permitted because cigarettes can be proved an absolute good, which they cannot, but simply because for the time being *we* happen to smoke them. We might call this giving professionals a taste of their own entitlement. Heaven forbid they choke on it.

ALIA VOLZ

Snakebit

FROM *The Threepenny Review*

> The phobia, which hoards the past, can be the one place in a
> person's life where meaning apparently never changes; but this
> depends upon one never knowing what the meaning is.
>
> —Adam Phillips, *On Kissing, Tickling, and Being Bored*

WE MEET A fat diamondback five minutes down the trail. He is
stretched across the path, dozing in the shade of a juniper bush.
I'm an adult, so I want to act like one, but I'm crying so hard
I can't inhale and snot is dribbling into my mouth. It takes me
twenty minutes to inch past the viper, while his tongue whips the
air. After that, I search out a long, heavy stick to thump on the
ground and jostle the creosote scrub before passing. My husband,
Kevin, and our two friends are sympathetic, but my pace is agoniz-
ingly slow, and they drift ahead. I hear them chattering, always
around the next bend, while blood bangs through my head like a
Taiko drum.

The whole park is rattlesnake color, and it's breeding season.
We camp among the mating snakes for three nights. We hear no
rattles, receive no death threats. Exhaustion renders my terror
quiet and viscous. "Snake," I breathe, as we ease past yet another
languid viper looped beside the trail. They're draped everywhere,
as in my dreams.

The last one we cross is pasted to the frontage road. It must have
bitten an oncoming tire; its mouth is spread open like a flower, the
tiny yellow points of its teeth splayed. The pink flesh of its throat is
turning to leather in the desert sun.

*

"Joshua Tree is such a powerful place," Dad says in our next *So how the heck have you been?* conversation. "Big energy there. I'm jealous you got to go."

Now that I'm grown, Dad and I are long-distance phone friends. We talk several times a year, our conversations clotted with jokes. We're both more comfortable this way, knowing we can hang up and return to our separate lives. I tell him about camping during breeding season.

"Oh, you must have loved that," he chuckles. "You used to cry if you had to walk past a rope on the ground."

"Remember the time you got bit?" I ask.

He hesitates. I picture his face squinting into the empty spaces eaten into his memory by the double whammy of epilepsy and psychedelic drugs. "Not sure I know what you're talking about."

"How could you forget? You showed me the fang marks when I was little and it scared me to death. I never got over it."

"You must be thinking of someone else . . ."

I don't believe him. We argue about it—politely, since we've both come to value our friendly distance. Then I call Mom, so she'll take my side. Dad forgets everything and she remembers everything. That's how it works.

"Not that I know of, honey," she says. "Your father did some dumb shit, but I think he steered clear of rattlesnakes."

Dad sits on the edge of his bed. I'm curled on the rug at his feet, an *Alice in Wonderland* pop-up book open on my lap. I am six years old and I do not understand why his eyes look so strange, his ice-blue irises walled behind dilated pupils. He has just returned from a week alone in the woods, what he calls a vision quest.

He's come home snakebit.

Dad rolls up the left leg of his lavender bell bottoms to show me the weeping punctures. His calf is swollen, the skin waxy and yellow like pork rind. Blue rings moondog the fang marks and raised gray veins jitter to his ankle.

I'm sweating in my footie pajamas, the canary-yellow ones that are so small they force my toes to curl. I've been told countless times that rattlesnakes are deadly, so I don't understand why he's still alive. He could die in front of me. The hot flannel constricts around my body and I tear at the metal snap at my throat.

How could this, possibly the most vivid memory of my childhood, inspiration for decades of ophidiophobic behavior, be false? This moment feels solid in my history, a flagstone lodged between our trip to Disneyland and the death of my first cat.

If I invented this memory, I don't know why or when. The question gets under my skin. I write essays about my father, scour childhood memories, and peek between my fingers at YouTube videos of snakes, scaring myself so badly one night that I run to find Kevin.

"You'll give yourself nightmares," he chides.

"I already have them."

Snakes take up inordinate space in my memory bank. I recall fifty-two specific encounters with wild snakes, a card deck of terror. Each image is crystalline. The snake's pattern. The sunlight gleaming on its skin. Whether its body was looped or unfurled or some disorienting combination of both. Whether it darted, oozed, or froze.

Equally sharp are times when I thought I saw a snake and it turned out to be something else—a lizard, a half-buried root—because my mind thought *Snake!* and triggered phobic hyperawareness. My highlight reel even includes photography from nature books and some truly awful YouTube clips. The viper whose decapitated head bites its own dying body. The snake that eats a spider, which then consumes it from the inside out. The infant who sleeps peacefully on a platform surrounded by hooded cobras.

I want to anchor my fear to a moment in time, but I can't find a sturdy one.

When I was a child, we lived in a former boardinghouse, a long-ago stagecoach stop on the Eel River in Northern California, an hour's drive from the nearest small town. The boardinghouse stood on wild land with majestic boulders, acres of mossy oak and dusty manzanita, and a cool green river, gentle in summertime. Peacocks nested on our shaded porch and we had a box freezer for making fruit slushies.

Behind the house was an empty chicken coop. My parents bought a dozen chicks from the feed store in town and brought them home in a cardboard box, together with a metal feeder and incubation lights. Peeping yellow puffballs with sharp little beaks. I gave them silly names like Fluffy and Muffy and Sunshine, though they were impossible to tell apart. I remember their smell—not fetid like grown chickens, but fresh and sweet. Miniature talons squeezing my fingers. Unearthly softness against my cheek.

One night, a snake crept into the coop and massacred the tiny chicks. It left one survivor flailing in bloody dirt. Half the chick's leg had been ripped away and its screams were tinny and tireless. Dad drowned it to end its suffering.

Traumatic indeed.

Only it wasn't a snake, Mom told me recently, but a fox.

A fox makes much more sense. A fox could cause frenzy in a chicken coop. A snake . . . well, couldn't. After two or three little chicks, a snake would look like a sock stuffed with tennis balls. It would be too sluggish and protuberant to slither back through the wire. Slaughtering eleven chicks would require a whole den of snakes. I have to remind myself of this. Because for me, it has always been a large brown snake pouring itself through the chicken wire and lurking in the straw until the first innocent blundered near.

I should have a fear of foxes: vulpophobia.

But I'm not afraid of foxes. I'm not afraid of spiders. I'm not afraid of rats. I'm not afraid of bats. I'm not afraid of needles. I'm not afraid of earthquakes. I'm not afraid of worms. I'm not afraid of germs. I'm not afraid of funerals. I'm not afraid of meteors. I'm not afraid of dogs. I'm not afraid of God. I'm not afraid of Satan. I'm not afraid of turbans. I'm not afraid to fly. I'm not afraid to die.

I'm not afraid to be bitten. I'm not afraid of the venom.

It's something else.

They are shape-shifters. Snakes materialize out of nothing—ordinary rocks, twigs, and leaves—reminding us that perception is untrustworthy. You can never tell just how long a snake is, where its body begins and ends. They may fold themselves three times, six times, a dozen times. They move like water and shine like grease, but their skin is dry as dust.

Snakes are deception, surprise, mutability. They violate the predictable. Snakes are agents of chaos.

My friend at the barn where I ride horses says she's afraid of snakes. She hates them, she says. Yet Diane tromps out into the grassy pasture like it's no big deal. She watches where she puts her feet, while talking of other things and enjoying the unseasonably warm weather. Spring has been coming earlier as the drought deepens. I saw my first snake of the year in January.

A wispy, harmless garter snake has darted from underneath a feed bucket and is now creeping around the barn, making my skin vibrate with dread. Where will I confront the snake next? In the feed room? In a stall? Diane finds it near the manure pile and grabs a pitchfork.

"What are you doing?" I say.

"I'm just going to carry it to the bushes."

"Please don't," I croak. "Please."

How can I tell her that the image of that strange, nimble body writhing between the tines will cycle on repeat through my brain for weeks? Even if I look away, I will know that it happened. The only thing worse than a snake on the ground is a snake off the ground: flying snakes and falling snakes and climbing snakes and swimming snakes.

Diane laughs, her expression bemused. I see that she is going to do it anyway, so I rush into the barn and wait it out in the dark, hands clamped to my face.

"Whoa, you're a fast little guy," I hear her say to the snake.

Breathe.

I am ridiculous, I know that. Among my worst fears is that my horse will unwittingly step on a small snake on the trail and I'll be forced to pick a bloody segment of its body out of her hoof. If I have to pee at the barn, I open the Port-O-Let's plastic door in minute increments, worried that a snake has squeezed through a crack to bask in the rank heat.

When Diane says she's afraid of snakes, she means that she is afraid of dangerous snakes, biting snakes, aggressive snakes. Delicate garter snakes don't qualify.

Fear and phobia are different planets, separated by vast, airless space.

Snakebite is easy to avoid. Don't step on a snake, don't taunt a snake, don't threaten a snake, and it won't bite you. I often fail to notice pretty butterflies and birds because my eyes are glued to the ground. A twig lying in my path will knock my lungs into my shoes. My chances of mindlessly stepping on a snake are practically nil.

Moreover, none of the snakes native to California could kill me with one bite. A perverse part of me hopes I'll get bitten so I can prove to myself that the worst-case scenario isn't that bad.

But venom—which is to say, real danger—has nothing to do with this. When a startled snake whips into action, the ground itself appears to move. Solid becomes liquid. Inanimate becomes animate. Nothing is what you think it is. Nothing is safe.

I keep returning to the false memory of my father's snakebite.

A grand mal epileptic with a penchant for going off his meds, he was profoundly unreliable and prone to sudden dramatic changes. He took LSD and peyote. He changed his name and then changed it back. When I was nine, he suffered a psychotic break, shaved all the hair off of his body and face, and plucked his eyelashes out.

Because my dad's instability disturbed me, I believed him snakebit. As if all things not what they seemed must be touched by snakes.

In dreams, I walk gauntlets of coiled snakes. Snakes tangle in my hair. They bite my hands or my feet. They wriggle into my open mouth. I find snakes in my bed, in the ocean, in the car, in the sky. They invade good dreams and bad. Sometimes they are beautiful.

At least one snake lurks in every dream I remember.

Which is to say that if I have a dream without a snake, it's forgettable, unimportant.

Isn't this persistent terror also a hope, also a call? By obsessing, I keep them close and present, inflating the importance of these humble, belly-walking creatures beyond reason. Again I think of my father, how parenthood temporarily transforms a half-broken person into a sort of god whose thoughtless gestures define his child's world. It's unfair to be a parent, unfair to be a child.

And what did any snake ever do to me? Nothing. I'm the stalker.

Kevin takes me to an upscale hotel restaurant offering a prix fixe menu of wild game. It isn't an anniversary or a birthday, but we dress up and celebrate, just because. Live jazz piano lilts through a room of low light and adult conversation. We sip a fine pinot noir bought on a road trip through Oregon before we married.

Our black-tie server arrives with the appetizer. Crispy rattlesnake pot stickers with persimmon chutney. I stare at the golden-brown pockets of dough and meat. *Just like chicken,* I think, my heart quickening. *Like chicken, like chicken.* Acrid saliva swamps my tongue. The fork feels so light, if I let it go, it will float up to the ceiling.

Kevin plucks his pot sticker barehanded, smears it through the chutney, and pops it into his mouth. "Mmm," he says. "You'll love it."

Being terrified of an appetizer is embarrassing.

The standard treatment for phobias is exposure therapy. Eating this snake—digesting it, absorbing it—could be a step in the right direction. Using the side of my fork, I slice the pot sticker open, releasing a ghost of steam, and lift the morsel to my lips.

It's hot and bland on my tongue. I taste nothing, not even the chutney. But when I blink, I see the meat regenerating into a diamondback that will live enveloped in my intestines, eating what I eat, dreaming what I dream.

Ducking, I spit the half-chewed bite into my cloth napkin, fold it tightly, and tuck it under my stockinged thigh. I push the plate toward my husband.

He shrugs and pops my pot sticker into his mouth. "Your loss," he says.

Kevin and I are at Diamond Caverns in Cave City, Kentucky, approaching the visitor center to purchase tickets for a cave tour. A jet-black snake four feet long whips across the footpath in front of me and slips into the center's decorative garden. I spin, making guttural noises, and speed-walk in the other direction. My husband grabs my shoulder, hoping to comfort me, but I cringe away from his hand. I feel turned inside out, as if my organs suddenly pulsed on the outside. I hyperventilate in the parking lot, until Kevin promises the snake is gone.

After the tour, I look out at the garden through a plate-glass window. Between plants, I see what looks like a looped black hose, but I know. I stand with my nose centimeters from the glass and watch the liquid black body wind through the flowers. It seems to touch everything, to be everywhere at once. In the afternoon sun, it looks dipped in oil. The snake pauses and lifts its head out of a bed of tulips. The face and neck are surprisingly delicate for such a hefty body. Maybe it's because of the pink tulips, but it strikes me as female. I watch her taste the air with her tiny vibrating tongue.

The snake has seen or heard or felt me watching; she watches me back with keen black eyes.

I've never subscribed to the idea that animals are dumb, nobody home, driven by mindless instinct—yet this is the first time I've sensed a snake's intelligence. She's just going about her afternoon business, maybe hoping to score a meal, while soaking up enough sun to stay mobile at night when she must avoid the owls. She is herself and I am myself, and we have nothing to do with each other.

My exhalations have fogged the glass, but I notice that I'm breathing calmly. I'm seeing past my own trickery. How I use snakes as scapegoats for terrors I will not face. How they are my favorite shield. The phobia does not end with this; walking through grass will always make my blood hammer. But I've been granted a reprieve here, a moment of empathy for this she-snake, and with that, compassion for my most stubborn parts. The parts that refuse to mend.

Contributors' Notes

*Notable Essays and Literary
Nonfiction of 2016*

Notable Special Issues of 2016

Contributors' Notes

JASON ARMENT served in Operation Iraqi Freedom as a machine gunner in the USMC. He's earned an MFA in creative nonfiction from the Vermont College of Fine Arts. His work has appeared in *Narrative Magazine, Gulf Coast, Lunch Ticket, Chautauqua, Hippocampus*, the *Burrow Press Review* (Pushcart Prize nomination), *Dirty Chai, Phoebe, Pithead Chapel*, the *Indianola Review, Brevity*, the *Florida Review, Atticus Review, Zone 3, New Madrid, Veterans Writing Project, Midwestern Gothic*, and *War, Literature & the Arts: An International Journal of the Humanities*. His writing has been anthologized in *Proud to Be: Writing by American Warriors* (volumes 2, 4, and 5) and is forthcoming in *Duende* and the *Iowa Review*. University of Hell Press will publish his memoir *Musalaheen* in 2017. Jason lives in Denver, where he coordinates the Denver Veterans Writing Workshop with the Colorado Humanities and Lighthouse. He can be reached at jason.arment@gmail.com.

RACHEL KAADZI GHANSAH is a contributing writer for the *New York Times Magazine* and author of the forthcoming *The Explainers and the Explorers* (2018). Her essays and articles have appeared in the *Paris Review*, the *Believer, Bookforum, Transition, Rolling Stone, Virginia Quarterly Review, Los Angeles Review of Books*, and other publications. She has taught writing at Columbia University, Bard College, and Eugene Lang College. Her profile of Dave Chappelle was a finalist for the 2014 National Magazine Award. She lives in New York.

ELIESE COLETTE GOLDBACH is a graduate of the Northeast Ohio Master of Fine Arts Program. Her work has appeared in *Ploughshares, Alaska Quarterly Review, Western Humanities Review, McSwee-*

ney's Internet Tendency, and other journals. She was the recipient of the Ohioana Library Association's Walter Rumsey Marvin Grant and a winner of the Ploughshares Emerging Writer's Contest. She lives and writes in Cleveland, where her latest project has been a memoir about working in a Rust Belt steel mill.

LAWRENCE JACKSON is the author of *Chester B. Himes: A Biography* (2017) and writes occasional essays for *Harper's Magazine* and *n+1*. He is working on a collection of essays called *Christmas in Baltimore*, and is Bloomberg Distinguished Professor of English and History at Johns Hopkins University.

RACHEL KUSHNER is the author of two novels, *The Flamethrowers*, a finalist for the National Book Award, and *Telex from Cuba*, also a finalist for the National Book Award, as well as *The Strange Case of Rachel K*, a collection of short prose. She is a Guggenheim fellow and winner of the Howard D. Vursell Award from the American Academy of Arts and Letters. Her fiction has appeared in *The New Yorker*, *Harper's Magazine*, and the *Paris Review*.

ALAN LIGHTMAN is a novelist, essayist, and physicist with a PhD in theoretical physics. He has served on the faculties of Harvard University and MIT and was the first person to receive dual faculty appointments at MIT in science and in the humanities. His essays and articles have appeared in *Harper's Magazine*, the *Atlantic, The New Yorker, Granta*, and other publications. Lightman's *Einstein's Dreams* was an international bestseller and has been translated into thirty languages. His novel *The Diagnosis* was a finalist for the National Book Award in fiction. His latest books are *The Accidental Universe*, a collection of essays about how recent developments in science have changed our philosophical and theological views, and *Screening Room*, a memoir about the South.

EMILY MALONEY'S work has recently appeared in or is forthcoming from *Harper's Magazine, Glamour, Virginia Quarterly Review*, the *North American Review*, and the *American Journal of Nursing*. She is at work on a memoir and a collection of essays about health care in America.

GREG MARSHALL is a graduate of the Michener Center for Writers. His essays have appeared most recently in *Sonora Review, Tahoma Literary Review*, and *Roanoke Review*. He lives in Austin, Texas, with his husband, Lucas, and is at work on an essay collection called *Leg: The Story of a Limb and the Boy Who Grew from It*.

BERNARD FARAI MATAMBO'S work has appeared in *Witness, Copper Nickel, Prairie Schooner,* and *Transition,* among others. He has received fellowships from the Blue Mountain Center and the I-Park Foundation, and has served as a visiting artist at Gallery Delta in Harare, Zimbabwe. His first book of poems was awarded the Sillerman First Book Prize for African Poets and is forthcoming in spring 2018. He is currently at work on a book of nonfiction from which the essay comes.

KENNETH A. MCCLANE is the author of seven books of poetry and two volumes of personal essays, *Walls: Essays, 1985–1990* (2010) and *Color: Essays on Race, Family, and History* (2009). His essays have appeared in many anthologies, including *The Best African American Essays; The Art of the Essay; The Story and Its Writer; Literature for Life; Bearing Witness: Selections from African-American Autobiography in the Twentieth Century; The Anatomy of Memory;* and *You've Got to Read This.* In 2012 he retired from Cornell University, where he was the W.E.B. Du Bois Professor of Literature.

CATHERINE VENABLE MOORE is a writer and producer based in Fayette County, West Virginia. She is a recipient of a MacDowell Fellowship in Long-Form Journalism, the Vermont Studio Center's Mountain State Fellowship, the Highlander Center's Appalachian Transition Fellowship, and a West Virginia Humanities Council Fellowship. She is also an honorary member of the United Mine Workers of America and is currently at work on a collection of essays. Find out more at beautymountainstudio.com.

WESLEY MORRIS is a critic at large at the *New York Times* and a staff writer at the *New York Times Magazine,* where he writes essays about popular culture. He also hosts the culture podcast Still Processing with Jenna Wortham. For three years he was a staff writer at *Grantland,* where he wrote about movies, television, and the role of style in professional sports and cohosted the podcast Do You Like Prince Movies? with Alex Pappademas. Before that, he spent eleven years as a film critic at the *Boston Globe,* where he won the 2012 Pulitzer Prize for criticism.

CHRISTOPHER NOTARNICOLA studies writing at Florida Atlantic University, where he also edits for *Swamp Ape Review.* His work has appeared in *SmokeLong Quarterly* and the *North American Review.* He lives in Pompano Beach, Florida.

MEGHAN O'GIEBLYN is the recipient of a 2016 Pushcart Prize, and her essays have appeared in *n+1*, the *Point, Ploughshares*, the *Guardian*, the *New York Times*, and elsewhere.

KAREN PALMER is the author of the novels *Border Dogs* (2002) and *All Saints* (1997). She has received an NEA fellowship and a Pushcart Prize, and her writing has appeared in the *Kenyon Review, Five Points*, the *Rumpus*, and the *Manifest-Station*. "The Reader Is the Protagonist" is part of a memoir in progress.

SARAH RESNICK is a writer who lives in New York. Since 2010 she has been an editor with the publisher and magazine *Triple Canopy*.

HEATHER SELLERS is the author of *You Don't Look Like Anyone I Know: A True Story of Family, Face Blindness, and Forgiveness;* two volumes of poetry, *The Boys I Borrow* and *Drinking Girls and Their Dresses;* a collection of short stories, *Georgia Underwater;* and three books on the craft of writing, *Page After Page, Chapter After Chapter,* and *The Practice of Creative Writing*. She teaches poetry, essay, and micromemoir at the University of South Florida. She's currently at work on a collection of essays.

ANDREA STUART was born and raised in the Caribbean. She studied English at the University of East Anglia and French at the Sorbonne. Her first book, *Showgirls*, was published in 1996. It was adapted as a two-part documentary for the Discovery Channel in 1998 and has since inspired a theatrical show, a contemporary dance piece, and a number of burlesque performances. Her second book, *The Rose of Martinique: A Biography of Napoleon's Josephine*, was published in 2003. It has subsequently been published in the U.S. (2004), in Germany (2004), in France (2006), and in Sweden (2006). *The Rose of Martinique* won the Enid McLeod Literary Prize in 2004. Her third and current book, *Sugar in the Blood: One Family's Story of Slavery and Empire*, was published in England (2012) and in the U.S. (2013). It was shortlisted for the OCM Bocas Prize and the Spears Book Award and was the *Boston Globe*'s nonfiction pick of 2013. "Tourist," a meditation on female sexuality, was published in *Granta* in 2014. Her writing has appeared in numerous anthologies, and her articles have been published in a range of newspapers and magazines.

JUNE THUNDERSTORM lives to rain on every single bourgeois parade. June Thunderstorm says what others are too fearful to say, too respectable to figure out. She seeks no blessings from parasitic professionals, nor caters to academic games of "reflexivity" (except maybe just now haha). Instead it's like: May the bourgeoisie just fuck off and die. Indeed we aim to inspire glorious, glorious class rage. Enjoy her heartwarming autobiographical debut "Able-Bodied Until It Kills Us" (2013), as well as her "Fuck Legal Marijuana Manifesto" (2017), both also originally published in the *Baffler.* The rest is yet to come (fyi send large checks now tx).

ALIA VOLZ is a native daughter of San Francisco. Her work has appeared in the *New York Times, Tin House,* the *Threepenny Review, Nowhere Magazine, Utne Reader,* the *New England Review,* and the recent anthologies *Dig If You Will the Picture: Remembering Prince* and *Golden State: Best New Writing from California.* The Squaw Valley Community of Writers awarded her the Oakley Hall Memorial Scholarship twice. *SF Weekly* named her among the "Best Writers Without a Book in San Francisco." To make up for that, she's currently working on a book.

*

Leslie Jamison would love to thank Benjamin Nugent for allowing her to cite his Writing After the Election lesson plan, as well as all the students—past, present, and future—who helped her articulate the possibilities of the essay: Marcus Creaghan, Nicholas Dilonardo, Lisa Factora-Borchers, Meghan Gilligan, Harrison Hill, Bethany Hughes, Joseph Lee, Jack Lowery, Taleen Mardirossian, Zoe Marquedant, Kristen Martin, Katherine Massinger, Kalle Mattila, Andrew Miller, and Heather Radke.

Notable Essays and Literary Nonfiction of 2016

SELECTED BY ROBERT ATWAN

W. ROYCE ADAMS
Hands, *Catamaran,* Summer
KIM ADDONIZIO
Blue Guitar, *New Letters,* vol. 83, no. 1
DANIEL ALARCÓN
The Ballad of Rocky Rontal, *The California Sunday Magazine,* August 7
MARCIA ALDRICH
Float, *The Normal School,* Spring
KENDRA ALLEN
When You Learn the Alphabet, *December,* Spring/Summer
SAM ANDERSON
David's Ankles, *The New York Times Magazine,* August 21
KATE ANGUS
When We Were Vikings, *American Literary Review,* Spring
JACOB M. APPEL
Why Get There from Here? *Fourth Genre,* Spring
AMELIA ARENAS
Sex, Violence, and Faith: The Art of Caravaggio, *Arion,* Winter
NOGA ARIKHA
Body and Soul, *Lapham's Quarterly,* Fall
PHILIP ARNOLD
Stereoscopic Paris, *Apt,* June

CHRIS ARTHUR
Crux, *Hotel Amerika,* Spring
POE BALLANTINE
The Wreck Up Ahead, *The Sun,* December
BILL BARICH
A Weary Desperado, *Narrative,* Spring
JUDITH BARRINGTON
The Walk Home, *Creative Nonfiction,* Summer
TAD BARTLETT
My Time with You, *Chautauqua,* no. 13
ELIF BATUMAN
Cover Story, *The New Yorker,* February 8 & 15
SOPHIE BECK
Returning the Gaze, *The Point,* Winter
DIANNE BELFREY
Adrift, *The New Yorker,* November 7
KAREN BENNING
One Way It Might Have Happened 1931, *The Chattahoochee Review,* Fall
LESLIE BERLIN
Where the Heart Is, *The American Scholar,* Winter

ANURADHA BLTOWMIK
High Stakes, *Copper Nickel,* Fall

SVEN BIRKERTS
Birkerts and I, *Agni,* no. 83

HEATHER BIRRELL
Further Up and Further In!
Canadian Notes & Queries, Winter

LUCIENNE S. BLOCH
What Is Left, *The Sewanee Review,*
Fall

SUSAN BLOCH
The Mumbai Massacre, *Blue Lyra
Review,* Spring

MARC BOOKMAN
The 14-Year-Old Who Grew Up
in Prison, *Vice,* July 20

JENNY BOULLY
Instant Life, *Story Quarterly,*
no. 49

SARAH BOXER
Reading Proust on My Cellphone,
The Atlantic, June

JOHN H. BRACEY JR.
The Coming of John, *The
Massachusetts Review,* Winter

CINDY BRADLEY
Death, Driveways, and Dreams,
Under the Sun, no. 4

NICOLE BREIT
An Atmospheric Pressure, *Room,*
vol. 39, no. 4

TRACI BRIMHALL
Murder Ballad in the Arctic,
Copper Nickel, Fall

TAFFY BRODESSERE AKNER
Tennis Lessons, *Racquet,* Autumn

KATHRYN BROWN
Attacked, *Baltimore Review,* Winter

JANET BURROWAY
Around the Corner, *New Letters,*
vol. 83, no. 1

AMY BURROUGHS
Two Strangers on a Train,
Jabberwock Review, Summer

JACK BUSHNELL
Writing on Water, *Tampa Review,*
no. 53

AMY BUTCHER
Flight Behavior, *The American
Scholar,* Summer

PATRICIA BYRNE
Milk Bottles in Limerick, *New
Hibernia Review,* Spring

KELLY GREY CARLISLE
The Dead Baby Window, *Cherry
Tree,* no. 2

LUCAS CARPENTER
Byron's Pistols, *Chicago Quarterly
Review,* Fall

TOM CARSON
True Fakes on Location, *The
Baffler,* no. 31

DOUG PAUL CASE
Elegy for a Photograph Deleted,
Whiskey Island, no. 67

BEA CHANG
The River My Father Promised,
Broad Street, Spring/Summer

EMILY CHASE
In Defense of Grudges, *Tusculum
Review,* no. 12

JAMES M. CHESBRO
Green Mazes, *The Collagist,*
March

ALEXANDER CHEE
Our Well-Regulated Militia,
Longreads, April 18

S. ISABEL CHOI
His Anger Is Not New, *Slice,* Fall/
Winter

CAITLYN LUCE CHRISTENSEN
Why a Girl Would Want To,
Indiana Review, Summer

KRISTA CHRISTENSEN
Etymologies, *New Ohio Review,*
Spring

GEORGE CRAIG
Aging: An Insider's Look, *Raritan,*
Spring

CAITLIN CRAWSHAW
Dark Spots, *Event,* vol. 45, no. 3

RACHEL CUSK
Coventry, *Granta,* no. 134

EDWIDGE DANTICAT
A Voice from Heaven, *Brown Alumni Magazine,* January/ February

GEORGE DARDESS
The Mosque Outside the Mosque: Aerosol Arabic and the One Experience, *Image,* no. 89

PWAANGULONGII DAUOD
Africa's Future Has No Space for Stupid Black Men, *Granta,* no. 136

CAROL ANN DAVIS
On Slaughter and Praying: An Essay in Two Parts, *The Georgia Review,* Fall

DAWN S. DAVIES
Keeping the Faith, *Chautauqua,* no. 13

COLIN DAYAN
The Old Gray Mare, *The Yale Review,* April

JENNIFER M. DEAN
Sounding in Fog, *Crazyhorse,* Spring

LARISSA DIAKIW
Mirror Land, *Brick,* no. 97

JAQUIRA DIAZ
Monster Story, *Ninth Letter,* Spring/Summer

NATALIE DIAZ
The Hand Has Twenty-Seven Bones, *Tin House,* no. 67

MARGARET DIEHL
And Then the Letting Go, *Alligator Juniper,* no. XX

LAURA DISTELHEIM
On Kindness, *The Briar Cliff Review,* no. 28

BRIAN DOYLE
The Stone Nose, *Ruminate,* Fall

JACQUELINE DOYLE
A Eulogy, Despite, *Full Grown People,* April 14

ANDRE DUBUS III
Carver and Dubus, New York City, 1988, *Five Points,* vol. 17, no. 2

IRINA A. DUMITRESCU
The Things We Take, The Things We Leave Behind, *Southwest Review,* vol. 101, no. 1

STEVE DURHAM
Human out of Me, *Opossum,* Fall

LUCY DURNEEN
All the Things, *Hotel Amerika,* Spring

ANJALI ENJETI
Identity Lost and Found, *Atlanta Journal Constitution,* September 11

ADAM EWING
In/Visibility, *Transition,* no. 119

ALTHEA FANN
What Flowers Mean, *Crazyhorse,* Fall

BETH ANN FENNELLY
Y'all's Problem, *The Chattahoochee Review,* Spring

GARY FINCKE
Hearts, *Ascent,* May 12

COLIN FLEMING
A Midshipman Lights Out, *Salmagundi,* Spring/Summer

MATTHEW GAVIN FRANK
On Naming Bones, or, How to Ship a Mosquito, *1966: A Journal of Creative Nonfiction,* Winter

JONATHAN FRANZEN
The End of the End of the World, *The New Yorker,* May 23

ERICA FUNKHOUSER
One Salt Marsh, One Hawk, One Swimmer, *Harvard Review,* no. 49

NEAL GABLER
My Secret Shame, *The Atlantic,* May

MEGAN GALBRAITH
Sin Will Find You Out, *Catapult,* March 1

J. MALCOLM GARCIA
If You Raise a Mexican Flag in America, *Latterly,* October

EMILY GEMINDER
Choreograph, *Agni*, no. 83

DIANA HUME GEORGE
In the House of Habakkuk,
Chautauqua, no. 13

DAVID GESSNER
The Taming of the Wild, *The
American Scholar*, Summer

DENISE GIARDINA
Candy, *Appalachian Heritage*, Fall

RENEE GLADMAN
Five Things, *The Paris Review*,
Summer

ERIK GLEIBERMANN
Soothing the Serpent's Tooth,
The Florida Review, Summer

ELIZABETH GOLD
So It Begins, *The Gettysburg Review*,
Spring

ANNE GOLDMAN
The Kingdom of the
Medusae, *Southwest Review*,
vol. 101, no. 2

RIGOBERTO GONZALEZ
Dias de los Muertos: A Oaxaco
Journal, *Apogee*, no. 8

ADAM GOPNIK
Feel Me, *The New Yorker*, May 16

EMILY FOX GORDON
Mr. Sears, *Ploughshares*, Summer

MICHAEL GRAFF
Man Alone, *Success*, September

PETER GRANDBOIS
Honor, *North Dakota Quarterly*,
Winter

SARAH GRIGG
Medicine Wings, *Boulevard*,
Spring

STEPHEN D. GUTIERREZ
The Case for Steve Gutierrez,
Waccamaw, Fall

DEBRA GWARTNEY
Into Every Life Some Rain Must
Fall, *Creative Nonfiction*, Fall

SHAHNAZ HABIB
A Letter to My Daughter About
Palindromes, *Agni*, no. 84

KATHLEEN HALE
Through the Looking Glass:
A Week at Miss America, *Mary
Review*, Fall

CLAIRE HALLIDAY
The Possible Universe, *The Sun*,
September

CAMERON DEZEN HAMMON
Infirmary Music, *The Literary
Review*, Summer

LARRY HANDY
What to Do When Grandma Has
Dementia, *Rivet*, no. 9

SILAS HANSEN
What Real Men Do, *The Normal
School*, Fall

RACHEL MICHELLE HANSON
Ways of Leaving, *American Literary
Review*, Spring

DANIEL HARRIS
The Kardashians, *Southwest
Review*, vol. 101, no. 4

STEPHANIE HARRISON
What We Have Left, *Colorado
Review*, Summer

NATHAN HELLER
The Big Uneasy, *The New Yorker*,
May 30

SARA HENDERY
Dangerous Language, *Creative
Nonfiction*, Summer

ARIEL HENLEY
White Noise, *The Rumpus*,
October 3

MICHAEL J. HESS
On the Morning After the Crash,
Sport Literate, vol. 10, no. 1

ERIK P. HOEL
Fiction in the Age of Screens,
The New Atlantis, Spring/Summer

BROOKE HOLMES
Tragedy in the Crosshairs of the
Present, *Daedalus*, Spring

ANN HOOD
Imagine, *The Normal School*,
Spring

LAUREN HOUGH
'The Shepherds, *Granta,* no. 137
CARLYNN HOUGHTON
Letter to a Stranger: US Route
17, New York, *Off Assignment,* May
12
PAT C. HOY II
Habitations, *The Sewanee Review,*
Summer
EWA HRYNIEWICZ-YARBROUGH
Little Bowls of Colors, *The
American Scholar,* Autumn
SONYA HUBER
If Woman Is Five, *River Teeth,*
Spring
BARBARA HURD
Glimpses, *Orion,* November/
December
SIRI HUSTVEDT
Sontag on Smut: Fifty Years Later,
Salmagundi, Spring/Summer

AMY IRVINE
Conflagrations, *Pacific Standard,*
July/August
DIONNE IRVING
Treading Water, *The Missouri
Review,* vol. 39, no. 2
LUCY IVES
Sodom, LLC, *Lapham's Quarterly,*
Fall

RONALD JACKSON
Camille: A Memory, *The
Chattahoochee Review,* Spring
HEATHER JACOBS
Seven Portraits/Siete Retratos,
Fifth Wednesday, Fall
LESLIE JAMISON
The Persephone Complex,
Water-Stone Review, no. 19
BROOKE JARVIS
When I Die, *Harper's Magazine,*
January
ANNA JOURNEY
Little Face, *Agni,* no. 84

GARRET KEIZER
Solidarity and Survival, *Lapham's
Quarterly,* Spring
RALPH KEYES
Inscriber's Block, *The American
Scholar,* Spring
ALISON KINNEY
History in Wax, *Lapham's
Quarterly,* April 11
WALTER KIRN
Crossing the Valley, *Harper's
Magazine,* April
CATHRYN KLUSMEIER
Crucifixions, *Crazyhorse,* Fall
KIM DANA KUPPERMAN
Memorial Daze (It Takes a Lot to
Laugh, It Takes a Train to Cry),
Aster(ix), Fall

JOHN LAHR
Hooker Heaven, *Esquire,* June/
July
LAURIE CLEMENTS LAMBETH
Going Downhill from Here,
Ecotone, Spring
BARTH LANDOR
Forty Passages for Shakespeare,
The Georgia Review, Summer
LANCE LARSEN
Heavenly Hits, *The Gettysburg
Review,* Winter
PETER LaSALLE
Driving in São Paulo at Night
with a Good Friend Who Has
Died, *The Southern Review,* Spring
LIZ LATTY
What We Lost: Undoing the
Fairy Tale Myth of Adoption, *The
Rumpus,* November 17
DAVID LAZAR
Five Autobiographical Fragments,
or She May Have Been a Witch,
River Teeth, Fall
ANNA LEAHY
Sweet Dreams Are Made of This,
Dogwood, no. 15

REBECCA LEE
    The Rules of Engagement, *Able Muse,* Summer
ALEX LEMON
    How Long Before You Go Dry, *River Teeth,* Fall
DINAH LENNEY
    A Longer Reach, *Los Angeles Review of Books,* November 28
JOAN LI
    Something That Lasts, *Chicago Quarterly Review,* Fall
MARGIT LIESÇHE
    The Ocean Between Us, *Chicago Quarterly Review,* Fall
ANYA LIFTIG
    Irretrievable Breakdown, *bioStories,* September
BRANDON LINGLE
    Turbulence, *The American Scholar,* Autumn
MEL LIVATINO
    Going Home Again, *Under the Sun,* no. 4
SONJA LIVINGSTON
    Spools of White Thread, *1966: A Journal of Creative Nonfiction,* Winter
PHILLIP LOPATE
    Red Relations, *Mount Hope,* Fall

DAVID STUART MACLEAN
    Golden Friendship Club, *Bennington Review,* Spring/ Summer
PATRICK MADDEN
    Missing, *Portland,* Spring
EMILY ST. JOHN MANDEL
    The Year of Numbered Rooms, *Humanities,* Spring
LUCAS MANN
    Trying to Get Right, *Guernica,* April 15
ALEX MAR
    Blood Ties, *Oxford American,* Spring

MARTINO MARAZZI
    Amelia, *The Carolina Quarterly,* Summer
STEPHEN MARCHE
    The Age of Ephemerality, *Brick,* no. 96
CLANCY MARTIN
    Seven Times Inside, *Vice,* November
DAVID MASELLO
    Building Friendships, *American Arts Quarterly,* July
REBECCA MCCLANAHAN
    Wren Boy, *River Teeth,* Spring
ELIZABETH MCCRACKEN
    The Container & the Thing Contained, *Harvard Review,* no. 49
LATANYA MCQUEEN
    After Water Comes the Fires, *Bennington Review,* Fall/ Winter
JOHN MCWHORTER
    Thick of Tongue, *Guernica,* March 15
DAVID MEANS
    The Old Man, *Harper's Magazine,* June
ANDREW MENARD
    Blind Spot, *The Georgia Review,* Spring
S. J. MILLER
    A Merry Little Christmas, *The Sun,* May
CAILLE MILLNER
    Four Murders, *Michigan Quarterly Review,* Winter
THOMAS MIRA Y LOPEZ
    Capricci, *Alaska Quarterly Review,* Spring/Summer
DAVE MONDY
    And We'll See You Tomorrow Night, *The Cincinnati Review,* Winter
DEBRA MONROE
    Trouble in Mind, *The Rumpus,* September 11

ANDER MONSON
Remainder, *Territory,* August 5
DAVID MONTGOMERY
The Living and the Dead,
The Washington Post Magazine,
December 18
DAN MUSGRAVE
Worry, *The Missouri Review,* vol.
39, no. 2
ALLISON GRACE MYERS
Perfume Poured Out, *Image,*
no. 89
ANDI MYLES
Impressions from a Vacuum,
Alligator Juniper, no. XX

MICHAEL NAGEL
Beached Whales, *Apt,* July
JOHN R. NELSON
Funny Bird Sex, *The Antioch
Review,* Winter
KERRY NEVILLE
After Divorce: Flight Path,
Huffington Post, September 20
JENNIFER NIESSLEIN
Before We Were Good White, *Full
Grown People,* December 15
JAMES NOLAN
Stairway to Paradise, *Boulevard,*
Spring

W. SCOTT OLSEN
Before the Breaking Wave: The
Duluth North Pier Lighthouse,
North Dakota Quarterly, Spring/
Summer

CARYL PAGEL
Alphabet, *Entropy,* September 8
LARRY PALMER
Urshel: The Beautiful Lost
Sheep, *Blackbird,* Spring
FRANCES PARK
"You Two Are So Beautiful
Together," *The Massachusetts
Review,* Summer

BRICE PARTICELLI
Take Me to the (Bronx?) River,
The Big Roundtable, June
ELENA PASSARELLO
Twinkle, Twinkle, Vogel Staar, *The
Virginia Quarterly Review,* Summer
COREY PEIN
Everybody Freeze! *The Baffler,* no.
30
EMILIA PHILLIPS
Excisions, *Story Quarterly,* no. 49
JOHN PICARD
The Accordion Polka, *Moon City
Review*
SAM PICKERING
Habituated Eye, *The Sewanee
Review,* Summer
MELISSA HOLBROOK PIERSON
Gimme Shelter, *Lumina,*
no. XV
SALLY POTTER
Naked Cinema, *A Public Space,*
no. 24
SHELLEY PUHAK
Detained: A Genealogy of
Whores and Wolves, *Columbia:
A Journal of Literature and Art,*
no. 54
LIA PURPURA
All the Fierce Tethers, *The New
England Review,* vol. 37, no. 3
JILL SISSON QUINN
Begetting, *Kenyon Review,*
September/October

ADRIANA E. RAMÍREZ
On Black Bodies, Metaphor, and
Mourning, *Literary Hub,* August
30
MICHAEL RAMOS
A Long but Incomplete List of
Some of the Things You Can't
(Don't) Talk About, *Fourth Genre,*
Fall
ADRIENNE RAPHEL
A Is for A, *The Iowa Review,* vol.
46, no. 3

WENDY RAWLINGS
Portrait of a Family, Crooked &
Straight, *Colorado Review,* Summer

SUE REPKO
The Gun Show, *The Southeast
Review,* vol. 34, no. 2

JIM RINGLEY
On the Smell of Certain Houses,
The Threepenny Review, Fall

WALTER M. ROBINSON
This Will Sting and Burn, *The
Sun,* January

JAMES SILAS ROGERS
Digging for Nothing, *Ruminate,*
Spring

KELSEY RONAN
Blood and Water, *Michigan
Quarterly Review,* Spring

DANIEL ASA ROSE
Separated at Birth, *Harper's
Magazine,* December

KENNETH R. ROSEN
Notes from My Suicide, *The Big
Roundtable,* March 10

NATANIA ROSENFELD
The Autonomous Land of
Prapruninma, *Michigan Quarterly
Review,* Fall

MARY ROSS-DOLEN
Diphtheria, *North Dakota
Quarterly,* Winter

MAURICE CARLOS RUFFIN
Fine Dining, *The Virginia Quarterly
Review,* Fall

SHARMAN APT RUSSELL
People Who Live Inside Us, *The
Threepenny Review,* Winter

SCOTT RUSSELL SANDERS
They're Neighbors of Mine, *Notre
Dame Magazine,* Winter

MARIN SARDY
Break My Body, *Guernica,* August
8

RICHARD SCHMITT
Not Knowing: The Rock & Roll of
Drinking, *Alaska Quarterly Review,*
Spring/Summer

BRANDON R. SCHRAND
Through the Glass Clearly, *The
Missouri Review,* vol. 39, no. 4

MIMI SCHWARTZ
On Stage and Off, *Prairie Schooner,*
Fall

SOPHFRONIA SCOTT
Why I Didn't Go to the
Firehouse, *The Timberline Review,*
Summer/Fall

JO SCOTT-COE
Listening to Kathy, *Catapult,*
March 30

WILLIAM HENRY SEARLE
The Hollow of Shell Bay, *Bellevue
Literary Review,* Spring

DAVID SEDARIS
The Perfect Fit, *The New Yorker,*
March 28

FREDERIC WILL
Eighteen Polarities from Within
the Self, *The Yale Review,*
January

PETER SELGIN
Noise, *Bellevue Literary Review,*
Fall

AURVI SHARMA
Apricots, *Gulf Coast,* vol. 28,
no. 1

MICHAEL SHEEHAN
On the Undiscovered Origins of
Everything in Waxahachie, Texas,
Agni, no. 84

FLOYD SKLOOT
He Had a Falcon, *Boulevard,* vol.
32, no. 1

LAUREN SLATER
It's Over?, *Elle,* May

ANDREW SLOUGH
Avoiding Hemingway in
Ketchum, Idaho, *Catamaran,*
Winter

PATRICIA SMITH
My Bricks Be Foul, *Prairie
Schooner,* Winter

CARRIE SNYDER
Why Give Yourself Away? *Brick,*
no. 96

JIM SOLLISCH
    The Foreskin and the Hindsight,
    The Washington Post Magazine,
    January 10
DOROTHY SPEARS
    Labor Day Weekend, *Epiphany,*
    Fall/Winter
KATHERINE E. STANDEFER
    Wilderness, *CutBank,* no. 84
ELEANOR STANFORD
    Grammar for an Unwritten
    Language (Cape Verde, West
    Africa), *Kenyon Review,* March/
    April
DAVID STEVENSON
    A Late and Uninvited
    Correspondent Responds to
    Maggie Nelson's Bluets, *Alpinist,*
    Winter
LAURIE STONE
    Montreal, *Ascent,* August 9
ROBERT STOTHART
    Magpies, *The New England Review,*
    vol. 37, no. 4
EMILY STRASSER
    Exposure, *Colorado Review,*
    Summer
ABE STREEP
    The Devil Is Loose, *The California
    Sunday Magazine,* August 7
SHEILA GRACE STUEWE
    Star Struck (1982), *Hunger
    Mountain,* no. 20
ANDREW SULLIVAN
    I Used to Be a Human Being,
    New York, September 19/
    October 2
JOHN JEREMIAH SULLIVAN
    Baby Boy Born Birthplace Blues,
    Oxford American, Winter
BARRETT SWANSON
    Calling Audibles, *Mississippi
    Review,* vol. 43, no. 3
JESSIE SZALAY
    Sloughing Off, *Gulf Coast,* vol. 28,
    no. 2

JILL TALBOT
    An Eye on the Door, *The Normal
    School,* Spring
ASHLEY P. TAYLOR
    After the Essay, *Entropy,*
    October 26
KAITLYN TEER
    Ossification, *Fourth Genre,* Spring
KERRY TEMPLE
    What's Best for Them, *Notre Dame
    Magazine,* Autumn
SALLIE TISDALE
    Gaijin, *Conjunctions,* no. 66
TOMMY TOMLINSON
    Our Old Dog, *Charlotte,* February
SAMANTHA TUCKER
    Fountain Girls, *Ecotone,* Fall/
    Winter
SARAH VALLANCE
    Heart Attack, *Post Road,*
    no. 31
JESSE MACEO VEGA-FREY
    Pigs, *Boston Review,* January/
    February
SARAH VIREN
    Advise Me, *The Iowa Review,* vol.
    46, no. 1
SCOTT VOGEL
    Gross Anatomy, *Houstonia,*
    December
ALIA VOLZ
    Chasing Arrows, *The New England
    Review,* vol. 37, no. 1

JULIE MARIE WADE
    Hourglass (III), *Southern
    Humanities Review,* vol. 50, nos. 1
    & 2
JERALD WALKER
    Thieves, *River Teeth,* Spring
NICOLE WALKER
    Revolution, *Barrelhouse,* no. 15
YUNGHSIN WANG
    Body, *Esprit,* Fall
KEEMA WATERFIELD
    You Will Find Me in the Starred
    Sky, *Brevity,* May

SARAH M. WELLS
    The Body Is Not a Coffin, *Under
    the Gum Tree,* April
ROSE WHITMORE
    Witness, *Colorado Review,* Fall/
    Winter
JOEL WHITNEY
    Fifty Years of Disquietude, *The
    Baffler,* no. 33
ESTHER K. WILLISON
    Askew, *Bellevue Literary Review,*
    Spring
GARRY WILLS
    My Koran Problem, *The New York
    Review of Books,* March 24
HEATHER GEMMEN WILSON
    Unpinned, *River Teeth,* Spring
STEVEN WINEMAN
    Erving and Alice and Sky and
    Elisabeth, *The Cincinnati Review,*
    Winter

DAVID WOJAHN
    On Hearing That My Poems
    Were Being Studied in a Distant
    Place, *Blackbird,* Spring
BRENNA WOMER
    Wusthof Silverpoint II 10-Piece
    Set, *Grist,* no. 9

AMY YEE
    Delhi's Current Flows On, *Electric
    Literature,* October 7
YIN Q
    The Home of Desperate Magic,
    Apogee, no. 8
ALISSA YORK
    In Memoriam Pompeius
    Maximus, *Brick,* no. 96

JESS ZIMMERMAN
    A Life in Google Maps, *Catapult,*
    September 12

Notable Special Issues of 2016

The Antioch Review, "Sex," ed. Robert
S. Fogarty, Winter

The Baffler, "The Virtue Cartel," ed.
Chris Lehmann, no. 33

Bellevue Literary Review,
"Reconstructions: The Art of
Memory," ed. Danielle Ofri, Fall

The Bennington Review, "Misbegotten
Youth," ed. Michael Dumanis,
Fall/Winter

Chautauqua, "Americana," eds. Jill
Gerard and Philip Gerard, no. 13

Conjunctions, "Affinity: The
Friendship Issue," ed. Bradford
Morrow, no. 66

Creative Nonfiction, "Marriage," ed.
Lee Gutkind, Spring

Daedalus, "What's New About the
Old," guest ed. Matthew S.
Santirocco, Spring

Ecotone, "The Country & City Issue,"
ed. David Gessner, Fall/Winter

Granta, "No Man's Land," ed. Sigrid
Rausing, no. 134

Gulf Coast, "The Archive Issue," eds.
Martin Rock, Adrienne Perry,
and Carlos Hernandez,
Summer/Fall

Hunger Mountain, "Edges," ed.
Miciah Bay Gault, no. 20

Lapham's Quarterly, "Luck," ed. Lewis
H. Lapham, Summer

The Literary Review, "Fight," ed.
Minna Zallman Proctor, Winter

Little Patuxent Review, "Myth," guest
ed. Patricia Jakovich VanAmberg,
Winter

Manoa, "Yoshihiko Sinoto: Curve of
the Hook," ed. Frank Stewart, vol.
28, no. 1

The Massachusetts Review, "The Music
Issue," ed. Jim Hicks, Winter

Midwestern Gothic, "Nonfiction Issue,"
eds. Jeff Pfaller and Robert James
Russell, Fall

The Missouri Review, "Family
Practice," ed. Speer Morgan,
Summer

New Letters, "Jazz," ed. Robert Stewart,
vol. 83, no. 1

North Dakota Quarterly, "McGrath at
100," ed. NDQ staff, Fall

Orion, "Coexistence," ed. H. Emerson
Blake, November/December

Oxford American, "Southern
Journeys," ed. Eliza Borne,
Summer

Prism, "Nonfiction Contest,"
eds. Jennifer Lori and Claire
Matthews, Spring

Room, "This Body's Map," ed.
Chelene Knight, vol. 39, no. 4

Ruminate, "Nowhere Near," ed.
Brianna Van Dyke, Fall

Salmagundi, "Arguing Identity," eds.
Robert Boyers and Peg Boyers,
Fall

Slice, "Enemies," eds. Celia Blue
Johnson, Maria Gagliano, and
Elizabeth Blachman, no. 18

Texas Monthly, "Guns," ed. Brian D.
Sweany, April

The Threepenny Review, "A Symposium
on Crying," ed. Wendy Lesser,
Fall

Tin House, "Faith," ed. Rob Spillman,
no. 69

The Turnip Truck(s), "The Road," ed.
Tina Mitchell, Spring/Summer

Under the Gum Tree, "Fifth Anniversary
Issue," ed. Janna Marlies Maron,
October

Vice, "The Holy Cow Issue," ed. Ellis
Jones, May

. . .

Note: The following essays should have appeared in "Notable Essays and Literary Nonfiction of 2015":

JASON ARMENT, Fear City, *Phoebe,* Fall
MICHAEL FALLON, The Other Side of Silence, *The New England Review,* vol. 37, no. 4
PHILIP F. GURA, To the Curator of Birds, *The New England Review,* vol. 37, no. 4
GARDNER LANDRY, The Song of Songs, *Cream City Review,* Fall/Winter
KATE LEBO, The Unsealed Ear, *The New England Review,* vol. 37, no. 4
SUSAN OLDING, White Matter, *The Malahat Review,* Winter